DREAMREADER

DREAMREADER

a novel

CATHY FIORELLO

WordCrafts

Published by WordCrafts Press
Cody, Wyoming 82414
www.wordcrafts.net

To Sam Fiorello,
for whom the impossible only takes a little longer.

I

GRACE

Glass orbs, rainbowed with oil slick, floated on the surface of the lake while sunlight winked through scattered clouds. A waterfall thundered in the distance. Somewhere far away, a violin played a soft and lilting tune. This time she was in a boat. Its bottom, a deep blue-green, began to shimmer and jump like cells dividing. Each jump made it more transparent until Grace could look through it into the water below. She saw fish swimming, tentacles, eels. On the bottom of the lake? A body. A tentacle wrapped around the body and carried it up to the surface of the water.

Clearly…it was her, eyes wide open—

Grace woke up with a start. Cold sweat prickled her arms and face. She pinched at her skin. Still here. Still alive.

She fought her way out of the quilt wrapped around her ankles and charged to the bathroom, hoping she wouldn't get sick along the way. Afterwards, she slid to the floor and lay down on the cold tiles, her breath frantic, her head pounding.

This had been her life since, two days before, she'd flipped over the handlebars of her bike on the way home from work and smashed her head into the pavement. She'd loaned her car to her sister, Mimi, to take her driver's test, foolishly thinking that riding a bike home in the rain would be *no problem*. Since then, watery nightmares had tormented her day and night. Each time, she saw herself under water, drowning.

Or just plain dead.

It had to be from the concussion or the pain meds, right?

She sat on the bathroom floor, her mind a jangle of thoughts. Why was she here, in her mother's house? Why had she moved home after graduation?

She'd been promised a job where she'd done her student teaching. A small, elegant private school in Boston. The students were motivated; the music program, top-notch. Sure, the pay wasn't ideal, but she'd had her apartment, her friends, her life. Why was she here, yet again, with her mother and sister? And now this.

She hadn't told them about the dreams. They had enough to deal with—both of them trying to finish out the school year. But they'd know soon enough.

She stood, shaky on her feet, and stumbled toward her bed and grabbed her phone. With trembling hands, she scrolled through her contact list. What was the name of the counselor she'd seen when her father died? Did she save the number by the first name, or last? After five minutes, she slammed her phone down. No way she could find it in her two-hundred-plus contacts.

She threw on a t-shirt and sweats and opened the front door to let in the morning air. The scent of newly-blooming jasmine and lilacs wafted into the house. On the way back into the living room, she glanced at her image in the mirror. Her blonde hair was dark and unwashed. Dried blood still clung to her stitches. Her face was bluish-purple around the eyes.

Of course she'd loaned her baby sister her car for the driver's test. Mimi couldn't park their mother's minivan to save her life. God forbid she'd have to take her driver's test more than once.

Protecting Mimi. It was the unspoken rule written in her parents' furrowed brows since the day Mimi was born. It felt like a life-sentence to Grace. When would it end? When Mimi had a husband to look after her? Or when she moved far enough away that Grace wouldn't know when she slipped on the sidewalk or locked herself out of the house?

Eve, Grace's art teacher mom, and Mimi had left for school long before Grace had gotten up, so the house was hers for the next six hours. She could unpack the boxes piled high in her room. Or maybe go to the music room and practice the piano. Instead, she flicked through mind-numbing shows on TV. Afraid to nap, she obsessed about her job playing piano in the lobby at Nordstrom's. Would she be able to focus tomorrow? Were three days off enough to repair the soft tissue of her brain that had slammed against her skull?

At around four, she started making chili. At five, Eve walked through the door tossing onto a chair a heavy, black bag decorated with puffy, colored glue. "Smells good, but you didn't have to cook. How's your head?"

Grace gingerly pulled her hair out of her eyes to gather in a hair tie, trying not to touch the crusty stitches that still hurt so much. "You've been out working all day, and I've been sitting home like a slug. It's the least I could do."

Her mother rolled up her sleeves to wash her hands in the sink. "You have a concussion. It's okay to be a slug."

"Never okay," Grace said.

"Now you sound like your father."

True. He'd taught her never to make excuses. "Be an example of what hard work can do," was his mantra. But then, when he couldn't handle his drive toward perfection anymore, he'd suddenly give up on everything. So would Grace. But not Mimi. She was the steady tortoise that would always win out. As long as Grace hovered, keeping the great darkness from swallowing her.

A few hours later, Mimi rolled in from her final *Footloose* rehearsal looking exhausted. Mimi, at seventeen, was a beautiful girl with long, dark hair. She took after Eve, while Grace had gotten their father's Swedish coloring—fair skin with blonde hair and blue eyes. They sat at the kitchen table after Eve went to bed, Mimi wolfing down chili while Grace cleaned the kitchen.

"Wait till you see Jay do his dance numbers," Mimi enthused.

"You're not gonna believe the choreographer got him to dance like that. Positively athletic."

"Scrawny little Jay?"

"Not so scrawny anymore. You haven't seen him for six months. He's been working out and has gotten pretty buff."

Grace grinned. "Apparently, you've noticed."

Mimi threw a dishtowel at her sister. "We're just friends. You know that."

"Then how come you're going to the prom together?"

Mimi shoveled in another mouthful. "About that. Can you go dress shopping with me? Mom can't do it."

"Not surprised. Who would volunteer for that kind of torture?"

"She's got meetings all next week. If you pick me up at school…"

"I'll let you know."

At eleven, Grace tried sleep again, and she did fairly well until about six a.m. Then was jolted awake—another dream. In this one, she was lying in bed with water raining down on her. Choking and sputtering like she was being waterboarded, she tried to get away but couldn't move. She opened her eyes and jumped out of bed. Bad move. Her head spinning, she had to grab the wall to keep from falling.

She eased herself downstairs and slid onto a kitchen chair. Eve spooned some scrambled eggs onto a plate and poured herself a cup of coffee. "You're up early."

Grace rubbed her head and winced. "Not on purpose."

"Pain?"

Grace nodded. Eve, dressed in a flowing Boho dress, fixed her eyes on her daughter with a single, raised eyebrow. "Why don't you call the doctor to see if you can get in sooner?"

Grace knew better than to argue with her mother, so later that afternoon she sat in a claustrophobic cubical at Dr. Dentmore's office while he looked over her CT scan. When he examined her stitches, he let out a low whistle. "You really did it to yourself. I must say, though, the ER doctor did some nice sewing."

He checked her pupils and reflexes. "How do you feel?"

"Weird, dizzy, in pain."

He glanced at the report again. "Concussions take a long time to heal, Grace. Take some time off from work. Don't do anything strenuous either. Otherwise, it'll take longer."

She didn't really want to talk about the dreams, but as he walked out of the room, Grace asked, in her most casual voice, "Is it normal that I'm having nightmares?"

"It's not uncommon after a head injury. They'll probably go away when you cut back on the pain meds."

On her way home, the dreamworld kicked up a notch and invaded her waking state.

This time, she saw herself behind a deafening, blue-green waterfall, thick and loud as Niagara. Drenched head to toe, with hair matted across her cheek like a scar, she was staring through cellophane-like, watery sheets.

She jerked the wheel to her right and almost slammed into the guardrail. Cars whizzed by at 80 mph, and she risked annihilation by getting out of the car to throw up in the bushes.

In less than three minutes, the whole episode was over. *Great, a new brand of crazy.*

Thirty minutes later, Grace stumbled into the house and flopped down on the couch. Eve, who sat in her red leather chair, was posting grades.

"How did your appointment go?"

"Okay, except I threw up on my way home."

Eve glanced at Grace as if seeing her for the first time. "You don't look so good. Was it something you ate?"

"No, I've just been throwing up since I hit my head."

"What did Dr. Dentmore say?"

"Uh, I didn't actually mention it."

Eve's eyes widened. "You didn't *mention* it?"

"It says online that vomiting can be a symptom of a concussion."

"You were at the *doctor's* office and you didn't *say anything*?"

Grace shielded her eyes from the afternoon sun pouring through the window. "Mom, I'm too exhausted to fight."

Eve looked like she wanted to say more but stopped herself.

"Besides, I have to drive over to Ben's, you know, to say goodbye."

Ben was Grace's on-again, off-again boyfriend and coworker at Nordstrom's where they traded shifts playing the piano in the lobby.

"What? Why? Where's he going?"

Grace sighed. "I told you, Mom. He's spending the summer in Germany at a piano symposium."

Eve grimaced. "This is the Ben who didn't even call you after the accident; the Ben who talks about himself non-stop; the one you thought was hitting on your sister?"

"He was just trying to figure out how she won the Governor's Award for music when she was only sixteen."

Eve closed her grade book and stood up. "Right. If you want my advice, say goodbye on the phone."

Grace walked upstairs to her room, grabbed a bottle of water and took a pain pill. She leaned back onto the heap of clothes piled on her bed. Ben had been strangely distant the last few days. Probably packing. She'd gotten him the job at Nordstrom's when she came home from Boston, and he'd enjoyed dazzling the old ladies with his renditions of musical theater numbers. But Eve was right. He could be a little self-focused. Egotistical.

She really wasn't in any shape for a one-on-one with him tonight. In a moment, Ben's picture came up on her phone. "So, how's my favorite accident-prone girlfriend?"

"Not too great today."

"Well, are you coming over?"

"Sorry, Ben, I don't think I can make it. I just took a pain pill."

"Grace," he whined, "you said you were coming."

"This concussion's got me beat right now."

He chuckled. "You know I could make you feel better."

Grace sighed. *He just wants a goodbye tryst.* "Can we video chat when you get to Germany?"

His voice turned hard. "Right."

And then the line went dead.

The next morning, Grace switched from pain meds to regular aspirin. Her head didn't hurt as much, and she barely remembered any nightmares. But something new was happening. A song had started to play in her head. It was familiar, but she couldn't place it. Not classical, not a pop tune, it was repetitive and beautiful. Normally, to identify the melody, she would've gone to the piano and played it out. But she couldn't do that. Nothing seemed to translate to her fingers these days.

That evening after supper, she got ready to attend Mimi's last high school show. Mimi was dressed to the nines in an expensive, little black dress, reserved only for music performances. She was also wearing makeup and wobbling on heels—a first for her. Her big brown eyes looked even bigger with mascara and eyeliner.

Maybe it was the pain or the momentous occasion, but Grace started to choke up. *How did this kid grow up so fast? Dad should've been here.*

When Eve spotted Mimi, she threw her arms around her and buried her face in her hair.

"You look wonderful, honey."

"Really? I had to do the eye liner three times."

Mimi put Herbert, her performance violin, in its five-hundred-dollar, titanium, temperature-controlled case while Grace stuffed the score into Mimi's backpack. Herbert was one of the last things their father had bought before he died. Mimi was only twelve at the time, but he'd watched the auctions and contacted violin sellers throughout the Northeast until he found a beautiful Franco Merlo. In her hands, it sounded like a Strad.

When they got to the show, Grace and Eve sat with their friends,

Dan and Cassie Castillo, the pastors of their church. Their six-year-old, Xavier, bounced in his seat when he saw Grace.

"Sit with me, Gracie, pleeeeese!"

She climbed into the seat next to him and gave him a hug. "You ready to see your big brother on stage?"

"Yup. He's been practicing his songs every day. I know all the words."

Cassie smiled at him. "But you're not going to sing along, right? The people came tonight to hear Jay and his friends sing."

Xavier put one finger in front of his lips. "Right. I'm just gonna listen, like Daddy said." Grace was glad she was sitting far away from Dan. Call it magical thinking, but he was so intuitive, she was convinced he could read her mind. She wasn't about to admit to anyone that she felt like she was going nuts.

When the lights went down, Grace sank low in her seat and closed her eyes so she could listen for her sister. Then the cellophane sheet of blue came between her and everyone else. Her pulse pounded in her ears. *Whoosh!* The water. She saw her face stare back at her, wet and scared. She tried to stay absolutely still, hoping it would pass.

The whole episode was over in less than a minute, but, like a seizure, it left her weak as a baby. *A baby?* Like the baby who lived in her head? Was *that* baby seeing all this? It had never seemed weird to talk to her, but maybe even that was crazy.

Grace closed her eyes again and tried to relax. But how, when she was turning schizo? Was her mental software crashing, or were these Ezekiel-style visions? Did she need a shrink, a neurologist, or an exorcist?

II

GRACE

By Monday, Grace was a total basket case. She'd had the blue vision/nightmare more than ten times, mostly when she was sleeping, but also in the daytime too. She had one when she was playing the piano, one when she mowed the lawn, one when she video called Ben. Fortunately, he was so absorbed in demonstrating his practice piece that he didn't notice her eyes glazing over.

When she finally told her mother how her nightmares had turned into visions, Eve immediately called her friend Paul, the neurologist, who scheduled an MRI for Grace the following day. Grace, who had never had an MRI, balked at the whole event—lying on a steel table, being slid into a giant Twinkie that clanked and banged like a toddler on pots and pans. Fortunately, her headphones saved her. She listened to a recording of her father playing a Schumann cello concerto, pictured him playing it just for her. Well, for her and the baby that lived in her head.

She thought about her father's last six months. Eve had lost it and would have gone completely bonkers if her friend hadn't hooked her up with Living Word Ministries. That's where they'd met Dan and Cassie who surrounded them with meals, gift cards, and respite time—everything that usually only family does. Eve and Mimi really got into the church, but Grace and her dad kept their distance.

Eventually her father said *the love* got to him, and he was baptized in their bathtub, his fragile bones angular under his T-shirt and sweatpants. He died on New Year's Eve.

The possibility of being crazy, or demon-possessed, was nothing compared to what he went through, so Grace worked hard to be brave during her test.

After the MRI, she had planned to go to work at Nordstrom's, since Stan, her boss, had been calling her every day, but the drive made her so anxious that she decided to just go home. She planned to take Mimi shopping for her prom dress on Tuesday. Maybe she'd have answers by then.

Grace woke up on Tuesday with an aching head, as usual, but cheerful that she was getting her stitches out. Before she left for Dr. Dentmore's office, Paul, the neurologist, called. "We're not seeing any abnormalities in your MRI. Just a slight bit of swelling at the point of impact that should subside within the next few weeks. I'm sending the results to your primary care doctor."

She knew the MRI would come back normal. Now what? Go back to the shrink she'd seen after her father died? But her life had been a mess then. Now, apart from the accident, her only problem was that she was living at home and couldn't find a teaching job. Nobody was dead—yet.

While she sat in line, waiting to pick Mimi up from school, Grace scrolled through her phone again, trying to find the name of her old shrink. They'd done a few sessions, and while they'd been helpful, talking to her pastor, Dan, had helped more. As she inched forward in the pickup line, someone behind her laid on the horn.

Grace had hated Eastchester High. Back then, she'd been the classic introvert, self-absorbed and shy, living in a private fantasy world with the baby in her head.

But Mimi was the opposite. Her first day in orchestra as a freshman, she was already somewhat famous. Their music teacher, Mr. Levinson, was beside himself, not quite knowing what he'd do with her but hoping the orchestra would place better in competition. Mimi had been nervous, carrying her practice violin and a backpack that weighed about fifty pounds. The concert master of the orchestra, a senior named Randy Moon, had played with her in the New York Youth Symphony. He was completely jealous and afraid she'd take his place. But she even won him over. By the end of the week, he offered to step down, but she wouldn't take his chair, even though Levinson said she could. She played second all year, and they became good friends.

Grace spotted Mimi as she walked out of the Music Wing, kibitzing with two other music geeks, Kimberly an oboe player and Jenna, a singer. When they reached the car, Jenna leaned down to talk to Grace through the window. "Mimi said you're taking her shopping for her prom dress. You guys should go shop at Jovani's. They have hundreds of dresses."

"Can I drive?" Mimi asked as she threw her stuff in the back seat.

Grace grimaced. "I'll tell you what, if you can make a decision without trying on two hundred dresses, you can drive home."

"We could go with you," Kimberly suggested. "Keep her supplied with dresses while she stays in the dressing room, trying them on. Might go faster."

All three of them looked at Grace expectantly, like a trio of superheroes ready for a mission. The very thought made her cringe. "That's okay, we'll be fine."

"How was your day?" Grace asked as they pulled out of the school lot.

Mimi pulled her hair away from her face and put it into a hair tie. "B-o-r-i-n-g. Our English teacher's on a rampage, so we're writing papers in class every day."

"What are you writing about?"

"Anything the loudest person yells out. Yesterday it was beer. The day before it was zombies. Today it's siblings."

"I hope you didn't write about me."

"No, I wrote about someone else's sister."

Grace pulled into a gas station, and Mimi jumped out to buy sodas and M&Ms while Grace pumped gas. When she got back in the car, Mimi asked, "You wanna hear what I wrote? I've got it with me."

"Sure."

She grabbed her notebook out of her backpack and began. "My Sister. It's hard to put into words what my sister is like because she's pretty changeable. Sometimes, she's very considerate, like when she buys me Dr. Pepper on the way to the store…"

"You just put that in!"

"To see if you were listening. Okay—sometimes she's very considerate like when she lets me drive her car or wear her clothes. Other times she's real moody and treats me like a ten-year-old. I don't think my sister is very happy, even though she has everything going for her, like beauty, brains, and talent. She's a lot like our dad who died awhile back—both intense and dramatic. When my sister gets an idea in her head, she won't let anything distract her. Like once when she was fourteen, she wanted to go to a concert in upstate New Y…"

"Not this again."

"The pianist was playing Rachmaninov's Third Concerto. It was about three and a half hours away, and she begged my dad to drive her. That day we had a huge ice storm. Everything was closed down—even the Thruway. But she didn't let up because, according to her research, nobody was playing the Rach III anywhere on the East Coast for a year. She finally convinced my dad. Only twelve people sat in the audience, and it took them ten hours to get home. My mom stayed up all night worrying about them."

"She stayed up all night?"

"Yep."

"Poor mom. You make me sound like a spoiled brat."

"You are." She continued, "My sister has a lot of spunk. She used to beat up anybody who teased me when we were little. One time she got kicked off the bus for a week because she hit three kids and made them all cry. Mom and Dad punished her, but not too much because she was defending me. When I was in the sixth grade, this kid hid my violin as a joke. I was afraid to tell my parents, but Grace knew. The next day she skipped out of her study hall at the high school and walked all the way over to the middle school. She told him that if he didn't return it in an hour, she was coming back to flush his head in the toilet."

Grace laughed. "I remember that. His mom told Dad she was gonna have me arrested for threatening. As I recall, that was your first good violin, that they told you not to take to school, which is probably why you didn't tell Mom and Dad in the first place."

"Nuh uh."

Grace went on. "Poor little, tortured musician, fragile as a butterfly. Did you say *that* in your little report? Did you say how you always set me up?"

Mimi answered by cranking up the radio and belting out the song it was playing.

After about ten minutes, Grace swung the car off the ramp. "There's Jovani's. Let's try to make this as painless as possible, Mi."

"Oh, I forgot to tell you—Mom wants us to send her pictures of the dresses before we buy anything."

Grace pulled into a parking space and stared at Mimi. "You're kidding, right?"

"No, she made me promise."

Grace felt her face redden. Is this what having high blood pressure felt like? "So, we have to wait around for her to text us back before we can check out?"

"She said she'd have her phone on her."

Grace got out of the car and slammed the door. "This is gonna be a freak show."

Mimi caught up to her. "Don't be mad. It'll be fun."

Jovani's was like a bridal warehouse on steroids—just as many dresses but in every color imaginable. Apparently, Mimi's goal was to try on every prom dress in her size in the store. Despite

Grace's initial mood, they actually spent a lot of time laughing. Once, when Mimi put on some scarlet thing that was cut down to her navel, she did a bump and grind that made Grace literally fall over. When they got to the point where they thought they might get kicked out of the store, Mimi spotted a shiny yellow dress that looked like it came off the red carpet. When she tried it on, the way it shimmered and set off her dark hair and eyes was simply breathtaking. Immediately Grace grabbed her phone, snapped a picture and sent it to Eve who called back in less than five minutes. Grace put her on speakerphone. "What else do you have?" Eve asked.

"This is it, Mom. It looks terrific on her."

"How much?"

"That's the best part! It's marked down from $400 to $250."

"What? That's *way* too much!"

"What are you going by, Mom? Have you seen the prices on prom gowns lately?"

"You only paid $150 for yours."

"That was five years ago! I'm telling you, it's practically the cheapest dress in the store."

"Then you're in the wrong store."

When Mimi slipped out of the dress, looking hopeless, Grace turned off the speakerphone and whispered, "Mom, she looks gorgeous in it. Let her buy it. I'll kick in seventy-five bucks. That'll bring it down to $175."

"You don't have any money, Grace."

"I've been making tons of money!"

"Not lately."

"I will again, once I get this head thing figured out."

"What did Dr. Dentmore say?"

"The obvious. He wants me to see a shrink. But I have a different idea. I'll talk to you about it tonight."

Eve said nothing.

"Everything's gonna be okay Mom. You'll see."

"You really think the dress is a good deal?"

"We've tried on every dress in this store. This is the best."

"Is it too low in the neckline? I can't tell."

"It's fine. It's a *no-cleavage* model."

"All right, run it as a debit."

Grace gave Mimi a thumbs-up which resulted in her doing a happy dance.

"I'll put some of it on mine."

"No, don't bother. I've got it."

Minutes later they left the store. Mimi laid the dress gently in the backseat. "You should've tried some on, Gracie. They make you feel like a princess. You need that right now."

Grace gave her a sideways glance. "How do you know what I need?"

Mimi stared straight ahead and played with her hair, her signature trait when she was upset. "I'm not stupid, Grace. I hear you talking to Mom. I know you're having a hard time. I just don't know what it's about."

Grace said nothing for a moment. Finally, she shrugged. "It's nothing."

Mimi glanced at her sister. "Something's been wrong since the bike accident."

Grace chewed on the side of her thumb nail—*her* signature vice when she was upset. "I'll figure it out."

She hoped that Mimi would stop the questions, but she was on a roll. "Can't you just tell me what's happening?"

Suddenly, Grace swerved over to the side of the road. "Out."

Mimi's eyes widened.

"It's time for you to drive, kiddo. You didn't try on two hundred dresses. You've earned it."

Mimi let out the breath she was holding and jumped out of the car. As she rounded the back, she met Grace and they high-fived, grinning. Without speaking, they both climbed back in and Mimi drove away.

III

GRACE

When Eve got home from work, she found Grace stir-frying chicken and veggies in her kitchen. "Cooking again? To what do I owe this?" Eve asked as she leafed through her mail on the kitchen table.

"Just trying to help out."

In the living room they could hear Mimi practicing the violin. She made Brahms sound like butter. "Has Mimi asked to borrow your car yet for the prom?" Eve asked.

Grace frowned. "No, and I'm not lending it to her. She can take yours."

"She doesn't want to drive a ten-year-old clunker to the prom."

"So?"

Grace poured rice wine into the wok which sizzled, spitting a sweet fragrance.

"How does your head feel now that the stitches are out? What did Dr. Dentmore say?" Eve asked.

"Still sore, but at least I can wash my hair. We talked about the dreams and the other stuff. He called the daytime events *waking dreams.*"

Eve looked up from her mail and stared at Grace. "I've never heard of anything like that."

Grace reached into her pocket for her phone. "I wrote down the technical name. It's called daytime para-hypnagogia or DPH, also known as *waking reveries.*"

"Like daydreams?"

"Sort of, but more intense."

"So, how do you get rid of it?"

Grace tasted the chicken and added some soy sauce. "That's the problem. Since they don't know what causes them, they don't know how to stop them. It sometimes comes from being sleep deprived, but I've been getting plenty of sleep."

"But what's the solution?" Eve persisted, queen of the bottom line.

Grace tossed the chicken for a minute, trying to put her thoughts into words. "Maybe it's not physical."

Neither of them said anything for a while, just listened to Mimi's beautiful music. "You mean like something spiritual?"

"Sounds weird, I know."

"Not really. My friend Alice gets dreams like that all the time. But why now, and why the constant repetition?"

"I don't know Ma, but I'd like to talk to Pastor Dan about it."

The next morning, Grace woke up cranky. There were the dreams of course, her new dream theme. She'd gotten used to them by now since they were all basically the same, her in trouble, lots of water, the falls, an odd blue-green wash over everything. Sometimes she was alone, sometimes other people showed up, but the fear, the sense of urgency stayed the same.

Stan hadn't checked in with her for two days. She'd found him two other music students to take her place for a while and thought maybe he liked them so much, he didn't care if she came back. They'd also cut her hours in jewelry down to only four, leaving plenty of time for teaching interviews. Only she hadn't had any in over a month.

After breakfast, Grace called him to ask him how the girls were working out. His voice was edgy and impatient. "I've scheduled them both for two weeks, but I think that's going to be the end of it."

Grace's stomach knotted. "Why?"

"Remember that visit from corporate last week? They've decided to pipe music in, like all the other stores. They'll keep the grand piano in the lobby for concerts, but they told me their research shows that *customers prefer high energy, recorded music* or some such malarkey."

"So, you're letting me go too?"

His voice softened. "Sorry, yeah."

Grace was actually relieved.

"I've got a spot in toys if you want it."

Grace chuckled. "Thanks, but I think I'm gonna take some time off to review my options."

"Are you still working in jewelry?"

"Only on Saturdays."

There was a long pause. "You know, you're actually a better piano player than any of them, including that boyfriend of yours. He had some great technical stuff going, but you have more heart."

Grace was shocked. *Better than Ben, the wonder boy?* "I appreciate you saying that, Stan."

After hanging up, she sat on the edge of her bed for a while.

Great, this is my life: no boyfriend, no work, crazy dreams. Time to call Pastor Dan.

Grace drove into the parking lot of Living Word Ministries and pulled up next to Pastor Dan's battered pickup, a hand-me-down from Cassie's minister/farmer dad. Inside, she followed the winding hallway to his office and knocked on the door which was slightly ajar. "Come on in," he called.

He was on the phone, so he waved for her to sit down. The desk he was sitting behind was piled high with bulletins, mail, coloring book pictures from kids, two stress balls, a Starbucks coffee cup and a few Kit Kat wrappers. On the corner sat his big green Bible.

A mountain of a man—over 6' 4" and at least 250 pounds, he didn't really look like a minister, at least not when he was wearing jeans and a Yankees T-shirt like today. He was more the trucker or contractor type, with calloused hands, a full beard and a weather-beaten face.

His son Jason was his biggest fan, although lately, according to Mimi, they'd been arguing more. Pastor Dan, a southern boy, was a big-time jock in high school and college, but he never forced that on Jason who was clearly not interested. He supported Jason's love for theater and music, while he and Xavier watched football and played soccer together. Jason took more after his mom who had a great voice and played the flute. According to Mimi, Cassie was not keen on Jay going into theater because she was afraid it would corrupt him. Pastor Dan didn't have the same concerns. He believed every profession—except maybe the Mafia—needed Christians.

After he hung up the phone, Dan walked to Grace and wrapped her in a great bear hug. "How's life?"

"Not so good."

"I figured as much from your phone call. Let's pray, darlin', before we get started."

Grace zoned out while he prayed, not hearing the words but focusing on the sound of his voice which was so masculine and kind—something she'd missed since her dad died. She felt tears well up from a tight little knot in her chest. Fortunately, the prayer didn't last more than a minute, or she would've turned into a puddle on the floor.

"So, what's going on?" he asked, sitting back down behind his desk.

He picked up his coffee, took a sip, and leaned so far back in his chair, that she was afraid he'd tip over and crack his skull.

It took her less than ten minutes to tell him everything. When she finished, he rocked back and forth in his chair, his fingers steepled in front of him. "Any pattern to these events, anything that seems to bring them on?"

"Not that I've noticed. I've had them while I was listening to music, while I was driving, while I was video chatting with Ben. I had one at the show last week. There doesn't seem to be any pattern to them."

"Do you listen to music while you drive?"

"Sure."

"Because, except for when you called Ben, it sounds like you were listening to music before each vision."

"Actually, there was music during that meeting too. Ben was playing me parts of his recital music."

Dan's brow furrowed. "Do you think about anything in particular when you listen to music?"

"If I'm practicing, I'm super focused. But if I'm just listening, I might think about my dad, wondering if he'd like what's playing."

She stopped talking and felt herself blush because the next thing was hard to say. "I also sometimes think about my sister who died. I call her *the baby in my head*. Dumb, huh?"

He picked up the blue stress ball, squeezed it in his massive left hand, switched it to his right. "Do you think about her much?"

"Not normally, but I have a little more since the accident."

"Why?"

She shrugged. "Don't know. She's like a song in my head. You don't notice it right away, but suddenly you realize you've been hearing it for a while."

Pastor Dan tossed the stress ball back onto his desk, picked up his pen, and twirled it. "Tell me again Grace, if you don't mind, what actually happened to her."

She took a deep breath and tried to get it all out at once, so it hurt less. "I'm not sure about the details because Mom never talks about it. Apparently, she was kidnapped from the hospital right after we were born. They never found her, but a month later a baby wearing her ankle bracelet turned up in a lake in Central Park. They never found the kidnappers. End of story."

He leaned back even farther in his chair. "That's funny."

Grace couldn't imagine anything funny about it at all.

"You didn't say she died; you said a *baby wearing her leg bracelet* was found."

"So."

"Did your parents believe that your sister was dead?"

"I guess. Yeah, of course."

She wished he'd drop it, but he was obviously on a roll.

"What about you? When you think about her, when she's like a song in your head, do you think of her as dead?"

Without warning, tears leaked out of Grace's eyes. She brushed them away, but they kept coming. She just couldn't talk about the little world that she and her imaginary twin inhabited. It was too weird, too personal. "Just like any kid with an imaginary companion, she seems real."

"That's not what I asked. Do you think of her as dead?"

Grace's ears burned, and suddenly she was mad. "No! I've never thought of her as dead. But that's my own stupidity. In my stupid little world, she's alive, because I want her to be."

Dan sat still while Grace angrily brushed her tears away with the palm of her hand. Eventually, he stood up, walked over to her, and crouched down in front of her chair. He was so big that he was still a head taller than her. "Maybe this is about her."

"Yeah, right," Grace said, dripping sarcasm, "maybe she's sending me a message."

"I'm just saying, you're in a transitional stage in your life where you may need to know more about what happened, so you can come to terms with it emotionally and move on."

That made Grace cry again because she had a ridiculous thought. *Maybe the baby in my head is finally talking back.*

"You okay?" he asked, after a few minutes.

"I hate talking about this stuff."

He nodded and sat down on the couch opposite her. "Sometimes in order to fix things you have to stir stuff up."

Great. Hand me the platitudes, she thought.

Suddenly his face brightened like a kid. "I have an idea. Cassie's brother, Kevin, is a New York detective. He's coming in from the city to have dinner with us tomorrow. Why don't you come and talk to him?"

She stared at him in horror. "No way, I don't want to dredge that whole mess up. What would it do to my mother?"

"This is about you, not her."

The very thought of talking to anyone about her dead sister literally made her nauseous. "I'd really have to think about it."

"Fair enough. But the invitation stands. If you do decide to come, try bringing anything you have about the crime—news clippings, pictures."

As he spoke, Grace could feel herself shutting down. What could a detective find out twenty-three years after the fact that wouldn't just make that horrible evil worse? She shuddered at the thought.

When Grace got home, she closed herself up in her room and threw herself onto her bed. She could hear activity downstairs but didn't answer her phone when her mother texted. She fell asleep and woke up with a start at 10:30 PM. Lying there in the dark, she tried to review her options, which she realized at once were limited and lame: go into therapy, get hypnotized, go on medication, or dig up some old crime. Even though talking to Pastor Dan's brother-in-law, Kevin, was her least favorite choice, she decided she should be prepared—just in case it was the one she ended up with. She knew her mother kept a box in the attic with clippings from the kidnapping that she could bring down to her room.

The attic stairs creaked, so she waited until midnight to go up there. Ducking under the eaves, she maneuvered through a minefield of junk until she found a clear, unlabeled plastic bin under a pile of Christmas decorations. One peek inside told her it was the one. After creeping back into her room, she slid it under her bed. Only then did she realize her whole body was shaking.

As Grace walked out to her car, she heard sounds coming from the back seat. Her heart pounding, she yanked open the door. There, sitting on the floor, she saw herself in a fetal position, soaking wet, crying, and holding a baby blanket in her hands.

She startled awake and glanced at the clock—four in the morning. She kicked off her blanket and stood up. Heading to the bathroom to get a glass of water, she paused at her hall mirror. Just two weeks past her concussion, she'd lost probably ten pounds and her eyes looked feral. She knew if she didn't do something soon, she was on her way to losing touch with reality. At that moment she decided what she was going to do.

IV

GRACE

The next morning after church, Grace waited in the hallway for Pastor Dan to finish greeting his crowd of admirers. When he saw her, he gave her a beaming smile and a hug. "Is the invite still on?" she asked.

Dan glanced at his wife, Cassie. "Sure."

Cassie put her arm through Grace's and walked her next door to the parsonage. The front hall was cool and dark with a gilded mirror on the wall. Nearby, an old iron umbrella stand held a collection of canes, some with animal heads carved into ivory, some twisted and bent, some decoratively painted. As they walked into the living room, Cassie said, "Come see what I just picked up at an estate sale."

Cassie loved buying antiques and refurbishing them to sell or add to her collection. She also liked moving furniture around a lot, so if you weren't paying attention, you could end up walking into stuff that wasn't there the week before. She motioned for Grace to sit down on a faded floral couch. She sank down into it, luxuriously. On the wall behind was an old Victorian sideboard, big as a coffin, made out of carved mahogany.

"They only wanted a hundred dollars for both! Dan and Jay weren't too happy about carrying them in—the sideboard probably weighs three-hundred pounds."

At that moment, six-year-old Xavier came bounding into the house. "Grace!"

He launched himself into her arms, knocking her back against the couch. Then he turned to his mother. "Is Uncle Kevin here yet?"

"Check out back," Cassie said.

He flew down the hallway. "I'm gonna get my rocket to show him."

After admiring the sideboard, Grace and Cassie followed Xavier out the back door. He was running, carrying a shiny spaceship in both hands. Kevin instantly scooped him up and swung him around. "Well, if it isn't the X-man! How are ya, buddy?"

Xavier didn't answer, just shoved his toy in Kevin's face.

"Cool!" Kevin exclaimed, turning it around in his hands. "Speaking of cool, who's your girlfriend?"

Xavier frowned. "Uncle Kevin, she's my babysitter!"

Cassie opened her arms to her brother. "Grace is one of our friends from church."

"I asked her to dinner so that she could pick your forensic brain. I hope you don't mind," Dan added.

"No problem. Hi Grace."

Grace found herself staring at a guy who looked like Cassie's twin. He had short, dark hair and a little stubble on his cheeks, but the mouth, nose, and striking, wide-set, blue eyes were just like hers.

She suddenly felt like this whole thing was a very bad idea.

They headed back to the house where Dan and Cassie began fixing lunch. Dan shooed Kevin and Grace into the living room to talk, but Xavier kept running in with toys to show Kevin. Finally, Cassie called him into the kitchen, and they were alone. Kevin was sitting on an overstuffed grey settee while Grace was buried in the floral couch feeling like a kid as it settled around her. At first, she felt horribly awkward, but small talk and his relaxed manner set her at ease.

"How can I help you?" he eventually asked, leaning back in his chair with one foot balanced on the knee of his other leg.

Suddenly, that simple question sent her back into a panic. She took a deep breath and tried to keep from running out of the room.

"Well, I've got a couple police-type questions for you. I don't know where to start, really."

He gave her an indulgent smile. "Take your time."

She swallowed hard. "Can you tell me when DNA testing was invented? I mean, when did police first start using it in their investigations?"

"I think it was around 1987, but it wasn't widespread until the mid-nineties."

"How did they identify bodies before that?"

"Dental records, mostly."

"How would they know if somebody was related to somebody else?"

"They didn't. Paternity testing didn't come until after DNA testing. Are you doing a paper on forensics? Is that why you're asking? 'Cause I have some books on the topic."

"No. It's a little more personal than that."

He gave her a half-smile which made her lose focus and feel like she wanted to jump into Cassie's Victorian coffin. "I'm trying to find out about a crime that happened twenty-three years ago."

Then like a girl on fire, she spilled out her story practically in one breath. When she finished, he didn't say anything for a while, just sat there smoothing the cuff of his Dockers. Finally, he looked up. "I'm really sorry."

At that moment Cassie called them in for lunch, so he didn't say another word. Grace felt naked as a newborn. Now that she'd spilled this much, she felt her gut burning. How could she go eat dinner and act normal? Somehow though, that little "I'm sorry" did something for her. No one had ever said that before. Most people would say things like, "Oh that's awful," or "How'd your family ever get over that," or "That's the worst story I've ever heard."

All those reactions would make her feel like she had to take care of *them* because they were so uncomfortable with a glimpse

of her world. But nobody had ever just said, "I'm sorry." It helped, just a little, to ease the heartache.

After dinner, Jay got ready to go to the movies with some friends while Dan and Cassie cleaned up. Dan shuffled Kevin and Grace out of the room. "Go finish your talk."

They grabbed their coffees, walked outside, and settled into wicker chairs on the deck. For a while they both just stared at the sky which was cloudless and blue. Why ruin a perfectly gorgeous day by talking about kidnapping and murder? But eventually, Grace inched back into her story. "I have a whole box of clippings and police reports, if you want to see them."

"I do, but not just yet. First, I want to know why you're trying to find out about this case now. What do you hope to gain?"

She realized that she couldn't tell him the full truth—the crazy factor being what it was. "If there's any test that can prove for sure that my sister died back then ago, it'll help my mom to accept it."

"Your mom?" he asked, meeting her gaze.

"Well, and my sister." That was an absolute lie. Mimi didn't care at all.

"What about your dad?"

"He died five years ago."

"But *you're* not interested."

"I have a little curiosity, but it's my mom mostly."

Grace swore he could tell she was lying. He took a sip of coffee. "Since this happened at St. Luke's, the files would be down in the 18th precinct. I think I can scare up some records. When do you want to know this stuff by?"

"No time soon." That was like three lies in thirty seconds.

He chuckled. "I get it. You mean yesterday."

What was it about police, pastors, and therapists? They could read you like you were a two-year-old. "You want to see the box?"

"Yeah, but I'd like to take it home with me if you don't mind."

"No, that's fine." Lie four.

"Give me your phone number, and I'll get back to you as soon as I know anything."

He handed Grace his phone so she could put her number in.

"I really appreciate this."

He nodded. "Now, I'd better pay some attention to the X-man, or he'll pout for a week."

They walked back inside, and in a minute Kevin and Xavier were a mass of arms and legs and shouts and giggles.

Grace didn't really want to hang around, but she helped Cassie serve the Chubby Hubby ice cream she had brought for dessert which kept her there for another twenty minutes. Jay's ride didn't pan out, and since she was driving right past the theater, she offered to take him.

Once Grace got into her car, she took a deep breath and let it out slowly. She and Jay chatted about Mimi and college until she dropped him off. *Now what? Cruise the streets of Tuckahoe?* Why did she think talking about her sister's death would help? The ugly reality of her family's past enveloped her like a choking fog. She had to get home. Taking the shortest route, she pulled into the driveway, relieved to see that Eve and Mimi weren't home. She took the stairs to her room two at a time. Once she got inside, she closed the blinds and sank into bed. She felt like she'd worked a twelve-hour shift and immediately fell asleep.

V

KEVIN

When the alarm rings for the fourth time, I drag myself out of bed and into the shower. I have to be across town and at my desk in one hour, which seems impossible, so I'm ticked off already. After my shower, I try to find a clean cup for coffee but end up having to wash one out. Listening to the morning news on TV, while brushing my teeth in the kitchen, I spit onto a bunch of garbage in the sink that didn't make it down the disposal from—Friday, probably. When I clear off the newspapers from my kitchen table, I see the box on the chair. Oh yeah. The favor for my sister's teeny-bopper friend. How do I get myself into these things?

She was a looker though—long blonde hair, gorgeous eyes, but a little too skinny and definitely too young. I really don't have time for this, especially now, but I pop open the box anyway. Lying on top of a batch of news articles, letters, and photos are two plastic baby ankle bracelets, one pristine, one brown and barely readable. At the bottom of the bin is a pink hospital blanket, some crumbling dried flowers, and a deflated Mylar balloon that says, "It's twins!"

When I first started on the force six years ago, evidence really upset me. It wasn't the gruesome stuff like blood-soaked clothes or murder weapons. What bothered me were ordinary things that, in a normal world, would have just been items in your house or car or wallet. The Dunkin' Donut's cup in the trash that a victim didn't know would be her last. The book on the nightstand or the backpack or the hockey tickets for next week's game—expectations of a future that never came. Now, as I look through this box that represents a life-not-lived, it barely registers a beat. I shove the top back on, throw it under my arm, and walk out the door, ready to brave the Monday morning clowns clogging the streets of Manhattan.

I inch over to 102nd Street, pull into the Precinct parking lot and jump out of the car with the bin, taking the outside stairs two at a time into the police station. The place is mobbed with people who were arrested over the weekend, most in handcuffs, some in leg irons getting ready for transport to court.

I dash past them into the elevator and ride to the sixth floor. When the doors open, I sprint over to my desk and sit down, like I've already been there for at least five minutes. The only hint otherwise is my breathing.

Bob, whose desk abuts mine gives me a look. "Way to slide in without being noticed."

Bob is thirty years older than I am, and a wise ass if ever there was one, but he's saved my butt more times than I can even remember. Why? Not because of his love for me, but because he hates our Sergeant, Carlton Hines. He'll do whatever he can to make him look bad. Carlton came to the department five years ago, a transfer from Texas. There's nothing that rattles the brotherhood more than when management brings in a young newbie from the great, non-New-York outer darkness to supervise veteran detectives. They come in with their "ya'lls" talking about soda pop and how nobody knows how to make good Mexican food. They know how things *should* work. Why, out in the Land of Oz, things run more smoothly when they have daily meetings and time cards and weekly expense account oversight.

Bob thinks he should have gotten the promotion to Carlton's position, so basically anything Carlton has to say is worthless. Too bad he turned out to be good at what he does.

Bob points to the plastic bin. "Whatcha got there, lover boy?"

"Were you on the force in 1995?"

"Who wants to know?"

"Infant kidnapping at St. Luke's. Do you remember it?"

Bob takes a swallow of coffee and unwraps his morning bagel. "A twin, right? Turned up in the Central Park Reservoir?"

"That's the one."

"Rudy O'Neil worked that case. He's a big shot now—assistant commissioner of transportation."

"What do you remember about it?"

"Not much. Never found the kidnappers. Baby died of exposure and then was dumped in the river."

"How do I get hold of Rudy?"

Bob leans over and flips through his ancient Rolodex. "He's at Worth Street. I probably have the number somewhere. You trying to reopen the case?"

"Maybe."

He jots down the number. "You're full of secrets today."

The door to Carlton's office swings open, and he crooks his finger at us. I pick up my clipboard and stand, but Bob doesn't move a muscle. "Someday I'm gonna break that finger right off his hand," he says.

After lunch I call Rudy's office, and surprisingly he agrees to meet me at Delaney's after work. By 5:00 PM I've interviewed eight witnesses, written four reports, and of course had an adrenal-pumping encounter with a perp. As they say, "Fifty-nine minutes of sheer boredom punctuated by one minute of sheer terror." It's not like I don't have enough to do without digging up an old murder, but the look of veiled desperation on that girl's face got to me. So, I drive the twelve blocks to the tavern, walk in, and see a short, sixty-something guy with thinning hair waving me over to a table by the window. "Mr. O'Neil?"

We shake hands. "Call me Rudy."

After we order beers and nachos, he says, "I recognize you from your picture. You broke the PS 31 stabbing last year, right? I still follow the department news. Only thing that keeps me awake during the day."

"I've heard that the D.O.T. is a pretty quiet place."

"It was hopping after 9/11, but by the time I came over, it was like going from real life to the morgue."

"When did you make the switch?"

"About thirteen years ago. I'd been going to Fordham Law at night for what seemed like forever. Jack Pullano was the commissioner then. He kept telling me that when I passed the bar, he was going to recommend me for his assistant. When he retired, Lois took over. We work well together, but it's nothing like police work—none of the adrenalin rushes. I don't take blood pressure medicine anymore, but the magic's gone."

"I hear ya."

"How's my old friend Bob Bernier? Still scrappy?"

"Worse, probably. He says hello, by the way. Told me you two worked the same precinct for eight years."

"We were in different departments, but I'd see him when we teamed cases. Have you seen his imitation of Carlton Hines?"

"Only a few times a day."

The waiter sets down our nachos which are piled high with melted cheese and jalapeños. "What can you tell me about the Maddox case? I know it was a long time ago."

"That was some case. Had the whole city in a panic. Why the interest now?"

"The victim's twin is a friend of my sister. She asked me to look into it."

He shakes his head and grins. "You never know when something's gonna get resurrected. Yeah, that was like twenty years ago. I was new to investigations. My own kids were little, so I really took it personally. How much do you know about the case?"

After stuffing a loaded chip in my mouth, I have to chew and swallow before I answer. "I know the kidnapping happened at St. Luke's before the kid was a day old. Police found her on an anonymous tip when they dragged the Central Park Reservoir a month later. No real leads on the kidnapper."

Rudy nods, takes a long swallow of beer, and wipes his mouth. "I lived and breathed that case for months. You can imagine how it affected people—a baby taken right from the hospital. St. Luke's almost went under. Only the absolutely destitute would go there to have their kids. I don't know why the parents didn't sue the pants off them. There was a lot of political posturing which made the investigation even harder. St. Luke's shut up like a clam. Nobody would talk to us. But it pretty much changed the way we handle hospital security. Now the babies get alarmed ankle bracelets."

A couple of guys walk into Delaney's that everyone seems to know. Suddenly the noise level jacks way up forcing me to nearly shout the next question. "When did the search for the kidnappers get dropped?"

Rudy moves his chair a little closer to mine. "After about a year. Since there was no note, no ransom, it fell into the domain of some crazy lady who wanted a baby but couldn't take care of it—at least that's what the shrinks said. But usually, we blow those cases open in a matter of days because somebody tips us off that a baby's appeared outa nowhere, and the mom's real secretive. Kidnappers like that are unprofessional and unbalanced enough to stand out. This was different. You gotta remember it was before Amber Alert, milk cartons—all that stuff popped up later."

"Was there ever any question that the baby they fished out of the river was really the Maddox kid?"

"No, because the parents IDed the baby."

"Yeah, but you know that a bloated corpse is barely recognizable. Did they run any tests to make sure?"

Rudy shakes his head. "DNA testing wasn't a big thing yet. A few years later we could've gone back, but the parents weren't interested. I think they just wanted to put it behind them. I guess they had another daughter a few years later. Saw some write up about her not long ago. Guess she's a real talented kid."

He takes a swallow of beer and looks past me like he's talking to someone else. "The case really bothered me because we had no leads on the kidnapper. I was told—forcefully—to drop it after six months. The department was getting pressure from the mayor's office. They wanted to shut down the media attention."

"Did they keep any of the old evidence?"

"Sure. Technically, it's an unsolved. All that stuff is down at the barracks on 53rd. I guess by now nobody would care if you checked it out. I tried to open the case up again about five years later, but some reporter got wind of that, and the iron fist came down again. That's when I got disillusioned. And you can see where that landed me: behind a desk in transportation."

He lifts his glass to me with a resigned smile.

"Why'd you want to open it up?" I ask, helping myself to all the jalapeños Rudy avoided on the nachos.

"New evidence. Three months before the kidnapping, a neonatal nurse resigned out of the blue. I thought there might have been a connection."

"That didn't come up at the initial investigation?"

"No. I'm telling you, the hospital closed in on itself. They were one uncooperative bunch. I'm sure they had pressure from the top. They wanted the thing to blow over once the baby turned up dead."

"How did you find out about the nurse?"

"A nurse on staff the night of the kidnapping called me after she retired."

"How can I find out her name?"

He gives me a half-smile. "Ask me."

"Okay—who was she?"

"Alice McMahon from the Bronx. She'd be in her 80s now if she's still alive."

"You've got a good memory."

"Not really. I looked it up after you called."

He pops another scraped-off chip into his mouth followed by a sip of beer. "I'd love to see you reopen this case because it always bothered me. When you called me today, I had one of those feelings—wishful thinking, I guess."

"What?"

Rudy grins. "That you'd validate what I'd tried to do—find out what really happened."

He looks down and stares at the soggy napkin under his drink. "I can't even imagine what those parents went through. Do you know how the other twin turned out?"

"She just graduated from college. Guess she's smart and talented too. Seems like a good kid. Goes to my brother-in-law's church."

"Good. Yeah, if you can find out what I was never able to, you'll be my hero. Anything else you want to know, just call me."

He pulls his card out of his wallet. "Call the cell phone. I always answer."

"Thanks, I appreciate your help. You want another beer or something?"

"Nope, gotta go. My wife and I are babysitting the grands tonight."

He stands up, shakes my hand and starts to walk away. Then he reaches into his pocket and comes back. "Almost forgot. This is Alice's phone number, or at least it was fifteen years ago."

As I back my car into a parking space at the 53rd precinct, I plan my strategy. Rosemary Turino, the dragon who guards the gate to the evidence room, is always looking for requisitions—in triplicate signed by everybody and his brother-in-law. Since I don't want to include Carlton in this fact-finding mission right now, I have to find a way to get a look at the evidence without making it official. But I certainly don't want to repeat my last run-in with her.

I take the elevator downstairs. When the doors open, I'm standing not ten feet from the chain-link pen which surrounds Rosemary's desk. She's talking to a uniform who's dutifully showing her his requisition.

"This ain't gonna fly," she says. "It doesn't matter if your staff sergeant signed this. I need the deputy detective's signature."

"I told you, the deputy's on vacation," he says.

"Who covers for him? It's that detective's responsibility."

Disgusted, the uniform pushes a phone number through the iron grid. "Look Rosemary, the staff sergeant is next in command in our office. Call him if you don't believe me."

She gives him an evil look over the glasses resting on her nose, punches the numbers into her phone and listens to a recording instructing her to leave a message. "This is the evidence room on 53rd. I've got an Officer Mannion here who says he works in your office. Call me when you get this."

She hangs up the phone and looks at Officer Mannion. "We'll just wait until he calls back. Next!"

The officer stalks off and pounds the button on the elevator. He's cursing her up and down.

I walk up to the chain link pen. "Hi Rosemary, how's life?"

As she looks up, a flicker of recognition crosses her face and rapidly spreads to a sneer. "What do you want?"

"Now, is that any way to treat an old friend?"

"An old friend who got me written up last month. Where's your requisition?"

"Well actually Rosemary, I don't have any paperwork, but that's okay because I don't want to take anything out. I'm only gonna look at it here. It's a twenty-year-old kidnapping/murder case. I just want to see the boxes and take some notes; that's all."

She chuckles like an old witch. "You gotta be kidding. You expect me to do you a favor?"

"Look, that whole shouting match was because I was late for court. I told you I was sorry. What else do you want?"

"Me? I don't want anything from you. You, on the other hand, want something from me."

"Come on Rosemary, I can come back on Thursday. You know Brian will let me in. Can't you just save me the second trip?"

She answers that question with a big, vindictive smile. I walk to the elevator, mumbling under my breath like Officer Mannion. Then I remember that Rudy said he'd help. Maybe he knows Rosemary. She's been at this post for at least ten years.

When I dial his number, he picks up right away. "Sorry to bother you so soon, but I'm trying to access the Maddox evidence, and Officer Turino at 53rd is being difficult. I don't suppose you could talk to her."

He laughs. "I'm not even to the Holland Tunnel yet. Let me talk to Rosemary."

I walk back to the pen and hand her the phone. "Somebody wants to talk to you."

She grabs the phone, a disdainful look on her face. "Officer Turino."

Within seconds, her voice softens. "Oh, hey Rudy. It's been a while. How'd you get hooked up with somebody as obnoxious as Kevin Jacobs?"

She's quiet for a while and then starts doodling on a pad. Slowly her face begins to change. The hardness melts, and though it seems impossible, she actually looks vulnerable. This guy is good. In less than two minutes, she's asking about his wife, Monica, and the grandkids. Were they friends at some point?

After she says goodbye, she hands the phone back to me. "I didn't know it was the Baby Maddox case. I don't like you, Kevin, but I like Rudy, and I remember that case. I'll see if I can get you the evidence."

I can't believe my luck. "Rosemary, you don't have to dislike me, you know. When I'm on a case, I'm a bulldog. I admit it. But that's not the real me. I'm really quite a nice guy."

She smirks. "I'll try to remember that. Lemme find out what stack it's in."

She types the name into her computer and then picks up the phone. "Billy, I need case number 21254 in stack 86. There are two boxes. Thanks."

"Have a seat, nice guy. He'll be a few minutes."

I hesitate to ask, but maybe she's still under Rudy's spell. "You mind if I use the conference room where I can spread out?"

"I'm gonna let you take the stuff. If you need it longer than a week, call in."

I'm completely disarmed. "Rosemary, I don't know what to say. Thanks."

She barely looks up. "Yeah well, solve the case. That'll be thanks enough."

"Were you involved in it too before you worked evidence?"

"Not really. It's just that," she gives me an odd look, "I was having a baby at the same time. It made an impression."

"Then your kid is twenty-three?"

She's silent for a good half-minute before answering. "No. He didn't make it."

What a jerk I am. "I'm sorry."

"Thanks. I have another son though. He's twenty."

I don't know what else to say, so I just sit there in silence.

Rosemary fills out my paperwork. "Rudy and Monica were good to me. They lost a kid once, too, so they understood. I'd just gotten back to work when the Maddox baby turned up dead. I wanted to see the kidnappers get the chair, but that didn't happen. Maybe they'll finally get what's coming to them."

I'm relieved to see Billy walking up the aisle pushing a cart. The last thing I want is for Rosemary to think I'm going to be her avenging angel. "I'm just looking into this for a friend. I don't know what'll come of it."

She buzzes the pen open, and Billy brings out the boxes.

"Thanks, Rosemary. You're a real trooper."

She tears off a copy of the form and gives it to me. "Yeah," she says.

When I get home, I drop the evidence and Grace's bin onto the kitchen table, put a frozen dinner in the oven, flip open a beer, and open the first box.

Box one contains police reports of the initial investigation at the scene—interviews with hospital personnel and the parents. Next are reports of numerous street and highway searches, interviews of extended family and friends, logged conversations with the typical street sources that line the underbelly of the city. There's a log of literally hundreds of telephone tips that came in over the course of three weeks, videos and transcripts of TV news reports and the Maddox's appeals. There's also a recording and a transcript of the final call that tipped the department off to where they found the baby.

Box two contains artifacts from the kidnapping and recovery scenes, pictures of her little naked body, an autopsy report, interviews of people in the vicinity of the lake, a detailed report on the location of the public phone used to call in the tip, interviews with officers in the City Parks Enforcement Patrol. There's also a report of the parents' reaction when they were told that the body had been recovered because apparently, they had always been considered suspects. There are newspaper and magazine articles on hospital security, a report on the new security policies at St. Luke's, and an interview with the president of the hospital.

Poor Rudy! He did his research well—the boxes represent hundreds of hours of work. Finally, there's the abrupt report dated 9/22/20

```
Case to be transferred to unsolved, inactive.
```

Clipped to that page is a sticky note with Alice McMahon's name and number. Since it's still early, I dial the number. I only get the answering machine, but the female voice sounds elderly, so I leave my name and phone number.

At the bottom of the box is a sealed manila envelope labeled "Samples." When I open it, I find two three-inch square, zip lock bags. One contains four tiny nail clippings; the other has about ten strands of fine, baby hair.

I finish up my beer and barely pick at the food which is cold and tasteless by now. Then I zone out watching baseball.

VI

GRACE

The radio pounded out an electric beat in Grace's little blue car as she drove into Manhattan. Her hair blew like a blonde stream out the window, and trees blurred as she rounded the curves of the Henry Hudson Parkway. The Hudson River sparkled to her right, while the George Washington Bridge loomed down river.

Suddenly, something blue hit her windshield. A suicidal blue jay? A loud whooshing sound enveloped her, while blue liquid spread over the windshield and into the car. Terrified and soaking wet, she jerked the car over and jumped out.

Grace awoke, heart pounding, to her cell phone ringing. Clawing for the phone, she yanked it out of the charger and onto the floor. She fumbled around under the bed to retrieve it. "Hi Grace, this is Kevin Jacobs." His voice was over-the-top a cheerful." Did I wake you?"

"No, I mean yes, sort of. Who is this again?"

"Kevin, Cassie's brother."

She took a deep breath and let it out slowly. "Oh, hi."

"Sorry to call this early, but I wanted to catch you before you went anywhere."

She glanced at her clock—7:45 AM, but the room was pitch black since she'd started draping a blanket over the window blinds.

"I've been looking over the records of your case. I still have some research to do, but I'd like to meet this week to talk."

"Sure, where?"

"Your house?"

Because her brain wasn't quite in gear yet, she agreed, instead of suggesting another place. But then she remembered that Mom and Mimi would be at choir practice on Wednesday. "Can you come tomorrow night at around seven?"

"Sure."

Grace stood up and pulled the blanket off the window. It was grey and wet outside. "How about a little preview of what you've discovered?"

"Actually, I'd rather talk about it in person, if you don't mind."

Even though she expected him to say that, it still made her stomach tighten. "Okay, I'm living at my mother's house, right now. I'll send you the address."

"I know where you live."

She should have figured that.

When she opened the door for Kevin, she was surprised to see that he was even better looking than she'd remembered. He was wearing grey slacks, a blue button-down shirt, and a yellow and blue striped tie. His hair was a little mussed, like he'd been driving with the window down, and the shirt nicely complemented his eyes. Grace glanced at the clock. "Right on time."

He grinned. "It's one of my strong points."

Those blue eyes were another one.

They walked into the living room. "Have a seat. I'll get us something to drink."

"Thanks. Your place is really nice."

Grace glanced around, trying to see it with new eyes. The walls were off-white, or what Home Depot called *Swiss Coffee*. There were splashes of color from her mother's paintings interspersed with black and white photos she'd taken during her last photography class. The furniture was a little shabby, but her mother, Eve, enjoyed flea market finds—old metal toys, a bicycle wheel made into a clock. In the center of the room sat her prized possession—an old, battered Louis Vuitton trunk that worked as a coffee table.

As she pulled glasses out of the cupboard, she saw Kevin walk around the room, staring at the walls.

"It's different. The paintings, the colors... it's beautiful."

"Well, they say your surroundings should mirror your soul."

"Then I'm in trouble. My apartment is pretty much a dark pit."

Grace slipped back into the living room with two iced teas and a plate of sandwiches on a tray. "I didn't know if you'd eaten. If you have, no problem."

Kevin looked delighted. "I'm actually pretty hungry, and I love the way you cut them into little triangles—makes me feel like I'm at a party."

Grace sat down across from Kevin and watched him devour three triangles. Then he leaned back, loosened his tie and pulled out a little pad. "I want to make sure I tell you everything. That way, you'll be fully informed in case you need to make some decisions."

What kind of decisions?

"Last week I met with Rudy O'Neil, the detective who handled your sister's kidnapping case. Nice guy. Believe it or not, he and everyone else I've talked to, still have pretty strong feelings about what happened. He said the case generated so much anxiety in the city that city officials shut it down prematurely once the deceased baby was found. Apparently, your parents didn't hound the department to keep it going."

He took a swallow of tea and went on. "Five years later, Rudy gets a call from a former St. Luke's nurse who wants to talk. Let's just say he wasn't encouraged to re-interview her. You following me so far?"

"It sounds so TV cop show. I can't believe that you're talking about my family. But, yeah, so he didn't follow it up?"

"Right. The nurse, Alice, worked in neonatal at St. Luke's when your sister was kidnapped. The hospital had been pretty tight-lipped during the investigation. Once she retired, she couldn't get some-thing off her mind. But by then, the police department wasn't interested. Rudy gave me Alice's number, so I called her right away. She called me back a day later."

Grace realized she was holding her breath. She made herself exhale.

Kevin must have noticed because he leaned over and touched her arm. "You okay?"

She nodded but kept gripping the arms of her chair.

He gave her a long look, then continued. "Alice is a spunky, eighty-year-old gal who gave me an earful. She told me that three months before the kidnapping, a neonatal nurse resigned, saying she was moving out west with her husband. That seemed strange to Alice because she knew this woman wasn't married, although she did have a live-in boyfriend. I figure it's not unusual for people to call their boyfriends their husbands, so that didn't mean much to me.

"On her last day of work the other nurses planned a party for her, but she called in sick. They'd already collected about a hundred bucks they wanted to give her, so someone tried calling her number, but it had already been disconnected. Since Alice was the only one who actually knew where she lived, they elected her to stop by her apartment just to give her a card with the money. When she got there, she discovered—"

"That she'd already moved," Grace said, taking her first sip of tea.

"Right! Not only had she already moved, but the neighbors reported that her boyfriend had moved out a month earlier and didn't look like he was going anywhere with her."

"So this lady was being secretive and maybe telling a few lies."

"Correct. Now here's the strange part. About a month later, one of the nurses says that she saw this lady coming out of an apartment building on the East Side—some classy place with a doorman."

"She moved, but not out of the city."

He nodded and took another sandwich. "Five years later,

after Alice gets her first computer, she looks this lady up on the national database of licensed nurses, and it's like she's disappeared off the face of the earth. The lady never again renews or transfers her license to another state, which, according to Alice is very unusual."

"Maybe she changed her name."

Kevin looked at Grace over the top of his glass. "Ever think of going into police work?"

She ignored the compliment. "Does Alice think this lady had something to do with the kidnapping? All this stuff is interesting, but it doesn't make her a criminal."

"Let me finish. A week before she resigned, she finished teaching a birthing class at the hospital. Your parents were in that class."

That stopped Grace cold.

"Her name was Angela Selverini. I did a search on her boyfriend, Frank Benedict, and found out he married somebody else, moved to Arizona, but after about ten years got divorced. Apparently, he came back East, got arrested a few times in Philly, then later in New York. Breach of Peace, DUI—that kind of stuff. Eventually he got arrested again and ended up in Putnam County prison which means I can go talk to him."

"What's he in jail for?"

"Trying to meet up with a fourteen-year-old girl on the internet."

Grace tried to process it all, but part of her was resistant to connecting dots that might make everything more real.

Kevin took a sip of tea and helped himself to another sandwich. Out of the corner of her eye, Grace could see him watching her. "I know this is a lot of information to lay on you all at once."

She ran her fingers through her hair, pulling it back from her face. "I guess I don't know what it all means."

"It may mean nothing, or it may mean we're closer to finding your sister's kidnappers."

"I'm not sure what I was looking for when I asked you to check into my sister's death. But I never expected to actually find my sister's kidnappers. Call me naïve, but I figured if that were possible, it would have happened already."

He polished off his drink and leaned back into the couch. "Grace, I have enough work to carry me through till Christmas. I don't need another project in my life, but if you want me to keep digging, I will."

"Why?"

He ran his finger around the rim of the glass that was still in his hand. "I don't know anything about you, Grace, except that you're important to four people who are important to me. I realize this is very personal for you, but to me it's a detective's dream—a giant puzzle with a bunch of missing pieces. If I can help you and have fun at the same time, I'm in heaven. Besides," he pointed to the party sandwiches, "I may get a few free meals out of it."

Grace's throat was dry with anxiety, but she forced herself to sound upbeat. "So, where do we go from here?"

"You don't have to make any decisions yet, but if I go to see Frank Benedict, you're welcome to come with me."

"Go to a jail? Why would I do that?"

"To see his reaction to you. If he had anything to do with the kidnapping, it would show in his eyes."

"How?"

"I can't give away *all* my trade secrets. But seriously, if it makes you uncomfortable, you don't need to come." He stood up. "Can you point me to the bathroom?"

"At the end of the hall."

As he closed the door, Grace thought about Frank and his girlfriend. If they took her sister and hurt her, what kind of monsters must they be? She physically shuddered and tried to block them out of her mind. In a few moments Kevin returned, but didn't sit down. "I've gotta get going. I told Xavier I would stop by."

On his way out of the living room, he stopped to look at her family photos. He pointed to a picture of Mimi. "I saw her at Jay's show. She looks a lot like your mom."

Grace nodded, but she was deep in thought. Finally, she said, "If it'll help, I'll go with you to see that guy. I just don't want my mom to find out. She's insanely protective ever since Dad died."

"When was that?"

"Five years ago."

Grace crossed the room and grabbed a picture off a shelf near the window. It was her parents' wedding picture—two carefree, twenty-somethings on a beach, barefoot and smiling, their hair blowing in the breeze.

"What was he like?"

"He was a cello player—taught Mimi violin until she got better than him. He was funny, kind—a perfect dad."

Kevin handed her the picture with a grim look. "You have no idea how lucky you are."

Not more than three minutes after he left, Grace heard her mother and sister pull into the driveway. When they walked through the door, Eve had a weird look on her face. "Was that Cassie's brother Kevin who just left?"

"Uh, yeah."

"Cute, isn't he?" Mimi said.

"I guess so."

But Eve didn't look happy. "Why was he here?"

"Somebody has a boyfriend," Mimi sing-songed.

Grace reached across her mother to try to swat Mimi, but she dodged out of the way, laughing as she went into her bedroom. Eve silently made a cup of tea without looking at Grace. Finally, Grace said, "I asked Kevin to investigate, you know, the case."

Remembering how her choice of words upon finding out about her dead sister had created havoc when she was ten, she avoided saying "kidnapping" or "murder." Her parents had tried to shield her from their sordid history, but a cruel schoolmate had told her when she saw an article in the newspaper about it.

Eve stirred her tea without responding, but her face said it all. She had that sad, bewildered look that Grace had seen every time she brought up her twin. She sat down at the table and grabbed Eve's hands.

"Mom, just for now, I want to do this alone. Is that okay?"

Eve lifted her eyes and stared out the window. Then she looked back a Grace. "Of course, I just wish you'd told me."

They didn't talk more about it. Grace tried to be cheerful for the next few hours, but felt wretched. When Eve went to bed, Grace opened the curtained, glass doors of the music room and went inside. Her father's cello sat in the corner, exactly where he'd left it five years before. She ran her fingers over the scroll, making a track in the dust. They'd always been a duo. She sat down at the piano and played quietly. Gershwin, mellow and low.

VII

KEVIN

When I walk into the office on Thursday morning, Bob is rifling through the papers on my desk. "Looking for something?"

"The sergeant's on my back about the Benson case. Have you got it?"

"Yeah, locked up where it's supposed to be."

"Well unlock it before the fool has a coronary."

I open my desk and go through the files in my drawer while Bob hovers over me. "Stop breathing down my neck. I'm on it."

"You take it in to him, or I'll say something I shouldn't."

I'm just about done with Bob's childish vendetta against our boss, but I take the file into Sergeant Hines' office anyway. He's on the phone, so I drop the file on his desk, but he waves me to sit. In a minute he hangs up and grins at me. "Bob flipping out?"

"Sort of."

"Good. It keeps him on his toes. What've you been up to? I know it's not the Benson case, because it would've been done by now."

"We just need to get two more statements from witnesses to send it on to prosecution."

"You didn't answer my question, Kevin. Rumor has it that you're looking into an old case—which wouldn't be so bad, if I'd given it to you. But I haven't given you a cold case since last year, which you solved nicely, I'll admit. So, either you talk, or I'll get it outta Bob."

I knew my time would come.

"I'm looking into an old kidnapping/murder case. The victim was the twin of my sister's friend. I'm just helping her put it to rest."

"And when were you gonna tell me about this?"

"With all due respect, Sir, why do I have to? It's on my own time."

Carlton's eyes narrow, and his voice turns hard. "There's no such thing as your own time in this department."

For a split second I want to blast him, but I don't need a reprimand in my file. "What do you want me to do, Sergeant?"

"I want the Benson case finished, and the Cramer case, and the shooting on West 57th street. I want you doing your *job*. It's bad enough having Bob around who does as little as possible to get by. If he thinks being three years from retirement means he can't get fired, he's got another think coming. I could ship him to Harlem where he wouldn't last a week. You're supposed to be the guy I can count on. You better bring it back, and fast!"

By the time he's done, he's spitting mad. "Is that all, Sir?" I say evenly.

His face turns red, and he shoves the file across the desk at me.

Bob is waiting when I get back. "He ream you out?"

"Just let off a little steam."

"Don't try to be Mother Teresa. I heard him."

"Then why are you asking, Bob?"

"'Cause I'm keepin' a list."

"If you heard him, you must know he's threatening to send you to Harlem."

"You think I'm afraid of him?"

I've had it with Bob. "Look, he sees us as a pair. I'm sick of getting treated like crap because you've got a chip on your shoulder."

"Why do you kiss up to him? Comes in here pushing his weight around like he's some kinda god…"

I slam the folder down on my desk. "We're supposed to be a team."

Bob sneers at me. "Why don't we all just sing, "We Are The World?""

I give up. Maybe I'm the one that needs the transfer.

At 5:10, after everyone's cleared out of the office, I knock on the sergeant's open door. "I've got those cases you asked for this morning."

After I hand them to him, I say, "I was outa line this morning. I'm sorry."

He puts the files in his briefcase. "Forget it."

"I *have* been spending too much time on this old case. I just can't believe they didn't follow up on some of the leads and really nail the kidnappers."

"It's okay. Keep working on it."

"What?"

"I did a little search of my own this afternoon—called Rudy O'Neil when I saw his name on it. He said city politics drove the investigation instead of good police work. The lead detective is always the fall guy when that happens. Who knows, maybe if you turn over a few stones, a snake or two will crawl out."

"I'll make sure it doesn't interfere with department work."

"If you guys dotted all your i's on the Benson case, you can pick it up on department time. Bob can work the Wall Street case on his own while you spend a little time on this."

"Oh, he'll love that."

He gets defensive right away. "Meaning…"

"No, really. He loves embezzlement cases, knows just the right questions to ask 'cause he has a background in finance. I screw him up more than help him on those."

Carlton shakes his head. "Don't worry, if I give him the case, he'll complain."

Since he's not steaming, I take a risk. "You might try to understand Bob, sir."

"I understand that he hates me."

"That's only because he'd been on the force for twenty-seven years when you came in—half his age—to run the whole department. It kinda made him bitter."

"Yeah, well, if he'd had a better attitude maybe they would've handed it to him."

"Bob lost his wife to cancer just before you came. His kids won't speak to him. He's been through a lot."

"You're his cheerleader now?"

"I know who he is under the crust, that's all."

Sergeant Hines picks up his briefcase and turns off the light in his office. "There's only one thing with the kidnapping case—it's not about what the family needs, it's about what *we* need—correct what was botched, get closer to the truth. The wrong focus makes you miss stuff."

"Gotcha."

"And I want to be kept informed."

This is too good to be true.

After he leaves, I call Jody at the Office of the Chief Medical Examiner. "Hi Jody, this is Sammy's friend, Kevin Jacobs at the 53rd precinct."

"Kevin who?"

"Jacobs."

"I don't remember you, besides I'm backed up the wazoo."

"We met at the Toys for Tots benefit in December. I was sitting at the table with you guys."

"Yeah, well, I still don't remember. What do you need?"

"How are you?"

"Like I said, backed up."

"I was wondering if I could stop by with some hair samples. I need a DNA match. Identical twins."

I hear her frustration on the phone. "I don't know when I can get to it…"

"What time are you working to?"

"Nine."

"How 'bout I bring up some Chinese food when I drop the stuff off."

"It doesn't mean I can do it tonight."

"That's fine. What do you like?"

She doesn't say anything for a while. "Where you going?"

"Probably Planet Thailand."

"Okay, General Tso chicken."

"Great! I'll be there in less than an hour."

Planet Thailand is on West 24th Street, four blocks from Forensic Biology on First Avenue. For some reason, the traffic is in my favor tonight, so it only takes me twenty-two minutes to drive the thirty blocks. All the while I'm trying to remember what Jody looks like, or her last name, so I don't make a fool of myself, but it's not coming. When I get to the building, the officer on duty calls Jody from his desk. "That guy you don't know is here."

He directs me to an office at the end of the hall. Thankfully, there's only one woman in the lab sitting at a table, labeling Petri dishes. She looks up without any recognition. "I still don't remember you."

"That's no surprise. I'm kind of an everyman-looking guy."

I put the bag of food down on a chair. "Sammy and I co-chaired the East Side toy drive. He introduced us at the dinner."

I can't believe I didn't remember her since she's a pretty good-looking woman. Over six feet tall, she's got red hair and green eyes, a full mouth and a nice, ample body that I would've noticed since I'm not keen on skinny women. Maybe knowing she was somebody's girlfriend made me screen out my impressions.

"You're not the guy who got disgustingly drunk, are you?"

"No, I'm the guy who got called out halfway through dinner to a homicide in the Village."

"That's probably why I don't remember you."

"How's Sammy doing? I haven't seen him in weeks."

"He's in Miami visiting his parents."

"Do you want to eat now, or save this till later?"

"I can eat now. Let's go to my office."

She leads the way to a cramped little room in the back with a desk and two chairs. After we sort out the cartons, I hand her a pair of chopsticks. "Well, this solves the problem of what I was going to eat. Thanks."

We talk about her boyfriend, Sammy, for a while. Then she tries again to jog her memory about the dinner, but it's not working. "If you can't remember me, let's just pretend this is the first time we're meeting. Hi, my name is Kevin."

She laughs. "I'm Jody."

"I see you work for the police department. What a coincidence, so do I! How'd you get involved in forensics?"

Apparently, Jody doesn't know how to use chopsticks, so she just takes one and stabs pieces of chicken with it. "My dad was a chemist at Bristol-Meyers. When I was a kid, he'd let me hang out in his lab on weekends. I'd play with the silica gel, fill the test tubes with Juicy Juice, look at dust mites under a microscope. While other girls were playing with Barbies, I was growing mold in my room. I didn't want to help develop drugs that cost $1,200 a pill, so I went into forensics. What about you?"

"I chose police work so that I *wouldn't* be like my dad."

"Why, what does he do?"

"He's a minister."

She laughs. "So, you're a preacher's kid."

"Yep—raised in Lancaster, Pennsylvania where we only associated with people just like us. I was a pretty sheltered, homeschooled kid, no TV, couldn't listen to pop music, play cards, read anything but classics. When I turned eighteen, I jumped ship and moved to New York. I spent the first six months overdosing on TV. Once I saw my first *Starsky and Hutch* rerun, I knew I wanted to be a cop."

"How'd your dad handle that?"

"Not well. I told him it could've been worse—I could've ended up on the other side of the law."

Jody takes a swallow of her bottled water. "Not to burst your bubble or anything, but in a way, you did turn out like your dad."

"Oh yeah?"

"Sure. On the streets, you deal with good and evil, you spend a lot of time counseling and you try to bring order to chaos. Ministers do that too."

As much as I don't like her conclusion, I grin and nod. "Well, if that's true, then I've got a congregation that's headed to hell on a high-speed rail."

Jody attempts to eat the rice with both her chopsticks but only succeeds in picking up two grains. "Didn't they give you any plastic forks with this stuff? I always get plastic forks."

"Sorry. I'll know for next time."

She pulls open her desk drawer and rummages around until she finds a plastic spoon. "You think I'll be bought this easily next time? In case you don't know, forensic scientists are the most highly courted people in police work."

"I'm not surprised."

She shovels a few mouthfuls of rice into her mouth and closes up the container of food. "How 'bout giving me a little background on the hair samples before I get back to work."

"Okay. About twenty years ago a dead baby that had been kidnapped at birth was fished out of the Central Park Reservoir. Looking through the evidence box last week, I saw that some forward-looking officer saved a hair sample. This baby had an identical twin that wasn't kidnapped. She's 23 now and wants to find out more about the case. I just wanna make sure that the baby who came out of the lake is really her sister."

"Why? Didn't anybody ID the kid?"

"The parents did, but you know how bodies look after they've been floating for a while."

"Don't they take babies' footprints when they're born? Stick their feet in ink and make decorative birth certificates for their parents?"

"Not at St. Luke's."

"Okay, so this twenty-three-year-old gave you a hair sample?"

"Not exactly. I obtained it with her, shall we say, unconscious assent."

Jody snorts. "Unconscious assent?"

"Right. See, I'm 99 percent sure it's her twin, so why bother asking for a sample? It might upset her."

"Are you in love with this girl?"

"What!?"

"Just asking."

"I don't know anything about her."

"Why would you care if it upset her? That doesn't sound like objective police work."

"I don't know, maybe because she's my sister's friend. Hey, remember I'm no ordinary guy. I'm a minister to the masses."

"So how *did* you get the hair sample? Wait, don't tell me. The less I know, the better."

I laugh. "I just pulled a few hairs out of a hairbrush when I was in her bathroom."

"Remind me never to invite you to my house."

"I behave better in most social situations."

"Sure, you do."

She grabs the box of her unfinished food and stores it in the fridge. I shudder to think about what else might be in there. When I give her the two labeled plastic bags, she holds them up to the light, then stuffs them into the pocket of her lab coat. "I don't know when I can get to this."

I hand her a card with my cell number. "Take your time. Just leave a message when you know."

On the way to work the next morning I call my buddy Freddy who runs the fitness center on 51st Street. "You want to do something tonight?"

"Like what?"

"They've got salsa music at Remy's tonight. Who's that girl that Becky knows? Maybe we can get them to go."

Freddy sighs. "Kevin, when are you gonna learn you can't just call up a girl and take her out the same night. She wants notice, bro."

"Then we'll meet some girls there. I don't care."

"Whoa tiger, I don't wanna pick up any girls."

"Not pick 'em up, just dance! I've had a rough week, and I want to blow off some steam."

"Let me see what I can do. I'll call you later."

I walk into the office twenty minutes later and see Bob talking to Carlton Hines in his office. When he comes back to his desk, I brace myself for the string of invectives Bob normally spews after any encounter with him. Instead, he says, "I guess I'll be workin' the Wall Street fiasco with Connie Wright while you do that old kidnapping case."

I'm surprised he's not fuming. "You okay working with Connie?"

He grins. "Sure. Unlike you, she gets numbers."

"What's up with you and Carlton? I didn't hear any yelling."

"Working with Connie puts me downstairs. What's to yell about?"

I don't know what's going on, but I don't want to jinx it.

"Hines told me to help you with the kidnapping case when I can. Do you need anything before I leave?"

"I wanna get a picture and some background info on a nurse named Angela Selverini who worked at St. Luke's back then. I've got a rap sheet printed up on her boyfriend Frank Benedict, but she's not in the system."

"Good luck gettin' anything out of St. Luke's. They probably only keep employment records for about six years—ten years if there's been disciplinary action."

"Then I'll just start looking through the phone book for Selverinis."

He stares off into space for a few seconds and then smiles. "But if she was treated there—even if it was just a blood test—they have to keep those records for forty years. You might not get a picture or a social, but you can get an old address and insurance info."

"According to her co-worker, she lived on Eldridge Street, but I can't find her actual address."

"What was her old boyfriend's name? Frank Somebody?"

"Benedict."

Bob types Frank Benedict's name into the computer, one finger at a time. "Okay, I'm seeing 114 Eldridge in 1994."

I write it down. "Does he have any other addresses on file?"

Bob scrolls down on his screen. "Let's see, 85 Buena Way, Phoenix, 201 Fairfield Road, also Phoenix, 70 Bridgewater in Philly, back in New York at 107 East 51st Street, and now he makes his home in the lovely, gated community of Putnam County Prison."

He hits print, gives the sheet of addresses to me, grabs his files, his coffee, and his bagel. "Call if you need me."

When I get St. Luke's on the phone, they transfer me to their off-location site for old hospital records. A guy named Nunzio takes my number and says he'll check to see if anything exists, but it'll take a while. Then I call Putnam County Prison to check on Benedict's parole date, and I'm surprised to find out he'll probably be released in less than a month.

I look up the phone numbers of Selverinis and Benedicts within a fifty-mile radius and start calling them. Nobody's ever heard of Frank, but after about two hours I find one woman in Brooklyn who says Angela is her cousin.

I tell Carlton I'm heading out to talk to her, then on to St. Luke's archived records location, and if it's not too late, Eldridge Street. He waves me off, saying that he's going uptown himself and probably won't be there when I get back. "By the way," I say, "Bob practically looked happy today,"

"That's because I'm taking your advice."

When I look blank, he adds, "Trying to *understand* him, remember?"

VIII

KEVIN

Delfina Selverini lives in an Italian neighborhood in Brooklyn. The houses are brick duplexes with chain link fences and white statuary. Inside her gate, there's virtually no lawn, but the yard is awash with yellow daffodils and tulips in every hue. I walk up the steps and knock on the screen door. The smell of something baking makes me realize it's almost lunchtime and I haven't had breakfast yet.

I show my badge to a heavy-set woman with dyed black hair and red cheeks. She's wearing an apron over slacks and a flowery blouse, probably in her early sixties. After inviting me into the kitchen she offers me anisette cookies and black coffee.

"No, thank you. I won't be here very long."

She swats away my answer. "You look hungry. And all police drink coffee, right?"

"Well…"

"No well. Sit. I just made these fresh this morning. You tell me if you like. Why's a nice, handsome boy like you a policeman? Don't you know you can get killed?"

I laugh at what I think is her joke, but apparently, she's serious. When I bite into a cookie, I want to marry this woman or at least be adopted by her. "I try to stay away from people with guns."

"You married?"

I shake my head.

"No wonder. Who wants to marry a policeman? You end up burying him and raising your kids alone."

"So, it's hopeless?"

She smiles. "Eat up, Mr. Policeman—while you can."

She pours me a steaming cup of demitasse coffee, thick as mud. "So, what you wanna know about Angela?"

"Anything you can tell me. Where she was born, where she lives now, does she have any other relatives around here?"

"Is she in some kind of trouble?"

"No, I'd just like to ask her some questions, but I have no idea where she is."

She shakes her head. "Sorry, I haven't seen her for many years."

I pull out my pen and pad. "What can you tell me about her?"

"Angie was a good girl before she hooked up with that crazy boyfriend of hers. What was his name?" She squints, trying to remember.

"Frank Benedict?"

"Yes! No Italiano, for sure. She was very smart. Went to college—nursing school. She shoulda married Vinnie Romanelli. He woulda treated her right. I liked Vinnie too, but he only had eyes for Angelina."

"What did you call her?"

"Angelina, it's her real name, but she goes by Angela."

"Was she born here in Brooklyn?"

"Yes. We were born in 1960. Nicolo Selverini and my father were cousins. Her mother's name was Maria Nard." She points to my pad to make sure I spell it right.

"Any brothers or sisters?"

"No. Zia Maria had trouble carrying her and couldn't have no more. Hey officer, how old are you?"

I don't look up from my pad. "Twenty-seven."

"My niece, Anita Bono, she's your age. Very smart girl. She's in law school. You wanna see a picture of her?"

"Uh, actually, I'd like to see some pictures of Angela, if you have any."

She walks into the dining room while she talks. "They would be very old. I haven't heard from her for maybe twenty years."

"You weren't close?"

Bending down, she pulls a few photo albums from the China closet. "We were very close before she got mixed up with that man. She'd come in from the city for Sunday dinner almost every weekend. I was taking care of my mother in those days, *Il dio reposa.*" She crosses herself. "They loved to see each other, but after the boyfriend, we were lucky to see her maybe on holidays."

She flips through the pages of an album until she comes to a high school graduation picture of an attractive young woman, unsmiling with large, dark eyes. "Wasn't she *bella*? Anita looks like her. But that boyfriend—what a strange one."

"Why do you say that?"

She puts her thumb up to her mouth pretending it's the tip of a bottle. "He drank too much. And he liked the ladies, that one. Angelina, she worked every minute. He didn't do nothing."

She lowers her voice like someone else is around. "They lived together. My uncle, *si reposa nella pace*, would have turned over in his grave."

"Was there any talk of marriage?"

"Once, when she thought she was pregnant, but when it turned out to be a false alarm, they went back to business as usual. The jackass!"

"Do you have any more recent pictures?"

She rifles through the album. "I think I have one of her with my mother, maybe a year before we lost touch. Ah, here it is!"

She hands me a picture of an older Angela with an elderly woman.

"How old would you say she is here?"

"Middle thirties. And here is a picture of my niece, Anita."

Sure enough, she looks like Angela, only smiling. We walk back into the kitchen. "You want more black coffee?"

"No thanks. I won't sleep for a week." I hold up her photo. "Do you mind if I take a picture of this?"

She shrugs.

"When was the last time you heard from Angela?"

"Long time. More than twenty years. She came over and said she was gonna move out West. We told her, 'There's no Italians out West. Why you wanna go there?' She said she wanted a new start. I said, 'Dump the boyfriend; that would be a new start.'"

"Did she say specifically where she was going?"

"Nevada, maybe? I can't remember. Mama and Angie, they both cried together. That was the last we saw her."

"She never called or wrote?"

"We got one Christmas card. But no return address, so we couldn't write back. I tell you; it was all—"

"The boyfriend?"

"Yes!"

"Did you save the card?"

"If I did, I don't know where it is. Now officer, you answer me a question. Why you wanna know all this? Angie's in trouble, isn't she?"

"I don't know, Miss Selverini. I just want to ask her some questions about a kidnapping at St. Luke's twenty-three years ago."

"The baby? Oh my God! I remember, but Angie left before that."

"How long before?"

"Maybe a few months."

"Did she ever talk about any other friends she had in the city?"

"No. Wait, maybe yes. She had a friend who lived on the east side. Tania or Tammy."

"Last name?"

"Something Jewish—Leibowitz, Berkowitz, something like that."

I pull out one of my cards. "Will you call me if you think of anything else?"

"Sure."

She puts the remaining cookies into a Ziploc bag and presses them into my hands. "Here, take these. I'm only gonna throw them out. Why don't you get a job in insurance? They make good money."

"Yeah, but then I wouldn't get to meet ladies like you."

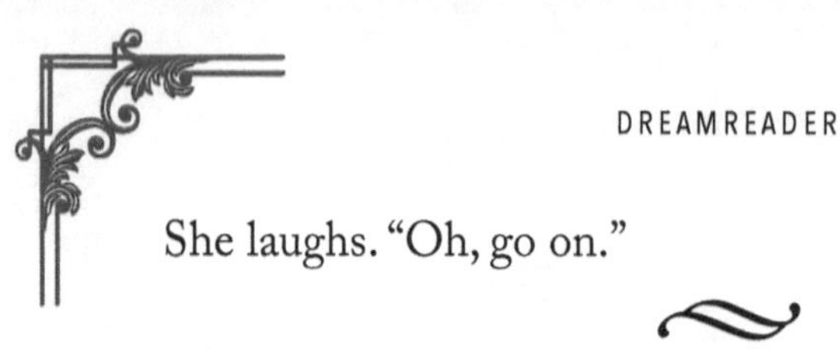

She laughs. "Oh, go on."

While I'm driving, I get a call from Nunzio, the records guy at St. Luke's. "You're in luck. We have a file," he says.

I drive over to the East Village and wait for him in a cramped, musty room. Inside the file is a copy of Angela's driver's license—same face; this time with a slight smile. There's a copy of her insurance card too, with her social security number. The file spans two years. Most of the blood panels were sent to Joseph London, MD, a gynecologist on Madison Ave. At least half of them in 1994 are to determine pregnancy. None are positive until May of that year. One month later, she's admitted for a D&C following a miscarriage.

I wonder if that's the pregnancy that was the "false alarm." When I check her emergency information, I expect to see Frank's name listed as her emergency contact, but he's not. Instead, it's Tamara Brodnavich, East 68th Street. Nice fancy neighborhood. I pretty much copy the whole file before giving it back to Nunzio.

Returning to the precinct, I call the number listed for Dr. London's office and leave a message. I look up Tamara Brodnavich but she's not living at that address anymore. There's a new number in public records which I try. I get an answering machine, and the lady, who has an accent, sounds old enough to be the right person. Again, I leave my name and number.

Next, I go on the Criminal Justice Information Site to pull up more information on Frank Benedict. Fifteen minutes later I get a call back from Dr. London's office. The receptionist sounds irritated. I explain to her that I'm looking for old records and would like to speak with the doctor.

"Dr. London is no longer a part of our practice. We have six doctors, none of whom were here before 2000. Besides that, we can't release any information without verification that this is a valid investigation."

"No problem, give me your fax number."

"Also, our old records are off-site. It will take us a while to access them."

"How long you talking?"

"Not until next week. Dr. London is retired, and all his old records are kept at his home."

"You've gotta be kidding!"

She doesn't answer.

"Then please give me Dr. London's phone number."

"I'm sorry, I can't do that."

"Why not?"

"We've been advised not to give it out."

"Look, this is a police investigation. I'll fax you the paperwork, and then I expect a call back with his number."

"No one is in the office but me, and I'll be leaving for the day in a few minutes."

I look at my watch. It's only 3:00 PM. "Well, I'm faxing this right now."

I hang up and look frantically through the blank forms in my files. When I find the right one, I scribble down the information and sign it. It's faxed within three minutes.

Ten minutes later she calls back. "Detective, the form you sent me doesn't have the signature of your supervisor. I can't process it."

This is like a déjà vu of Rosemary Turino. I take a deep breath and ask quietly, "Who am I speaking with?"

"This is Melissa Sand."

"Melissa, do you know what the charges are for blocking a police investigation?"

She is silent.

"Would you like to come down to the precinct and wait till my supervisor gets back tonight to sign the form?"

"Dr. London lives with his daughter in Parsippany, New Jersey."

She proceeds to give me the number and tells me that Dr. London is not always lucid, that he shouldn't have brought his old files to his home because anyone could look through them and that his daughter is a shrew. The last time she gave out his number, she got yelled at for twenty minutes.

"I understand completely Melissa. I'll be gentle on the old man and firm with the shrew. And I won't throw you to the wolves. Thanks, and have a nice weekend."

I dial Dr. London's number and a kid picks up. "May I speak with Dr. London?"

The kid drops the phone and gives an earsplitting yell, "Grampy, telephone."

For what feels like a full five minutes, I hear the squeals and pitter patter of children running through the house. Finally, I hear a female voice with a strong *New Joisey* accent yell, "Who knocked the phone off the hook?"

"Hello, hello," I say, but she hangs up.

The shrew.

I call right back and when she picks up, I ask for Dr. London again. Unfriendly to the core, she demands to know who I am. "This is Detective Kevin Jacobs from the 56th precinct, Manhattan."

There's a pause. "He's taking a nap."

"Well then, I'd like to leave a message. I need to question him about a patient he had twenty years ago."

"That's impossible. My father has dementia. He would never remember a patient from twenty years ago."

"I'm sorry to hear that, but if he's not able to speak on the phone, I'll have to make a trip out to your home. I understand he stores his archived medical records there."

"Who told you that?"

"Who am I speaking with?"

"Sylvia London Proctor. Did his office tell you the records were here?"

"If I can't speak to your father, Mrs. Proctor, please give me your street address."

Again, a long pause. "I'll see if he's still awake."

Like her child, Sylvia drops the phone. In less than a minute I hear an elderly man's scratchy voice say, "Hello?"

"Hello sir, sorry to disturb you. This is Detective Jacobs."

"My daughter said you need—uh—information. About a patient."

I slowly explain about Angela being his patient, stopping every now and then to make sure he's understanding me. "I don't suppose you remember her?"

"No."

"Could you check your old records and give me any information you can?"

"I can try. They're down in the basement. Will you give me your number and spell her last name slowly? My handwriting…"

His voice trails off.

As far as I can tell, the guy's slow but lucid. I hang up and go back to CJIS to print off fingerprints and a picture of Frank. Then I go to the Public Records database to see when he married.

I'm having trouble staying online and keep having to reboot the computer. By now it's after four and the office is just about empty. Bob never returned today. Neither did Carlton. I can't say I miss the stress. In about fifteen minutes, my phone rings. It's Dr. London.

"I found the—records. I—remember—uh—Angela Selverini."

I lean back in my chair and cover my eyes with my hand. Might as well slow myself down so his frustration with trying to find the right words doesn't drive me crazy. I can barely hear him because of the racket going on in the background. No wonder he's confused.

"She was a nurse, worked at St. Luke's. I had hospital privileges there. I remember her in the neo—"

Long pause.

"Neonatal unit?"

"Yes. She had her thyroid tested because she had several—uh—unsuccessful pregnancies. Change to: between 1987 and 1994, I have record of at least three first trimester pregnancies that were spontaneously—you know,"

"Aborted?"

"Yes. It's difficult for me to concentrate."

"Sounds like you're in a lively household."

"Yes, I think I'll go back downstairs. The light isn't good, but it's quieter. Hold on, please."

I hear him walk down the creaking steps. Then I hear a door open and close. "That's better. Now what were we talking about?"

"Angela Selverini."

"Oh, yes, my patient. Uh, I have her records right here. I'm not sure exactly what you're looking for Officer."

"Do you remember anything about her—other than the printed record?"

"Well, she was a floor nurse at St. Luke's."

"In neonatal."

"Yes. I—I think that was difficult for her."

His voice is starting to fade in and out.

"Because she couldn't get pregnant?"

"Yes. And she seemed more determined than other women. I have a memory—it might have been her—I can't be sure."

I wait for him to go on, but he doesn't. "Doctor?"

"She said that her marriage was shaky, and she thought having a child would help them. I told her having a child didn't usually fix a troubled marriage. But she didn't seem to believe me. I recommended counseling, but I never heard if she went."

"Did you ever meet her husband?"

"I don't remember ever meeting him, which is strange."

"Why?"

"I always met the husbands."

"Anything else you can tell me?"

"Let me look at the record. The light is—very poor down here. Maybe—maybe I should go upstairs."

My head is pulsing behind my eyes. "Please, doctor, if you could just read it there—the upstairs was very noisy."

"Yes, right. My last entry is—uh—June 12, 1995. I can't seem to read my handwriting. Hmmm—'follow-up exam after miscarriage and D&C. Recommended patient abstain from attempting to become pregnant until she contacts a maternal fetal specialist.'"

I hear him shuffling pages. "Patient seemed distraught. Suggested an appointment with Dr. Simmons."

"The specialist?"

"No—a psychiatrist. But I don't think she went."

"Why do you say that?"

"We were friends. He would have told me."

I hear what sounds like a door bang open, accompanied by laughter and shouting. "Mama, we found Grampy!"

He starts to laugh but ends up coughing. This goes on for a while. Finally, he wheezes, "Is there anything else?"

"Not at this point. Thanks for your time, sir."

After I hang up, I go back to saving and printing every page I find on Frank Benedict. When the page containing his marriage information comes up, I stare at it for a while, feeling like I'm missing something. I flip open the pad that I used to take notes at Delfina Selverini's house to look for the maiden name of Angela's mother. That's what I thought: Nardi. And what did she call Angela? It was Angelina. In front of me on the public records search is the date of Frank Benedict's marriage. The name of the woman he marries in New York City on June 12, 1995 is Lena Nardi.

Angela Selverini dropped out of sight and Lena Nardi took her place. No wonder Alice couldn't find her.

IX

GRACE

Grace opened her eyes to the sun flooding into her room and the sound of Eve and Mimi in the kitchen talking loudly about the prom. Oh, yeah. Today was the big day. She stumbled down the stairs to see her mother before she left. She figured Mimi wasn't going to school. Now that Mimi had her license, they were trying to jockey two cars among the three of them. Eve looked flustered. "Grace, can you pick me up at school today at four? Mimi needs my car to be at the hair stylist at three."

"Sure, Mom. I'm watching Xavier today from ten till two. That'll give me enough time to get you."

Mimi threw some clothes on to drive their mother to school. Before leaving, Eve kissed Grace on the cheek. "After Mimi leaves for the prom tonight, do you want to go get dinner, or maybe see a movie?"

Grace didn't really want to. She'd become a hermit since the dreams and visions had started, but she knew she should be there for Eve, especially after their last non-conversation. She smiled and nodded.

After they both left, she headed for the shower. When the temperature was right, she stepped in, closed her eyes and let the water pour down on her. But when she opened her eyes, she was staring into her own face, sheets of blue water drenching them both.

"Get away!" she screamed.

The face disappeared instantly but left in its place panic that tightened her throat, robbing her of air. A wail welled up from deep inside, "God, God, God!"

She stood there until she ran out of hot water and her teeth were chattering. Wrapping a big towel around herself, she crawled into bed. She pulled the blankets up over her soaking wet head and faced the wall. She felt cocooned, protected.

She was walking along the shore of a huge, narrow waterfall. She'd lost something—no, someone—in the water. She splashed into the lake up to her waist and heard someone crying, or was it the sound of a bird? "Me, me, Ma-m-m-a!"

She whirled around scanning the shore but saw no one. "Me, me, Mama!"

There was a flicker of motion behind the waterfall. "Anyone there?" she yelled, swimming toward the falls. As the water grew more turbulent, the spray blinded her. Someone was behind the waterfall. Through the froth, when she saw an opening in the falls, she swam toward it. The water was beating on her head so hard it was like being pelted with rocks. It drove her under, and she swallowed water. But then suddenly, she was on the other side. Straight ahead was a girl crouching down on a long flat rock. Grace swam to the rock, climbed out on it and laid her hand on the girl's shoulder.

She woke up to Mimi pounding on her door and shouting. "Grace, call Cassie. She's been trying to reach you!"

She grabbed her phone and saw that Cassie had called her six times. Grace poked her number into the phone, and Cassie picked up on the first ring. "Where are you, Grace? I thought you'd be here by now. Dan and I are due at the doctor's office in ten minutes."

"I'm sorry, Cassie. I'll be right there."

Grace jumped out of bed, dressed and threw opened the door of her room to find Mimi was standing right there. She screamed out. "What are you doing? You scared me the life out of me!"

Mimi held up her hands in a *don't shoot* gesture and backed away.

Later, Grace called her from Cassie and Dan's. "Sorry for yelling."

Mimi brushed it off. "Whatever. Nothing can ruin today."

But Grace still felt guilty. "I have some time before I pick up Mom. You need anything?"

"Uh, can you get me some M&Ms? They'll calm me down."

"Sugar doesn't calm people down, Mi."

"You asked if you could do anything. Help me out here."

"Okay, okay. I'll see you later."

"With the candy?"

"With the candy."

How Grace wished she was seventeen and all her problems could be solved by M&Ms.

When Grace and Eve walked into the house, Mimi was in her underwear in the living room, painting her toenails. Her dress, shoes, shawl, and beaded bag were lying on the couch. Her hair looked gorgeous, piled up on her head with wispy tendrils falling from the sides and back. There were tiny yellow flowers pinned here and there into her curls. Grace gasped at how beautiful she looked. But tearful eyes immediately gave way to a fearful churning in her gut.

Mimi was almost grown up. Who would protect her now?

Eve's eyes leaked a bit too. "You look like Cinderella. You should have one of those thingies around your neck, you know, a choker. Then you'd really look like her."

Mimi continued to paint her toes. "Except that Cinderella is blonde and her hair looks like a helmet."

Grace snorted. "Besides, chokers make you look like your head is sewn on."

Mimi laughed. "I like that idea, maybe I *will* wear one. Do bowties make guys look like their heads are sewn on too?"

"Only if they're not wearing shirts."

Mimi grinned. "Cinderella meets Chippendale."

Grace threw the bag of M&Ms on the table. "Your makeup looks good. Did Cindy do that too?"

"No, I did it myself. But I had to use your eyeliner because mine ran out. I hope you don't mind."

"Mimi, you can't use somebody else's eye makeup. That contaminates it."

"Sorry, I didn't think you'd make such a big deal."

"It *is* a big deal! Now I have to buy more."

"You mean you'd just throw it out? That's ridiculous!"

"Tell you what, you can keep the eyeliner as your very own and give me the money to buy some more."

"Guess we'll have to do the same with your mascara."

"Mimi!"

"Ma, can you give me twenty bucks? I owe Grace some money."

"If you're going to walk around like that, you should put the shades down," Eve said.

"But I need the breeze. I'm sweating already."

Mimi fanned her toenails. "I can't do my fingernails, Mom. Can you help?"

Eve took the nail polish and shook it until you could hear the metal balls rattling against the bottle. She painted Mimi's nails like a manicurist—two strokes per nail.

"Sis, can I borrow your car tonight, or do I have to drive that ratty, old van to my one and only prom?"

Grace ripped open the bag of candy and poured some into a paper cup for her sister. "I would have said yes if it hadn't been for the eye makeup."

Mimi poured a dozen M&Ms into her mouth. "You know, I put up with a lot when we were little. You were incredibly bossy and controlling. That should be worth a little contaminated eye makeup."

"But that was my job, right, Mom? You always said watch out for your little sister."

Eve capped the nail polish. "You may have overdone it a little."

After her nails were dry, Eve and Grace helped Mimi into her dress. When she was ready, she looked shimmery and lovely. Instead of a Cinderella choker, Eve brought out a locket their dad had given her when they were dating. They all got a little misty-eyed. Then they took a bunch of pictures and waited for Cassie to show up with Jay.

KEVIN

I look at my watch. It's after five. I know I should go home and chill out till I hear from Freddy, but I can't resist doing a search on Lena Nardi Benedict. She has no police record, so she's not in the New York State or FBI databases, but when I go to public records, I see that two of her last three addresses match Frank's: Buena Way and Fairfield Road, both in Phoenix. The third address, Solano Drive, looks like it may be her current one.

After that, I do a search on her social to see where she's worked in the last twenty years. In 1996 she started out at the Phoenix Children's Hospital. She was there for twelve years, and then worked for Visiting Nurses for six years. Her last job was at Lincoln Valley Hospital.

I gather up all the pages I've printed, throw them into my messenger bag and head toward my car. Before I get home, Freddy calls. "Becky and her friend Janelle are gonna meet us at Remy's for drinks at around nine-thirty."

"Why so late?"

"They gotta ditch their other dates first, which, by the way, they're already on. No wonder you don't have a girlfriend, Kevin. You don't know how to play this game."

"I wouldn't talk if I were you."

"Why, because Becky's dating other guys? She'll wake up soon enough."

"Yeah, when she learns to love wrestling and monster trucks as much as dinner and dancing."

He ignores me completely. "You want me to pick you up?"

"No, thanks. I'll meet you at the club."

I need to get this case out of my head for a few hours, and Remy's is the perfect place.

When I get there, I'm in heaven. The music is blaring, the beat throbbing. Becky's friend Janelle is a good dancer, so we're on the floor the whole night. I'm teaching her the spot turn and the *enchufla* when I feel my cell phone vibrate in my pocket. "Sorry," I shout over the music, "I've gotta take this."

She nods and walks back to our table while I sprint outside so I can hear.

"Kevin, this is Jody from Forensics."

I glance at my watch. It's nearly eleven. "Hey, Jody. You're up late."

"It's called the night shift. So, about the hair samples…"

"They a match?"

"Are you sitting down?"

"No, I'm standing outside Café Remy with all the smokers."

"Well, they're *not* a match. Not even close."

"What are you saying?"

"I'm saying that the kids aren't identical twins. They're not fraternal twins. They're not even related."

For then next several seconds I don't say anything. Finally, my voice returns. "You're sure?"

"Without getting all scientific on you, the DNA bands of the baby don't even *slightly* match the bands of the twenty-three-year-old. Siblings would resemble each other. Identical twins would match exactly. These samples don't even come close. If you want to come to the lab, I can show you."

I look at my watch again—10:58. For some reason, I want to remember the time I hear this news.

"Kevin, you there?"

"You just totally altered my investigation."

"You're welcome."

"I mean it, Jody. Unless this is some kind of a sick joke."

There's an edge to her voice. "I don't fool around with DNA."

"You know what this means?"

"Sure. It means you're going to have to find out what happened to the other kid."

"That's right. Can you put this all into a report?"

"I've already faxed it to your office."

"Thanks. I owe you, Jody."

"More than you know."

I stick around outside for another five minutes, just standing there with the smokers, trying to think this through. Cars stop at the light, horns blow, and tires screech. When they roll on, I hear the thudding of music. People keep leaving and arriving at Café Remy. Each time they open the door, I hear the salsa music and remember the feel of Janelle against me.

How do I tell this kid, Grace, that I don't know what happened to her sister? What will that mean to her and her family? I don't want to ruin the night, so I put my phone in my pocket and walk back into the club.

But the magic's gone. I can't get back in my zone. Janelle gets ticked because we only dance for another twenty minutes, and she wants to go on all night. Becky and Freddy are fighting about something. They've both had too much to drink. I look at my watch. It's quarter to one.

"I gotta get going," I tell Freddy.

Freddy gives me a desperate look.

I feel bad, so I order another drink, but just as I do, my phone vibrates again. When I look at the number, I see it's my sister Cassie. I put my hand over my ear and answer it.

"Kevin," she sobs, "Jay's been in an accident. Can you come right away?"

X

GRACE

The call came in around 1:00 AM. They didn't give much information except that there had been an accident, and the kids had been taken by ambulance to Lawrence Hospital. Eve ran upstairs and pounded on Grace's door. In a moment Grace was head-splittingly awake. They both dressed and tore out of the house.

I should have protected her. This is my fault. This is my fault.

She held Eve's hand while she drove, praying out loud with her. When they finally got to the emergency department at Lawrence Hospital, Grace dropped Eve off and then ran to catch up with her after she parked the car. A nurse led them through a maze of hallways into the surgical waiting room. Pastor Dan and Cassie were there already, and they ran into their arms. The nurse let them talk for a few minutes but then led them into a curtained area where Mimi was lying completely still on a gurney, her face white, black eye makeup streaking her cheeks. Her hair was glittery with glass, with some of the yellow flowers dangling. The beautiful dress was cut open and lay crumpled on a chair. When Eve gently touched her shoulder, Mimi jerked and opened her eyes.

Then the tears came.

Eve kissed her cheek. "It's all right, baby. Everything will be okay."

"My hands, Mom. I can't feel them."

Grace and Eve looked down and saw that her arms and hands were lying at odd angles by her side. Grace felt a chill go through her body. She leaned over and whispered to Eve, "We've got to get a hand specialist in here."

"Where's Jay?" Mimi asked, her tongue thick with pain meds.

"He's in surgery, honey."

Mimi's tears slid down into her blood-matted hair. "I'm sorry Mom. It happened so fast. He was right on us."

"I know. Dan and Cassie told us."

A short, stocky woman with grey hair and kind eyes walked into the room and introduced herself as Dr. Kramer. She motioned for Eve to follow her out into the hallway. Grace moved closer to the bed. She didn't know where Mimi hurt, so she didn't want to touch her. The old tapes were running louder than ever: *Watch out for your little sister; don't let anything happen to her.*

As if reading her mind, Mimi turned to look at Grace with a lopsided grin. "It's a good thing you didn't let me use your car. We would've been flattened by that monster truck."

Grace choked back tears. "Are you in pain, Mi?"

"A little. They gave me some kind of a shot because I was screaming when I got here. Now I'm mostly numb. The front of his grill smashed our window. Thank God the airbags went off, but my hands got pinned to the steering wheel. It took a while to get us out. They used some big machine, really loud…"

Grace glanced at Mimi's dress on the chair. "Where are your shoes and purse?"

Mimi closed her eyes. "Don't know."

Eve came back in and sat on the other side of Mimi, her face etched with dread. After about twenty minutes, Cassie and Dan peeked around the curtain, so Eve and Grace went out into the hall. Cassie looked awful—her hair was sticking up, her eyes ringed with fear. She kept twisting a tissue in her hand.

Eve lowered her voice to a whisper. "Do you know any more about what happened?"

"The guy swerved into their lane and hit them head on," Dan said. "They think he was drunk. It was one of those huge pickups.

It crashed through their front window and pinned them in the car. Jay's got head and neck injuries. His legs are broken too. They just tore in here and took him straight into surgery. Mimi's hands got hurt."

Eve covered her face and sobbed, a broken, childish sound, unrestrained and pitiful. Cassie embraced her, and they cried together. "At least they're alive, Eve. The police say it's a miracle. They had to be cut out of the car."

"What happened to the other guy?" Grace asked.

"Barely a scratch. He's being checked out at Mt. Vernon Hospital. His truck is like a tank," Dan said.

Eve roughly wiped her tears. "How is Jay?"

"He's been in surgery for over an hour. We don't know." Cassie broke down again.

Dan grabbed his wife's hand. "They're hoping there's no spinal cord injury. We've got the prayer chain going."

"Where did this happen?" Eve asked.

"They were on their way to the all-night prom party on Fourth Avenue."

"They weren't—drinking, too—were they?"

Cassie shook her head. "The police didn't say anything about that."

Eve choked up again. "They're calling in a special doctor to operate on Mimi's hands. I can't tell you guys how sorry I am about all this. I should have driven them instead of letting her take the car."

Cassie grabbed her hands and stared into her eyes. "It wasn't Mimi's fault, Eve. It could have been so much worse. They could have gone down the embankment into the river. There is *no* blame."

Eve nodded but didn't look convinced.

Thus began the waiting game. Dan and Cassie went back to the surgical waiting room while Eve and Grace sat by Mimi. Time flowed like molasses as doctors came in and out to talk about x-rays and options. Grace nodded off, but around 4:00 AM she startled awake, stood, stretched, and walked down the hall to where Dan and Cassie were. Cassie's brother Kevin had arrived. The three of them were huddled on the couch, half-dozing. She gave Kevin a grim smile.

He stood. "How's Mimi?"

Without wanting to, Grace teared up. "Her hands are a mess. Maybe ten broken bones in each one. I saw the x-rays. Some of them are crushed. They're calling in some big-time hand surgeon from Westchester Medical to operate. The doctors here don't want to touch her, you know, because…"

Kevin motioned to the couch. "Here, sit down."

She flopped down next to Cassie who put her arm around her. Instinctively, Grace put her head on her shoulder and closed her eyes, tears leaking out onto Cassie's shirt. "Try to sleep, Gracie. It's almost 4:30."

But Grace's eyes popped open. "Roy Kulick. That's the doctor's name. He's supposed to be the best hand doctor in New York."

Dan nodded. "We're just going to keep praying."

Grace wondered if Kevin was a praying man, or if he thought that they were all just kidding themselves.

Cassie gently stroked Grace's hair. "Kevin talked to the police. They're taking the other guy into custody after he spends the night in the hospital. His blood alcohol level was way over the legal limit. He's just bruised up a little."

"I'm going over to impound later to look at the car," Kevin added.

"When you do, could you look for Mimi's purse? She doesn't have it."

He nodded. "Grace, there's a bunch of kids out in the waiting room. I think somebody should talk to them and tell them to go home. You want to come with me?"

As Kevin guided her through the maze of hallways, they saw a tall, thin man being escorted to the surgery wing. The nurse buzzed a surgical tech. "Dr. Kulick is here."

Grace glanced at Kevin. "I hope he's as good as they say."

When they got to the ER waiting room, they saw a half-dozen kids in various states of sprawl in front of an annoyingly loud

TV. Kimberly, Genna, and their dates were there, all still in their wilted prom getup.

When they saw Grace, they both stood up and hugged her. Tony, Jay's best friend, looked stoic, but his jaw was clenched. "We were right behind them when that jerk plowed into our lane. We saw the whole thing and stopped just short of slamming into Mimi."

Kimberly nodded. "Mark and I were supposed to ride with them, "but at the last minute, we decided to go with Kurt and Genna. We were all headed to the same place, so it didn't matter who we rode with."

There was silence for a moment while everyone seemed to ponder the thought that sometimes it very much matters who you ride with.

Grace handed the girls a scrap of paper. "Please write down your phone numbers so I can call you with any updates. We think you guys should go home. Mimi will be going into surgery soon. We have no idea when she'll be out, or Jay for that matter. There's no point in you hanging out here when you could be home sleeping."

Tony nodded and pointed to his date. "She's gotta take the SATs in," he looked at his watch, "three hours."

"Me too," mumbled a few of the others.

After they'd gathered up their stuff, Grace and Kevin walked them outside. It was surprisingly cool, and getting light. When Grace unconsciously began to hug herself, Kevin took off his jacket and wordlessly draped it over her shoulders. Standing side by side, they watched the kids get into their cars.

Grace called out, "Be careful."

Kevin pointed to a bench near the ER doors, and they both sat. The crazy litany took up residence in Grace's head again—*I should've protected her. I'm a terrible sister. This is my fault.* She turned to Kevin. "You must see this kind of stuff all the time."

He stretched out his legs and looked down at his shoes. "Yeah, but it's always somebody else's family."

After a while, Kevin let out a huge sigh and stood up. "I'm gonna go check the impound."

Grace pulled his jacket off her shoulders, but he shook his head. "You keep it. I won't be gone that long."

As he walked away, Grace said, "I haven't even asked how things are going with finding out about my sister."

Kevin turned around. "I've found out a few things, but—now's not the best time to talk."

"Well, I'm not going anywhere, so maybe we can talk later."

Kevin looked away, as if he was trying to choose his words carefully. "I'll find you."

As Grace walked back into the hospital, she thought about his response. It seemed subdued. It had to be because he was preoccupied with his family. And yet—she considered herself an expert in reading people. She'd always had to be in order to protect Mimi. Either she was getting a false reading, or he no longer saw the case as a *giant puzzle* and *a detective's dream*. If anything, he looked a little—scared.

XI

GRACE

After spending twelve, mostly sleepless, hours at the hospital, Grace decided to go home to shower. Both the kids had gotten out of surgery at around 8:00 AM. Jay was taken directly to ICU and Mimi was put in a private room on the fourth floor. When Grace left, Eve was dozing in a recliner and Mimi was out cold, her hands elevated on pillows.

At home, she stripped down and stood in a steaming shower for a full twenty minutes. Afterwards, she dressed, tied up her hair, and checked her voicemail.

Apparently, the accident had been in the morning paper and on the news because there were dozens of messages—mostly church people and Mimi's friends.

She grabbed the scrap of paper out of her purse to call Mimi's friend Genna Benson. Her mom answered, her voice scratchy and deep. "Genna's sleeping. She cried for hours when she came home, then had to take her SATs on no rest at all. How are Mimi and Jason? We've been so worried."

Grace was matter of fact because she had no emotion left. "Mimi has broken wrists, hands, and fingers. A hand specialist came in to operate and set the bones in place. She's also got a concussion and some cuts. We might be able to bring her home in a day or two. Jay has some fractured vertebrae. They operated on his back and put in pins to hold the bones in place while they heal. We don't know if there's any spinal cord damage because the swelling is so bad. We should know within the week."

"That's awful. What can we do for you?"

"Could you make some calls?"

"Give me the numbers," Mrs. Benson said.

She gave her four, including Mr. Levenson's, Mimi's music teacher. "Anything else I can do?"

"Maybe call my mom in a day or two. She might need to talk to somebody."

"Is it okay for Genna to visit Mimi tonight?"

"I think so, maybe this afternoon. She just can't stay long."

After the call Grace made two tuna salad sandwiches, grabbed two apples, and headed back to the hospital. When she arrived, Eve wasn't in the room. Mimi was still pretty drugged-up and couldn't carry on much of a conversation, so she sat in one of the chairs and ate her sandwich and an apple. After about thirty minutes, Eve came back and flopped into the recliner, exhausted. Her face was lined with worry and lack of sleep.

Grace handed her mother the sack with the other sandwich and fruit. "You should eat," she said. "You look wasted. "Were you upstairs to see Jay?"

"Mostly sitting in the ICU waiting room with Dan and Cassie," Eve said between bites. "They only let you in on the hour, and you can't stay very long."

"How is he?"

Eve glanced at Mimi's closed eyes and lowered her voice. "He's all hooked up and unconscious. It's pretty scary."

"And Dan and Cassie?"

"As best as they can be."

"Where's Xavier?"

"Kevin just brought him in when I was leaving."

"Does he understand what's going on?"

"Not really. Cassie's doesn't want him seeing Jason until he looks better. She thinks he'll get scared."

"Why don't you go home and lie down for a few hours? I'll stay here."

"I'll just get a shower and come back."

Grace handed Eve her car keys. "I asked Genna's mom to return some of the voicemail messages, but I think we should call Andre and Auntie Elaine ourselves. Can you think of anyone else?"

Eve kissed Grace's forehead. "I'll call them both and my principal too."

After she left, Grace tried to read a bit, but it wasn't long before she fell asleep. When she awakened, Kevin was standing over her.

She sat up and wiped drool from her mouth. "That must've been a pretty picture, me sleeping with my mouth open."

He smiled. "Actually, it was."

Apparently, he'd gone home to change too and was now wearing a pale grey shirt and black pants with a badge clipped to his belt. He still had that windswept, casual look, like he should've been in shorts and carrying a beach blanket. He pulled a chair over and sat down in front of her, his knees grazing hers. Lowering his voice, he asked, "How's she doing?"

"They say the surgery went well. No promises, though. And Jay?"

"He hasn't come to yet. They have him heavily sedated."

Panic knotted Grace's stomach.

Kevin patted her knee. "How are you holding up?"

"Me? Don't worry about me. Worry about Mimi and my mom."

"Why? Shouldn't someone worry about you?"

She waved away his question. "I always land on my feet."

"That's not a reason."

Grace reached for her water bottle on the window ledge. "My mom doesn't complain, but you should've seen her face when we got the call last night."

"Are you one of those people who's so busy caring for others that you don't know what's going on inside you?"

She peered out the window and watched the trees in the hospital courtyard shed their late spring blossoms. Tiny pink flowers littered the ground like confetti, mounding into piles in the gutter. "Oh, I know. I just wait a decade or two before falling apart."

He smiled. "People who fall apart sooner usually do better."

Just what she needed—armchair psychoanalysis. She took a long swallow of water and capped the bottle. "So, you're a shrink, too? Don't bother. I've been analyzed, scrutinized, hypnotized, tranquilized—you name it."

"You put up quite a fight when someone asks how you are."

Time to change the subject. "Did you ever get your jacket last night? I don't remember where I was when you came back."

"You were sleeping on the couch with your mouth open."

"Great."

"I gave Mimi's purse to your mom. We actually had a nice talk. She's a neat lady."

"And the car?"

He cocked his head and looked at Grace. "You've seen the paper, right?"

"No. Is there a picture?"

He stood and headed toward the door. "Lemme go find one."

Grace glanced at Mimi, but she was still out cold. When she came to, she'd try to fix her hair and take off her make-up. They'd probably be doing everything for her for a while. How does someone manage with *two* broken hands? The inconvenience didn't bother Grace. It was the other part. She'd seen the x-rays.

When Kevin came back, he showed her the picture on the front page of the paper. It showed a truck with its tires resting on the dashboard of her mother's van. It had jumped the hood of the van and smashed through the windshield. When she saw the picture, Grace burst into tears. "Oh my God! How did they get out of that alive?"

She kept crying in fits and spurts, apologizing in between. Poor Kevin looked helpless and grabbed her a box of tissues. Half a box later, she handed it back. "I guess you know how I feel now."

He looked down. "Whenever I see Jay, I feel like crying too.

Even if the spinal cord isn't injured, there'll be therapy, a body cast." His voice trailed off.

"Mom and I pray for him every hour or so. Mimi did too, last night, when she was more awake."

He was silent for a moment. "You guys seem really close."

"We only have each other."

"That's the way it is with Cassie and me."

"Aren't your parents still around?"

"They live in Pennsylvania, but we're not close. I've just got Cassie and Dan and maybe two friends in New York."

"Girlfriend?"

"No time for that."

"Church?"

"Nope."

Grace cocked her head. "Isn't your dad a minister?"

Kevin's voice was emotionless. "A toxic person who soured me on church."

He checked his watch and gave her a grim smile. "We're about to be graced by the Reverend himself. They should be getting here in a couple of hours—probably to tell Dan and Cassie that this is the wrath of God coming down on them because they let Jay act in musicals and go to proms."

"They'd say that?"

He looked embarrassed. "I'm sorry. I'm not trying to knock your faith."

"That's okay. Somebody once said that if religion doesn't make you a much better person, it can make you a much worse one."

Grace sensed that Kevin wanted to change the subject. "Do you have any more information about my sister's kidnapping?"

"I have a little more work to do over the weekend. Can we get together Monday?"

"Sure, but if Mom and Mimi are home, I don't want to meet there."

Kevin glanced at his watch. "Okay. Hey, I should get back. I'm supposed to watch Xavier while Dan and Cassie go in to see Jay."

She watched him leave the room. *Why does he keep avoiding my questions?*

XII

KEVIN

Riding in the elevator, I suddenly realize that I didn't want to leave Grace. It actually bothers me that she's down there by herself. What is *wrong* with me? I'm acting like a teenager—spilling my guts, flirting. But that smile, those gorgeous eyes—I keep getting distracted.

When the door opens to the ICU wing, I practically trip over Xavier's toys which are strewn about the waiting room. Cassie and Dan are sitting on the couch together, talking and holding hands. I love watching them. They're the definition of soul-mates.

But Cassie looks exhausted, and even Dan looks like he's wearing out fast. As soon as Xavier sees me, he grabs my hand and drags me to the couch where I sit down next to Dan and Cassie.

"How's everything going?" I ask.

"About the same," Dan says. "They're letting us visit every half-hour now. We even took Xavier in for a few minutes. He did fine. In fact, he thought all the hook-ups were cool."

I grab Cassie's hand. "And how are you, sis?"

The pain in her eyes is almost unbearable. "What can I say, Kev? Nobody knows anything yet."

Dan puts his arm around her. "The doctors are going to keep him under for at least a few days to give the brain a chance to heal itself. Cassie wants to stay at the hospital, so I'm going to take Xavier home until your parents arrive."

"Why don't you let me take Zave? I have to go into the city for a few hours, but he can come with me. Tomorrow's Sunday, so I can even keep him overnight."

Dan looks at Cassie. "What do you think?"

"You don't mind, Kevin?"

"Not at all."

"Don't you want to wait until Mom and Dad get here?" Cassie asks.

"Not really. I'll see them tomorrow when I bring him back."

"They might need you," Cassie says.

"They never have before."

"This is different."

"I can't do it Cass. Not right now."

She doesn't respond. She just leans into Dan's shoulder and sighs.

"Will Xavier be okay overnight, or will he cry for you guys?"

Dan smiles. "Probably both."

I explain the plan to Xavier who's delighted and wants to leave immediately. After I tell him we're going to the police station, he's beyond excited. "Can I see the lockup, Uncle Kevin?"

"If you're good."

We stop home for his clothes and then head out toward the city. Xavier chatters the whole way. When we get to the station, I ask Shelly, one of the uniforms, if she'll take him for a tour of the station, including the lockup.

Upstairs at my desk, I see I have a message from Tammy Brodnavich. When I call her back, I find out that she's moved to West 54th Street which is just a few blocks from the station. I put her on hold and page Shelly. "Do you mind stretching out that tour? I want to go interview a witness."

"No problem. He's a charmer."

In just a few minutes, Tammy is buzzing me up to her apartment. The building's not in a bad neighborhood, but it's a far cry from an East Side apartment with a doorman. When I knock, I hear a couple of yappy dogs being put in another room before she invites me in.

The furniture in the living room is old and elegant, antiques, mostly. Tammy, a tiny woman in her sixties, has an entitled, almost regal presence. Her face is drawn, and her cheekbones jut out. You can see the vestiges of beauty, but there is bitterness in her large, brown eyes. Wearing slippers and a red silk kimono, she offers me her hand. "Can I get you a cup of tea?"

She speaks with a strong accent that's hard to place. "Thank you, but I'm on a strict schedule this afternoon."

She gestures for me to sit down on a cracked leather couch.

"What can you tell me about your friend Angela Selverini?"

"I can tell you she stopped being my friend about twenty years ago."

"Why?"

"Angela and I met at a miscarriage support group. We were close for about five years. My husband, Michael, and I saw her through some perfectly horrid times she had with her boyfriend. Twice, when he assaulted her, she came to stay with us, but she always went back. I told her she deserved better, but she never listened."

She puts a bejeweled hand to her jet-black, obviously dyed hair, and tucks a strand behind her ear. I hear an unhappy dog whine in the bedroom. "When Michael and I divorced in 1995, I took a trip to Budapest to see my father who was ailing. Since I didn't know how long I'd be away, I left Angela a key, asking her to pick up my mail and check on the apartment every week or so. She had done this before when we were away, so I assumed I could trust her."

Up to this point, she seemed emotionless, almost serene, but now her eyes darken and she speaks more rapidly. "While I was in Hungary, my father died, and it took me six months to settle his estate. At first, Angela and I spoke regularly. But then, suddenly, she stopped calling. When I tried her home phone number, I found it disconnected. When I tried her at work, I was told she had resigned and left no forwarding address. I was concerned about her, of course, but also about my apartment because I had many valuables. The anxiety ruined my last six weeks in Hungary!"

"What happened when you got back?"

She waves her hand in front of her like she's shooing away a fly. "Gone! She'd disappeared. But I discovered she had been living in my apartment for over three months."

"How did you know that?"

"Hans, the doorman in my Eastside apartment. He said he enjoyed his daily conversations with my tenant."

The dogs must sense she's upset, because the yapping begins again.

"If she had simply asked, I would have gladly offered her the apartment, but to do it without permission and then disappear without an explanation—well, it upset me very much."

Her face becomes more pinched and angry-looking as she pondered the betrayal.

"Mrs. Brodnavich, this is very important. Do you remember exactly when Angela was living in your home?"

"I don't know when she moved in, but I know the day she left."

She walks across the room and opens up an ornate secretary by the window. After rummaging through a lock box, she returns with a yellowed envelope. "The last day she was there, she left my key in this envelope for Hans."

She hands me the envelope which says, *key to apartment 417.*

"Since Hans thought I was subletting, he assumed the date she left would be important to me. Turn over the envelope, and you'll see that he dated it."

The date is 9/23/1995. "Out of curiosity, why did you save this?"

"I don't know, really. Maybe as proof that she had been there. I felt so violated, so deceived. I thought if I ever saw her again, I would confront her. But of course, she never called or wrote. That hurt worst of all—the fact that I wasn't worth an explanation."

Tammy looks like a woman who expects explanations. As I leave, her obnoxious dogs bark madly again.

Back at the station, Xavier is having the time of his life, coloring, devouring candy, and endearing himself to everyone. I take advantage of his celebrity status to slip away and look through my notes for the date the Maddox babies were born.

Sure enough, it's September 23, 1995, the day Angela Selverini—or Lena Nardi—left Tammy's apartment.

By the time I leave the station, it's after three, Xavier has a stomachache, and he's asking for his mama. For the past hour, I've been feeling more and more like a heel for beating it out of there before Mom and Dad arrived. Not for them, but for Dan and Cassie. I'm worried that Dad will pull some garbage with them. That's the last thing they need. I ask Xavier if he wants to go back to the hospital, and he says, "Yes, please."

Within five minutes, he's asleep. That clinches it. I'm not staying up all night with a six-year-old who's had a nap at four o'clock. I head back to Tuckahoe, turning over in my mind all the information I've gathered. But there are still missing pieces.

If Angela Selverini kidnapped Grace's sister, changed her name, moved to Arizona and married Frank, where did the baby in the reservoir come from?

And how could a nurse with no previous criminal background execute such a brazen, calculated felony and not get caught? Women who kidnap children to raise as their own are usually so unstable that they're caught in a few days. Masterminding such a seamless crime would require a chilling logic.

The answer has to be with Frank. I need to see him before his release. And I need to bring Grace with me to catch him off guard.

When I get back to the hospital, I try to rouse Xavier, but nothing doing. The sugar high has become a post-sugar low. I carry him onto the elevator and up to ICU. When we get to the waiting room, only Dan is there, leaning back on the couch, his eyes closed. I lay Xavier near him, and he opens his eyes. "I knew you'd come back."

"Why?"

He smiles. "I know my kid."

"Are they here?"

"Yeah. They just went in."

"How—you know—are they acting?"

"Like normal grandparents—stunned, afraid."

"Is he behaving?"

"You mean has your father said anything inappropriate? Not yet. He actually looks really worn out."

"I haven't been there much for you guys, but I'll be damned if I'm gonna let the old man crucify you."

Dan has a quizzical look on his face, and then breaks into a grin. "You came back to protect us? Kev, I appreciate that, but it's not necessary. I understand where your dad's coming from."

"He's coming from the devil," I say, more forcefully than I expect.

Dan smiles. "No Kev, your dad's theology comes from his own fears of not measuring up. His demanding god is probably based on the relationship he had with his own father."

"I don't care where it came from. The man has done a lot of damage."

"I don't deny that, Kevin. But a lot of that damage has boomeranged back on him. He's lived an unhappy life. The only way he'll ever change is by being exposed to non-judgmental love."

"Go for it, Dan, but count me out."

He pulls Xavier into his arms and kisses his sleeping face. "So, my dear brother-in-law, how did you knock out my son?"

"What can I say? The kid can't hold his liquor."

"Cassie will be glad he's back. She's been worried about him."

"She's the one I'm worried about."

"She'll be okay. She's trying not to let her mind go places, but it's hard. He opened his eyes about an hour ago for just a split second. The doctors said it didn't mean anything, but it meant something to us."

The door to ICU opens and Cassie walks out with her arm around Mom who's crying. Behind them is Dad, stony-faced as ever. When Cassie sees me, she smiles through tears. I walk over to my mom and put my arms around her, surprising myself by getting choked up too.

"Oh, Kevin, it's been so long," she murmurs.

I hold her tight and close my eyes. I love her smell—fresh bread and autumn. I look over her shoulder at my dad who is staring at us. Longing rises up, but it's quickly replaced by something cold. I let her go and shake his hand. He looks like he's about to hug me, but I straight-arm him so he can't get any closer. I nod at him. "Dad."

"Son."

We all sit down. Dan passes Xavier over to Cassie, and she gently tries to wake him up. "Grandpa and Grandma are here, honey. Do you want to say hello?"

"Hi," he says sleepily. He nestles into his mother.

We exchange awkward pleasantries for a few minutes, and when I can't stand it anymore, I ask, "Can I go in to see Jay?"

Dan stands up. "Sure. I'll go with you."

Jay is in the second bed on the right in a massive circular room with small cutouts for the patients, each of whom is hooked up to a million dollars' worth of equipment. Jay's eyes are closed, and he's on a ventilator, but Dan acts like he's conscious and can understand every word. He encourages me to talk to Jay.

I grab his hand. "How you doin', buddy?"

I don't expect a response because of the tube down his throat, but there's a slight squeeze of my hand. I squeeze back. Dan talks softly to him, telling him how much he loves him, how his friends have been calling, how Mimi's been asking for him.

When he prays for him, he takes a drop of oil from a tiny bottle and makes a cross on his forehead. Jay is still and white as marble, but the oil shines under the light.

XIII

GRACE

By the time Eve got back, the nurse and Grace had cleaned Mimi up and washed all the grit and glass out of her hair. Aside from bruising and some lacerations on her face, she was looking like herself, but all the activity had tuckered her out, so she drifted in and out of sleep. Eve looked better too, having showered and put on some makeup. When she came in, she kissed Mimi on the forehead. "How does everything feel, sweetie?"

Mimi didn't open her eyes. "Hurts."

Eve's brows creased as she glanced at Mimi's arms. Everything was wrapped up except two fingers on each hand which were so swollen and discolored they look like old sausages.

"Did you make any calls?" Grace whispered.

She nodded. "I talked to Auntie Elaine, and she'll be coming up Monday night. André was another story. He's beside himself. He wanted to come to the hospital right away, but I told him to visit her at home instead. She doesn't need that right now."

"Let him come," Mimi mumbled.

Mom looked at Grace who quickly shook her head. André, Mimi's neurotic violin teacher, forbade her to play softball, for heaven's sake. How would he react now?

"I don't think so, honey? You know how he'll carry on."

"Might as well get it over with," Mimi said without emotion.

When Mimi nodded off again, Grace motioned to Eve that she

was going to ICU to see Dan and Cassie. Upstairs, Dan introduced her to Cassie and Kevin's parents. Mrs. Jacobs, a frail-looking woman, was sitting on the couch with Xavier, distractedly listening to him babble on. Mr. Jacobs, a stern, stoic-looking man who had Kevin's eyes, was sitting by himself. Kevin, who looked desperately uncomfortable, offered to take her in to see Jay.

As soon as Grace saw Jay, her heart broke. The last time they'd been together was when he'd come to their house all decked out in his tux, nervously playing with a corsage box. Now he looked like a broken child. She hoped he wouldn't look like this by the time Mimi saw him. Kevin stepped in close and grasped his hand.

Grace kissed his cheek. "We love you, Jason."

Back out in the waiting room, Dan asked about Mimi. "She's better," Grace said. "She may be going home in a few days. They don't know if there's been nerve damage or if she'll be able to—you know."

Cassie stood up and embraced Grace. "We have to keep praying. I don't think God would give her that kind of gift just to let it be robbed from her like this."

"The Lord giveth and the Lord taketh away," Mr. Jacobs mumbled.

Dan spoke with forced cheerfulness. "Let's not assume He's taking anything away, right now."

Grace glanced at Kevin who was staring at his shoes, his face and body tense. Finally, he looked up. "Grace, I have to show my parents how to get to the house from here. Would you like to ride with me? There's something I need to talk to you about."

"Uh—sure."

When they got to Cassie and Dan's, Kevin carried in his parents' bags and beat a hasty retreat. Just before they got back to the hospital, he said, "Remember when we talked about going to see Frank Benedict at prison? We need to go as soon as possible because he's up for parole soon, and if we miss him, he'll be harder to find. I know this is a really difficult time for you, but we should go this coming week."

"I don't think I can go right now, Kevin. Mom and Mimi need me."

He pulled up to the hospital lobby to let her out. "Please consider it, Grace. That's all I ask."

Later that night after Mimi was asleep, Grace talked to Eve. "Kevin and I need to spend some time going over stuff about the case. But I don't want to leave you holding the bag with Mimi."

Ever since Grace had told Eve what Kevin was doing, whenever she mentioned *the case*, Eve would get a weird look on her face that was halfway between sadness and surprise—a look that made Grace want to stop the whole process. But it was just her face. Her voice was composed, almost cheerful.

"If Mimi gets released tomorrow, we should be into a routine by Monday, so feel free to get together with him then."

"I don't want to abandon you."

"I can handle it, Grace. You need to do this *now*."

When Grace got home that night, she called Kevin to tell him. "I'll pick you up at noon on Monday," he said. "We can talk about everything on the drive, and then we'll see what Frank adds to the mix."

That night, Grace couldn't hold back a flood of tears. She couldn't shake the feeling that she was responsible for Mimi's injuries. The worst part was that she couldn't talk to anyone about it because she knew it was crazy. She kept asking God to forgive her, but her prayers hit the ceiling. The only good thing about the last few days was that she hadn't had one nightmare, waking or asleep. But she'd rather have non-stop watery blue dreams than have her sister suffer like this. She'd always known that Mimi's future was way more important than hers.

When Kevin arrived at the house on Monday, he first went in to see Mimi. She was happy to talk to anyone besides her mother and sister. After they chatted for a while, Kevin and Grace left, picked up coffees, and headed out to Putnam.

For a while Grace felt awkward and didn't know what to talk about. Fortunately, Kevin seemed relaxed as he maneuvered them onto the highway. "Your sister looks better, and her attitude is pretty good."

"That's Mimi. She's incapable of feeling sorry for herself. How's Jay doing?"

"They haven't taken him off the Propofol yet, that's what keeps him unconscious, so he's still out cold. But they're going to cut it back tomorrow. My sister, however, is a mess."

They both nursed their coffees while they drove, without talking.

Grace eventually broke the silence. "We don't know if Mimi will able to play the violin once she heals. "Even if she can, it may still mean her career is over. I know that's small potatoes compared to whether someone can walk or not, but it's been her life up to now."

Kevin grimaced. "They're such good kids. Why them?"

"I wish I knew."

Again, they sank into silence.

Now or never. "You promised to tell me everything you found out about my sister's kidnapping."

"Yeah, I plan to do that, but I have a couple questions first."

Unconsciously, she held her breath.

Kevin glanced over at her. "I'm a student of human behavior. I have to be in my work, and I gotta say, I don't think you're being upfront with me. You keep saying things like, *It's really important that I know; I can't tell you why; it's a long story,* yada, yada. If you don't want to explain any of that to me, that's cool. But this whole thing could get a lot more complicated than we thought, and it would probably be good if we could trust each other."

Grace knew this would happen. "What's to tell? I've just been thinking about it a lot."

"That's the short story. I want the long version."

She looked out the window at the fences and trees blurring by. *He'd never understand.*

She took a deep breath. "Look Kevin, you seem like a black

and white kinda guy who believes in what you can see and touch. Am I right?"

He nodded.

"Well, that's not me. I've always had people in my life try to explain away what I thought and felt, telling me that I'm a little off, a little screwed up. You're right, I don't trust you. It's because I'm sick of being humored or written off as some wacko."

Kevin chuckled. "I'm not stupid enough to think I have all the answers, so if there are things that you're not telling me 'cause I'll think you're whacked, you're seriously limiting this investigation. I need every possible detail about a case before I can build a hypothesis. Besides, you've got me pegged wrong. I may look black and white, but I've got an emotional side and a spiritual side too. You may not believe this, but sometimes I'm able to crack a case because of an insight that just pops into my head outta the blue. Other times, I have a dream that gives the solution. In fact, last night I had a dream about *this* case. It doesn't make any sense to me, but it might later, and I'll take all the help I can get—even from my subconscious."

Grace felt a chill go through her. "You had a dream?"

"Yeah."

"What was it about?"

"You were in it, that much I know. Let's see, I'm walking down this dry, dusty road, and I'm really thirsty. I hear water running somewhere, so I walk toward the sound. When I come around this bend, there's a waterfall, I mean a huge waterfall, like a hundred feet straight up! I lay down on the bank to take a drink, and when I look into the water, I see your face instead of mine. Sounds silly, but that doesn't surprise me at all. I'm talking to you, but the waterfall is making such a racket, I can't hear what you're saying back."

Grace broke out into a sweat, and a wave of nausea washed over her. "Pull over! I think I'm gonna be sick."

Kevin didn't ask any questions. He just put on his police flashers, swerved to the right, and stopped. Grace opened the door and leaned out. Heat rose up from below the car. The smell of exhaust was choking. With her head spinning, she lurched out of the car like it was on fire.

"You all right?" he called.

"I just have to walk for a minute."

Okay, God, what are you doing? Now this guy's in my head! I'm so scared. I'm so scared. Are you messing with me? I love you, but I'm going crazy. And now somebody else is involved. Are you gonna give me some answers?

She walked the length of the car, back and forth a few times while Kevin watched her, a look of alarm on his face. When she climbed back in, she leaned her head back and sat with her eyes closed for a few minutes.

Trust.

That was her answer—one word.

Trust. Trust who? Trust what?

Trust.

She buckled her seat belt. "Okay, let's go."

"You sure?"

"Yeah."

He pulled back into the flow of traffic and switched off his lights. After they drove for a few miles she said, "Kevin, I've decided to trust you."

"I'm glad to hear that."

She looked out the window and tried to gather her thoughts. "That dream you had—it's very similar to dreams I've been having. Three weeks ago, I got a concussion from a bike accident. Since then, I've been having dreams—lots of them—and something else, too—visions."

"Visions?"

"That's where it gets weird."

"Visions?"

"I'm just going along, minding my own business, when I feel

my skin crawl, and I have trouble breathing. Sometimes it comes on gradually, sometimes it just blindsides me. Usually, I see a blue waterfall and my face. Sometimes I'm speaking, but I can't hear what I'm saying."

Suddenly, Kevin was all ears. "Have you been writing this stuff down?"

"No."

He straightened up in his seat, looking really energized. "You should start. Now, as best as you can, tell me everything you can about all of it."

Time stopped for Grace at that moment. *Could he possibly be taking me seriously? Who is this guy?*

Slowly at first, she began—first with the one on the highway. Then it all came out in a rush, down to the last one in the shower on Friday. When he asked questions, they were clipped and incisive. "And there's always bluish water?"

"Almost always."

Kevin was silent for a few minutes, but she could practically hear his mind whirring as he started doing a drum beat on his steering wheel. "It can't be a coincidence that I had that dream."

"No kidding! That's what's freaking me out."

"What do *you* think is going on?"

"Before, I thought it meant I just needed to process the past, which is why I thought knowing more about the kidnapping would help. But that doesn't explain why *you* would have a dream. Part of me is relieved that someone else might be able to understand what I'm going through, but part of me is really scared that my craziness is rubbing off on you—like I'm contagious."

"Has it *rubbed off* on anyone else?"

"No."

"Then it wouldn't follow that you're infecting me. If you were somehow telepathically communicating this dream, why would it be to me, and not your mom or sister?"

"I don't know."

"And these dreams and visions scare you?"

"Of course, wouldn't they scare you?"

"No, Grace. That's the point. I wasn't scared, only curious."

"Does that mean something?"

"I don't know. Unless…"

"What?"

"Your family isn't helping you find out the truth, but I am. Maybe I had the dream because *together* you and I are gonna find out what really happened."

Tears sprang into Grace's eyes. "I really hope so, because I don't know how much longer I can take this."

They drove on in silence for a while, the turnpike getting less crowded as they headed north. "It's a good thing you decided to trust me."

Grace smiled. "Yeah?"

"Yeah, 'cause I'll probably ask you to do things you won't understand."

"Like going with you to meet this guy?"

"Right."

Grace let out a big, ragged sigh. "Now that I've spilled my guts, are you gonna tell me what you know?"

He shifted in his seat, checked his mirrors and took a swallow of coffee. "Fair enough. Everything I've seen, everyone I've talked to, all seem to be pointing to this Angela Selverini aka Lena Nardi as the lady who may have walked off with your sister. I can give you all the gritty details later, but basically, she resigns from St. Luke's in June, right after meeting your parents. She tells people she's moving out west, but she doesn't go right away. Instead, she stays in New York and marries Frank, even though she tells two different sources that he wouldn't marry her unless she had a child. Then he moves to Arizona, looking like he's stepped out of her life. The day you guys are born, she disappears and ends up in Arizona with Frank. She may have planned to raise your sister as her own child."

Grace had no words. Her eyes blurred with tears. But in a moment, she brushed them away with fury. "How horrible! What an evil woman! And then something went wrong, and my sister died?"

"That's the part where you have to trust me."

"What do you mean?"

Kevin pulled off the highway and headed for the Putnam County Compound. "I'll explain after we get out of here."

Grace said nothing more, and neither did Kevin. As they got cleared to go through the gates, he grabbed her hand. "Don't worry. It'll be all right."

She tried to believe that.

KEVIN

Arthur Kill Correctional Facility is a medium security prison. When we enter, we're directed to a lobby where about twenty other people are waiting to visit inmates. I show the guard my ID, and he directs us to another room with two lawyers and a police officer. The guard asks for Grace's ID and then explains that she can't take in her purse, sweater or cell-phone. He directs her to a wall of coin-operated lockers. "You'll also have to take off all your jewelry and the barrette you have in your hair, Miss."

"Even though I'm with a detective?"

"That's right."

Grace looks at me for reassurance. I nod.

After we store her things, we walk through the metal detector and get patted down. Again, Grace is startled by the process. Poor kid! She doesn't get that in this place, everyone is suspect. They usher us into another room where we wait for a good twenty minutes. I try to distract her by talking, but she's obviously nervous and fidgety. The guard calls my name, and we're led through a set of electronically controlled doors down a corridor to another room with several tables and chairs. Six people besides us are waiting for the inmates to come in.

"Grace, do you mind waiting at another table until I call you over?"

"Where should I sit?" she asks, her eyes wide.

"How about over there by the window?"

She sits down looking so vulnerable, so alone. I know I'm setting her up. But it has to be this way. I hope she can handle it.

Frank is escorted in by a guard who then stations himself by the door. Frank is a slight man, about five feet, six inches with a belly. He's wearing a sagging, orange jumpsuit, his number printed on a strip of cotton over the breast pocket. He's got stringy grey hair tied in a ponytail and watery blue eyes. I stand up to shake his hand.

"Hello, Mr. Benedict, my name is Kevin Jacobs."

He sits across from me, hostility etched into his face. "Who are you?"

"I'm a detective from the 53rd precinct in New York City."

His eyes are wary. "Whadaya want?"

"Actually, I'm not here on official business. I'm just a friend of someone who wants to see you."

"Who?"

"She's over there, sitting by the window."

He glances in Grace's direction.

"Do you recognize her?"

He watches her for a bit. "No."

"I know she's a lot older than the last time you saw her."

I motion to Grace to come and sit with us. As she walks toward us, I study Frank's reaction. He gives her the once over, his eyes lingering on her legs and breasts. At first, he looks confused. Then his mouth curls into a smirk. "Well, well, you certainly have turned into an eyeful, Brandi. Come to visit your old man?"

Grace grabs my hand and moves closer to me. "My name isn't Brandi."

"Then, who the hell are you? Her twin?"

As soon as the words leave his mouth, a wave of realization

flickers in his eyes, and he jumps up. "What's going on? If you're trying to pin something on me, you're all wrong. I had absolutely nothing to do with it."

I keep my voice nonchalant. "With what?"

"Guard, I want to go back to my cell!" His voice is ragged, his movements jerky.

The guard approaches us, but I show my badge and wave him back.

"Mr. Benedict, I understand you're going before a parole board in about three weeks. I plan on being at that hearing. Now, I can either tell them that you fully cooperated with me, or I can tell them that I believe you were an accomplice in a kidnapping/murder case. Which is it?"

"I'm not talkin' to anyone without a lawyer."

"Suit yourself. I already got what I came for. I'll see you at the parole hearing."

Frank sits back down and leans over the table, pleading. "Wait a minute! I'm telling you, I never had nothin' to do with it. I've done some stupid things in my day, but I'd *never* do anything like that!"

I glance at Grace who looks like Bambi caught in the headlights. "You decide, Frank. You tell me now, or it comes out at the hearing."

He stares me down, looking like he'd just as soon twist my head off as look at me. "All right. Whadaya wanna know?"

"Hang on."

I lean toward Grace and whisper, "Do you want to hear this, or would you rather wait in the lobby for me?"

The fear in her eyes turns to fierceness. "I'm staying."

I grab her sweaty hand. "Okay Frank. Tell us what you know."

"About the kid, right? The kid that this one looks like a grownup version of?"

"That's right."

"What do you want to know?"

"Why don't you start from the beginning?"

He licks his lip and pushes stray strands of hair behind his ears. "Okay, so Lena wanted to have a baby, but she couldn't 'cause there was somethin' wrong with her."

"Why are you calling her Lena? I thought her name was Angela?"

"Angelina. Out in Phoenix, she wanted everyone to call her Lena, insisted I do too. Lena wasn't somebody you crossed."

"Okay, go on."

"Like I said, she wanted a baby real bad. She told me one day that she had a chance to adopt one, but we had to get married first. I didn't wanna marry her, but she pushed, so we did. Right after, I mean the *next day*, she said she wanted to move out west. She knew some guy in Phoenix, so she gave me some money and told me to go out there and find us a place to live. We packed up the apartment, and she went to live with her friend. She said she had to stay in New York until the baby was born.

"About a month later, she drove out with a kid. We named her Brandi. I thought it was strange that they let her take the kid out of state, 'cause I know it's a while before adoptions are finalized, but I didn't ask no questions 'cause she was happy as a clam. About a week later, I was watching CNN and saw that a baby girl, a twin, had been kidnapped from St. Luke's which is where Lena worked. I got real scared. Lena could get violent if she got mad, but I needed to know if Brandi had been, you know, kidnapped. When I brought it up to her, she wasn't upset or nervous or anything. She said that it was really sad, that she felt bad for the parents and hoped they got their baby back.

"A few weeks later, I saw that the kidnapped kid turned up drowned. I kinda breathed a sigh of relief. But," he turns to Grace, "now that I see you—I don't know."

"Did you ever see Brandi's birth certificate?"

"No. Lena took care of all that stuff."

"Do you have any pictures of Brandi?"

"No. I kinda left in a hurry, and never stayed in touch."

"Why'd you leave?"

Frank glances around the room, beads of sweat gathering on his upper lip. "It's a long story."

"We got time."

He shifts uncomfortably in his chair. "Lena never had a drinking problem before we moved out west. But once we got to Phoenix, she started drinking like a fish. I drank too, but she could really put it away. We fought—a lot. My boss, Ray, and Lena went way back, and I could tell he was sweet on her. As much as I told him to knock it off, and as much as I told her to stay away from him, they just seemed to like tormenting me with their flirtin'. One night—Brandi was about ten—I got really mad. I told Lena if she thought she could do better with somebody else, she could just leave. Well, she'd had a few, and she actually came at me with a knife, so I got the hell outa there. I tried to go back, but she said it was over. She wouldn't let me see Brandi.

"Of course, I lost my job 'cause Ray had been looking for a chance with Lena. I had no money and nowhere to go, so I came back East and lived with my brother until I got back on my feet. I went to a lawyer here, and he said I had a right to see Brandi, so I called Lena and told her I wanted Brandi to come east for two weeks in the summer. How's this for a lovin' wife? She said if I tried that crap, she'd put a hit on me. She was psycho enough to do it. She mailed the divorce papers to me. I signed them, so that was that."

"And you never saw Brandi again?"

"Nope. I missed that kid."

"What are you in for, Frank?"

"Why?"

"Just curious."

"Some internet scam."

"Didn't you meet up with somebody you thought was a fourteen-year-old girl?"

"What's your point?"

"But you never tried anything with Brandi."

His watery eyes turn dark. "I tell ya, I never touched her! We were buddies. I was even afraid to leave her with Lena."

To my surprise, Grace leans across the table. "Can I ask you something?"

Frank turns to her with an odd look on his face. For a moment he isn't wearing his con-man mask. There's a flicker of something like tenderness. "Yeah."

"It's about Brandi. What was she like?"

"Well, it was a long time ago, but she was smart and funny. She was learning the guitar, and she loved to sing. I can't hold a tune, so I liked that."

Grace doesn't say anything.

"I missed her, but I wasn't about to go against Lena. She's a wacko. I had to get away from her."

"Where do you think they are now?"

"Don't know. Lena worked at the Children's Hospital in Phoenix. For all I know, she's still there."

I give him my card. "If you think of anything else that might be important, call me. I'll pay for the call."

"What's gonna happen to Lena?"

"That's not up to me."

As we stand up, I see he's staring at Grace. "Uh, what's your name again?"

"Grace."

"Yeah, uh, Grace, I'm sorry 'bout what happened. If Brandi is your sister—uh—I just want to say, don't expect too much from her. Unless things have changed a lot, she probably wasn't raised by the kinda people that raised you."

Grace's eyes soften. "Thanks for talking to us, Mr. Benedict."

He looks down at the card I gave him. "Uh, Jacobs—you still comin' to the hearing?"

As much as the guy makes my skin crawl, I say, "I'll write the board—tell them you helped the investigation."

XIV

GRACE

When they got back to the visitor's waiting room, Grace went to her locker to pick up her stuff. Kevin had to hold her arm as they walked out of Arthur Kill because she was shaking so badly, her legs like spaghetti. When they got to the car, she tried to strap herself in, but suddenly she was so nauseous she had to get out of the car. After she threw up in the parking lot, Kevin ran over to hold her up because she was about to collapse.

She wailed, her cries like howls, jagged breaths in between. She bent over and threw up again.

"Oh, God, oh God," was all she could say before she would start howling again. Poor Kevin patted her arm, handed her tissues, and kept saying, "It's okay, it's okay. Try to breathe."

Finally, she just collapsed in his arms, her tears and runny nose staining his shirt. She didn't know how long they stayed like that. It seemed like there couldn't be anymore tears, but then there were. When she finally managed to stop crying like a two-year-old, he awkwardly disentangled himself from her and helped her back into the car. She sat with her back against the door.

"I'm so sorry Grace. I don't know what I expected. It was a rotten trick to bring you here. I never should've done it. I'm really, really sorry."

When she saw the look of misery on his face, she tried to smile. "It's okay. I mean, it was terrible and wonderful at the same time. If this girl, Brandi, is my sister, it means that she made it to at least ten years old. Maybe she's still alive."

When they got back to Tuckahoe, she asked Kevin to drive around for a while. "I don't want to go home yet. I have so many questions."

He gripped the steering wheel tighter. "Ask away."

"How can we know for sure this girl is my sister?"

"I don't know, Grace. We'll have to find out."

"And what about the baby that died? If Brandi is my sister, who's buried in my sister's grave?"

"I don't know that either. I only know she's not your sister."

"How can you be sure of that?"

"We did a hair test."

"You had a sample of her hair?"

"Yes. And a sample of yours."

"Mine?"

Kevin gave her an embarrassed grin. "I got it off your hairbrush when I came to your house. Sorry."

"How'd you know it was mine?"

"Two brunettes and one blonde living together—it wasn't hard."

In spite of herself, she smiled, but then caught her breath. "Kevin, what do I tell my mother?"

He shook his head. "Nothing yet. We'll do it together when the time is right."

"Even if we find out that Brandi is my sister, it doesn't mean she'll want to connect with us. You heard Frank—she was raised by a psycho."

"That's probably true, but I wouldn't believe everything he said. What's your read on why he left Lena and Brandi?"

"I don't think he touched her."

He shot her a skeptical look. "How do you know?"

"Not sure. I just don't think he did."

Grace cranked up the air conditioner and pointed the vents directly at her face while they drove on in silence. Her mind raced through pictures of Brandi at various stages of her life. Did she feel safe as a child, a teenager? Did she have friends? Did she like school? She begged God for ideas about how to move forward.

"What do you think about me going out to Phoenix to find out what happened to her? If she's there, I could find out what's she's like and whether she wants to have any contact with your family."

But Grace's thoughts were miles away. "Uh huh."

Kevin looked confused. "Do you have a better idea?"

"No. I just wonder what it will be like for Brandi to find out her mother is a kidnapper. Will it put her in danger? Will Lena get arrested? Will Brandi still want a relationship with her? And if she meets us, what will that be like? Joy? Grief over all the lost years? How will Mom handle it?"

Kevin ran his fingers through his short hair. "I guess I don't think the way you do. In that sense, you're right, I *am* black and white. I just think a great wrong has been perpetrated that needs to be corrected. If it were me, I'd want to know the truth."

Grace smiled sadly. "Really? What if you found out something awful about your family—like your mom cheated on your dad, and he's not really your father. Your *real* dad is a drunk, and your mom isn't who you thought she was. You might wish you'd never found that out."

"First off, I've always wished I had a different dad, so that wouldn't bother me. As far as my mom, sure, I'd be surprised, but no matter what she did or didn't do, I'd still be me."

Grace shook her head. "I don't believe you'd be that casual about it, Kevin."

"Doesn't it say in the Bible that knowing the truth will set you free? Brandi gets to meet her real family. Lena has to face the consequences of her actions. We find out who the baby is that's buried in your sister's grave. Maybe there are parents somewhere who have no idea what happened to their baby. Shouldn't they learn the truth?"

"Way to know enough Bible to make a point."

He looked irritated. "You have no idea how much I know."

Grace glared at him. "Do I even get a choice in how this gets handled, or is it all up to you?"

Kevin sighed. "Look, I'm trying to get your input now, so that I can go in with a plan. Without a plan, my boss will be calling the shots. If that happens, I can guarantee that justice will be served with little regard for collateral damage."

She turned away from him to stare at nothing outside the window. "I just can't think right now."

Instead of responding, he flicked on the radio, and they mindlessly listened to music. When they got to Grace's house, he walked her to the door. "I know this has been a really hard day. Sleep on it, and I'll call you tomorrow."

As if sleep would help. As if sleep had been giving her any peace at all.

Instead of going straight to her room, Grace sat down on the couch next to Mimi who was watching TV, her arms propped up on pillows. She felt like a secret as big as a continent lay between them. "Where's Mom?"

Mimi didn't look at her. "She went out to get something for supper."

"How are you doing?"

Mimi shifted her body and winced. "Terrible."

"In pain?"

"What do you think?"

"Can I get you something?"

Mimi turned her head to face Grace. "You can take me to the hospital to see Jason."

Grace noticed Mimi's pupils were hugely dilated from the pain meds. She tried to talk a little slower. "Mom's got my car right now, Mi, otherwise I would."

Mimi didn't respond. Instead, she heaved herself up and nearly fell over. When Grace reached out to steady her, she pushed her hand away. Then, leaning against the wall, she stumbled to her room and kicked the door shut.

Grace sighed and went into her room where she stripped down, fell on her bed, and closed her eyes. The insides of her eyelids felt like sandpaper from all the crying. She tried to pray but found she could only say, "Please God," with nothing after that.

She was in a large, crowded room trying to find Brandi. Finally, she located her and saw she was holding a cat that looked just like Alfred who died when she was twelve. Grace was so happy to see him. Maybe he didn't really die but just went to live with Brandi. When she reached her sister, Brandi asked, "Do you want your kitty back?"

Grace nodded and Brandi put him in her arms. But he wasn't Alfred, just another cat who looked like him. While she scanned the crowd to find Brandi again, the cat struggled to get free and bloodied her arms with his claws.

She woke up to the sound of knocking. Stumbling to her door, she opened it and saw Eve on the other side. "Come on in," she said as she sat back down on the bed and pulled a pillow to her chest. "Did everything go well with Kevin today?" Eve asked.

How on earth could she answer that? "Yeah, sure," she said, without looking up.

Eve seemed to wait for her to elaborate. When Grace didn't, she added, "Do you want to talk about it?"

"No."

Her mother looked momentarily hurt, then her eyes hardened.

Grace backpedaled. "There's a lot to tell, but you know me. I have to get things right in my own mind first."

"I know," Eve said, and with that she walked out the door.

Grace sighed. She didn't want to emerge from her room, but it was obvious neither Mimi nor Eve was doing well. She wrapped herself in a robe and followed her mother downstairs into the kitchen. "How are you doing, Mom?"

"Just ducky." Eve slammed a few drawers and tore open the bag with the takeout food. "One daughter's having hallucinations; the other one is completely broken. I don't have a car or the money to buy a new one. Everything's *fine*."

Grace sighed. "Do you want me to get Mimi?"

"No, when I called her, she announced that I took *too* long, and she's *not* hungry anymore."

Grace shook her head and chuckled. "Well, I'll eat with you. I'm starving."

Eve grabbed plates and silverware while Grace poured drinks. They sat down and held hands to pray. Grace looked at her mother's bowed head for a long time. Then she said, "God, thank you for this food. And I gotta say, we're in trouble. Mimi's hands are crushed. Jason's in a coma. Mom needs a car, so I can have mine back. And I can't even go into what's happening with me. Please help! We really could use a miracle or two. And help us take care of each other."

"And Dan and Cassie, too," Eve mumbled. "And Aunt Elaine who should be here any minute. May she not drive me crazy."

"Amen."

KEVIN

After I drop Grace off, I race back to the city to talk to Carlton Hines. Luckily, he hasn't left the office yet. "How'd it go today?" he asks.

I can barely contain myself. While I tell him about Benedict, he interrupts constantly to ask questions. Afterwards, he lets out a low whistle. Then I drop the bomb. "I'd like to fly to Phoenix to meet Brandi."

"When?" he asks.

"As soon as possible."

He cocks his head and stares at me. "Is this the right time, given your family situation?"

"The best thing for me is to stay busy. I can't just sit around the hospital. My parents are here watching my nephew, so things are pretty much under control. The sooner I can finish this case, the better. I didn't tell you this, but the other kid who was in the accident with Jay is Grace's sister—the girl who got me into this. Believe me, those people could use something positive right now."

He doesn't look convinced, but I can see he's softening. "You'd need to connect with the Phoenix PD. I don't want you out there without backup. A sixty-year-old lady may not seem dangerous, but you don't know what she's capable of. Who do you want to take with you? Bob—Tony?"

"What I'd like to do is take Brandi's twin with me. I'm hoping if they meet, she'll realize this isn't just about closing an old police case, but about a family that loves her. If we just go in all blockbuster and try to arrest her mother, she could get in the way—maybe try to help Lena escape. Seeing her twin sister might help her want to cooperate."

Carlton shakes his head. "I can't imagine the red tape we'd have to wade through to make that happen."

"She's next of kin. Technically, she'd have a right to go and identify the victim."

"Still."

"What's the harm in asking?"

Carlton reddens. "The harm? My head would be on the block if anything went wrong!"

"You *know* I can protect them both, Sergeant. Besides, I'll have cops there to back me up."

"I'll ask, but I can't guarantee anything."

"Could Rudy have some pull?"

"I don't know, but I'll call him. Maybe somebody owes him a favor."

"Thanks, sir. Call me when you know, no matter the time."

After eleven that night I get the call. Somebody owed Rudy a favor.

XV

GRACE

Two days later, Grace woke up to her phone ringing.

"Grace, it's Kevin. Hope I didn't wake you."

"Don't you ever call people at normal hours?"

"No time to chit-chat. Would you like to go to Phoenix with me?"

Grace sat up in her bed, fully awake. "I-I don't know."

"I mean, can you get out of work for a while?"

"I'm not working. It's on hold since the accident. I figured I'd need to help my mom with Mimi. But Mom is taking a leave of absence from school, and my aunt is here, so they haven't needed me much. But Kevin, I'd have to tell my mother what's up, and we can't do that! If everything fell apart, it could be disastrous."

"Does she know about the dreams and visions you've been having?"

"Yeah, why?"

"Well, a guy I grew up with works at some inner healing center in Arizona somewhere. We could tell her you're going there for some treatment."

Grace was skeptical. "And what would be your purpose in going?"

Kevin sounded frustrated. "I don't know—introductions, a body guard—just tell me, do you want to go?"

Grace didn't hesitate. "Yes."

"Okay, then leave the rest to me."

"By the way, how much coffee have you had this morning, Kevin? You sound like you're on crack."

"Just be ready when I come to pick you up today at noon."

"What? Are you kidding?"

"I'll talk to Eve."

And then he hung up.

Grace jumped out of bed and grabbed a carryon from the top of her closet. She threw clothes in it before she got in the shower. Suddenly, she felt a flicker of hope rise in her chest—and fear.

By the time she packed, showered, and came out of her room at nearly 11:00, Kevin was already in the kitchen, talking to Eve. Grace didn't know how he did it, but Eve was nodding and smiling. "Kevin told me everything, and I think it's a great idea. And how nice that he has some police business to take care of in Phoenix so you don't have to go alone."

Grace exchanged glances with Kevin. "Uh, right."

Before she could say anything else, Kevin jumped in. "I'm not sure how long it'll take, so I got open-ended tickets."

"Well, my daughter's peace of mind is the most important thing to me. You two stay as long as she needs to."

Grace knew she should at least try to protest. "But Mom, what about Mimi? Don't you need help with her?"

"Aunt Elaine and I can manage." She took Grace's hands in hers. "Besides, we prayed yesterday for miracles. Maybe this is one of them."

Grace didn't know what to say now that she felt like lying scum, so she just hugged Eve, then walked into the living room to hug Aunt Elaine and Mimi. "Bring me home something with a scorpion on it," Mimi yelled as they walked out the door.

After they drove away, Grace got a chance to really look at Kevin. His eyes were ringed from lack of sleep, his hair was wet, and there was stubble on his face. He was even peppier than this morning. "When was the last time you slept?" she asked him.

"I'll sleep on the plane."

"What did you tell my mom? I think she would've been okay with you taking me to Mars today."

He grinned. "First, I put on my professional detective voice; then I did a little Columbo thing where she had to finish my sentences. But basically, I told her about the Christian Trauma Institute where my buddy works—that they specialize in issues like yours."

"I feel awful, with you lying like that."

"I wasn't lying! I've already connected with Gary, and it's all set up. They're meeting with you tomorrow at four."

"What? I thought this was just a ruse to get to Phoenix!"

Kevin smiled wickedly. "Au contraire, my dear. I also guaranteed her that you'd come back completely different. I didn't tell one lie."

Grace shook her head. "It's not what you said that bothers me; it's what you didn't say."

"Just doing what you told me, Grace, getting the facts before we tell her anything."

"Did you ever consider going into sales, Kevin? I think you could make a cool million in no time."

He laughed, obviously delighted with himself. "No, I've never thought of that. Besides, what would I sell?"

"Snake oil."

KEVIN

When we get to the airport it takes us over an hour to go through airport security. They keep checking and rechecking my credentials even though I called last night to alert the TSA that I was traveling armed. At the departure gate we have another thirty-minute wait before we board the plane, so we get coffee and sandwiches at Starbucks.

Between bites, Grace gets this serious look on her face. "I can't believe how much you've thrown yourself into this, Kevin. Even if we never find Brandi, even if she's not my sister, I want you to know how much it means to me."

"Save your thanks until something good happens. Up to now, it's all been bad news."

She takes a sip of coffee and looks pensive again. "Remember that day at the hospital when you asked me why I wouldn't let you worry about me? I want to know why you won't let me thank you?"

When I don't answer right away, she smiles innocently. "You've been babbling on your caffeine high all morning. Now you're quiet? It's a simple question."

"Okay. When you thank me, it makes me afraid that now I'm gonna screw up."

She stares at me for a moment. "Where does that come from?"

"Who knows? Maybe from never getting a straight compliment from my dad. It was always, *You got this right, but you messed up over here.* Stupid, huh?"

She takes a tiny bite of her sandwich. "Not really."

"What, that we all just keep reacting to our *childhood wounds*?"

She raises her cup. "Let's toast to that depressing reality."

We tap cups. "But not for you, right? Your parents were great."

She chuckles. "Let's just say, mistakes were made."

"Like what?"

"Like they never told me what happened to my twin."

"What?"

"At my fifth birthday party, I found them in their bedroom, crying and hugging each other. I had no idea why. They were trying to protect me I guess, but it made me think *I* was what made them unhappy. Later when Mimi was born, that dark cloud lifted—which only confirmed my suspicions that I was the bad seed while she was the bright star. When she turned out to be a prodigy, there was no way I could measure up."

"That's not what Cassie says. She thinks you're just as talented as Mimi."

Grace doesn't say anything for a moment. She takes another bite of her sandwich and a swig of water, then says, "When they finally told me all the details, it got worse. I decided I was responsible for her death."

"What?"

"I was in the NICU with breathing problems when she was taken. That's why it was her instead of me."

"That made you responsible?" I ask, incredulous.

She shrugs. "What can I say? It's how kids think."

"Didn't your parents explain that wasn't true?"

"I kept it a secret. But from then on, I made it my mission to take care of Mimi—protect her like I didn't protect the baby. I was her shadow. More and more I put my own life on hold in order to keep her *safe.* By the time she started going to competitions and playing all over the place, it got crazy. Finally, my mom put a stop to it and insisted I go away to college, which I did, trusting she'd be all right without me. And she was, until—"

A tear rolls down her check which she quickly brushes away. She pastes a fake smile on her face and goes back into hiding. "Enough about me. So, you say you have a lot to tell me. Well, I have a few things to tell you, too. I did a little search on the internet a few nights ago. It kept me up till four, but it was worth it."

"What did you find out?"

She grins. "You're not the only detective around here."

"Come on. Spill it."

"I checked to see if Brandi Benedict has a Facebook account."

"Why didn't I think of that?"

"Maybe you're too old."

I ignore the dig.

"I found a bunch of Brandis, and I gotta say, that name generates some weird personalities—porno stars mostly."

All of a sudden, the reality of this girl being something completely different from her sister hits me.

"She's not one . . . is she?"

"No. But there was no Brandi Benedict. Then I wondered if Lena remarried and Brandi had another last name, so I looked up *all* the girls named Brandi on Facebook. Care to know how many there are?"

"Seventy-five?"

"Over seven hundred."

"Why didn't you just narrow it down to Phoenix?"

"Because sometimes people set up accounts in a different city to protect themselves. You'd know that if you were a girl."

"Did you find her?"

"I think so. The picture's not very good, so I can't tell for sure."

"Show it to me."

"When we get on the plane I will."

"Why?"

"'Cause it comes with a little surprise."

Which makes me wonder what else she may have done. "You didn't send her a message, did you?"

"No, I was afraid to."

"Thank goodness! Don't do *anything* on your own. You hear me?"

"Yeah, yeah, yeah."

"I'm serious, Grace."

She pulls her hair out of her eyes and looks away, like she's bored. "I'm sure you are."

When we're finally seated on the plane, I say, "Okay, tell me what you found out."

Grace grins. "You first."

"You are so exasperating. Okay, I called the Phoenix police department this morning. They told me that Brandi and Lena Benedict live at separate residences in the Phoenix area. Neither of them has any police record, but they were associated for a while with a guy named Ray Morgan who lived with Lena and served time for selling drugs and tax evasion. They referred me to FBI special agent Lewis James who'll be coordinating the case. I faxed him a report of everything we've learned to date, and he's supposed to reserve us a car and hotel rooms and meet us when we land. After we meet with James and his team, they'll plan a strategy."

"This is getting scary."

"What Lena's done is scary."

"When do you think I'll get a chance to see Brandi?"

"I have no idea. It depends on FBI protocols. By the time we get there, hopefully they'll have more information on where she works and hangs out, her friends, that kind of stuff."

Grace fidgets with her seatbelt trying to get it tight around her hips. "If the FBI takes over, does that mean they get to run the show?"

"It depends. Lou James didn't sound like the kind of guy who has to be in control. I think I'll have a lot of input. Their primary concern is that no one gets hurt."

She sighs. "People have already been hurt."

I wait a minute before I go on. "I won't pretend there's no danger. We might even need you to play a part in all of this. Are you ready for that?"

Her response is immediate. "Yes."

While we're talking, the plane taxis down the runway. The engines begin a soft rumble that turns into a roar. Suddenly she grabs my hand and squeezes hard. In less than a minute we're off the ground and looking down on New York. In another five minutes we're above the clouds looking at a beautiful blue sky with a white, wooly haze beneath us. She loosens her grip, and the frown lines disappear.

I gently extricate myself, acting like it's no big deal that we've been holding hands. I'm keenly aware of how fragile Grace is, and I don't want to take advantage. "What's your news?"

She locks my eyes with her own, milking the moment. Why does she have to be so pretty? "I think Brandi is in a band."

"That's better than being a porn star. What makes you think that?"

"There's a picture of her on stage, playing the guitar."

"Are you sure it's her?"

"Not one hundred percent. The image is a little blurry. But she's from Arizona."

"Phoenix?"

"No, a suburb called Chandler."

"What's her last name?"

"Heismann."

"We can do a public records search under that name. Maybe she's married."

"I don't think so."

I shake my head. "You don't even know if it's her."

She gets that sneaky look again. "Guess what the band is called?"

I shrug and shake my head.

"*Turning Blue.*"

Okay, now she's hooked me and is obviously on a roll. "The band doesn't have a website, "but it has a Facebook page. The pictures were better there but still not clear enough to make it official."

"Lemme see."

She pulls out her phone, and I scrutinize the pictures. There's one with four band members, including a girl on guitar with a mic blocking most of her face. The other two are farther away, probably taken with somebody's phone. Something about her reminds me of Mimi. It's confidence. She obviously owns the stage. She's blonde like Grace, about the same height and build, but her face is blurry. "Hmmm."

When she takes her phone back, I can't help but give in to the intense exhaustion that's been dogging me all morning. Squirming around, I try to find a comfortable position to sleep in. I'm drifting off when she says, "Are we doing the right thing? It's not like we're just going to find a long lost relative. Her mom is a criminal. What if meeting her ends up ruining her life? She doesn't deserve it. She didn't do anything wrong."

I'm so tired, I barely know what I'm saying. "Maybe she's always known something wasn't right. Maybe instead of ruining her life, you're the answer to her prayers."

XVI

KEVIN

I wake up three hours later to find Grace staring at me. "I can't believe you slept the whole way. We're getting ready to land."

After enduring the bumpiest landing of my life, I call Agent James, but I get his secretary instead. She says he's not able to meet us, but he's reserved a rental car and rooms at the Sheraton Grand Hotel for us. So much for an FBI welcome.

We pick up a red Hyundai Elantra and drive to the Sheraton in the frying Phoenix heat. Unfortunately, our rooms are a floor apart instead of side by side. When I complain at the desk, they tell us it's because they're hosting a national elevator conference and the place is booked solid.

That night we have dinner at a place across the street called Mi Amigos. Either the food is fantastic or I'm ravenously hungry. Conversation is a little awkward, not only because we're both wiped out from traveling but because we barely know each other. The only thing we really have in common is Cassie and Dan's family and our determination to find out the truth about Brandi. I try to remind myself this is not a date. Grace is vulnerable and obviously under stress. I see her staring off into space a lot. I can't imagine what she's feeling, but I want to make it as safe for her as possible. We both decide to turn in early. Before I go to bed, I call my sister.

"How's Jay?"

"He's in and out of consciousness, but his vital signs are good. They're reducing the Propofol every few hours."

"How are Mom and Dad doing?"

"Dad had to go back, but Mom is staying to take care of Xavier."

"Any problems—with Dad?"

"No, he's been pretty helpful."

"Probably an act."

Her voice sounds weary. "Kev . . ."

When she asks how Grace is doing, I make sure to remember our cover story and tell her we're going to the Trauma Institute tomorrow.

"Take good care of her, Kev. She's a very special girl."

"I can see that."

After we promise to keep in touch daily, we hang up, and I suddenly feel like the loneliest man on the planet.

First thing in the morning I call Lewis James and leave a message on his cell phone. "What can you tell me about Brandi? Where does she live, where does she work, and where can I find her? I know we're slated to meet this afternoon, but I don't want to waste a whole morning. Please get back to me as soon as you can."

I also call and leave a message for Carlton Hines. "Either things are a lot slower out here in the desert, or the FBI isn't being cooperative. They didn't meet us at the airport, and they can't see us until this afternoon. Let me know what I should do."

Within twenty minutes, I get a call from Lewis James. "Sorry about the mix-up at the airport. Is everything all right—the car, the hotel?"

"Yeah, it's fine. I just want to make contact with Brandi as soon as possible, hopefully before we meet this afternoon. Do you have her address and phone number?"

"Well, that's just it, Detective," he drawls. "We have to go slow on this. There are some additional factors I need to brief you on later today. We'd rather you not contact her directly yet."

"Can I at least get a look at her? Meet her undercover?"

"As long as she doesn't get tipped off to who you are."

I bristle at that. It's not like I didn't work undercover in the biggest city in the country, as opposed to this little desert outpost. "Don't worry, Agent James, I know what I'm doing."

"And the sister—what's happening with her?"

"She'll stay on the sidelines until we need her."

"Okay. Brandi works at George's Music, 359 Roosevelt Street."

I immediately call Grace and tell her I'll be at her room with coffee in an hour. The gig is on.

Two hours later, outside George's Music, Grace is whining like a two-year-old. "I wanna go in with you! Can't I wear a wig and sunglasses or something? It's not fair that I have to hide out in the car."

I try to be patient, but she's getting on my nerves. "If you'll just listen, I can make it work for you."

I rummage through my messenger bag in the back seat and pull out a lipstick cam and a tablet. "This is a wide-angle video recorder and transmitter. You'll be able to watch everything I say and do on the tablet. I'll probably start by picking her brain about—I don't know—conga drums, just to get her talking. Got any last-minute advice?"

"Yeah, don't flirt. That might scare her. And don't act like a cop, either."

I try to hide my annoyance. "What's that supposed to mean?"

"All pompous and official sounding. Just act like a musician who's looking for a good deal. Do you know anything about drums?"

"Not really."

She looks incredulous. "Oh, that should make you really look legit."

"Okay, Miss Know-it-all, educate me."

"Ever hear of Pete Escobedo?"

I shake my head.

"How about his daughter, Sheila E.?"

"Nope."

"She's a big conga player. Try throwing her name around. She played a lot with Prince."

I hook the cam to my belt and climb out of the car. Just before I get to the store I turn around. "Can you hear me?" I whisper.

She gives me a thumbs-up.

"Text if you need me." And then I open the door.

XVII

KEVIN

After I walk in, I begin milling around, when I hear somebody talking in the back of the store. "Can you file these piano books? I've gotta unpack the new guitars."

A voice answers, "No problem, Rosie."

It sounds like Grace's, only with a soft, southwestern twang. Brandi carries a box out toward the sheet music racks.

I don't want to scare her, so I fiddle loud enough with a guitar I've pulled off the wall for her to hear. She startles, anyway.

She puts on her retail face.

"Can I help you?"

Once I get a full view of her, I can't believe it. Her hair, her eyes, her body height and shape—I'm seeing Grace. I smile. "I don't know, can you?"

"What are you looking for?"

"Drums."

She's all business. "Any particular kind?"

"Bongo, conga, that kind of stuff."

She leads me to a section where they have hand drums, maracas, and other percussion.

"Nice selection."

She pulls her hair away from her face the same way Grace does. "I know, right? And if you can't find what you're looking for, we can order it."

Trying to keep her talking, I ask, "If I was gonna buy a pair of conga drums, is any brand better than another?"

"Depends on what you're using them for. We've got LP, Remo, Tycoon, rope-tuned, African. They come in fiberglass or wood. LP—Latin Percussion is the highest quality drum we sell."

She really knows her inventory. "Do you play the drums?"

"A little."

What was that girl drummer's name? Shelly, Sherri? "So, you're not like that girl whose last name starts with E, the one who played with Prince?"

"Sheila E? I wish!"

I'm losing steam, so I point to her nametag. "Your name's Brandi?"

"That's right."

I hold out my hand. "My name's Kevin."

Her handshake is stronger than Grace's—more committed. "Do you play in a band?"

I suddenly feel embarrassed. "Not yet, but I want to."

"You might wanna look at the eleven-inch LP Aspire series. They're a good beginner to intermediate drum."

"You like salsa music?"

"It's okay, but I'm more into rock fusion."

"What's that?"

"It's a combination of genres, folk/punk, jazz/rock."

I laugh. "Yeah, well I only know what I like."

She smiles, too. "Most people feel the same way."

"So . . . do you have to be a musician to work here?"

"Not really, but I am."

"What do you do—play or sing?"

Right then a wall goes up, and she backs up imperceptibly. "A little of both, I guess."

I take the hint. "Well, I'm going to try out some of these congas."

I start banging on a set of LPs. My technique is terrible, but my rhythm isn't half-bad. "I don't want to take up your time, but I'm probably gonna be here for a while."

She seems a little more relaxed. "We're used to that."

She goes back to filing sheet music. In between trying out different drums, I talk quietly to Grace. "What do you think?" I whisper.

She texts back,

Overwhelmed!

"How am I doing?"

You scared her off. Slow down!

After another ten minutes, Brandi comes back to the practice room. "Need any help?"

"I've got a few questions about the music scene in Phoenix."

She glances at her watch. "Okay."

"What kind of live music clubs do you have? I'm here on business for about a week."

"There are a few jazz bars, some Irish clubs, and the Salsa clubs."

"Got any suggestions?"

"Joe's Grotto, and the Steel Horse Saloon for salsa."

"Are you in a band?"

I can tell she's getting wary again. "Yeah."

"Performing anywhere?"

"Not to be rude, but I've got to get back to work."

I try to look apologetic. "Oh sure, I didn't mean to bother you."

She walks away and Grace immediately texts,

FAIL!!

"I'm just trying to act like a friendly musician," I whisper.

She thinks you're an axe murderer.

I play a few more sets of congas and watch Brandi out of the corner of my eye while she waits on customers. When the store is empty again, I walk out of the practice room and put on my boyish smile. "I have one more question, and I promise I'm not trying to come on to you. If I buy a set of congas, can you ship them to New York?"

"Sure. In fact, if you live near a George's Music you could pick them up there and wouldn't even have to pay shipping." She pulls a laptop off of the counter. "Where do you live?"

I laugh. "Now who's getting too personal?"

She blushes. "I'm just trying—"

"I know. I'm messing with you. I live in Manhattan."

I study her as she goes on the computer. When she's concentrating, she does this little crooked thing with her mouth that I've seen Grace do. How can something like that be purely genetic? "Looks like the nearest George's Music is in the Bronx. Is that close to you?"

"Yes. Listen, I'm truly sorry if I came on too strong before. I'm actually here in Phoenix with my girlfriend. If I went to hear your band, it would be with her."

She looks relieved. "Oh, that's okay. Sometimes my band plays at The Black Swan. But it's really a dive."

"Do they serve food?"

"Yeah, and actually, the food's not bad. It's the clientele."

"We don't care about that."

"I'm not sure how to tell you this. They've got *dancers*—if you know what I mean."

She raises her eyebrows really high until I get her drift. "Your girlfriend might not feel comfortable. But they don't come on until nine, so I suppose you could leave before that."

"Yeah, she'd definitely want to go early then. You guys performing anytime soon?"

I can tell she's about to ward off this new question, but suddenly her boss is behind me saying, "Tomorrow night, at seven."

Brandi looks past me and gives her the evil eye.

I turn to see a lady who's casually drinking a bottle of water, her grey-flecked curly hair hugging her head. I have no idea how long she's been there.

"What?" the woman says, all innocence. "Brandi's band is awesome—even though they mostly play in dumps. If you want to hear a rising star before you have to pay $100 a ticket, I suggest you go listen to them."

Brandi's face pinks up. "*Rosie!*"

Rosie walks away saying over her shoulder, "What? It's the truth!"

Brandi sees the grin on my face and shakes her head.

"Looks like you've got a great boss."

"Oh, she's something, all right."

"I want my girlfriend to check out the drums before I buy them. She knows a lot more than I do. Maybe we'll come back tomorrow."

Rosie, who's helping out a new customer, waves cheerfully when I leave the store. As the door closes behind me, I walk toward the car with a huge grin on my face.

XVIII

GRACE

When Kevin went into the store, her heart was pounding. She took a few deep breaths, trying to ward off a panic attack, but then she got nauseous watching the camera jiggle with every step. She couldn't see Brandi's face when he started talking to her, but when he moved, it came into view, only fuzzy and distorted because of the wide-angle lens. Then suddenly, it was clear.

It was her—her sister! If she went into the store and switched places with her, no one would know the difference. *Her sister.*

Brandi's hair was the exact same length—no bangs—and she tucked it behind one ear the way Grace did.

But it wasn't just her appearance. It was everything—the way she talked, the way she moved. And then, that indefinable thing—like her heart was home.

Grace cried, of course, and ended up being a mess the whole time Kevin was in the store. Now and then she would touch the video display to trace the outline of her face. When Brandi laughed, she couldn't help but laugh too—even though she was still crying. Brandi clearly had a sense of humor and a funny, southwestern twang.

Maybe it was the *her heart was home* part, but Grace couldn't get over how lovely Brandi was. *She's so beautiful,* she thought. *She looks like Mom.* She had never thought she looked like her mother. Suddenly she realized she did.

Instantly her stomach knotted up again. *Will she want to be a part of my life the way I want to be a part of hers? What if she doesn't need a sister? And what about all the warnings and images of waterfalls?*

While Kevin was pounding on the conga drums, she turned the sound way down. But then she realized he was talking to her, so she turned it up. She texted,

> *Don't be so pushy! She's getting edgy.*

When he asked her how to get Brandi to talk more, she texted again,

> *Ask if she plays in a band, but don't interrogate. Musicians like talking about themselves if you don't look like a stalker.*

The rest of the time he was in there, Grace fluctuated between crying and laughing.

She wished Eve and Mimi were there. If only they knew what was happening right now. All those terrible years, all the pain—the end of a nightmare. She wondered if her dad was seeing this.

Before Kevin left the store, he texted,

> *Slide down in the seat, so if anyone's watching, they'll think I came alone.*

She scooted down right away.

In a few minutes, he climbed into the car and pulled away without a word. When they were a block away, he said, "I knew it! That boss lady was watching out the window when I drove away!"

They drove a few more blocks and parked the car at a strip mall where Grace cried again. He smiled and grabbed her hand.

"You okay?"

She tried to pull herself together, blowing noisily into a tissue. "What now?"

He looked away from her. "I don't know yet."

He started the car and pulled out onto the road. Then he playfully slapped her on the arm. "And why would you lead me into a trap? *Musicians like to talk about themselves.* That was a disaster."

"Not my fault! I told you not to interrogate. Seriously, you police types need some instruction on casual conversation."

He grinned. "Maybe *you* should do the talking at the Black Swan tomorrow night. We can pick you up a black wig at the station."

"Right, like that's gonna help! In case you haven't noticed, we're identical."

"We can get you some big, tinted glasses."

"We're going to a dark nightclub. That reeks of disguise"

He laughed. "You don't think people wear disguises when they go to a strip club? Don't you worry. Police engage expert makeup artists. Just a few minor adjustments and you won't even recognize yourself."

He pulled back into the hotel parking lot. "Don't forget, after we talk to the FBI, you've got your appointment at the Christian Trauma Institute at four."

Grace groaned. *Why did I agree to this charade?*

When she got back to her room, Grace saw that her quazi-boyfriend, Ben, had tried to video-chat her on the laptop. She called him right back, sitting against a white wall so he wouldn't think she was anywhere outside of New York. "How's it going over there?"

"Lousy. I'm working on my pieces, and the program director tells me my technique is *scratchy*, and that I should attend grad school here to perfect my attack—whatever that means."

"I heard college is completely free in Germany."

"So, what," he grumbled. "I don't need some wiener schnitzel telling me how to play the piano."

At that point the video froze and Grace had to wait a few minutes for it work again. When they were live again, Ben was more than cranky. "This isn't working."

"It's because your WIFI is so terrible. Should we just wait to catch up when you get home?"

He stared at her; his eyes dark. "Catch up like what? Like friends catch up?"

"I guess so. It's not working in more ways than one, Ben."

"Fine with me. I gotta go anyway."

And just like that, he hung up.

Tears sprang to her eyes, but in less than a minute, she was just plain angry. *Who am I kidding? Ben isn't for me. I just couldn't stand being alone.*

She went out to the soda dispenser in the hallway and came back with a Dr. Pepper. Then she called her mother. "I'm taking Mimi to the doctor in about an hour," Eve said.

"That's good, right?"

"Not really." Eve choked up. "He isn't sure she'll ever be able to move her fingers like she did before."

Grace wished she could give her some good news, but she knew it was too early. "On a good note," Eve said, "Mimi's been reading to Jay at the hospital. She wants him to know his Shakespeare for the English exam. This morning, he gave her a half smile."

"That's awesome Mom! And how's it going with Auntie Elaine?"

"So far, so good. She's cooking and cleaning while I cart Mimi around. When she starts cleaning out the closets, I'll know it's time to kick her out. But enough about us. How are you doing out there?"

"Pretty good. I'm going to the Christian Trauma Institute later today."

"Great. But have some fun too, Grace. Go sightseeing. I hear it's beautiful out there."

"It is. The mountains are gorgeous, but it's too hot to do much during the day."

"Well, don't come back until you feel better, sweetheart. I want things to be different for you."

Grace sighed. *You have no idea how different things are already.*

The Phoenix police department was bright and airy, and everyone was very cordial. They directed Kevin and Grace to the FBI head-quarters on the seventh floor where they met Agent James. A tall man with a greying butch haircut, he didn't look much like an FBI agent, wearing a blue polo shirt and tan shorts. Actually, everyone in the office was in casual dress.

After introductions, he pulled three water bottles out of a little fridge. "The weather is murder in June. Most days are in the hundreds. Took me years to get used to it."

Kevin twisted open his bottle. "Where are you from?"

"DC. They sent me out here because of my background in synthetic drugs. I interned as a chemist for Pfizer."

Kevin drank half the bottle in one swallow. "What can you tell us about Brandi, Lena, and any other people I should know about."

Lewis slid four grainy pictures across the table. "Here's a current picture of Lena. And this is Anton Morgan. His uncle, Ray Morgan, Lena's old boyfriend, owned the Black Swan over on South Central Avenue for about three years until he died last September in a car crash. These other two guys are with Anton all the time, bodyguards, bouncers for the club. They're his enforcement team."

Kevin looked at Grace. "The Black Swan—that's where Brandi is playing tomorrow night."

But Grace was fixated on the picture of Lena. She had grey hair, deep set, dark eyes, a long nose and thin, unsmiling lips. She didn't look like a happy woman, but she didn't look like a monster either. She was a nurse, for heaven's sake. Someone that helps people. But someone who kidnapped her sister. *How does such a normal-looking person steal a child?*

Kevin's voice interrupted her thoughts again. "Who's Anton, and how is he connected to Brandi?"

"He and Brandi grew up together," Lewis James said. "His Uncle Ray lived with Lena for a while. Apparently, Ray was not a nice guy, and when Lena drank too much, Anton kind of became Brandi's protector. As they got older, they drifted apart, but when Ray died, they caught up at the funeral."

Brandi's protector. I'm glad she had someone. But Anton doesn't look like a nice guy either. And why does he need bodyguards?

James pulled out a picture of the Black Swan. On the sign was a big, gaudy swan, flanked by two black silhouettes of women. "Ray left the Black Swan to Anton. It's still a strip club, but local bands perform there occasionally, bringing in a different clientele. Brandi and Anton dated for a while, but she recently ended it. Rumor has it she discovered he was dealing drugs."

Oh, my poor sister! These are your people?

"We've had our eye on Anton for a while. We believe he heads a ring that sells a type of synthetic marijuana called *spice*. It's cheap, but it's laced with all kinds of chemicals that can kill people."

Grace squirmed in her chair as images of her dreams scrolled through her mind.

"The other thing they sell is a substance called *25i*. This stuff comes from China. Very dangerous. Kids think they're taking LSD, but they're not."

"Why isn't this guy behind bars?" Kevin demanded.

James sighed. "A few reasons. First of all, he and his boys mostly traffic to Native Americans who live on reservations. This creates multi-levels of prosecution complexity. According to the Indian Country Crimes Act, the State of Arizona can't prosecute a suspect when the victim is Native American. And since tribal authorities can't prosecute non-Indians, it becomes a Catch-22. The FBI can prosecute, but in order to do that we need admissible evidence, which is hard to get. Not to mention that we don't have enough manpower to cover the entire state. Sometimes agents have to travel six hundred miles to get a bloody handkerchief."

Kevin nudged Grace. "We're not in Kansas anymore."

James continued. "Those are just the prosecuting issues. Whenever one of these drugs gets outlawed, the chemists change the compound slightly which makes it legal until the government gets wise to the new formula. There are thousands of changes they can make that still yield the same results. These guys are slick. And somehow, they get the stuff onto the reservations in ways we can't pin down. The FBI isn't always welcome there."

"Brandi's not involved, is she?" Grace asked, her heart pounding.

"We don't think so. Like I said, when she got wind of this, she backed away really fast. Her mother, though, is a different story. Lena helped finance the original purchase of the Black Swan, and she has an interest in it today. Our sources say that monies from the club and from the drug business are one in the same."

"Has Brandi ever been in trouble with the law?" Kevin asked.

Grace held her breath, praying that the answer would be no.

Lewis shook his head. "Surprisingly, she's pretty clean. She was picked up for shoplifting when she was fourteen, but the charges were dropped. And she missed a lot of high school, but she managed to get a high school diploma. After high school she moved out of her mother's house and started working full-time at a music store. Two years ago, she enrolled at Arizona State. She's actually the one who might be the key to breaking this case."

Kevin looked wary. "Why do you say that?"

"She's got intimate knowledge of these people, and we believe she hates the drug trafficking. One of our contacts heard her threaten to go to the police if Anton didn't stop distributing to children. At the very least, she could be our eyes and ears on the inside."

Grace couldn't hold back. "What would cause her to rat out her old boyfriend and her mother?"

"Maybe when she finds out Lena's not her mother."

Grace's face reddened. "Let me get this straight. We've come here to tell her what could be the most traumatic thing anybody could hear, and you want to use it to close your case?"

Agent James gave her a half-smile and began talking to her like she was a nine-year-old. "Grace—may I call you Grace? We've been working on this case for over a year and haven't been able to make any headway. When Kevin called us, it seemed like the break we'd been waiting for. Honestly, what are the chances that your girl would be connected to our case? Maybe finding out she was kidnapped will make her angry enough to help us."

Grace resented his condescending tone. "Agent James, I just came here to find my sister. Not to sound anti-FBI, but that's more important to me than your case."

His eyes hardened. "A thirteen-year-old Native girl died last week from a synthetic drug distributed by these guys. She was probably somebody's sister too, certainly somebody's daughter." Lewis looked at Kevin. "Have you got any other ideas?"

Kevin ran his fingers through his hair. "I don't know. My main goal is Brandi's safety and Lena's capture. But give us a chance to talk about it a little more."

"Okay, but time is running out. Who knows how many unsuspecting kids might get access to tainted drugs before tomorrow night?"

"I'm assuming you have a wiretap on Anton's cell phone?"

"Yes. And now because of your investigation of Lena, I can get a tap on her phone too. It's possible we can break this open without Brandi's help, but that's not likely."

Coping with a decades-old kidnapping was scary enough for Grace. Drug dealers, the FBI using her sister as an informant—this was way over Grace's head. When she looked at Kevin, he must have gotten the message because he whisked her out of there in minutes. When she got outside, she took a deep breath of the scorching air and shivered.

XIX

GRACE

As they rolled up to the Christian Trauma Institute, Kevin and Grace argued about their meeting with Lewis James. "I don't want you to take offense," he said, "but you're a little naïve about police work. We have to let them feel like they're in control. Otherwise, they won't play nice. Just let me deal with the FBI."

"In other words, keep my mouth shut when they want to put my sister at risk in a sting operation that has nothing to do with her."

Kevin shook his head. "You're missing the point. But let's talk about it later. Right now, you should calm down or this counseling session may not work."

"Right," she scoffed. "Like it's some magic elixir I need to be in a trance-state to drink."

In tense silence they followed a long, winding driveway to a large stucco house with a red tile roof. In the front yard, yellow and pink flowers and some fat round cactuses surrounded a gurgling fountain. Several people were sitting on high-end, cushy lawn furniture under wide umbrellas. It looked more like a spa than a mental health treatment center.

Kevin dropped Grace off at the front of the building, then went to look for his friend. Inside, a woman asked her to fill out a few forms before showing her to a waiting room next to a small chapel. The stained glass in the chapel was beautiful and intriguing. Windows and doors had colorful panels depicting desert scenes with a religious theme. One of them showed a lamb caught in a thicket with a shepherd about to extract it. Another showed the risen Christ surrounded by wildly blooming cactuses. One more was of a starry night over a canyon with a white dove in flight.

"What do you think of our artwork?" a male voice behind her asked.

She turned and found herself about eye level with an older man sporting a white ponytail, a cowboy shirt, and jeans.

"They're beautiful."

He held out his hand. "I'm Dr. Francis, director of CTI. Please call me Stephen."

"Grace Maddox, from New York."

Stephen smiled. "Welcome."

As they walked toward his office, Grace's heart pounded. *How am I gonna explain my crazy dreams and visions?*

The room, which had a cathedral ceiling and a skylight, was sparsely decorated and bright. Two tan couches with a coffee table between them took up most of the room. On the table was a tissue box, a few brochures, and a small wooden cross.

Stephen motioned for her to sit. "How did you hear about us?"

"A friend of mine set this meeting up. He knows someone who works here. I think his name is Gary."

"Oh yes. Gary is one of our interns from Pennsylvania. We have Master's level interns from all over the country who are working toward licensure in Christian counseling and trauma work.

"Only Christians can come here?"

"No. Everyone's welcome."

"Does it work—I mean, what you do?"

Stephen smiled. "*You* do the work. We just facilitate."

Grace let out a frustrated sigh. "I don't know what kind of work I'm supposed to do."

He looked at her with kind eyes. "Just tell me your story."

She launched into the whole mess—the bike accident, the concussion, the visions, Mimi and Jay's car crash, her twin's kidnapping, seeing Brandi. By the time she finished, she was crying and highly embarrassed. "And that's another thing. I keep crying, and I don't even know why."

"You don't? I'd say you have every reason to cry. How else is all that pain going to come out?"

He handed her the tissue box like it was just another day at the office to him.

Grace used up a wad of tissues and dropped them into her purse. Waiting until her voice wasn't shaking, she asked, "What's my work?"

Stephen sat quietly for a moment. "Probably preparing to meet your sister. I mean, it's great that you came here to the center, but it sounds like your detective friend was simply using it as a ploy to get your mother on board."

Funny, I don't remember mentioning that.

He went on. "There are so many possibilities. God may be trying to warn you in these dreams and visions, or maybe your subconscious pain is coming out in pictures."

"You don't think I'm crazy?"

Stephen leaned back in his chair. "No, but I think you've been traumatized more than you realize. The accident probably triggered some physical problems, but those will heal over time. Maybe your work is to be sensitive to how God is guiding you."

Grace teared up again. "I'm trying."

"It's an exciting journey, isn't it? Like finding a missing part of yourself. But you say the police are involved. Is it safe?"

"I don't know. There are complicating factors."

Stephen laid his hand on her arm. "Grace, you're welcome to spend some time with us if you want, but even if you don't, I'd like to pray with you for protection and guidance. My colleague, Sister Ann, is especially good at that. May I ask her to come in?"

When she nodded, Stephen left the room and returned with a petite woman who was dressed like a nun and had a smile that melted Grace's defenses.

"Is it all right if we anoint you with oil, Grace?" Stephen asked.

Grace nodded.

Sister Ann gently touched Grace's shoulder, while Stephen made a sign of the cross in oil on her forehead. As Sister Ann began praying quietly, her hand got warmer and warmer. The warmth spread to Grace's chest and down her arms. At the same time, a sweet smell of something like roses wafted into the room.

She peeked out between her eyelashes to see if the windows were open, but like the rest of Phoenix, it was a thoroughly air-conditioned room. The things Sister Ann prayed about sounded like Stephen had told her everything she'd said, but she knew there wasn't time for that. Either these people were legit, or they had a really smooth operation going.

After a few minutes, Sister Ann stopped praying and addressed Grace. "My dear, do you have anything you want to confess or forgive? That's an important part of any healing prayer."

Confess? For sure. I hoodwinked Mom, but that was to protect her. All the petty ways I'm selfish and narcissistic. Isn't everyone? Forgive? Definitely. Ben, Lena, the police who stopped the investigation too soon, myself for not protecting Mimi. Even Kevin. "I don't know, I guess I have to think about that."

Sister Ann smiled. "Don't think too long. Your prayers can get blocked with that kind of junk."

"I know you're right, but it's too hard right now."

"Can you try?"

Gradually, it all came pouring out. After an hour, Grace felt cleaner, but her heart ached, and she could barely catch her breath. They sat and talked casually for another fifteen minutes. Stephen and Sister Ann asked about her music, her plans to teach. All Grace could think about was the stained-glass picture of the lamb stuck in a thicket.

I think that shepherd is on his way to me.

"How much do I owe you for your time?" she asked, embarrassed to bring up money.

Stephen chuckled. "We don't charge for prayer. We only charge for therapy, and we go through insurance for that."

"But you spent so much time with me. I feel like I should do something."

"Come back again to tell us how things went, or just write us a letter when you get home."

They both walked her to the door where Grace impulsively hugged them. When she walked outside, she found Kevin dozing under one of the big umbrellas. She tapped him on the shoulder. "Did you see Gary?"

He yawned and stretched. "Yeah, we got a coffee together." He glanced at his watch. "You were in there for a while. How'd it go?"

"Good. Very good."

"Are you gonna come back?"

"Maybe."

"I'm sorry we argued," he said.

"Me too."

As they drove away, he sniffed and smiled. "By the way, you smell like flowers."

The next day Kevin talked to Lewis about getting a disguise for Grace. They dug up a wig with long dark hair, a baseball cap and tinted glasses. Someone from the department applied dark make-up to make her look more tanned. They showed her how to change her stride and voice, and suggested that she keep her head down a lot. They were going for a Latina look which she thought was great, because the only acting class she remembered from college was in accents. She was totally psyched to *get her Chicana on*.

Kevin kept staring at her as they drove to the club that night. "I'm impressed. Not only do you look completely different, you sound different too. How'd you get the Southwestern twang?"

"Magic, chico."

When they entered the Black Swan, they slipped into a darkened booth near the back. The speakers overhead were playing a particularly annoying type of screamer rock. Kevin scanned the place for Brandi and pointed her out setting up equipment on the stage.

He glanced at Grace. "You okay?"

She lied. "Yeah, sure."

He grabbed her hands and looked into her eyes. "Remember, you don't have to do or say anything. Just hang."

"I'm trying."

"I'm going to say hello to Brandi. If the waitress comes over, order me some nachos and a Coke."

He slid out of the booth and walked to the stage. When he got to Brandi, she looked blank for a second and then said something back. Kevin pointed to Grace sitting at the table. They talked a little more while she kept unrolling cable and plugging in mics. In a few minutes he was back at the booth. "Well, that went badly."

"What happened?"

"She was very standoffish, probably thinks I'm a stalker."

"You look like one."

"Thanks."

"No really, you don't have much of a way with women, do you?"

He stared at her. "You're kidding, right?"

"You seem to have trouble getting rid of the police persona."

He looked offended. "You're crazy. Girls love me."

Grace snickered. "Really? You're a poster child for uptight. It's like you're always on the job."

"I am on the job!"

Grace nodded. "That's true right now, but you haven't been on the job every minute since I met you. Not to be critical, but it's like you're trying to control everything. That really puts a girl off. Also, you take everything too seriously."

He scrunched his eyebrows like an angry toddler. "Well, since we're getting personal, you don't come off very relaxed either. You're hypervigilant, always looking over your shoulder, waiting for someone to sneak up on you. Skittish as a colt."

At that moment the waitress brought their drinks. After she left there was an awkward silence between them. Grace vigorously stirred her Coke with the straw. "Now that we've insulted each other..."

Kevin leaned back in the booth, a smug look on his face. "Mine wasn't an insult, just an observation."

Grace glared at him. "Way to judge my personality during the most stressful month of my life. Yeah, I'm skittish. And now with Lewis trying turn this into a federal case—"

Kevin gave a mirthless laugh. "Grace, it was a federal case before we ever met him."

"Not for me!" she said through gritted teeth.

Kevin's voice turned into a hoarse whisper. "Look, I'm sorry this isn't just a nice little meeting between two long-lost relatives. It's also a crime. When Lewis said that Lena might be involved in something shady, you think I was surprised? That's her MO. She, or somebody else, substituted a dead baby for your sister, for heaven's sake. Where do you think that kid came from? And this is the woman who raised Brandi!"

He leaned in closer, his eyes on fire. "The fact that Brandi's not in jail or an addict is a miracle. Yes, I see this case very differently than you do. You're scared and excited, but I'm mad. Damn mad."

Unwillingly Grace's eyes filled with tears. "Oh no, I can't cry. It'll ruin my tan."

She tried to blot her eyes before white rivers ran down her face. He reached for her hand. "I'm sorry. I guess I'm a little edgy today. This situation's got me—" He stopped mid-sentence and stared at his fists. "I just want to beat someone to a bloody pulp."

Grace took a deep breath and willed herself to stop crying. "I get it. You hate the injustice. Broken family, lost years, lies. But for me, being here is the answer to a prayer I never prayed. Something I don't understand led me here. To me that's amazing."

Kevin spent the next minute swirling the ice in his glass. Then he sighed. "Did you order?"

"Yeah, nachos and some barbecued chicken."

"You think I'm a control freak?"

"About as much as you think I'm a horse."

"I never said—"

The waitress appeared at their table again with their food. They both dug in like they hadn't eaten in days. In a while their attention was drawn to the stage where Brandi had strapped on an Ovation acoustic/electric guitar and was testing her mic. Eventually, the house lights dimmed. "Hi everyone," she said. "It's a beautiful night in Phoenix!"

There was a smattering of applause, and thankfully, the management turned off the background music. "We're gonna begin with a few covers tonight. Afterwards, we'll do a little original stuff, play for about an hour before the other entertainment comes out. You guys with me?"

She nodded to the drummer, a guy with long blond hair tied in a ponytail, and he began a cymbal beat and a few drum rolls leading into a solid 4/4 rhythm. The lead guitarist looked like a kid who wasn't shaving yet. He launched into a whining, melodic riff, his distortion pedal turned up so high that the low notes sounded like a bunch of clashing pans. All the while the bass guitar was doing a funky groove to keep the beat and add support.

Brandi was playing rhythm but popping in and out with sparse chords as she readied herself to sing. Thanks to Mimi, Grace knew all the pop songs they played, but they added their own spin, making it hard to hum along. They were good, but not awesome.

But when they got to their own stuff, something happened. Brandi's voice went silky and low, half-whispery, evoking colors and scents. When she closed her eyes, it seemed like she was singing to herself. As the musical tension and her confidence mounted, she burst into a gritty blues. The intensity of her singing, even though it seemed effortless, was magical, otherworldly. It made Grace feel like she lost her one true love, but that was all right because she was going to heaven—*today*.

Sizzling with energy, foreboding yet ethereal, Brandi was a complete paradox.

Grace glanced at Kevin who was mesmerized and totally unaware of her. For the rest of the song, all she could feel was the ache of being ordinary.

Brandi was another Mimi.

They stayed for an hour, during which Brandi introduced the band: Gary on drums, Robbie, on bass and Larry on lead guitar. Grace and Kevin were the only ones exploding with applause between each song. The rest of the clientele seemed unimpressed.

When they launched into their last song, Grace leaned over to Kevin. "I want to leave."

He frowned. "Why?"

"My disguise feels stupid, and I'm worried she might come over to the table when her set is done."

He gave her a searching look. "Okay."

As they walked to the door they were stopped by a buff-looking guy wearing a buttery, leather jacket and cowboy boots. His curly hair was close-cropped, he had a sculptured light beard, and he seemed to know how good-looking he was.

He grinned at them. "Leaving so soon? You're gonna miss the best part of the night."

Kevin lifted his eyes and met his gaze. "We came for the band."

"Oh them, they're just a local group. But the dancers—"

Grace was suddenly indignant. "I thought they were fantastic."

He looked down at her, and she tilted her head a little lower. "I'll have to tell them you said so," he said with a slow drawl. "The lead singer is my girlfriend."

Not good. Could this be a new boyfriend—or Anton? No one can spot similarities better than a boyfriend. But Kevin was oblivious to the situation.

"I just met her yesterday at the music store. I stopped in to buy some drums," Kevin said.

"Yeah, she's been working there since high school. But I'm surprised she told you she'd be playing here tonight."

"Her boss told me. She was a little tight-lipped."

The guy nodded. "That sounds like her."

Kevin stuck out his hand to introduce himself.

"I'm Anton," the guy said.

Yup, this just got worse. "I have to make a pit stop before we leave. Can you point me to the ladies' room?"

Anton gestured to the back of the club. As she pulled open the door, she glanced back and saw they were talking like long-lost pals. The ladies' room was black with some bling around the mirrors. It smelled like cranberry potpourri.

Grace took off her glasses and stared into the mirror to check her makeup, but when the door opened, she slipped into one of the stalls. She stayed there for the next five minutes while two girls came in, did their thing and left. Apparently, the set was finished because the screamer rock was back on the overhead speaker.

Finally, when she was sure no one else was there, Grace ventured out. At that exact moment. Brandi walked in. Her hair was damp, and she was trying to put it into a ponytail.

"Hi."

Grace looked down, the brim of her baseball cap hiding her eyes. "Uh, great music," Grace stammered.

Brandi smiled. "Thanks."

Grace hightailed it out before she did anything stupid, but a little smile played on her lips. *I talked to my sister!*

When she walked to the front, Kevin was nowhere in sight. Anton nodded toward the door. "He went to get the car."

Outside, the air was a little cooler. She stared up at the night sky and took a deep breath. Kevin pulled up, but they didn't speak until they were over a block away. He was as excited as a puppy.

"I had to tell a few white lies, but I found out Brandi's got another gig tomorrow night at The Brass Mill. By the way, you've been upgraded from a girlfriend to a fiancée. I didn't want him to think I was making a play for her."

Grace pulled off her wig, hat and glasses. "I'm not going."

Kevin was silent for a while. "I thought you might say that."

Grace started to fume. "How long are we gonna keep this circus going? Do you even know what your next move is?"

"In theory, I get close enough to her to tell her what's going on. If you want to speed things up, come to the store with me tomorrow."

"I can't wear this stupid get-up again."

"You sound cranky."

"I saw Brandi in the ladies' room."

"Do you think—"

"No, she barely saw me. But I can't keep doing this, Kevin. It's too hard. I want to talk to my sister!"

"I'm sorry, Grace."

"Actually, I did talk to her. I said something stupid like, *Great concert.* Then she said, *Thanks.* Impressive first words, wouldn't you say?"

A tear leaked out, then another. "I don't want her involved in this sting operation. I'm so afraid something terrible is going to happen."

Kevin was silent while she wept and blew her nose, her makeup smearing onto the tissues. When they got back to the hotel, she put the dark glasses back on, took the elevator to her floor and mumbled goodnight. Twenty minutes later, there was a knock on the door. When she looked through the peephole, she saw Kevin with a bag in his hand.

She let him in, and he handed her the bag. "A peace offering."

Grace peeked into the bag and saw two cartons of Ben and Jerry's Chubby Hubby ice cream. He handed her a spoon. "I remembered this was what you brought to Cassie and Dan's the day we met."

They sat down and tried to poke plastic spoons into the mostly solid blocks. "I keep forgetting how this is for you. I'm so used to the chase, to putting pieces together, one break leading to the next. Naturally, you're taking the whole thing much more personally. Grace, I wonder if it was a good idea for you to come. Lewis and I can handle it from here. Why don't you fly back home?"

She continued to eat her ice cream in silence, shaving off paper thin layers, one at a time.

"I admit these covert operations are way over my head."

She watched him eat for a while. When he looked up, he grinned, his mouth was full of ice cream. "My kind of early breakfast."

"Seriously, how long do you think this is going to take?"

"It's hard to tell, a week, a month?"

"Then maybe I should go. It's too stressful waiting around. But I'm worried about Brandi. If she's anything like me, once she finds out the truth, she'll probably freak out. Add that to finding out you guys want to use her as a rat."

"We're not going to use her—"

"Come on, Kevin! What else do you call it? Asking her to be a narc, a snitch, a squealer?"

"A squealer? Where do you get this stuff?"

"You think I don't read detective novels?"

"What, from the forties? Next, you'll say we're trying to turn her into a stool pigeon or a weasel."

"That too."

"Do you want me to put the kibosh on Lewis's plan?"

"Can you?"

"I can try. But I know what he'll do. He'll say we should let her decide."

"I can only hope she's as big a chicken as I am."

He leaned over and grabbed her hand. "Grace, I *promise*, I won't let anything happen to her."

She pulled her hand out of his. "I hate it when people say that. You can't promise that bad things won't happen."

At first, he seemed shocked that she didn't accept his little platitude, but then he added, "That's true. But I can tell you this. I've devoted my life to protecting people, and I'm pretty good at it."

"I don't have much faith in the police right now."

He grinned. "Come on Grace, you know that if I'd been on this case twenty-three years ago, I would have found your sister."

"Cocky, aren't you?"

"Seriously, let me take care of this. Go take care of your mom and Mimi."

She didn't say anything because, suddenly, she felt incredibly exhausted.

"How 'bout I get you a flight out of here tomorrow?"

Standing up, she capped her ice cream and put it in the tiny freezer of the room fridge. "Okay."

After he left, she threw herself onto the bed and cried.

XX

GRACE

She was on the pebbly red beach with a gun in her hand. Kevin was nowhere around, but her sister was standing nearby. "Run," Brandi screamed.

Grace took off. As she ran, she was enveloped in sheets of blue cellophane. Then, suddenly, Brandi was alongside her, riding on the back of a black bear. She scooped Grace up in front of her, and they took off faster than a train. They rode over mountains and deserts, rivers and cities, but behind them, a car was chasing, and someone was shooting at them. Grace looked for the gun but couldn't find it. She glanced back at Brandi whose grip around her waist was loosening. She'd been shot. Slowly she tipped off the bear. Grace tried to grab her hand, but it was slippery with blood. Finally, Brandi dropped to the ground while the bear kept running. When Grace looked back, the car had disappeared. They had only been after Brandi. Once she was gone, they left too. Grace burst into uncontrollable tears. Then the bear turned into a plane, and she heard music playing… just like the ringtone on her phone.

She jolted awake and grabbed her phone.

It was Kevin, his voice upbeat. "Ready for some breakfast, kiddo?"

"No, Kevin, no!" Grace shouted.

"No breakfast?"

"No, I'm not going home!"

"But I've already put you on a flight. It's leaving at eleven."

"Just come to my room."

She hung up and threw on some clothes.

In a few minutes, he was banging on the door. Grace opened it and flung herself into his arms, crying.

He awkwardly stroked her hair. "What's going on?"

But Grace couldn't talk yet. She just kept seeing Brandi's stricken face and kept feeling her slide out of her grasp. Eventually, she broke away from him and said, "I had another dream. I can't go home without her, Kevin. I can't. Please don't ask me to."

They sat down on the bed where she told him the whole story. "We're so close to what we came for. That girl is my sister, and I can't leave until she knows she has me in her corner."

"Look Grace…"

"Don't try to talk me out of this, Kevin. Something bad is going to happen to her if I leave. I know it."

He ran his fingers through his hair, still wet from his shower. "Okay, let's go back to Lewis and see if we can step this up. We're probably going to have to tell him all about your visions and dreams, you know. And he's going to think we're both wackos."

"That doesn't bother me. I only care about my sister."

"I'll meet you downstairs in thirty minutes with coffee and a bagel."

"Give me forty-five and make sure the coffee is hot."

Lewis was more than a little amused by the story of Grace's visions and dreams. Once he heard that Kevin had a complementary dream, he sobered up somewhat. "What are you guys, psychic?"

Kevin shook his head. "I've never had anything like this happen before."

Lewis laughed. "Well, you're in the right place. Arizona is chock full of new age weirdos."

Kevin gave him a disgusted look.

Then Lewis glanced at Grace. "I thought you told me she was flying back East."

Grace stood and tried to look confident. "Not anymore. I'm sure my sister is in danger, and I'm not leaving until I know she's safe."

Lewis didn't bother to address Grace. He looked at Kevin. "I don't need a loose cannon ruining a year's worth of work."

Grace's face reddened. "A loose cannon—"

Kevin put his hand on her arm to cut her off. "Technically Lewis, this is *our* case, and you were supposed to assist *us*."

"Well, yeah, but..."

"I know you've been working your *related case* for a while. But our primary concern is making sure this girl isn't put in any kind of danger. She's already had twenty-three years stolen by a dangerous person, possibly a murderer. If we can't work together, I'll call my boss, he'll call yours, and our collaboration will end."

Lewis pursed his lips, looking grim but resigned. "What do you want from me?"

"I want you to find out everything you can about Brandi—where she goes, who she hangs out with, how much contact she has with Lena, with Anton. And I don't want her railroaded into helping the FBI."

"Okay, I'll get you that information. But as far as Brandi helping us out, let's let her decide what she wants to do. Deal?"

Kevin glanced at Grace. "Deal?"

She nodded, but just barely.

That night in her hotel room, Grace sat on the bed watching Kevin's nauseatingly bumpy lipstick camera. She'd convinced him to put it in his jacket breast pocket so that she wasn't getting constant views of people's crotches. Every once in a while, he would put his hand over his mouth and talk to her.

She shot him a text;

```
People are going to think there's some-
thing wrong with you if you keep doing
that.
```

He texted back;

It's better to talk than text. I don't want evidence of our conversations, dear.

Dear?

Remember you're my fiancée.

Can't we just erase them as we go?

Sure, but criminals are better at technology than we are.

Where is she?

Not here yet.

Aren't they supposed to be going on in like 5 minutes?

Yeah, the rest of the band is all set up, but she's not here.

Is Anton?

Nope. But I'm pretty sure his two goons are sitting at the bar.

What will you do if she doesn't show up?

Go look for her.

He spoke again into his hand. "Wait a sec—looks like Lewis is calling. I'll get back to you."

She could tell he was walking outside. When he stopped texting, Grace's heart beat like a crazy drum solo.

KEVIN

"Lewis here. We've got a problem. You know that guy you met at the jail in New York, Frank Benedict? He called Lena this afternoon."

"Isn't he still in jail?"

"Due to be released next week."

"Far as I knew, Lena wanted nothing to do with him."

"We thought so too. But he left her a weird message, and the next time he called, she picked up."

"What was the message?"

"*The goose is in flight.* Mean anything to you?"

"Nope."

"When he talked to her, he repeated that phrase and said he would be out soon and could meet her where they honeymooned. She hung up, left the house, made one stop in Phoenix, and started driving south. My guess is she's on her way to Mexico. Do you want us to pick her up?"

"I've actually got bigger problems than that right now. Brandi hasn't shown up for her gig. Anton's not here either. Something's fishy."

"I can issue a BOLO on her car."

I remember my promise to Grace. "Do that, but I'm gonna look for her too."

"At least let me send someone to help you, Kevin. You don't know the area."

"Okay. There's some kind of a shopping mall nearby."

"Metro-center Mall."

"Tell your guy to meet me at the theater entrance."

"What about Lena?"

"Alert the border guards. If she tries to cross, they can detain her. Meanwhile just keep track of her."

As I walk toward the car, I see that Anton has just arrived, so I slip back inside to watch him. He walks straight up to the bar and talks to Frick and Frack. In less than a minute the three of them leave together and climb into Anton's car. I call Lewis back as I jump into mine. "Instead of sending someone to meet me, keep looking for Brandi. I'm gonna follow these guys for now."

GRACE

After hanging up with Kevin, his camera went dead, and for the next fifteen minutes Grace heard nothing from him. She told herself it was probably a tech failure, or that he'd gotten involved in a conversation with someone at the club, or he was in the bathroom—any excuse she could come up with. After a while she turned on the TV and tried to watch a cooking show which made absolutely no sense without sound, but she couldn't risk missing his phone call.

In her nervousness, she lathered up her hands with hand lotion—a trick she'd discovered that stopped her from chewing on the skin around her fingernails. By the time the phone rang, her hands were so slippery it slid out of her hands and landed on the floor. She dove for it and slammed her knee into the nightstand.

She was wincing in pain when she picked up the call. "Where've you been?"

His voice was urgent. "Listen carefully, Grace. Brandi's missing."

Her skin went clammy, and her heart returned to pounding.

"She never showed up at the club, so Lewis is out looking for her. I'm following Anton and his boys. Lena got tipped off by Frank and is probably heading for Mexico. I need you to text me pictures of all the journaling you did on your dreams. Maybe there's some clue to where she is."

"Come pick me up!"

"Sorry, I need to stay with these guys."

"Who's watching out for you?"

"Don't worry about me. I'm staying in touch with Lewis."

He sounded distracted and tense, so she grabbed her journal, took pictures of the pages, and texted them to him.

"I'll keep in touch. "Don't answer the door, and don't let anyone in!"

After she hung up, she felt her chest constrict. She tried to do deep breathing, but it still turned into a full-blown panic attack.

"God, please protect her," she kept saying over and over. After lying on her back for twenty minutes, tears running into her ears, she suddenly knew what she needed to do.

She changed her clothes, put on some makeup, and called a cab.

XXI

GRACE

Grace arrived at The Brass Mill at about ten-thirty. She was wearing frayed jeans and a tucked-in shirt, similar to the one Brandi had worn at The Black Swan. The place was packed and thankfully pretty dark. Brandi's band was up on stage playing without her. The guy who had done harmonies the night before was singing lead. They weren't doing any original music, just covers for pop songs, and people were dancing.

She recognized the songs they were playing, even if she wasn't clear on all the words. She found herself feeling grateful for having a teeny bopper sister who always insisted on controlling the car radio.

At eleven, the band took a break. Just then Kevin called, but she sent him to voicemail and texted

`I'll get back to you.`

When she was absolutely sure that Brandi wasn't there, she swallowed hard and walked over to where the band was huddled, popping open water bottles. The singer guy looked up, his face mirroring his anger. "Where the hell have you been?"

Trembling, she said in her best non-Brooklyn accent, "Give me a break. I had to take Rosie to the hospital, and I couldn't use the phone."

"She okay?" asked the drummer, who was much less ticked off.

"Yeah, some kind of gallbladder attack, but they're keeping her overnight."

The bass guitarist who had a wedding ring on said, "We've got another hour to go. What do you want to do?"

Gary, Robbie, Larry, but who was who? "Let's do some more covers, but I wanna sing harmonies, if you don't mind. I feel a cold coming on."

The drummer looked shocked. "You want Larry singing melody?"

Larry gave him a snide look. "Why is that so hard to believe, Gary?"

Great! She knew their names now: Larry was the singer on lead guitar; Gary was the drummer and Robbie was on bass. Robbie piped up, "Because you guys argued about that last week, don't you remember?"

"Listen, it's okay, I've been listening for a hot minute, and Larry's doing an awesome job." Grace turned to him. "Larry, do you mind?"

Suddenly, he wasn't so hostile anymore. "Are you kidding? You know I've been itching to sing lead."

"Where's your guitar?" Gary asked.

"Left it at the store in all the hubbub. But it's okay, I'd rather just sing."

Larry handed her a tambourine. "Don't upstage me."

Bass player Robbie gave her a bottle of water. She took a swallow, and they were off.

By the end of the hour, Grace felt fantastic! She loved singing with the band, wailing on some numbers, humming and beating that old tambourine when she didn't know the words. At first, performing without a piano made her feel naked. But the night's desperation was a great distraction. As they packed up after midnight, she asked, "Can anyone give me a ride home? I took a cab from the hospital because I left my car at the store."

Robbie, bass player, nodded. "I can drop you there to pick it up."

She tried to think fast. "That's the problem. My keys are locked in the store. Wait," now she was trying to cover the last lie, "that means I don't have my house key either."

At that, they all gave her a quizzical look. Drummer Gary broke the silence. "Isn't the back door unlocked?"

"I think I might have locked it yesterday. But we can give it a try."

"I'll give you a ride," Robbie said.

When they got in the car, he stared at Grace for a long time. "What's wrong?" he asked.

"Huh?"

"We've known each other since we were kids. You're not yourself. You would never miss a gig, even if someone was dying. And don't lie."

"I'm sorry, Robbie, I can't talk about it. It has to do with my mom."

That seemed to satisfy him for the moment. He nodded knowingly as he started the car. "You know she's a psycho. Don't let it bother you."

Grace settled down in the seat, now only slightly panicked. "How are you doing?"

Fortunately, he wanted to talk, so he told her about his son, Robbie, Jr., and his wife, Maya, the problems with the bathroom renovation, and his job at the post office. She discovered he was a vet, that Junior had an ear infection, and that the pipe didn't fit under the sink. Maya was fed up with her sister, and they hoped that Brandi was coming to Junior's birthday party next Friday.

When he got to the house, Grace checked the back door. Sure enough, it was open. She waved him off and snuck in, praying that nobody, especially Brandi, was there.

At first, she flicked on a table lamp. When she saw he was gone, she turned it off and pulled out her phone to light the way. There was a voicemail from Kevin. "When you get this, text or call me. I want to update you on what's going on."

As she crept through the apartment, she noticed two tiny bowls on the floor, both empty. Since she heard no barking, she assumed they were for a cat, but no such creature appeared. The place was small, only three rooms, so she combed them all, including the bathroom. When she was done, she texted Kevin.

Hey.

Were you sleeping?

Not exactly. What's happening?

Been following Anton for two hours. Stops at bars. His boys are in and out in minutes. Then they hit next the one. Been driving all over Phoenix.

As Grace texted, she continued to look around. She wasn't sure what she was looking for, but she hoped to find some clue that would help to locate her sister.

Do you think they're looking for Brandi?

Don't know. Maybe making drug deals.

Has anyone talked to her boss at George's Music yet?

Don't know. Coming back to hotel to sleep for a few hours.

Before he suggested getting together, she quickly tested:

OK, talk to you in AM

As Grace continued to wander around, she had the eerie feeling that she was looking at her own stuff. Brandi's clothes, books, even the food in the fridge looked like things she would buy. In the bedroom, which was a mess, there was a picture of Brandi with two other girls. On the back of the picture, it said, "Friends Forever, Jess and Robin."

She looked through the books on her shelves to see if she could find a high school yearbook. Not there. What would she have done with it? She checked the closet for boxes. Sure enough, it was in a plastic bin, way in the back, with old notebooks, letters and pictures. She tucked the box under her arm and called a cab. In less than thirty minutes, she was back in her room at the hotel. She wanted to go through the bin right then, but it was three in the morning, and she had nothing left. She lay down on the bed and fell asleep instantly.

The next morning, in spite of having a headache and sore muscles from tension, Grace showered and dressed before eight. When she checked her phone, she saw that Kevin had texted her a few minutes before.

 Can I bring you coffee and a bagel in about twenty minutes?
Yeah, thanks.

She put her hair up wet and opened the yearbook. She figured Jessica and Robin were probably seniors when Brandi was—maybe involved in music stuff? She was wrong about the music, but they both graduated with her: Robin Blackbear and Jessica Mendoza.

She got onto Facebook and found them both. Robin Blackbear was attending Arizona State like Brandi and listed her current city as Phoenix. Jessica listed hers as Anaheim, California. Grace did a white page search on both of them and had directions to Robin's house by the time Kevin knocked.

"Don't get mad," was the first thing she said to him as she opened the door.

He handed her a coffee and a bagel. "Because you got up late? So did I."

"No, not that."

"Then why would I be mad?"

"I went out last night."

His face turned red. "I told you to stay—"

"I know, but I couldn't."

"You just don't get it. We're dealing with dangerous people, Grace. What did you do, go across the street for food?"

"Worse than that."

He stared at her, expectant, obviously irritated.

"I pretended to be Brandi at The Brass Mill."

"What?!"

"I know it was wrong, but I had a hunch—"

Kevin slammed his paper cup down on the desk. Coffee sloshed out through the tiny hole in the cap. "You have *got* to be kidding."

Grace said nothing.

He stalked away from her, his words terse. "I knew I should have sent you back to New York!"

"Now, come on Kev—"

By now his face and neck were a mottled pink. "Why would you do something as stupid as that?"

"It was impulsive, I know, but it actually paid off."

"What are you talking about?"

"Robbie brought me back to Brandi's house."

Before he could flip out even more, she added, "It wasn't locked. I just knew if I went there, I'd find a clue to help us locate her. And I did."

He sat down in a chair and put his head in his hands. "I'm out chasing down drug dealers, and you're breaking and entering."

"Also stealing."

"What?"

"I took a box of Brandi's high school stuff that was buried in her closet."

Kevin threw up his hands. "Oh, this just keeps getting better."

"But here's the deal. I think I might know where Brandi is. At the very least I think we can find someone who'll know. It looks like she may have two close friends. One is in California, and one is still in Phoenix going to the same college where Brandi goes. I've got her name and address. Maybe we can look her up this morning."

"Grace, I'm telling you, if you do anything like this again, you are definitely going home. And I would have no trouble handcuffing you to an agent to make sure you got there. Do you understand what I'm saying?"

She nodded, looking as penitent as she could. And then, suddenly it occurred to her that she might be falling in love. But Mr. Uppity himself was on a roll. "How could I ever face your mother if something happened to you? If you can't manage to worry about your own safety, think of your mom. Can you imagine what it would be like for her to lose two daughters?"

"Okay, okay. You can put away your tiny violin now."

"You're so exasperating."

She grabbed her purse off the chair. "But you love me, right?" When she turned back around, he was a deep shade of red. "What's the matter?"

Without saying a word, he grabbed his keys and coffee and walked out the door.

And she followed him, like a puppy.

XXII

GRACE

Robin Blackbear lived in a development of tiny stucco houses within spitting distance of each other. Preschool age kids were playing on the sidewalk, darting into each other's yards. When they knocked on the door, a middle-aged Hispanic woman opened it. Instantly, her face lit up, and she threw her arms around Grace.

"I knew you'd come back, Button. Come in, come in. Who's your boyfriend?"

Speechless, Grace looked to Kevin.

"Thank you, ma'am," he said, walking inside. "I'm Kevin. You're Robin's mom?"

"Yes, and you're not from around here. I can hear it in your speech."

She held Grace's hand and led her to a chair in the kitchen.

"Is Robin home?" he asked.

"No carino, she's gone for a few days to visit her grandparents. What do you kids want? Eggs, pancakes? I was just cleaning up from Papa. He'll be so sorry he missed you, Button."

Grace looked at Kevin for direction, and he gave her a slight nod. As tenderly as she could, she said, "Mrs. Blackbear, I'm not Brandi... I'm her twin sister, Grace."

She waited for that to sink in before going on. Mrs. Blackbear chuckled as if she were used to practical jokes. "Kevin and I are

166

from New York. We've come to find her. Right now, our only good lead is your daughter, Robin, so we want to speak to her."

Mrs. Blackbear still had a half smile on her face. She was not going to be fooled by her *Button*. They sat still for a few minutes while Grace looked into her eyes. Suddenly, Mrs. Blackbear's face darkened, and she looked at Grace as if she really had never seen her before. "Let me see your ankle," she demanded.

Before Grace could respond, Mrs. Blackbear was on the floor lifting up her pant leg and running her fingers over her right ankle. When she looked up, her eyes were clouded with tears.

"No scar."

She sat back down at the table looking stunned. "Brandi fell off her bike right here in front of my house. There was glass in the street, and it cut her ankle pretty deep. But her mom was out of town, and I didn't know if I should take her to the ER to get stitches. So, I cleaned it up and put a butterfly bandage on it. It healed nice, but there was always a little scar. You, carina, don't have that scar, which means ..."

Mrs. Blackbear began to cry. "O dio mio, but I am not surprised, carina." She took Grace's hands in hers. "I prayed the Rosary so many times for my Button. She had such a deep sadness. I knew something was wrong, but I never knew what. Now I know. She was missing her other half."

She leaned over and hugged Grace again. In spite of herself, Grace teared up too. It felt like her mother's arms around her. They sat like that for a while until Mrs. Blackbear jumped up to grab some tissues.

"It's not right to ruin your shirt with my tears," she laughed as she dabbed her eyes and blew her nose. "Tell me, what happened? Were you split up at birth and adopted by different parents?" She frowned. "Is that how they do it in *New York*?"

Grace looked at Kevin who quickly shook his head.

"That's a long, complicated story, Mrs. Blackbear," Grace said.

"Oh, please, carina, call me Mama B. Everyone else does."

Grace saw that Kevin was champing at the bit. She said to him, "Maybe you can explain things better than I can."

He dove in. "I'm a New York detective, Mama B. Anything you can tell us about Brandi would be appreciated."

"She's not in any trouble, is she?"

"No, not at all. I met her earlier this week, but now she's gone missing. We thought Robin—or you—might be able to help us locate her."

"I haven't seen Brandi for over a year. She and Robin had an *argumento* over Brandi's boyfriend. Robin thought he was no good. Robin tells it like it is. She gets that from me—her Latina side. Her looks she gets from the Native side. She told Brandi that someone had been giving drugs to nine-year-old babies in the Native community—can you imagine! There were even some *deaths* from *drogas malo*. Robin told her everyone was saying Anton was the dealer. Brandi didn't believe her, so she stopped coming around. That was so sad for me. I practically raised her because her mother worked long hours and wasn't always nice to Brandi when she was drinking."

"Is it possible that they've been in contact recently?" Kevin asked.

"I don't think so. They're both *obstinado*."

"When did Robin leave to see her grandparents?"

"Three days ago. She has a week off."

"Where do they live?"

"Supai village up north, on the reservation, about three hours from here."

"Does she have a cell phone number so we can get in touch?" Kevin asked.

"I can give you her number, but you won't be able to reach her. There are no towers up there. And the phones with the wires never work either. The place is so *remoto* you have to hike eight miles from the last parking lot before you can get to the reservation."

"Wow!" Grace said. "And Robin doesn't mind doing that?"

"She goes to clear her head as much as to see her grandparents. Do you know any *indigene* carina?"

Grace looked at her, confused.

"Native Americans."

"No."

"They're different from the rest of us. They need quiet. They need nature. At least that's what I've seen being married to one."

Kevin stood up. "Thank you, Mama B." He gave her his card. "Please call us if you hear from Robin. But if Brandi gets in touch, please don't tell her about Grace. That's something Grace needs to do herself."

"I understand. But carinos, you haven't had anything to eat or drink yet! And I need to get to know my Button's sister."

"We'll come back," Grace said. "I want to get to know you, too. Thank you for everything you've done for Brandi. I'm sure she loves you and your family very much. I know I would."

"You're always welcome here, Grace. You too, Mr. Detective."

After they left, they drove over to George's Music, but it was closed on Monday.

Kevin slammed his steering wheel, frustrated. "That's just great. Well, what about that other girl? The one in California."

"Jessica Mendoza? I wasn't able to get her address or phone number. Do you think you can?"

In answer, Kevin spun the car around and tore back to the police station. In no time he had Jessica's phone number and had left her a message. He also got Rosie and her husband, Howard's, address so he could go talk to them.

He waved a Post-it note in front of Grace. "Guess what their last name is? Heismann."

"The name Brandi goes by on Facebook? Do you think they adopted her?"

"There's no record of an adoption."

"Why would she do that?"

"No clue." As they left the station he said, "I'm taking you back to the hotel."

"Why? I want to come with you."

"I'd rather interview them alone."

"But I may get something that you would miss."

"I promise I'll tell you everything when I get back. Just relax and take the afternoon off."

Grace couldn't help but think he was punishing her for doing his job.

After he dropped her at the hotel, Grace called Eve who picked up on the first ring. "Grace, I've been trying to get you since last night! Where have you been?"

She sounded frazzled and a little angry.

"I'm sorry Mom. I didn't see any calls come through. Is everything okay?"

"We're fine." But her voice didn't sound fine at all.

"What's going on?"

"Some new options have opened up for Mimi. Andre knows of a doctor in Cleveland who's an expert hand surgeon. He works with a lot of musicians. After looking at her x-rays, he thinks he might be able to do bone grafts on each of her fingers. It's a series of very difficult, long surgeries, but there's a greater chance that she'll be able to play again. We're trying to decide if we want to do it."

Grace's heart ached for her sister. "Is there a downside?"

"She'll be out of commission for a lot longer. She'll need to be very careful until the grafts take. If some of the grafts don't take, they'll have to go back in again. They harvest bone from other parts of her body which is very painful. And it's *very* expensive."

"Doesn't insurance cover it?"

"Only partially. Dr. Hermani is out of network. Plus, we'll have to fly out there several times, stay in hotels, rent a car—all that's extra."

"I've got money, Mom. I've saved about $6,000. Would that help?"

Eve sighed audibly. "I don't want your money, Grace."

"But I want to give it!"

Eve was silent for a moment. "Andre says he can do a fundraising concert for her. But I'm afraid—"

"That he'll think she owes him?"

"Yes, and if after all that, she's not able to play again, well, think how awful it would be for her."

Poor Mimi. Her teachers had always been possessive, but Andre was the worst. "What does Mimi want?"

"She's not sure. She's worried about the money."

"Tell her to forget about that. We'll figure it out."

"Also, she's not sure she even wants to play again if Jay won't be able to walk."

"That's crazy! Jay would want her to play just like she'd want him to walk."

"I know, but she's not thinking clearly right now."

"Can I talk to her? Is she there?"

"No, she's at the hospital with Dan and Cassie."

"Tell her to call me later when she has some privacy."

Eve gave another big sigh.

"You sound tired, Mom. Do you want me to come home?"

"No," she said vehemently. "I want you to stay there as long as you need to. I can barely manage Mimi. If you were here, struggling, I don't know what I'd do."

"What about Auntie Elaine? Is she still there?"

"I had to send her home. She was driving me nuts. Cleaning every minute, lots of unwanted advice. No, Mimi and I are doing fine by ourselves. I don't have to go back to school. They got a substitute to finish out my year. I just need to do grades."

"What's Mimi going to do about her exams?"

"They're letting her take them orally. Everyone's been great about it."

"And graduation—I need to be there for that."

Another long pause. "Mimi says she doesn't want to go. She was supposed to play, remember? But that's two weeks away. Maybe she'll change her mind by then."

"We're a mess aren't we, Mom?"

"We've been worse, I guess."

The lady's got guts, thought Grace. "How's Jay?"

"Better, but I'll let Mimi give you the details. Tell me about the trauma center. Did you like the people? Did they help you?"

Oh, right, the reason I'm here. "Yeah, Ma, they were a big help. I may go back again, but first I have to process it all."

"Well, don't give up. This will all work out, you'll see."

Grace felt her defenses melting. She wanted to tell her mom everything, but she knew she'd have to wait just a little longer.

Please God, help us to find Brandi.

XXIII

KEVIN

I knock on the door of a modest home on the outskirts of Phoenix, then stop to look around and admire the yard. Almost nobody in Phoenix has a lawn—just rocks and sand everywhere. But this house has a neat little patch of green grass and a few flowers. You can tell someone has worked hard to keep the desert at bay.

Within a minute, a grey-haired man opens the door. I pull out my badge and identify myself. "I'd like to ask you some questions about Brandi Benedict. May I come in?"

Howard stands at the door, frozen. For a second it looks like he doesn't understand what I'm saying. "Of … of course. I'll get my wife."

He waves me into the living room. The furniture is plain and sparse. There are some framed awards on the wall and pictures of bands, their years labeled across the top. The only thing that stands out is a shiny, black, grand piano in the corner. "Rosie," he calls, "it's about Brandi."

Rosie hurries into the room looking just like she did at the store, slightly disheveled, flushed. When she sees me, there seems to be a glimmer of recognition, but her expression quickly changes to worry.

"Is she alright? I was just heading back to the hospital to see her."

I'm confused but try not to show it. "I just want to ask you a few questions."

"Well, I can tell you right off the bat the accident wasn't her fault.

She's a very careful driver. I've ridden with her many times, and she never goes over the speed limit."

"I can corroborate that, Detective. She is a safe driver," Howard says.

I pull out a pad and pen and write down, *accident.*

"If you ask me," Rosie continues, "I think it's very convenient that the other guy refused to take the breathalyzer or the blood test."

I keep writing. "He did?"

"That's right. He refused for *religious* reasons. Sounds like a cover-up to me."

"When did you find out about the accident?"

"Last night at about nine-thirty. The police called me while she was in the ambulance. When I got to the hospital, the doctor said she'd broken her collarbone. They decided to keep her at least overnight for observation."

"Was the other driver at the hospital too?"

"No, they said he refused medical care."

"Do you happen to know his name?"

"No. I'm sure the police officers at the scene took down his information."

She looks at me quizzically. "But you should know all that."

"Actually, I'm doing a private investigation."

She tilts her head and squints at me over the top of her glasses. "Do I know you?"

I stand up and head toward the picture window. "That's not likely. I'm not from Phoenix."

Mr. Heisman takes over. "The other driver hit her broadside on 46th street—jumped the light. Besides the collarbone, Brandi is pretty bruised up. The car, of course, is totaled."

Meantime out of the corner of my eye I can see Rosie still watching me with that squinty look. "What exactly are you investigating?" she asks.

"I just want to make sure she's okay. Her band members were concerned."

She shakes her head and her curls frizz out. "I tried calling Robbie last night, but he didn't pick up, so I left him a message to call me back. I haven't heard from him yet." Again, her eyes narrow. "They hired you?"

"No, I just happened to be at the club when she didn't show up, so I said I would find out what happened. Except for the broken bones, she's okay?"

"Hopefully. I'm heading up to Saint Joseph's now to see how she is."

"I'd like to follow you there."

"Sure, just give me a minute."

She waves Howard to follow her into the kitchen. I can hear their muffled voices. She probably has figured out where she saw me, so I find myself cooking up a story. I don't want to tell anyone the truth until I speak to Brandi first. Then it will be her decision who she tells. Everything that's going on with Anton and Lena means she's at risk. Until she's safe, the less said the better.

When Rosie returns with Howard trailing behind, her movements are jerky and her mouth is set. There's not even a trace of friendliness on her face. Howard is wearing a nervous smile that seems to say, "Sorry buddy, I can't control what she's going to do next."

"Ready to go?" I ask.

"Not quite. May I see your badge? My husband said you showed him a badge."

She puts on her reading glasses which magnify her eyes to large blue marbles.

I take it out and hold it up to her eyes. She scrutinizes it, my face, and the badge again. Her voice turns to ice. "Let me see if I understand. You're a New York detective who just wants to help out some band members he doesn't know—a New York detective who met Brandi at our store two days ago and went to two of her performances?"

"That's right," I say in my calmest voice.

"Well, I just got off the phone with Robbie, and he doesn't

remember you at all! What he does remember is Brandi coming late to the gig, acting strange and telling him that *I* was in the hospital. Brandi couldn't have been there! She was at the ER all night. And you, *if* you were at The Brass Mill at all, never even spoke to the guys in the band. I think you owe us an explanation, young man!"

XXIV

GRACE

Afraid that when Kevin came back he'd insist they return Brandi's memory box, Grace hastily spent an hour rifling through it. The yearbook was the biggest item in the box. Besides that, there were three greeting cards—two from friends and one from Lena—several pictures—two of her high school band at Disneyland—and a picture of a cat with the name Willow written on the back. She also had a picture of Lena, Frank, and her at the beach. She looked about seven. Lena and Frank were wearing sunglasses and smiling, but she was just squinting.

There were a bunch of report cards. The early ones were great until the fourth grade. That year the grades weren't bad, but the teachers' comments were:

Brandi would do so much better if she didn't act like a clown.
Brandi distracts the other children.
Brandi was sent to the principal three times this marking period.
Not working to potential.

The comments got better during fifth grade but slumped during sixth. When she got into seventh grade, Howard Heisman appeared as her band teacher and Beth Ackerman as her chorus teacher. She started earning straight A's in those classes. Her behavior must have improved too because there were no teacher comments.

By her sophomore year she was doing well in all her classes. There were jazz band and chorus certificates for every year. She found a yellow grading sheet from a tryout for Arizona all-state chorus, 159 points out of 162! Grace had never gotten more than 140 in New York, and she still had made the cut.

Brandi's high school diploma was in the box and an acceptance letter from Arizona State. There were a few well-worn toys, a set of Russian nesting dolls, a beanie-baby-sized blue unicorn with a green iridescent horn, a deck of cards with puppies on them, and a pink Polly Pocket case with tiny dolls and furniture inside.

At the bottom of the plastic bin was a batch of papers that were clipped together. They looked like they'd been torn out of different notebooks. Some of them were dated. The most current were on top and they went back to 2005. The top one was dated January 5, 2018:

> *Pick up books for Stat class and Chemistry*
> *Take the car to Hogan for the rattle*
> *Pay rent*
> *Pay landlord to change the locks*
> *Find a new guitar strap on sale $$*
> *Dinner this weekend at Howard and Rosie's—bring salad*
> *Look up the definition of stalking. THEN break up with Anton*
> *Introduce Gary to the band*
> *Practice!!!!!*
> *Get a new phone*

The rest of the pages seemed to be diary entries.

November 29, 2017

> *I'm movin' on out! Rosie found me a little three room on 55th street about a mile from the store. The rent is $700 a month. Mom's pissed off because she says I should be saving my money, but I can't take the arguing anymore.*
>
> *Between the store and the band, I know I can swing it. Food may only be Ramen noodles and canned peas for a year or so, but I'll have some peace. Robin and I always said we'd get an apartment together, but we're not talking since she*

trashed Anton. Screw her. She's just jealous because she and Wes didn't work out. She'll get over it.

August 28, 2017

Can't believe I'm starting school. I'm soooooooooooooo excited! First semester: English, Dummy Math, Bio and Art class. Woohoo! I hope I can handle it all with work and the band. Rosie says I can study in the back room when it's slow at the store. She's an angel.

June 6, 2017

Played our first real gig tonight at Funky Monkey! I screwed up the lyrics on Mine but other than that it was pretty good. We actually got paid instead of just earning food and drinks like we do at the Black Swan. I hate the atmosphere and customers at that place, but at least I get a good meal once a week. After tonight, I have a feeling we'll be getting more gigs.

April 2, 2016

Do taxes!!!!

Find out when R and I are going to Supai and get the time off from work

Buy Mom's bday present

Talk to Felicia at Arizona State about their music program 602.285.7558

Clean room! yuck

Get Uncle Bob's number

The Language of the Living—Am Bb Em DChorus: D Cm D A

I didn't pay for the dirt on my skin

But you must know where I've been

Heaven and hell don't tempt me like you

The pain of love cuts deep blue

Chorus: Fire, fire is the language of the living

Fire, fire in the act of forgiving

Don't blink now it's all getting buried

Cover up the grave, make sure you hurry
All's forgiven here, let's just disappear…
December 25, 2014

Today sucks. I wish I was someplace where it snows. It never really feels like Christmas in Arizona. Jessica is home from college. We're gonna go out tomorrow night with Ro, 'cause they're both with their families today. Ray and Mom had a big brawl last night, so neither of them is talking. I made pancakes for breakfast thinking we could be a normal family. How stupid am I! I watched SpongeBob SquarePants and ate by myself in the living room. There are a few presents for Mom and one for Ray under the tree waiting for them to stop acting like babies. I don't want anything they have for me, but I guess I'll have to wear a smile and be grateful. Mr. Heisman and Rosie asked me to come over tonight. I can't wait to get out of this place. I just want normal. Did I ever have it or was it a dream? Happy birthday, Jesus. Too bad we're still treating you and each other like crap.

April 20, 2014

Mom and I actually had a good day today. We went to the mall and picked out a dress for graduation. Then we went out for burgers at Red Robin. She says I have to get a job after graduation since I'll be paying for gas, insurance, clothes, pretty much everything but rent. I don't mind. I just wish she was like Mama B. who says the same things, only more like a mom and less like a prison warden. Tomorrow starts spring break!! Robin and I are going to Supai for a few days. I can't wait! I love her gram and gramps.

The next two pages didn't have a date and read like a story. In fact, there were red corrections in the margins like it was something she had handed in.

Abby heard the morning news blaring from the TV as soon as she woke up. She pulled herself out of bed and walked into the living room. Her mother, Gail, who worked the three to eleven shift at the hospital was sleeping with her mouth open on the couch. The place smelled like stale smoke and beer. There was a dark, wet spot of Bud on the rug under a tipped-over bottle. Gail must have lit a cigarette that burned down completely because there was a little ash tube that disintegrated when Abby picked up the ashtray. She flicked off the TV and dumped the ashes and bottles in the trash. Then she grabbed a dishtowel, threw it on the rug by the couch and stepped on it to soak up the beer. "Come on, Ma," she said, "let's get you to bed."

Gail was so small she could have carried her, but she didn't have the energy this morning. "You gotta walk, Ma."

Her mom wobbled to her feet, opened her brown eyes and looked at her like she was in another world. Finally, she said, "Gotta go to bed. You too, Abby."

Abby shook her head and walked her mother toward her room. "I'm going to school in a little while."

Gail's boyfriend Tom was sprawled out in the middle of the bed. Just looking at him made her sick. She sat her mother down on the edge of the bed.

"Light me a cigarette," Gail said.

"No mom, you're too tired. Just lie down."

She flopped backward onto the pillow, and Abby swung her legs around. "You want to get undressed?"

"No," her mom mumbled.

As she pulled the covers over Gail, Tom shifted. When she walked away Abby felt an iron grip clamp down on her wrist. Tom's eyes were open and he was staring up at her. "Ya shoulda left her on the couch. She smells like a brewery."

Abby felt her heart pounding out of her chest. "Let go!"

He released her with a grin and rolled over.

After leaving their room, she glanced at the clock. Fifteen minutes behind schedule. She took a quick shower, threw on some clothes, grabbed a Pop-Tart, and ran out the door. She pulled her bike off the front lawn and peddled to her best friend Rose's house. When she got there, Rose's mom was just pulling out of the carport.

"Come on Abby," she called, her round, brown face smiling.

Rose swung open the back door of their beat-up Ford wagon. Hopping in, Abby offered her half of her Pop-Tart. Rose wrinkled her nose. "How can you eat that stuff?"

At the bottom of the page a teacher had written, "Great details. This could be the beginning of a good story. A-"

The next few pages were undated and looked like they were torn out of a kid's journal. The handwriting was nothing like the hurried scribbles and bullet points of the first pages. The ink was green and the i's were dotted with hearts.

Dear Diary,

I got you for Christmas and I promise I will write every day!!!! I am hiding you in an Unknown Place, where no one will find you. I'm going to name you Sam. I am thirteen years old, and I am in the 8th grade at school. I am good at music. For the Christmas concert, I got the solo in chorus instead of Carlita who thinks she's the next Madonna. Bobby McArthur, he wants to go out with me. He is really cute. Today he told me to go to the lav at exactly 1:15 PM and he would meet me there. He did and he kissed me real long and put his tongue in my mouth which was disgusting but okay. My best friend is Robin. She comes over every day after school because Mom says I can't be alone, and she doesn't get home until 4:30. My mom has a boyfriend named Ray. I hate him. He's such a jerk. She says I should be grateful because he helps out with the bills. I'd rather live on the street. He runs a club which I've been to a few times. I guess it's only open at night (more about that later). My mom is pretty nice, but she drinks beer a lot and never wants to do anything. She's also very old—48, I think. She comes from NY and says we don't have any relatives, but I don't believe her because we are Italian. On TV it always shows Italians with lots of relatives. When I'm sixteen I'm going to buy a car and drive out to NY to find my dad and meet my relatives.

Every day when Robin and I come home, we have a snack and watch As the World Turns. Then we do our homework. Robin lives down the street with her mom and dad. When we turn 18, we are going to get an apartment together.

The last page, also from a journal, was dated November 6, 2005.

After daddy went to work today, Mom said he's leaving us and moving back East. She said that he never loved us. That is why he is leaving. I DONT BELIEVE HER! Shes always mean to daddy.

Last night I had a dream, or maybe it was real. Daddy woke me up and said shhh be quiet. I dont want your mother to hear. He said I have to go away, but I dont want to leave you. He said I can go to NY to visit him when Im bigger. He gave me a piece of paper with his brother Bob's address on it. He said you can write to me. Then he said dont worry if you dont get any letters from me cause maybe mommy will throw them out and say I don't care about you. I was crying but he said dont cry just be brave. I hate my mom.

XXV

KEVIN

"Who are you *really* and what do you want with Brandi?" Rosie demands.

"Mrs. Heisman, I plan to explain it all. But first I need to see Brandi."

Rosie sits down and crosses her arms. "We're not going anywhere until you talk to us."

Feisty lady—annoying, but admirable. I walk toward the door. "Then I guess I'm going to St. Joseph's without you."

"I told you I know the doctor, right? Brandi will be discharged before you get there. Then you'll have a hell of a time finding her."

Mr. Heisman kneels in front of her. "Rosie."

She waves him away. "No, Howard! This whole thing is fishy. How do I know he didn't have that badge made downtown, and he's one of Anton's henchmen?"

I stop with my hand on the doorknob. "I'm not one of Anton's henchmen."

She tosses her grey curls. "*Humph!*"

"Listen, I know about Anton and his late uncle Ray. That's why I need to talk to Brandi."

"Not until you tell me why you, a detective from New York, knows about any of this."

I choose my words carefully. I don't want to reveal too much, but I'm getting impatient with Rosie's game. "I've been working with

184

the local police. They think that Anton is a less-than-legitimate businessman, and Brandi may be at risk."

"Any fool knows that! But why are *you* involved?"

"Because some of this involves a New York crime."

Mr. Heisman finally speaks up. "We believe Ray was a drug dealer, and Anton is carrying on the family business. We tried to talk Brandi out of getting involved with him, but she isn't always easy to convince."

"She's still dating him?"

Rosie jumps on that. "See, Howard, didn't I say he knows more than he's telling us?" She turns back to me. "No, she's *not* still dating him. We didn't press the issue. She finally saw it herself. I'm a very keen observer of people, Mr. Jacobs,and I can tell that the way you're talking to us in dribs and drabs shows you have a lot up your sleeve. We have no way of knowing that you're not one of them."

She says *them* like it's a curse word.

"Mrs. Heisman, I'm an officer of the law. I am trying to protect Brandi."

"Why would a New York detective come to Phoenix to *protect* Brandi?"

"I told you. I have to speak to Brandi. Then she can tell you whatever she wants."

"You want us to trust that you're looking out for her best interests? We're not hillbillies! We watch *60 Minutes*. We know all about dirty cops. You started by spying on her. Then you lied about talking to her band members. Listen, Brandi is more important to us than anyone. We would have adopted her if we could have. Instead, we're her substitute parents. That may not mean anything to you New York City cops, but it means something here."

"I don't doubt what you're saying. I'm sure you *are* like parents to her. But she's over eighteen. Even in Arizona that means she's an adult."

I look at Howard in utter frustration. "Look we're wasting

precious time. I'd hate to have to dispatch officers to keep Brandi from leaving St. Joseph's before I get there, but believe me, I will."

Howard puts his hand on Rosie's shoulder, but she pushes it away. "We'll see who wins this war."

"So you're willing to risk a charge of obstruction?"

Her face turns scarlet. "Yes."

With a helpless look, Mr. Heisman slumps down next to her on the couch and takes her hand. Though an unwilling participant, he'll still support her.

Suddenly I find their love for each other and for Brandi more touching than annoying. They are her de facto parents. Without them, who knows who or what she would have become? "All right. I'll tell you what I can, but you need to promise me something."

"What?" Rosie snaps.

"Don't talk to Brandi about this until I say so. If you care about her as much as I think you do, you'll soon understand why."

She glares at me over the top of her eyeglasses, but finally she nods.

GRACE

Grace put everything back in Brandi's box just the way she found it. She didn't cry until she was in the shower.

All the times I've complained about my mom, and acted like it was such a burden to have a little sister. So we had to share a room. Big deal. So Mom and Dad were overprotective. At least they loved each other.

She cried so hard she had to keep cold water pounding down on her face, knowing that if she didn't, her eyes would puff up like balloons.

When she finally got out of the shower, she was freezing. She dressed, did her hair, put on a bit of makeup, and waited for Kevin to get in touch, but he never did. She lay down for a few minutes and woke up three hours later to Mimi calling her.

After saying hello, the first thing she did was tell Mimi how much she loved her.

"What's wrong?" Mimi demanded

"Nothing! Can't I say I love you?"

"Mushy isn't your style."

Grace ignored her. "Are you still at the hospital?"

"Uh huh, I've been reading *King Lear* to Jason."

"He's awake?"

"Yeah, didn't Mom tell you?"

"No! She just said he was better."

"They've been gradually reducing the drugs that kept him in a coma while his brain was healing, but he was having trouble coming to. Yesterday morning it broke. At first, he was confused and angry, but once he got used to his surroundings, he calmed down."

"Is he okay? I mean, is he really upset?"

"He's depressed. And sometimes he cries cause he's in pain. Other times he curses."

"Jay curses?"

"Yep, we've started having cursing contests."

"I guess things have changed since I left."

"Usually we're angry at the beginning, but then we end up laughing."

"How is he really doing, I mean his legs?"

"That's actually the *really* good news. He's wiggled his toes. At first, they thought it was just reflexes. They told Dan and Cassie that he fractured his back at L5 in addition to smashing his legs. But it looks like that fracture hasn't affected the nerves."

Grace tried to keep herself from crying again. "Wait a second."

She went into the bathroom, soaked a washcloth in ice-cold water, and put it over her eyes, makeup and all. "Okay, I'm back."

"You sound all muffled. What's happening?"

"Nothing, just go on."

"He can't move until it heals, so they've got him on this waterbed with weird balloon thingies on his legs that fill up with air every few minutes to keep him from getting blood clots. The next step is a body cast. They have a great team of doctors, so Pastor Dan and Cassie aren't as freaked out as before."

"How are you doing, Mi? Are you hurting?"

"Not so much now, but I suppose Mom told you what's in the works for me."

"Cleveland and Andre doing a fundraiser? What do you think about all that?"

"Could we video-chat? I need to see your face, Gracie."

"Why?"

"When we talk, I need to know what you're really thinking."

"I tell you what I'm thinking, Mi."

"No, you don't, Grace. FaceTime me back."

She hung up, so Grace had no other choice but to pull the washcloth off and face her sister. She was right, of course. Grace couldn't fool Mimi when she was looking at her. She picked up on the first ring, and in a few seconds, Grace could see her huge smile, but the rest of her looked pretty awful. Her gorgeous, curly hair was flat and unwashed. Her face was blotchy. She was wearing the same t-shirt she had on when Grace had left. Grace felt love surge up in her. "Hi imp."

"What's wrong with your eyes? Why are they all puffy?"

"See, this is what I was afraid of. You're just freakin' nosey."

"I'm sorry that I notice when my sister looks like a puff adder."

"I'm gonna hang up on you."

"All right, all right, keep your secrets." Her voice grew quieter. "I miss you, Gracie. Mom's acting so weird."

"What do you mean?"

"For one thing she looks puffier than you, so I know she's crying all the time. And she's worried about you. Actually, she's worried about everyone."

"Poor Mom."

"She's so intrusive."

"You know what Mi, be thankful for that. She's a real mom, a real good mom."

Mimi was silent for a moment. "What's gotten into you? You're the one who always says how intrusive she is."

"I know, but let's just say I'm missing her, and you too, squirt. So, you're gonna go to Cleveland and have the surgery, right?"

"I don't know."

"Why not? If the doc says you'll have a better chance with your fingers, you need to do it Mimi. Music is your life."

"Not anymore."

"What are you talking about?"

"This whole mess is changing me. I mean, how significant is a performance career when people can die any second? These nurses and doctors, now they're really doing something important. They're saving lives. Me, I'll just be playing for rich people who can afford concert tickets. How does that help anybody?"

"You can't be serious, Mi. We're talking about a God-given gift here. Those doctors and nurses are doing their thing because they're good at it. They don't faint at the sight of blood. They don't mind touching people's clammy skin. That's their gift. You were given something else. Besides, you know how important the arts are. Why patch people up if they don't have anything to live for? Your music brings people joy. It brings you joy. You're the only person I've ever met who feels joyful practicing for six hours a day."

"Get off your soapbox, Grace."

Grace felt around for her hand lotion on the nightstand. When she couldn't find it, she picked at the skin around her thumb nail. "Mimi, do you think music is in our genes?"

"I don't know, I guess so. But you know as well as I do, you have to practice like a slave to develop the skills. I guess not practicing right now is showing me just how much of a slave I was."

"But a happy slave, right?"

"I can't be what Andre wants me to be."

"You don't have to."

"Grace, his eyes look worse than yours and Mom's. He's acting like he's lost something valuable, like I'm some kind of extension of him. Do you know he yelled at me because I never insured my hands! *They're your livelihood,* he said. What a jerk."

Grace could feel a doozy of a headache coming on because Mimi was probably the most stubborn person she knew. It never paid to try to convince her of anything; it just made her dig in deeper.

"Okay, I'm not going to argue with you. You've got to figure this out on your own. Just think about a couple of things. Our dad was a great musician. It was in his bones. We picked that up from him. It wasn't just because he taught us. It's because we had an *aptitude*—like some people have a gift for math or technology or politics. So, think what it would be like if you had this amazing ability, but there wasn't anybody there to nurture it because you were—let's say, in the wrong family."

Mimi was quiet for a bit. "I guess that would make it harder."

"Hopefully, your ability would eventually come out, but who knows? I don't think it was some accident that you got dumped into our family, Mi. And we're not even talking about when you got prayed over at twelve and your talent jumped up twenty notches. That was some kind of extra helping of magic."

"You said what happened was bunk."

"I was jealous."

She was silent for a minute. "Your puff adder eyes say you're telling me the truth."

Grace took a deep breath as she thought about what she was going to say next. "On to other things. I have something to tell you that is gonna make you forget all about your so-called bondage to Andre and your longing to be a part of the medical profession, God help us."

Mimi grimaced. "I doubt it."

"Only you've got to promise not to breathe a word of this to anyone upon pain of death."

"Death doesn't frighten me," Mimi said dramatically.

"Mi, stop it. Getting a splinter frightens you."

"You too, big shot."

Grace let out a long, loud sigh. It sounded like the hiss of a puff adder.

XXVI

KEVIN

Rosie and Howard are speechless when I tell them the story. Literally, their mouths are hanging open. Finally, Howard clears his throat. "I knew she couldn't have been Lena's daughter. Brandi is such a compassionate young woman. Lena is cold as ice."

Tears fill Rosie's eyes. One slides down her cheek and onto her blouse. "That poor child. That poor family! But why is Brandi in danger now?"

I explain to her how Brandi once told Anton in a fit of anger that she knew *what else* he did. Now that there were deaths associated with the Native youth, she was the most likely person who could incriminate him.

"Do you think he might have had a part in the accident?"

"With Lena no longer around, anything's possible."

Suddenly Rosie's eyes grow large. "Wait, are you saying that her twin was the one who showed up last night at The Brass Mill?"

"Yes."

She puts her hand on her cheek and stares at Howard. "They must truly be carbon copies of each other if even her closest friends couldn't tell them apart. Doesn't that mean that this Grace is in as much danger as Brandi? Anyone who would see her would assume—"

Leave it to Rosie to see what I had missed. If Anton got suspicious of me, if they led me on a wild goose chase just to tire me out and follow me until I lost patience and went back to the hotel, they would know where I was staying. Then if they saw Grace—

How could I have not seen it? I told Grace the bad guys were always smarter than the good guys. How stupid I've been.

GRACE

"Where are you in the hospital?"

"In the café."

Mimi leaned to the left, so Grace could see behind her. There were about fifteen people around eating lunch.

"Can you go someplace more private?"

"Sure."

She shuffled down the hall to a private waiting room, shut the door and propped the phone up against a table lamp. When she sat down, Grace got a fuller view of her and her poor hands still wrapped up like big burritos. The way Mimi slumped into a chair made her chest ache.

Sitting up against the headboard of the bed, Grace stopped biting her nails and tried to look mature. "I'm just gonna dive right in here, Mi. But please be patient with me, because this is not easy."

Mimi leaned closer to the screen, her eyebrows arching in alarm. "What's wrong?"

"If you want to know why I have puff adder eyes, it's because I've been crying for probably the last three weeks. Ever since I started getting those weird dreams, asleep and awake, I've been on the edge of craziness."

"Mom said you went to Arizona to get that fixed."

"Right. So, these dreams take place at a beautiful but scary lake. When I couldn't figure them out, I went to talk to Pastor Dan. He said that maybe they had to do with the way my twin sister died because they found her in a lake. He suggested that I find out more about that case, that it might quiet my mind. In walks Kevin Jacobs—the guy who's gonna help me get over this. You following me so far?"

Mimi grinned. "He's cute, isn't he?"

Grace sighed, indulging her sister. "Yes, Mi, he's cute. So, Kevin starts researching the case. Come to find out, it was botched beyond belief with leads being ignored and a rush to close it after the baby was found. The main detective wanted to reopen it, but he was shut down. People wanted to forget what happened, understandably, I guess. But Kevin, bloodhound that he is, started following the leads that were dropped. I can tell you all the details another time if you want, but let me just say that he found out the baby they fished out of the reservoir wasn't our sister."

Mimi who had been pulling at a thread on her sweater, suddenly looked up, her eyes wide. "Who was she?"

"We don't know yet."

Grace hated the way she looked just then, all confused and scared. She wanted to get to the happy part. "Can I keep going Mi, or do you need to process?"

"Go on."

"Finding out she wasn't my twin led to more discoveries. The guy is amazing!"

"That, plus maybe God was helping him," Mimi said.

"I don't doubt that at all. To make a long story short, the clues led to the possibility that our baby sister didn't die but was raised by her kidnapper here in Phoenix. We came out here to check it out—and Mi, it's her. It's our sister."

Mimi's eyes grew large, but then turned angry. "I don't believe you, Grace!"

"I am not lying. Her name is Brandi Benedict, and she looks just like me—just like us, actually. She's our sister!"

At first, Mimi was open-mouthed, stunned. But then, her face went through a series of changes. Her cheeks got pink, she looked dismayed, then she turned white, and finally erupted into tears. In less than a minute, the tears had turned into a full-blown wailing fest. Grace waited patiently for her to get control.

She smiled to herself. *If it takes all day, so be it.*

Little by little Mimi settled down, but then she would start crying again so pitifully that Grace ached to wrap her arms around her. After three or four minutes of that, her mood changed, and she jumped up and did a happy dance. "Thank you, God, thank you, thank you."

She laughed until she couldn't stand up, so she flopped down onto the couch looking totally spent.

"What did she say when she met you?"

Grace took a deep breath. "I haven't actually met her yet."

"What? Why not?"

"There are some complications. She's been mixed up with some bad people, and we want to make sure she stays safe."

Mimi suddenly turned into a girl on fire and shot questions at Grace for the next several minutes, most of which she couldn't answer. Grace tried to tell her about Lena, about Brandi's friend Robin, about Anton, but she became increasingly alarmed that Mimi, in her current mood state, wouldn't be able to keep from blabbing the story to Eve.

"Mimi, you've got to promise me that you won't tell Mom about this. With everything she's going through right now, she might have a heart attack. Kevin and I have to make sure that Brandi hasn't turned out to be some brand of crazy before we let Mom in on this. Can you imagine what it would be like if she turned out to be a sicko like her mother?"

Mimi shook her head forcefully. "That woman's not her mother. You said so yourself. She's got our genes."

"Yeah, but anybody brought up by a psychopath is bound to have some problems."

"We're gonna have to pray that she doesn't."

This is where Grace had a problem. *If it's already there, how can God go back and make it different?* But she didn't bring that up to

Mimi because she didn't want to shake her faith by asking existential questions. "Do you agree not to tell Mom?"

She looked alarmed for a moment. "Can I at least talk to Pastor Dan?"

Grace hesitated, but when she remembered that he had started her on this journey, she said, "Yeah, okay, but swear him to secrecy too."

"He's a flippin' pastor. He doesn't need to swear."

"You know what I mean."

Then Mimi really surprised Grace. "I'm gonna have the surgery in Cleveland."

"What? Why?"

Her eyes were glistening. "Because of this. To honor the genes. To honor Dad—and Brandi."

Grace's eyes filled up too. "Why are you trying to make me cry again? Don't I look bad enough?"

"I love you, Gracie. And I love the fact that you're listening to God."

"Sometimes it's feels more like I'm listening to the devil."

"Just be careful. Don't do anything stupid like you usually do. This is different. There are real bad guys around."

"Thanks for the vote of confidence, Mi. I love you too."

KEVIN

I dial Grace as Rosie and I rush out to the car. By the time we pull onto I-30, I'm already going too fast. The inside of the car is like 120 degrees so I have the air conditioning on and the windows down, but it's still not cooling off. Grace isn't answering. I hit redial at least ten times but it keeps going straight to voicemail. Finally, I leave a message. "Grace, you might be in danger. Don't leave the hotel room. Don't open the door for anyone. And this time *do as I say!*"

Frustrated, I punch in Lewis James' number, but he's not picking up either. Finally, I call the Phoenix PD. "This is Detective Kevin Jacobs from New York City. I've been working with Agent James from the FBI, but I can't get him. Can you give me any help with that?"

The officer sounds like he just woke up. He puts me on hold while I'm still talking. When he gets back, he says that Agent James is out of the office.

"I know that! Look, I need you to send an officer to the Sheraton Hotel on Fourth Ave, room five twenty-two. Grace Maddox is there. She needs protection. Please put somebody outside her door until further notice. Also, send someone to St. Joe's and without making it obvious, please guard Brandi Benedict's room. She's in..." I look over at Rosie.

"Three twenty-four."

"Did you hear that?"

"Yup, Three forty-four."

"No! Three *twenty*-four."

"Okay."

"We have reason to believe three perps, Anton Morgan and two other guys, might try to harm her. While you're at it put out a BOLO on Anton. And the guy who hit Brandi last night, find out if he has any connection to Anton."

The officer seems to be doing a lot of typing in the background. "We don't have any reports of a Brandi Benedict being assaulted last night."

"Not hit like punched. She was in a car accident!"

"I don't have access to the motor vehicle database right now. It'll take me awhile to get his name."

"All right, just make sure you get on the other things quickly."

"Not to be a pain, but I have to check all this out with my boss. Can I have your badge number and the name of your supervisor in New York?"

I shake my head in rage. "You have got to be kidding? The protection details need to be sent out immediately!"

"I understand sir, but I don't have the authority to send those officers out."

"Then let me speak to someone who does!" I roar.

"Hold on, please."

I pound the dashboard so hard it hurts. Then I glance at Rosie whose bravado has worn off. She looks terrified. "I'm sorry. I just don't want anything to happen to these girls."

"I understand. Is there anything I can do to help, like hold your cellphone so we don't have an accident?"

I give her my phone. "Thanks."

GRACE

After hanging up with Mimi, Grace saw she had a voicemail from Kevin, but when she listened to it, he sounded like he was in a wind tunnel. She couldn't make out anything but her name. She tried calling him back, but it went into his voicemail. "Hi, it's me," she said. "Have you found out anything about Brandi? I'm going to *Mi Amigos* for lunch. Call me as soon as you can."

Mimi's reaction to finding out about Brandi made Grace realize this whole thing meant almost as much to Mimi as it did to her. It had always been the two of them, fighting but then making up, putting up walls, but then sharing secrets, grousing about Mom but then being supremely protective of her. They would take up each other's causes and sometimes try to fight each other's battles. They were a magic duo.

But now, with the possibility of Brandi being part of their family, would things change? She was so sweet to want to do something to honor Dad and Brandi.

Grace wondered, when they met, if they would recognize the gift they shared? Mimi was classically trained, and Brandi was self-taught, but that spark, that angel dust was on both of them. Broken fingers could never take that away from Mimi just like what happened to Brandi couldn't take it away from her. Two amazing talents.

After lunch, she walked back to the hotel and stopped in the gift shop to grab a *Vogue* magazine and a bag of Reese's Pieces. On the way to the elevator, there was a guy who looked a lot like Anton. She'd tried not to at look at him when they had met at the Black Swan, so she wasn't sure. But when he turned around their eyes meet. It was him. *What could he possibly be doing here?* She darted back into the gift shop, her heart pounding.

But he didn't follow her. She waited another five minutes before poking her head out of the gift shop again—no sign of him. So, she sprinted to the elevator, but just as it closed, someone put a hand in to stop the doors—Anton!

"What the hell are you doing here?" he asked.

In that split second, Grace had to make a decision—pretend to be Brandi or act like she didn't know him. Pretending to be her would probably get her into trouble fast, but what could she do with the fact that they looked exactly alike? Only one thing differentiated them—the New York accent that she'd tried to tone down for ages but could easily pull out when needed.

"Excuse me?" she said, trying to sound as nasty as she could. She pointed her finger in a circle, a sneer on her face. Moving from side to side like she had some kind of ghetto swagger, she said, "Who do you think you're tawkin to?"

He looked confused for a moment, but then a smirk spread across his face. "Nice try."

"Listen buddy, I don't know what you're thinkin', but I don't know you."

"Don't give me that," he said, grabbing her arm.

The elevator was barreling up, and no one else has gotten on. But touching her was the worst thing he could do because her fear morphed into volcanic rage. "Get your hands off me, you pathetic jerk, before I call the cops!"

Surprised, he dropped his hand. But in a moment his bravado

was back up. "Keep messing with me, babe, if it makes you happy."

At that moment, the elevator opened onto the floor where the pool was, and Grace saw a group of wet people waiting to get on. "Get outa my way," she said, pushing him aside and practically climbing over the people to get out of the elevator.

He tried to follow her, but she'd already gotten her key card into the pool access door. She yanked the door open and slammed it behind her. The elevator closed on Anton and the swimmers, and she found herself face to face with a towel guy who had muscles the size of grapefruits. When she flashed him a big smile, he returned it with interest.

She hurried into the ladies' dressing room, and with shaking hands, ripped her phone out of her pocket. Yet again she could only get Kevin's voicemail. She called Agent James and waited for what seemed like twenty rings for him to pick up.

"Lewis," she whispered, "Anton came to the hotel and saw me. I'm hiding out by the pool, but I'm sure he's going to come back."

"Grace?" he asked.

"Yes! I just saw Anton, and he thinks I'm Brandi. He grabbed me in the elevator. I'm scared, Lewis, and I can't get hold of Kevin."

"Calm down. Where are you?"

"In the Sheraton at the pool. I'm scared."

"Stay where you are, Grace. Don't worry. I just got a call from the Phoenix PD. They told me that Kevin ordered a protection detail sent to the hotel. They should be there in a few minutes. I'll tell them where you are."

While she waited, she tried to become best friends with the towel guy. It only took five minutes to find out that his name was Steve, that he worked part-time at the pool and he hated rich people and kids.

"I'm expecting a police officer or two to come looking for me," Grace said. "Don't worry when you see them. They're just here to protect me."

"Are you in trouble?" he asked.

"No, not really. It's kind of a complicated story."

"So, when they come, I should let them in?"

"Yes."

In a few minutes, two men appeared at the pool area door. They weren't wearing uniforms, so she assumed they were detectives. Like Agent James, they were only wearing slacks and short sleeve shirts. One of the guys had short blond hair and the other one had a shaved head. They both looked kind of familiar. When the bald guy held up a badge against the glass, Steve let them in.

"We heard someone was harassing you in the elevator," the bald guy said to Grace. "We'd like you to file a report at the station."

"Okay," Grace said.

They took the elevator downstairs and out a side entrance into an idling, nondescript car. Blond guy got into the front passenger seat while bald guy got into the back with her. As they backed out, the driver turned around and looked straight into Grace's eyes.

Anton.

XXVII

KEVIN

When we get to the hospital two officers are already standing outside Brandi's room. Rosie goes in first, and I watch her give Brandi a gentle squeeze. Brandi is wearing her street clothes and is sitting on the edge of the bed, her arm in a sling. "How're you feeling honey?"

She gives a half-smile. "Sore."

Different from the girl I met the other day, she looks confused and battered. She's got a black eye and scratches up and down her arms. I greet her with a slight nod.

Rosie points to me. "Remember this guy from the store the other day?"

"What's he doing here?"

"You won't believe me if I tell you. But first things first. When is Dr. Sanchez releasing you?"

"He already has. They're just doing the paperwork now."

Rosie grins. "That's great! Then we'll be out of here soon. Honey, Howard and I want to take you back to our house for a few days, just until you get back on your feet."

"Thanks Rosie, but it's not necessary. I need to go home and take care of the cat."

"Howard will feed and water her while you're with us."

Brandi winces in pain and then sighs like she knows no one ever wins an argument with Rosie. As she stands up, suddenly, her face registers alarm. "Why is this guy here? Why are there cops out in the hall? Is it my mom? Is she all right?"

Rosie puts her arm around Brandi. "Don't worry, dear. She's fine."

I walk into the hall and tell the officers where we're going. They agree to stay with us until the Feds get to the house.

From the doorway I hear the nurse talking to Brandi. "Since you're going to be sore for a while, Dr. Sanchez has ordered some pain medication. Check in with your doctor in a week. In the meantime, rest. No work, no driving."

Brandi sighs. "That shouldn't be hard since I don't have a car anymore."

Rosie has started gathering Brandi's things when the nurse comes back with a wheelchair. Brandi gingerly lowers herself into it looking as forlorn as a lost child. Rosie leans down and pats her knee. "Kevin's driving us home. Once we get there, I'll make you a nice cup of tea, and if you're up to it, he has a few questions for you."

I smile and try to make small talk, but she eyes me with suspicion. After I bring the car around, Rosie eases Brandi into the back seat. She helps her with the seatbelt and then takes her hand in her own. "Everything's going to be all right. You'll see."

Brandi nods and turns her face toward the window.

GRACE

As soon as Grace saw Anton's eyes, she remembered Mimi's warning, *Don't do anything stupid. There are real bad guys around.*

Too late for that. What should I do? Play along? Lie?

She breathed a silent prayer, decided it was probably safer to act like she thought they were officers, so she reinvented herself again as the brash New Yorker. "What, you again? I don't care how cute you are, your dating skills suck."

He chuckled and kept watching her in the rearview mirror as he drove.

"Okay, I get it. You're a cop. You had me going there for a while. Am I supposed to be guilty of something?"

"Gary, check her purse for a wallet," he said to bald guy.

Gary, the guy next to her opened her purse. "Let me know if you find any money in there," she said.

When he fished out her license, he read, "Grace Maddox, Tuckahoe, New York."

"Get her phone and give it to Carl."

Gary grabbed her phone and tossed it to blondie in the front seat who checked her contact list and recent calls. "I don't see Brandi or Lena here," he said.

"I've heard of Brandi, but who's Lena?" she asked, grateful that she had listened to Kevin and never tried to make contact on her own.

The blond guy, Carl, went to her Facebook account, looked at her *About* page, and scrolled through her photos. "Yep, she's from New York; it says she went to Boston University but moved back to New York last year. She's got pictures of a mom and a sister, and maybe a boyfriend."

Grace acted irritated. "You know, you could've asked me those questions yourself."

Gary, the bald guy in the back, kept giving her lecherous looks which she tried to ignore, but nausea was creeping into her throat. "This is gettin' a little old, ya know."

"We just want to make sure you are who you say you are."

"Who else would I be?"

"What's the name of the guy you're with?"

"What guy?"

"Grace Maddox," Anton said, like her name was a joke in his mouth. "Some guy from New York appears in Phoenix to listen to a girl in a band who looks just like you. Coincidence? I don't think so."

Carl, who'd been scrolling through her recent calls, piped up, "She's been talking a lot to a guy named Kevin. New York number."

"Is Kevin your boyfriend?"

"Why? You wanna date him?"

Carl added, "Her last call, though, was to somebody named Lewis. That one's a Phoenix number."

Anton's eyes appeared in the rearview mirror again. "Who's he?"

"You know, dude, I'm done answering questions. Take me to the station and arrest me if you want."

"Hit redial," Anton said to Carl.

"Okay, okay! So, I'm two-timing my boyfriend. I'm a piano player, and Kevin, who's also my manager, was searching the 'net one night like he always does, looking for talent to make him rich. He comes across this singer who he says looks just like me. Brandi Something, out in Arizona. He says she could be my twin. I think, yeah right. But then when I see her, I think, wow, she's my double! I was adopted, so Kevin says maybe she was too and we're twins."

Grace pulled closer to the car door to get away from the lech and really started improvising. "Kevin's eyes turned into dollar signs after that. Two musicians who find out they're sisters and start performing together. What a gimmick. So, he convinces me to fly out to this desert hole in the wall to meet her. But he says he has to check her out by himself first, so he connects with another guy in the business and goes to some club to hear her sing. I'm back at the hotel, sick of sitting in my room, so I go downstairs for a drink, and I meet Lewis who's hanging out after his conference. We talk until about one AM. When Kevin rolls back in, he tells me he's gonna go see her sing the next night at another club. When I ask him if I should go too, he says no, it's too soon. I'm fine with that because I've already gotten interested in Lewis."

Anton laughed. "Sweetheart, you're not the only one who's steppin' out. I met Kevin at The Brass Mill on Tuesday, and he introduced me to a Hispanic chick he said was his fiancée."

Grace pretended to be shocked. "That jerk!"

Gary turned to Anton, a sneer on his face. "You don't believe any of this, do you?"

"Hey, go to my YouTube videos if you think I'm lyin'."

Gary opened the YouTube App and typed in Grace's name. Fortunately, there were videos of her senior recital at Boston where she had played three jazz pieces with an ensemble. Mimi had uploaded them without her permission and then refused to take them down.

Music filled the car while Anton and Gary watched the video. Before they got to see that the videos weren't taken at a club, Grace said, "Wait, so back at the hotel, is that who you thought I was? Brandi? Do I look that much like her? Is she in some kind of trouble?"

KEVIN

When we get back to the Heisman's from the hospital, Howard jogs out to help Brandi inside. As soon as she flops down on the couch, she asks for a pain pill. "I need to get out of these clothes and take a shower, too."

After bringing her water and a pill, Rosie escorts Brandi to the bathroom and gives her towels and a toothbrush. She waits outside the door for Brandi to send out her clothes which she takes downstairs and loads into the washer. When she comes back, she says, "I should go to her house to pick up some things for her."

"I'll send a female officer to do that."

"You think people are watching her apartment?"

"I'm sure they are."

"I don't know if Brandi is ready to hear your story. She may need to rest or eat first."

"That's fine, I'm not in a hurry. In fact, I want to drive back to the hotel to check on her sister."

"When are they going to meet?"

"Not until I'm sure Brandi can handle it."

GRACE

"Yeah, she's in trouble," Anton said.

Apparently, he had decided to use her cop ruse to his advantage.

"Your double, Brandi, is a drug mule that we've been tailing. Problem is, nobody's seen her since yesterday. So, if boyfriend number one knows where she is, you need to tell us. Carl, text her your phone number so she can get in touch with us. If we don't hear from you by tomorrow, we'll call you."

Grace gave a hoarse laugh. "Sucks for her, but hey, this is exciting! Is there anything you need me to do? Impersonate her, maybe, for your investigation?"

Grace was getting weary of trying to pretend these guys were cops, but if they bought it, maybe they'd eventually let her go.

"We might need you for a little sting," Anton said.

She noticed both Gary and Carl suppressing smiles.

But Anton was starting to get into his role. "The thing is, you can't tell anybody you're working for us. Not your boyfriend or your other pal, Lewis."

"Don't worry about that. I'm great at keeping secrets."

"You sure? Because if you're lying, we'll know."

"I'm sure."

All the time that Anton had been driving, he'd been staying in the neighborhood because when he finished his spiel, they were back at the hotel. "Remember, if you tell anyone about this, you'll be prosecuted for impersonating a drug runner."

She heard Carl snort.

Grace grabbed her purse and phone as she got out of the car. "Don't worry, I'll call as soon as I know anything."

She tried to look casual as she walked into the hotel lobby, but after she saw that they'd driven away, she ran into the ladies' room and threw up. After that, she called Kevin.

Kevin found her in the lobby watching the door, pretending to be buried in a *Vogue* magazine. As soon as she saw him, she smiled and grabbed his hand, praying that, if anyone was watching, they wouldn't be able to see that she was shaking.

He walked her into the lounge where it was dark and suggested a drink to calm her down. "I can't," she whispered, "I'll throw up again."

Kevin put his hand on her back. "You're doing great. Just try to look cool, since we don't know who's watching."

"Those two guys sitting by the gift shop look suspicious."

He chuckled. "They're cops, Grace. I recognize them from the station."

"A lot of good they did for me when I needed them."

He leaned in and brushed a strand of hair out of her eyes. "Tell me everything."

Grace told him about her conversation with Mimi, his indecipherable, tornado voicemail, lunch, the elevator, the kidnapping, the trip to the john and why her mascara was a mess. When she finished, he stared at her with wide eyes.

Grace shifted uncomfortably in her chair. "You're mad 'cause I didn't stay in my room, right?"

"Well, yes—but Grace, I'm in awe! What other, untrained twenty-three-year-old could've pulled off what you did? You may've saved your life! If you had fallen apart, who knows what would've happened?"

She was totally floored that he wasn't yelling. "Thanks Kevin. I honestly didn't expect that response."

"Have you ever considered doing police work?"

She couldn't tell if he was being serious or sarcastic. "I have to say, I took a page out of Mimi's book and prayed my little heart out."

He gave her a look she couldn't read. "If anything had happened to you, I don't know what I would've done."

"Now don't go all mushy on me. Tell me what's happening with Brandi."

After he explained about Brandi's accident, she was furious. "I wouldn't put it past those punks to have orchestrated it just to scare her. Let's go nail these animals."

He put his hands up. "Whoa girl, you're not going to *nail* anyone. You got your free pass. Now you leave it to the professionals."

She thought this was probably not the right time to argue with him. "Okay, okay, just tell me when I get to meet Brandi."

Kevin shook his head. "Not yet. I want to talk to her alone first. She's fragile and in pain, so I need to be cautious. Depending on how she responds, we'll take the next step."

Grace frowned. "You can't leave me again, Kevin. I'm fragile, too."

"Don't worry; I've got this under control. Lewis's people are gonna move you into a secure location. You'll be safer there."

"Unless the bad guys pose as Feds."

"Grace, believe me when I say I will *never* let anything happen to you."

"You're doing it again. Bad things have already happened to me. You can't foresee every situation. Don't promise anything you can't deliver."

He let out a bitter laugh. "That's what my dad used to say."

"So, it's not a new problem."

Grace regretted her remark as soon as she saw the look on his face. "Sorry."

"It's okay. Let's get out of here."

He steered her out of the lounge into the lobby.

"Where are we going?"

"I told you, to a safe house."

"What about my stuff?"

"The police will get it. Mine, too. This time we'll bunk in adjacent rooms. I don't want to risk you being here another minute."

"But what if Anton and his goons follow us?"

Kevin smiled. "Grace, I know how to lose people. Remember, I'm a cop."

When they got to the car, he called Lewis who gave him an address which he typed into Google Maps.

"Ask him to return Brandi's save box," Grace said. "It was in the back of her closet."

Kevin hung up, and they drove in silence, him checking his rearview mirror constantly. The only one talking was the female voice of Google Maps on his phone. Grace finally broke the silence between them.

"Why would your father say that to you?"

"How should I know? Maybe because I always had big dreams. He was an expert at shooting them all down."

"How?"

"Really? We're running from criminals, and you wanna talk about my troubled childhood?"

Grace shot back, "Listen, I know practically nothing about you, while you know almost everything about me. It won't kill you."

He sighed and shook his head. "When I was sixteen, I worked bailing hay all summer. My first paycheck, I took my parents out to dinner. We never ate out, so I had no idea how much it would cost. Turned out I didn't have enough money, so my dad had to loan me ten bucks to pay the bill. He laughed about it for years. You'd think Mr. Sensitivity would've been proud of a kid who wanted to spend his first paycheck that way. Another time when I was seventeen, I wanted to borrow his truck to take a girl out on a date. I asked my dad at the beginning of the week if I could use the truck on Friday night. He said if he finished his planting by then I could. Naturally, I was pumped. I told her to be ready at six. It ended up raining in the morning, and he didn't bring the truck home till nine that night."

"I'm sorry, but maybe it was unavoidable."

"He could've told me ahead of time, but no, he loved seeing me lose face."

"Really, Kev?"

He slammed his hand against the steering wheel. "Your dad loved you. You can't possibly know what I'm talking about!"

"Why would a dad not love his son? I want to understand."

Kevin's jaw tightened. "He wanted me to be just like him. A farmer, *a lover of the land*. If I heard it once, I heard it a thousand times. *This land has been in our family for a hundred and fifty years.* He thought it was our God-given mission to work that land. Well, he made me hate the land. I couldn't wait to escape. On my eigh-teenth birthday, I got the hell outa there and came east."

"To Cassie and Dan's?"

"Yep. I worked two jobs all through college until I got accepted into the police academy. At least that was one thing the old S.O.B. taught me. How to be tough. They try to break you, but I wouldn't quit. I wouldn't give my dad the satisfaction. And now, thank God, I don't have to have anything to do with him."

Grace didn't respond for a few minutes, but then couldn't hold it in anymore. "I'm no shrink, but I think trying to prove something to your father at your age means you're still pretty much tied to him."

Kevin laughed out loud. "You're right. You're no shrink."

"Yeah, but I've seen enough shrinks to know that when you don't forgive someone, they get away scot-free while you drink the poison meant for them. It's like carrying around a rotting corpse on your body. Kinda compromises your love life, if you know what I mean."

"And where did you pick up that charming image?"

"Your brother-in-law, actually. He told me the Romans used to do that to murderers. Killed them in the end."

"Well good for Dan! He knows forgiveness works. Did it ever occur to you that he has to say stuff like that? He's a minister, for heaven's sake!"

"I know parents make mistakes. My friend's mother would sit around praying while her father would beat her. Talk about having something to forgive! And even when they don't do stuff out of cruelty or stupidity, they still let you down. My dad said he would always be there for me, and he up and died. It took me a long time to get over being angry at him for that."

"But it wasn't his fault."

"Maybe your dad's personality wasn't completely his fault either. What did he learn from his father?"

"Oh, he was a piece of work! Didn't even attend my parents' wedding because my mom wasn't German." He heaved a great sigh. "Look, we can talk psychobabble for hours, but that's not gonna keep you or Brandi safe."

"Right, because *you're* going to make sure nothing bad happens to me."

"Cheap shot, Grace."

"You're right, I'm sorry."

They drove on in silence until he said, "Even if I forgave him, I could never trust him."

"I'm not saying you should."

He gave a bitter laugh. "No, *everything's all sweetness and light* between us? Isn't that what you people believe?"

"I don't know who *you people* are, but I'm no fool. I've forgiven people that I would never trust again. Trust and forgiveness are different issues."

He stared straight ahead, his hands gripping the steering wheel like he wanted to snap it off, his mouth a grim line.

Grace's voice softened. "Let me ask you a question. When you tell Brandi the truth about what Lena did, how do you think she's gonna feel about her?"

"I don't know. She'll probably hate her."

"Maybe, but *kidnapper* Lena isn't exactly the same as *Mom* Lena. Even if it wasn't often, there had to be times when Lena was there for her. What's Brandi gonna do with the memory of Lena holding her hair back when she puked in the toilet?"

"What?"

"It's a girl thing."

He glanced her way. "You're so weird."

"Maybe, but you better believe Brandi's gonna have lots of conflicted feelings."

"Your point?"

"Maybe one day she'll forgive Lena, but nobody's saying she'll ever trust her again."

XXVIII

KEVIN

I hate to talk *feelings*, but Grace seems to have a knack for it. She's so annoying when she tries to drive a point home. Especially when it comes to my father. What does she know? She didn't grow up with a weak mom and a cruel dad. That horrible combination destroys so many families. Sure, her parents were probably a little off. Who wouldn't be with what they went through? But her mom was strong, and her dad sounds like he was a good guy. Maybe what she's saying would make sense to somebody else, but not me, not now.

After I drop her off at the safe house and drive back to the Heismans', I try to focus on my strategy with Brandi. I wish I'd brought a social worker with me, like somebody from the Trauma Center. They know how to deal with this kind of stuff. Grace is right. It's gonna be murder for her to reconcile her feelings about Lena. How will she react when I tell her about Grace? Just because *I* know the Maddox family is wonderful, I can't expect her to believe that, sight unseen. She's going to have to take it on faith.

Faith.

In spite of myself, I breathe a little prayer. *Help me paint an accurate picture of her real family—and help me be compassionate.*

I park and introduce myself to the agents in the car out front. Then I circle the house. There's a six-foot high stone fence surrounding the back area. There's no gate, so I grab the top and hoist myself up to look inside. The back door to the home opens into a well-tended courtyard complete with a bubbling fountain and comfortable looking outdoor chairs. *Anyone trying to get in or out from the back is going to have a hard time of it*, I think.

I walk back to the front and enter to find Rosie and Brandi in the living room on the couch drinking tea. Howard nods to me, mumbles something about having to get ready for a meeting, then disappears down the hall. Brandi is dressed, although her hair is still wet, and she looks ten times better than when I last saw her.

"You ladies look comfortable."

Rosie stands. "We were just relaxing until you came back. Have you had lunch, Kevin?"

"Actually, no."

"Then I'll make you a sandwich."

"You don't need to—"

But she's already gone. Brandi looks down into her cup of tea like it has a secret message for her. "Rosie said you've got quite a story to tell me. Is that why you came to the store on Tuesday?"

"Sort of. I needed to get a look at you first."

"So, you were lying about wanting to buy conga drums."

I grin at her. "Not really. I am going to take lessons. And I do want to be in a salsa band."

"And coming to our gig Wednesday night, that was fake interest?"

"Actually, all of these things are connected."

Brandi stares straight into my eyes. There's defiance in her voice. "Okay I'm listening."

"Can I ask a few questions first?"

"I guess so."

"What's your relationship like with your mother?"

Her expression hardens. "Strained."

"Why?"

She looks down at her cup again. "She's not an easy person to get along with. She can be really moody, and she has a problem with alcohol."

"Has it always been that way?"

"Pretty much."

"What about your dad?"

"He left when I was ten."

"Do you know why?"

"He was probably tired of her abuse."

"How did you get along with him?"

"Better than with her. But I never heard from him again, so I guess we weren't as close as I thought."

"What if I told you they weren't your real parents?"

She looks up from her cup. "You mean like I was adopted?"

"No."

She seems confused but waits for me to go on.

"What if you were kidnapped?"

The color drains from her face, and she stares me down. "I'd say you were lying."

Put yourself in her place, I tell myself.

"My parents may be jerks, but I know they're not kidnappers."

"Not your dad—your mom."

She's silent for a long moment. "My mom is basically a good person," she begins, but then her voice trails off.

"If anybody knows her, Brandi, it would be you. But is there anything you remember about your childhood, unexplained things, red flags?"

Her lower lip trembles. "Why are you doing this?"

"I'm looking for the truth."

She brings her tea mug to her lips. Then her eyes narrow. "Whose truth?"

I don't say anything.

"I've never talked about this before."

I nod.

"She never let me play outside."

She winces as she shifts her position on the couch. "After Dad left, she did let me have a friend, Robin Blackbear. Her mother,

Mama B, watched me when Mom worked second shift. But some-times Mom would drop me off at Robin's and not come back for a few days. I knew it wasn't planned, but Mama B never said a word to me—just acted like she already knew about it. After a while she always kept a few sets of clothes for me at her house."

"Do you remember anything else that was unusual?"

Brandi gets more agitated. "I remember something that made me mad enough to try to run away."

"What happened?"

"In the beginning of my freshman year. Mr. Heisman, Howard, encouraged me to try out for the all-state music festival in voice—just to get the experience. Amazingly, I got in. But I knew that Mom wouldn't agree since it was going to cost about five hundred dollars. When I told Mr. Heisman, he managed to raise music department money so I wouldn't have to pay a thing. I went home to tell her, but she still said no. I freaked out and threatened to run away."

"Why wouldn't she let you go?"

"I think it had to do with my birth certificate. She said she couldn't find it and wouldn't be able to get a copy in time. I thought that was completely bogus, so I went ballistic. Normally, I was a pretty compliant kid, so that really surprised her."

"Did she ever find it?"

"Yeah, I have a copy somewhere."

"Anything unusual about it?"

"Well, it was filed when I was five years old. Mom said I was born at home, but the midwife never filled out the paperwork and then suddenly left the state. She told me that one of the times she went away it was to look for her."

"Did she ever find her?"

"No, because one of her doctor friends verified the birth even though he wasn't there at the exact moment." She stares at me. "You think it's a fake, don't you?"

"I can only tell you what our investigation has turned up."

"Which is?"

I take a deep breath. Here goes. "We believe you were kidnapped from a hospital in New York City hours after your birth. Within a day or two, we think Lena brought you out to Arizona."

Brandi's face reddens, and she shakes her head. "I don't believe you."

"I don't blame you."

She slams her cup down on the coffee table and looks like she's going to walk out of the room. But instead, she stares out the window, refusing to meet my eyes. Finally, she turns and gives me a withering look. "I suppose you have some kind of proof?"

My heart goes out to the kid. She's trying so hard to believe that her life hasn't been a complete lie.

As if on cue, Rosie returns to the living room. "How's everything going?" she asks with what seems like forced cheerfulness.

She sets my sandwich and a tall glass of water down on a TV tray beside me.

"Rosie, have you heard this guy's story?"

"Not entirely. I got the *Cliff's Notes* version this morning."

"What do you think?"

"It's possible, that's all I can say." She turns back toward the kitchen. "I'll let you finish your conversation alone."

"Please don't go," Brandi pleads.

Rosie looks at me for direction.

"I'm fine with you staying."

She sits down next to Brandi who leans her head on Rosie's shoulder. Her voice is vulnerable, childlike. "I don't believe that my mom kidnapped me. I know she's a little crazy, but to steal someone's baby? I can't believe she'd do that."

I take a bite out of my sandwich to give her some breathing space. Then I down the water and head to the kitchen sink to refill the glass. When I come back, I ask, "Do you know where Lena is now?"

Brandi looks at Rosie but doesn't respond.

"You're not in trouble, Brandi. You wouldn't be, even if you tried to protect her. But there are other factors here, factors that suggest she might not be safe. Please try to remember."

I lean over to take another bite of my sandwich. It's like I'm in a bad movie. This poor kid is hearing for the first time that her mother is a criminal while I'm eating a ham and cheese sandwich.

Rosie whispers something to Brandi. There's another excruciating pause.

"Yesterday she stopped at my apartment while I was at work. She left me an envelope with a key and a note asking me to get her mail. The note said she was going away for a while and didn't know when she'd be back."

"And the key?"

"It's in my purse. She said it opens a little safe at the house."

"Have you heard from her since then?"

"No. I left a voicemail after the accident, but she hasn't called back."

I swallow some water. "We think she may have gone to Mexico."

"No way, she hates Mexico."

"She may be meeting your dad. Do you, by any chance, know where they spent their honeymoon?"

Brandi runs her fingers through her blonde hair. "No idea. I remember her once talking about being in Belize, but I don't think it was with him."

"She might be trying to disappear."

Brandi's face turns red. "How would she know how to do that? This is my mother, not some international criminal."

Rosie pats her hand. "Take it easy Brandi. We'll get to the bottom of this. But right now, I think it's safe to assume you don't know your mother as well as you think."

Brandi's face and voice hardens. "I wanna hear the so-called *proof* you have that my mother is a monster and has told me nothing but lies."

"I'm trying to get there—"

"Look Mr.—whatever your name is."

"Just call me Kevin."

"Okay *Kevin*," she spits out, "everyone I know will tell you I'm a bottom-line kind of person. All this scene-building is wasted on me. If you've got proof that I was kidnapped as a baby, give it to me now without trying to sugar coat anything."

Rosie and I lock eyes. She gives a slight nod.

"You have an identical twin sister who's been searching for you."

XXIX

GRACE

After Kevin dropped Grace off at the *bungalow*, she waited inside with a closed-mouth agent until a young couple dressed like tourists drove into the driveway.

They carried her suitcase and about five others inside. Inside their suitcases were laptops and other techie gear, which they hooked up to at least ten surveillance cameras surrounding the house and street. They had bulges under their shirts that looked like gun holsters.

The girl cop was a no-nonsense blonde named Jenny; the guy, named Dave, had curly red hair and dimples. They both looked like they were about nineteen even though they were probably in their thirties.

Grace watched them set up their gear, mesmerized by their silent precision. They looked like they'd done it a thousand times. She tried to stay out of their way by wandering around the house, checking out the cupboards, the fridge, the back rooms. In the kitchen, apparently their command center, she watched them finish up. "Is this what it means to be *hiding in plain sight*?"

Jenny looked up from her laptop. "Sort of."

Dave broke open a bag of Cheetos and offered her and Jenny some. Grace shoved a few in her mouth. "How long do I have to stay here?"

Jenny licked orange off her fingers. "That's up to Agent James."

"Do you know why I'm here, why I'm being *guarded*?"

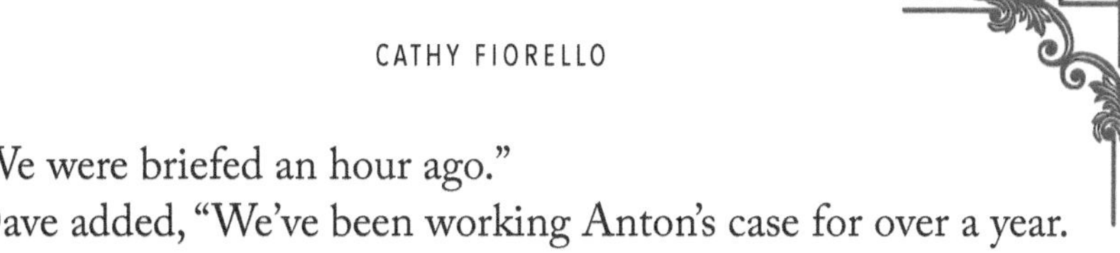

"We were briefed an hour ago."

Dave added, "We've been working Anton's case for over a year. Having another case tie in, especially one like yours, isn't something we expected."

Grace gave an ironic smile. "Tell me about it. A month ago, I wouldn't have dreamed of where I am right now."

As soon as the words were out of her mouth, she realized it wasn't true. She did dream of this—not being in a safe house but being someplace dangerous.

"What do you want me to do while I'm here?"

"Relax," Dave said. "Read, nap, snack, anything you want. You just can't leave."

"Can I call my mom and sister in New York?"

"Sure. We brought in a burner phone for you."

"What should I do with my own phone?"

"You can keep it. Just don't make or take any calls," Jenny said as she grabbed a new phone and powered it up.

Grace studied the phone. "Can I check in on Facebook and Twitter with this thing?"

"You can observe if you want. We've set up fake social media accounts for that. Just don't post or comment."

Grace put the phone in her pocket. "Just how dangerous are Anton and his boys?"

Dave and Jenny exchanged a split-second look.

"His goons have put people in the hospital," Dave said. "One guy's not going to walk again. And they may be linked to a murder. We believe Anton's responsible for at least six deaths through trafficking dirty drugs."

The reality of Brandi's unsafe life hit Grace hard. Anton, the tough punk who lived in Brandi's world, was now living in hers.

KEVIN

I wait for the reality of Brandi having a twin sister to sink in before

I say anything else. It's perfect timing because I've just finished my sandwich, so I go back into the kitchen to get another glass of water. When I return, Brandi and Rosie are talking, their heads almost touching. Rosie is holding Brandi's hand; a box of tissues lies in her lap. She'd be the one to hold back Brandi's hair if she were puking into a toilet. She and Mama B.

I just want to kill Lena. *How could she have been so selfish, so callous?*

"You okay?" I ask Brandi after a few minutes.

She twists the tissue in her hands. "No. First, you tell me my mother is a criminal. Now you tell me I have a twin sister I've never seen. Any other revelations before we go on?"

"I know this is a lot to take in."

"Ya think?"

She stands up with effort, a grimace of pain on her face.

"It's okay to take a break. I can come back later if you want."

She steadies herself on the side of the couch. "I just need to walk around a little, clear my head. Then I want you to tell me everything you know. I don't want any more surprises later on."

Rosie stands too. "I'm afraid your life is going to be packed with surprises for a while honey, no matter how thorough Kevin tries to be today."

Brandi says nothing but starts toward the kitchen door. Just before she puts her hand on the doorknob I say, "You really shouldn't go outside."

That's when everything falls apart. Brandi whirls around with fire in her eyes. She starts calling me every name in the book, cursing me, fate, God—anybody she can name for this assault on her world. Her tirade goes on and on. I don't blame her.

At one point I want to say something, but one look from Rosie tells me I'd better keep my mouth shut. As Brandi's rage begins to subside, she collapses into a kitchen chair, far away from Rosie and me. From there she starts to wail in anguish. Her tortured sobs are heartbreaking, full of helpless misery. Still, neither Rosie nor I intervene.

Finally exhausted, she stops crying and her face turns masklike, totally blank. After a few minutes she wobbles to her feet, and heads toward the guest room. "I need to lie down."

She slams the door behind her.

Rosie heaves a great sigh and goes into the kitchen to wash my plate and cup. "She'll be all right. She just needs time."

I could use a break too, so I step outside. The air feels like the inside of an oven. It's almost painful to breathe. Not a breeze, not a cloud—my definition of hell. I walk around the perimeter of the house and listen to the traffic sounds on the street behind the house. Then I go over to chat with the two agents, Paul and Dennis, who are sitting out front in a black car.

"Seen anything unusual?" I ask.

"Nope," Dennis says. "We haven't heard any chatter about Anton either."

"How can he disappear into thin air?"

"They've probably ditched the car and left town."

We talk about Anton's associates, his competition, his previous run-ins stretching back to when he was fourteen. Then we talk about baseball and the hideous weather which they don't seem to mind at all.

After a while there's nothing left to say to people I don't know, especially when the heat is melting my brain.

"We're gonna pick up some lunch soon. You want anything?" Dennis asks.

"No thanks, I just ate."

I walk back to the house, sit down on a stone bench in the front yard, and dial the safe house. Somebody named Dave answers the phone. "How's Grace doing?" I ask. "Can I talk to her?"

"She's all right. We gave her a burner phone if you want the number."

I call, and she answers on the first ring. "That's creepy," she says. "I thought I could only call out on this thing. I never expected someone could call me."

Her naïveté makes me smile.

"How's Brandi?" she asks. "Did you tell her?"

"I told her some of it. I told her about you. But it's not going well right now. She's in so much physical pain, it's hard for her to cope."

"Meaning..."

"She had a bit of a meltdown. Understandable. She's resting right now."

"I need to be there, Kevin! If there was ever a time that she needs a sister, it's now."

"I don't think she's ready yet, Grace. I'll ask her though, after she starts talking to me again."

"I shouldn't need to say this, but don't leave her alone. In times like this, people can do crazy things."

"Grace, I'm a police officer. I know these things."

"Yeah, but you don't have our genes. You don't know what it means to be me—or her."

After we hang up, I go back inside. Rosie is not around so I sit back in an easy chair. I can wait Brandi out. I can wait anybody out.

Twenty minutes later I awake to the sound of Rosie making coffee in the kitchen. I jump up, embarrassed and sticky with sweat.

"Would you like a cup of coffee?" she asks.

"Thanks. Where's Brandi?"

"Still in her room. I think she's sleeping too."

"I guess I dozed off. I'm sorry. Have you been around the whole time?"

"I went downstairs for a while to fold some laundry."

I run my fingers through my damp hair and glance at the clock on the wall. The afternoon is slipping away fast. "We need to get started again. Do you want to knock on her door, or should I?"

"What if she's still sleeping? She needs rest."

"I just need to ask her a few more things before I can report to my boss. It shouldn't take long."

Rosie gives me a disapproving look, but she taps on Brandi's door. "Brandi, may I come in?"

When she doesn't get a response, she knocks a little harder, "Brandi?"

Finally, she cracks open the door. The room is dark. She calls her name again. No response. Something's not right. I shoot past Rosie into the room and flip on the lights. She's gone.

XXX

GRACE

After lunch, Grace called Eve who sounded excited. "I'm at the hospital. Jay's being moved to New York Presbyterian for rehab. They have a great team of physical therapists who will work with him when he's ready."

"He must be happy about that."

"Definitely! He's so anxious to get back on his feet, he'll do just about anything."

"How are Dan and Cassie doing?"

"Dan, as usual, is upbeat. Cassie looks like she hasn't slept or combed her hair in two weeks. She's been at the hospital pretty much round the clock. But she won't be able to do that at the rehab hospital—which is probably good."

"Do the doctors think he'll get back full use of his legs?"

"They're taking a wait-and-see approach. A lot depends on how badly he wants it."

"I sense a *but* in there."

Eve hesitated. "It's going to be a long haul, Gracie."

"How's Mimi doing?"

"I don't know. What did you say to her this morning? Afterwards, she told me she *will* go to Ohio for the surgery. And she must have spent some time with Dan this afternoon because he told me to go easy on her."

Maybe she shouldn't have told Mimi.

"What about you, Grace?"

"I'm okay, Mom. Things are coming together."

Grace didn't realize she sounded discouraged until she heard Eve say, "I wish I could be there with you, honey. You don't sound so good."

"I'll be home soon, Mom. Then everything will be all right."

Suddenly, she surprised herself by choking up. "I miss you, Mom."

"Me too. Just do what you have to do to get better."

Grace pulled herself together. "I'll tell you one thing, I'll never complain about the weather in New York again. This place is a sauna. I've drunk more water here than I have my entire life."

"Is Kevin doing okay?"

"Yeah, he's fine. Just a little controlling, patronizing, annoying."

"So, you're falling for him."

"Why would you even *say* that, Mom? He drives me crazy."

Eve chuckled. "Just teasing."

"Well, don't."

"I have to go, honey. They're moving Jay now, and I'm the part of the mule team that gets to carry everything he's accumulated here."

Grace hung up, wishing she was home instead of being guarded by a bunch of strangers.

KEVIN

Brandi isn't in the guest room. I check all the other rooms in the house. I can't find Howard either. "Where's Howard?" I ask.

"He had a meeting at school. He must have left while I was downstairs."

"Call him," I yell over my shoulder.

I run outside to Dennis and Paul who are eating McDonald's in the car.

"She's gone! Did you see her leave?"

They both jump out of the car and check the perimeter of the house. "We went to grab lunch, but we were back in less than ten minutes. We never saw her come out the front. Maybe she slipped out the back."

"We'll find her," Dennis says, and he and Paul take off.

I also cruise a six-block perimeter of the house, but there's no one out in this 110-degree hell.

I leave a message for Lewis. "Brandi's taken off. Put out an all points for her. She's wearing jeans and a blue t-shirt. Her arm was in a sling, but she might have taken it off. Get back to me ASAP."

I end the call and the phone immediately jangles. It's Paul. "I checked with every taxi company in the city along with Uber and Lyft. There haven't been any pickups around here."

"Keep looking. Without wheels, she can't be far. And get Dave at the bungalow to see if he can track her phone."

I head back to the house and see Rosie pulling out of the driveway in her large, black sedan. I shout out the window, "Where are you going?"

"The music store, maybe she went there or left a message on that phone."

Yeah, sure, or maybe's she's just disappeared for good. How could I have been so dumb?

GRACE

It had only been three hours, but being stuck in Neverland Bungalow was driving Grace crazy. She finally asked Jenny to take her to a local store so she could at least pick up some drinks and food. Apparently, Jenny was bored too, so she agreed. They entered the only store nearby—a super Walmart. "Just don't walk away from me," Jenny said with a smile, "or I might have to use my gun."

Grace saluted her and threw a bunch of stuff into the cart. Sugary breakfast cereal, candy bars, chips, and instant mac n' cheese found their way in, like she was a child whose mom was away for the weekend. She also threw in sunglasses, two tank tops and a bathing suit. But Jenny was always a few steps behind, and this kind of shopping wasn't fun at all. It was like picking up supplies before going to jail. She got in a lengthy checkout line while Jenny went to wait for her at the register. Then her new phone rang. Kevin.

"I'm not sure how to tell you this," he began.

By the time he finished, Grace couldn't tell if she was angry with Brandi or proud of her. "Give me her phone number," she demanded.

"I don't think that's a good idea."

That was it. She felt like the top of her head was about to blow off. "You know what Kev, I don't care what you think right now! We've been playing this game by your rules from the start. Anytime I had a gut feeling, you ignored it. The times I didn't listen to you, we ended up further ahead of anywhere you and your team of experts got, so give me her number, or I'll get it from Rosie!"

He let out an exasperated sigh. "Grace—"

"No, Kevin. My guard-chick and I are on our way to George's Music if you don't."

The phone was silent. Finally, he said, "I'll text it to you."

As soon as she got the number, she dialed it. Of course, Brandi didn't pick up. When the chance to leave a voicemail arrived, she froze. What could she say? *Brandi, this is your sister, call me back. Brandi, the police are looking for you, get the hell out of Dodge?* When she realized she'd waited too long, she hung up. *Kevin and the Feds are screwing this up royally, and here I am,* she thought, *being guarded like I'm the prisoner. Brandi must be feeling this way too. We haven't done anything wrong, yet we're the ones being watched while the real criminals are out prancing around.*

I need to talk to my sister to sort this whole mess out, she thought. *If only I could slip away.*

Grace could see Jenny waiting for her at the end of the checkout line. Four more people in front of her. Just then Jenny glanced down at her phone.

Should she?

She left her cart in line and walked into the women's clothing section, moving as quickly as she could without drawing anyone's attention. When Jenny looked up, Grace watched her through a maze of sundresses. The look on Jenny's face actually made Grace feel sorry for her.

She discovered that it's really not that hard to *give someone the slip*. She was glad she wasn't a crook, because there was something very satisfying about it. She ended up several aisles behind Jenny so she could watch her every move. Her only chance of getting away was to do it before backup came. Grace jogged to the garden section because she knew they usually have an extra exit there. When she spotted it, she walked fast without looking back.

Outside, she ran to the back of the store and called a cab. Fortunately, it turned up in less than five minutes. When she got in, she called Brandi again. This time she left a message.

"Hey Brandi, you don't know me, but I look a lot like you. I'm actually in Phoenix, flew here with Kevin on Monday. Kevin and his posse have been guarding me from a guy named Anton, but I kinda lost my girl-cop a few minutes ago. I'd like to meet up with you to see if between us we can get this whole mess sorted out. I'm not familiar with Phoenix, but I know where the Sheraton is, and a little restaurant across the street named Mi Amigos. Let me know if you want to meet me at either of those places."

As the driver pulled out of the store parking lot, her pounding heart started to slow down. "Just head for the Sheraton," she told him.

But when misgivings crept in, Grace began to feel like a woman without a country.

Maybe I should just give up and have the driver take me back to the bungalow. Then she heard a ping on her phone. It was a text coming from another number. It said:

`Mi Amigos in 20 minutes.`

XXXI

KEVIN

I'm driving around searching for Brandi when my phone rings. I pick up, hoping it's Dennis or Paul telling me they've located her, but it's Jenny, Grace's *guard-chick.*

"What?!" I shout into the phone when she tells me what's happened. "Well, find her, and fast—and get Dave to track the burner. As soon as he gets it, tell him to text me the location."

I dial the phone Grace is carrying, but it goes straight to voicemail. "Grace, please call me. I don't know if you ditched Jenny at the store or if you were kidnapped."

I bang the phone against the dashboard of the rental so hard the case falls off. Since by now I'm only blocks from the Phoenix PD, I drive there and screech into the parking lot. Taking the outside stairs two at a time, I race inside and pound the elevator button for the seventh floor.

The eyes of several FBI agents are on me as I stride to Lewis' office and pound on the door. When he opens it, his face is grim. "Two girls missing, three drug dealers on the loose. How the hell did this investigation go bad so fast?" he shouts.

But I've had it with him. "What's the matter, Lewis? No foreplay first? Where's my bottle of water and my small talk?"

"Your sarcasm is out of line, Detective. How are you going to fix this?"

I'm about to punch this guy. "How am *I* going to fix it? I came here with only two goals—contact Brandi and see that Lena gets sent back to New York. That was it! *You* complicated this with your convoluted drug sting. If anything happens to either of those girls, *you're* responsible, not me. This screwed up, backwoods operation is all yours, Lewis."

Lewis walks away from me and plops down in his desk chair. He steeples his fingers and stares at a spot over my head. Finally, he spins his chair around, grabs two water bottles from his fridge, and tosses one to me.

"Thanks," I mumble, twisting it open.

Lewis rocks his chair back and forth. "The worst part is that we can't find Anton. We had him in our sites yesterday, and now he's disappeared."

I take a huge swallow of water. "Everybody's disappeared—Lena, the girls. The only people left are us, with egg on our faces."

Lewis gets his far-off look again. But then he stands up and paces with purpose. "That's not true."

He starts ticking off on his fingers, "We've got the people who work at the Black Swan. We've got the Native kids who buy from Anton. We've got Brandi's friends, the Heismans, the Blackbears, and the band members. Somebody's got to have a piece of this puzzle we've overlooked. And that Robin Blackbear kid—we've got to find her!"

"I can't understand why both Brandi and Grace ran off. Don't they realize we're trying to help?"

He shrugs. "They're scared. I see it all the time. We come in waving our badges thinking that people are going to listen to us, trust us. But they don't. Sometimes they see us as the enemy. Sometimes they think we're just bunglers and that they can handle the situation better than we can."

"Which in this case may be true."

Lewis ignores me and continues. "When we get involved with everyday people who aren't criminals, it completely disrupts their view of *normal.* You don't know how they're going to react when their world stops making sense. People are unpredictable, and that usually puts them in danger."

I know he's right. Carlton would always say that our normal isn't the normal of the people we're trying to protect. He would tell me to make sure I was in tune with their reactions so that I could predict what they might do next. But I didn't listen. I was smug, emotionally detached, handling my cases like a TV cop where everything wraps up nicely in an hour. But now that there are two girls missing, it makes me sick to my stomach. If anything should happen to Grace...

It's as if Lewis can read my thoughts. "Look, it's not your fault. Until they learn how to live their new normal, they're going to be all over the place."

"Which wouldn't be so bad if we knew where Anton was."

"Yeah, I've been thinking about that. What if he's gone, not because he thinks we're after him, but because he had someplace to be? Like maybe his product doesn't get shipped to Phoenix. Maybe he picks it up somewhere else, someplace we'd never think to look."

"So, if we look into his connections outside of Phoenix, we might find him."

"And if we can catch him with his stuff, we won't need Brandi anymore. She could start living her new normal without police presence."

"That would be great, but Anton's your gig. My responsibility is Grace and Brandi."

When I'm back outside in the stifling heat I see the pinks and purples of a gorgeous sunset. The time on my phone is almost eight PM which makes my stomach knot up. I'm just about to call Jenny again when my phone rings. The caller ID says Jessica Mendoza, Brandi's high school friend. I fumble with the phone, my hands shaking. "Detective Jacobs."

There's a brief pause, and I hear a timid voice say, "This is Jessica. You called me?"

"Yes! Thanks so much for getting back to me."

"You said I might be able to help Brandi Benedict?"

"That's right. I met with her earlier today, and we just want to make sure she's safe."

"I would have called you when I first got your message, but then I decided to talk with Brandi first, just in case, you know, you weren't legit. After I spoke to her, I realized she's really scared and does need help."

"When did you talk to her?"

"About an hour ago."

GRACE

The cab driver was too talkative, but he was fast, so Grace got to Mi Amigos in less than fifteen minutes. She stepped inside and stood for a moment to allow her eyes to adjust to the dim lights. A hostess greeted her, and Grace asked to be seated where she could watch the front door.

The waitress brought menus and two glasses of water. Grace gulped down both and asked for more. Her heart was pounding again, and she was lightheaded. She tried to relax, holding the icy glass up to her cheek. She waited, said a little prayer, and waited some more. The prayer was pretty juvenile: *God, don't make her hate me.* If she'd had more time, she would've called Mimi to pray a smarter prayer than that.

She thought about all the times she'd waited for things, knowing that once they happened, everything afterwards would be different. Like getting her high school diploma, or when her dad was dying. This was the same thing—the minute before you meet your sister and then the rest of your life.

But it was turning into more than a minute—more than five

or fifteen. Eventually, it was more than twenty minutes, so she texted Brandi.

Waiting for you at Mi Amigos. ETA?

In less than a minute, the phone pinged.

Already here.

Grace looked around but couldn't find Brandi.

Where?

At the bar.

Behind her; the lights were lower at the bar. Sure enough, there was a girl with her back to Grace. She started to walk back there, but as she did, someone grabbed her arm and yanked on it. She whirled around. It was Anton, with a sick smile on his lips.

KEVIN

As I try to crank up the air conditioning in my oven of a car, I end up stumbling over my words. "Y-you just spoke to Brandi?" I ask Jessica.

"Yes."

"Is she all right? Did she tell you where she is?"

"She's okay, but she told me she was in an accident a few days ago and broke her collarbone."

"Right. Did she sound drugged or like someone was with her?"

"No, but she was pretty emotional, which isn't like Brandi."

"What else did she say?"

"Wait a minute," she says, her voice shaky. "Before I answer your questions, I have a few of my own. Why are you looking for her? She tried to explain, but she wasn't making much sense. Something about a kidnapping?"

Sighing, I launch into the two-minute version of the story, barreling toward today's disappearance and Anton's threat. "This guy is dangerous. We want to find her before he does."

"If you're trying to protect her, why did she run away from you?"

I take a deep breath and decide to tell her the truth. "I threw a lot of information at her this afternoon without thinking about how it might affect her. I guess she doesn't trust me, not that I blame her. I wasn't being very sensitive. But I want to make that up to her, and I especially want to keep her safe from Anton."

"I guess your story pretty much matches hers—without all the F-bombs. But I don't think she knows that Anton may be out to get her."

"That's because I didn't get a chance to tell her that before she walked out on me."

"I mean, she knows he's a jerk, but she doesn't think he would hurt her."

"Did she say that?"

"No, that's just Brandi. She's a little naïve. That's why Robin has always tried to protect her."

"What else did she say?"

"Nothing much. She was actually acting kind of weird, reminiscing about the old days when our lives were simpler. Oh, and she asked about Robin—when I heard from her last."

"And when did you?"

"Robin texted me this morning around ten. She's on her way home from her grandparents."

"Did you tell Brandi that?"

"Yes. She asked if I thought Robin hated her because of their fight over Anton."

"What did you say?"

"I said I'm sure it's all water under the bridge. Robin loves her."

"Do you know where Robin is now?"

"When she texted me, she was in Peach Springs which is only about three hours from Phoenix. Unless she made some stops, she should be home by now."

"What about Brandi—did she tell you where she was?"

"No. I asked, but she wouldn't say. She's paranoid that her phone is bugged."

"Any idea where she might be?"

"Not really. I'm kinda out of the loop since I've been at college."

"If she calls you, *please* tell her we're worried that Anton is going to try to hurt her. Give her my number so she can call me."

"Okay."

"One last thing, did she happen to tell you how she got out of a house being guarded by three officers and a nosy boss?"

Jessica chuckles. "She hid underneath Rosie and Howard's bed until you all left to go look for her. Then she just walked out the door."

"Great," I say, contemplating my stupidity yet again.

XXXII

GRACE

Grace was speechless at the sight of Anton. There was only one thing she knew: she wasn't going with him, no matter what. "Come on," he said, yanking her toward the door.

Grace raised her voice. "No way! Get your hands off me."

Anton looked around at the other diners and smiled. "You wanna see your sister, don't you?"

But Grace planted herself back at her table, ready to create a scene. "I don't believe that Brandi's with you."

"No? How do you think I got her phone?"

"Then where is she?"

"Out in the car. If you walk over to the door, you'll see her."

"You're such a liar. I don't believe a thing you say."

He shrugged his shoulders. "Have it your way."

At that moment the waitress came to their table, so Anton let go of her arm and leaned back in his chair. "What would you like to eat?" she asked as she snapped her gum.

He locked his gaze on Grace. "Nothing yet."

"Take your time," she drawled, "I'll be back."

Grace couldn't stand the way he was sitting there, so self-assured, so convinced that he could get whatever he wanted. "What makes you think I'm her sister?"

"Come on," he sneered. "Are you kidding?"

"Maybe we're cousins."

"Listen, Brandi told me everything. I know you're sisters."

"Did she tell you how she ended up in Arizona?"

He hesitated. "I don't have all the details yet."

"Liar! I don't know how you got her phone, but if you don't get out of here, I'm gonna start screaming."

"Whatever, girl, I just figured since you came all this way, you'd want to spend some time with her. After today, that ain't gonna happen."

"Why?"

"Me and her are gonna split. Get away from all you people."

"If that happens, you'll be taking her against her will. Just another thing for you to go to jail for."

He grinned. "First of all, it ain't against her will. And second, I'd like to see you try to find us."

Grace felt desperate. *Why is Kevin never with me when I run into Anton?* "You bring Brandi in here if you want me to believe you."

Anton smirked. "Now why would I do that?"

"Because if you don't, I'll call the police. They'll be here before you get back to the car."

"Those clowns? They couldn't find me if we were in a bathtub together."

"Maybe so, but do you want to risk that? I can get them here in a heartbeat, and I will if I think you're gonna hurt Brandi."

His eyes darkened. "I would never hurt her."

"That's not the vibe I got when you thought I was her."

He shrugged his shoulders and stood up to leave. "Too bad your little quest didn't work out for you." As he walked away, he threw a phone on the table. "I guess she won't be needing this anymore."

KEVIN

My phone starts ringing. It's Grace's burner, and my heart skips a beat. "Are you okay? Where are you?"

"I'm at Mi Amigos across from the hotel."

"Stay there. I'm coming to get you."

"Kevin, Anton was here. I think he has Brandi."

I tear onto Route 10 and floor it. "When did he leave?"

"Less than a minute ago."

"I'll alert Lewis, but you stay in the restaurant, around people. Don't go to the john or anything."

"Okay."

Her voice is small, like a little kid. I want to say something comforting, but then I remember how mad she got when I told her that I'd protect her. "Just sit tight and tell me what happened."

She makes these weird noises, like she's holding back tears. "I texted Brandi and asked her to meet me here. But Anton showed up instead. How would he get her phone if she wasn't with him?"

"I don't know. But right now, my main concern is you. I'll be there in ten minutes."

"It's all my fault. I never should have come here. If we hadn't gotten involved, the FBI would've figured out how to land Anton six months from now, and Brandi would be safe."

"We don't know that. This was a bomb set to explode at any time. You didn't cause anything to happen."

She's silent.

"Let me call Lewis. I'll be right there."

"I'll never forgive myself if—"

I cut her off. "Grace, we'll work this out together. We've been a good team so far, right?"

I make sure not to add, *when you're not doing stupid things like impersonating Brandi or running away.*

I hang up and call Lewis. "Have your people look for Anton near the Sheraton hotel. He was last seen at Mi Amigos. He may have Brandi with him."

I pull into the restaurant parking lot, jump out of the car, and run inside, my hand on my gun and my badge clipped to my belt. Grace is in the middle of the room looking forlorn. I rush over, and she stands up and falls into my arms. I hold her tight as she clings to me. I feel—what is it—the thrilling sensation of not being a disappointment.

I throw some money on the table, and we walk out, our arms around each other. When we get to the car, she freaks out, blaming herself for everything. I just hold her hand and think there's nowhere else in the world I want to be right now.

Once she calms down, we sit in silence for a moment. Finally, she says, "Kevin, I am so sorry. I've been a jerk, I know. I'll understand if you want to ship me back to New York. But please, please don't!"

"I'm not going to ship you back. But I gotta be honest, I don't know what to do with you."

"You could lock me up."

Her half-grin makes me think she's not completely sincere.

"I would if I didn't think you'd find a way to break out."

She ponders that for a minute, looking pleased with herself. "All right, what do we do next?"

"Not sure. Lewis has his guys looking for the vanishing Anton. We need to find out if Brandi is with him."

"I know he had her phone, because he dumped it onto the table when he left."

"Are you sure it's hers?"

"How would he have been able to respond to my texts if it wasn't?"

"It's possible. There are all kinds of Spy Apps that let you read other people's texts. I think I remember you saying that the texts you got came from a different number. Did you save the number?"

"Yep."

"Then call Dave at the safe house and give him the number so he can track it."

She grimaces. "Call Dave? I don't think so. I doubt Dave and Jenny will ever want to hear from me again."

"Sorry, kid. If you want to be an investigator, you have to acknowledge your screw-ups and make nice."

"Who says I want to be an investigator?"

"Your actions. You haven't stopped sleuthing since I met you."

Reluctantly, she dials Dave, offers a lame apology for giving Jenny the slip, and gives him the number.

"Good job, Grace. See, despite evidence to the contrary, you can play well with others. Now, we work on finding Brandi. Her friend Jessica says she might reach out to Robin."

"I'll call Mama B."

There's no answer, so she leaves a message. "What next?"

"Where's the phone Anton gave you?"

She pulls it out of her purse and spends a few minutes checking it out. "Now that I look at it, I don't think it is Brandi's."

"Why do you say that?"

"It has no pics, no interesting Apps, an ugly background. It isn't personalized at all—just doesn't have the vibe of a twenty-three-year-old female."

I suppose she knows, better than I, what the average woman is like, but how average is Brandi?

GRACE

Kevin made an abrupt turn into a gas station. "I need to hit the can. Come into the store with me, so you can pick out some drinks and snacks."

While he spoke, he motioned for Grace to leave Brandi's phone and her purse in the car. When they got inside, he practically dragged Grace back to the customer bathroom, pulled her inside and locked the door.

Her eyes widened in alarm. "What's happening?"

His voice was clipped and urgent. "Something occurred to me while we were talking about Brandi's phone. If Anton's capable of spying on her through it, he could have done the same to you. Is your phone in your purse?"

Grace nodded.

"Did he ever have access to it during the time you were in the car with him and his thugs?"

"Not him personally, but the guy in the front seat. I think his name was Carl. He looked through my phone, checked my contacts, my Facebook page, my recent calls."

"You only need access to a phone for a few minutes to set up the spyware. That means he could be hearing and recording all your conversations, reading all your texts, taking pictures of you when it's out of your purse, even listening to our conversations through your microphone."

"What a slimeball!"

"Which could be the reason he's always one step ahead of us."

"So, what do I do now, dump my phone and just use the burner?"

"That's one solution," he said, pacing.

But then he got a sly grin on his face. "Another one is to use his spying to our advantage. Talk about things we *want* him to hear. Lead him where we want him to go. Only problem is we have to be careful not to leave the phone behind—like we've just done, or he'll catch on. We need to have a way to communicate privately and still use the phone enough for him not to suspect."

"Are you saying that even when my phone's in my purse, he still might be able to hear us?"

"Yes."

"We could text each other on your phone."

Kevin chuckled. "Or write notes like they did in the olden days before you were born. But we can only do that while we're also having normal conversations so there aren't any questionable gaps."

"What exactly do you want him to think is our next step?"

It looked like he was shuffling through several possibilities. "I'm not sure, maybe that we suspect Brandi and Robin are heading to the Havasupai Reservation to hide out."

"But what if they *are*, and Anton goes there to find them?"

"We'll let the reservation police know ahead of time. Once he's there, it's a confined enough area that we can watch him and keep him from intimidating Brandi."

"And if he already has her?"

"Then he won't follow us there. As soon as he knows we've left Phoenix, he may come out of the woodwork here."

Grace's skin started to feel clammy. "I'm so scared, Kevin. I don't want anything to happen to her, but things keep getting screwed up."

His look softened, and he took her hand. "Look, real police work isn't like the movies. It's frustrating and time-consuming with dead ends and blind alleys. I told you the bad guys are sometimes smarter than we are, but they're also greedier. And they're arrogant, which is what usually gets them in the end. If you can wait them out, they eventually cut their own throats. We can beat this guy."

She didn't want to cry, but she could feel her eyes stinging. "As long as Brandi doesn't get hurt. We can't let anything happen to her."

"I know you hate what you think are empty promises, but I really believe this is going to work."

He pulled out twenty bucks. "Grab us some snacks and something to write on. Then meet me back at the car. Just remember, if I'm right, he can hear everything we're saying. Take your phone out only when we want him to have a visual. The rest of the time, keep it in your purse. Same with Brandi's phone. Don't take any calls you think would hamper our plan. And do all this while acting like you haven't got a clue what's going on. You think you can do that?"

"I'll try."

Grace stepped out of the restroom while Kevin called Lewis. She picked up snacks, drinks, and a writing pad and got on the line for the checkout, scanning the place as they inched forward. A typical convenience store, it had a few touristy elements—Arizona magnets, key chains, postcards, even little cactuses. A display of travel brochures sat near the front door. Wishing this was a vacation instead of a stakeout, Grace reached for a brochure called *Guide to Havasu Canyon*, hoping it might say something about the Havasupai Reservation. When she pulled it out, she almost

dropped everything in her hands to the floor. On the front cover was the waterfall from her dreams.

KEVIN

As I dial Lewis, it occurs to me; maybe Grace's phone isn't the only one that's been hacked. How else would Anton constantly be able to escape detection while he's literally under our noses? Either that or he's got somebody on the inside at the FBI.

But how could a small-time hood like Anton have connections at the FBI? To be safe, I call Lewis' office instead of his cell. As soon as he picks up, those are the first two questions I ask him: could Anton be paying off an agent, and has Lewis ever left his cell phone unattended in public.

Lewis' answers are curt. "Absolutely not to the first question. Everybody here is above reproach. As far as the hacking question, can it be done remotely?"

"I don't think so. They probably need to have the phone in hand."

"Most of us keep our phones on us all the time. I know I do."

"Never left it on a bar or a table in a restaurant for a few minutes? That's all they'd need."

Lewis sounds impatient. "I can't say *never*. I guess the techies will need to look at all our phones."

"Don't do anything yet. Right now, he's priding himself that he's ten steps ahead of us and that we're a bunch of screwups. If we play this right, it might give us an advantage."

Once I tell Lewis my plan, he's completely on board. He says he'll contact the tribal police in Supai. "What else do you need?"

"If and when we get there, we'll need undercover people in Supai already."

"Done."

"I know *my* phone isn't hacked, so you can call me anytime. Just do it from a landline. If I'm with Grace, just know I'm not gonna say much."

"Okay, but I want to be kept informed. Touch base with me on your way into the reservation. And be careful."

I get out of the bathroom to find that Grace is still waiting in line to pay for our stuff. As soon as I see her, I know something's wrong because her face is ashen, and she can barely get her words out.

She hands me a brochure. "It's the place."

A bright trifold has a full-page picture of an enormous waterfall spilling into a turquoise blue lake surrounded by brick-red soil—exactly where we're headed.

GRACE

Kevin grabbed Grace by the arm and hustled her out of the store. "We've already been away from the phones too long."

"I guess we shouldn't talk about the waterfall if Anton and his buddies are listening, right?"

Kevin nodded. "Right. The dreams and visions are warnings. Nobody besides us should know about that."

"But we told Lewis James about them already."

"Yeah, but we can trust him."

"I hope so," Grace murmured.

As they drove, she poured over the brochure. Havasu Falls was one of the main tourist attractions of the Havasupai reservation. Thousands of campers and hikers traveled there every year to see the blue-green water. In fact, the word Havasupai meant *People of the blue-green waters*. The falls looked spectacular but treacherous.

Grace borrowed Kevin's phone and browsed the reservation's website to learn as much as she could about the place. It was a remote, fragile environment where the river was subject to flash flooding during the rainy season. The falls made it lush and beautiful in spots, but the rocky descent to the village could be deadly. She felt both exhilarated and terrified, knowing this was where she'd been headed from the beginning.

KEVIN

After fifteen minutes of zipping through the back streets of Phoenix, I turn off the radio. "We need to check out of the new hotel," I say to Grace, using quote signs with my fingers so she knows we're headed to the bungalow. "No use keeping our rooms if we're going to stay in Supai for a few days."

"Are we gonna be roughing it? Because, you know, I'm a city girl."

"An eight-mile hike from the trailhead. I don't know, is that roughing it?"

"It says in this brochure that they also have a helicopter that flies in and out twice a day. Can't we do that instead?"

"You got three hundred and fifty bucks to drop for no reason?"

"No reason? My health and welfare is no reason?"

"If your sister can do it, I'm sure you can too."

"Have you forgotten that we've been raised a little differently?"

While she's talking, her phone rings. Pulling it out of her purse, she shows me that it's Mama B. "Here," she tosses it to me like it's a hot potato. "You talk to her."

I say hello, trying to think out the conversation three steps ahead. I wish we had called her on my phone so only one side of the conversation would be available to Anton—if he's listening..

"Hi Mama B, this is Kevin Jacobs. We met on Saturday. I know you were returning Grace's call, but she handed me the phone. How are you?"

"Not so good, Mr. Jacobs. My Robin isn't home yet from her grandparents. I expected her hours ago."

"She hasn't called you?"

"She left a message on the home phone while I was at work saying she had a few things to do and would get back to me later. I tried calling her, but her phone goes right to voicemail. I don't know if she's out of range or just not picking up."

"I'm sure she's fine. Would you please tell her to call me when you hear from her again?"

Grace motions for me to give her the phone, and they have a brief conversation. "Don't worry about anything, Mama B. We're heading up to Supai. If she's still there, we'll let you know and make sure she gets home safely."

Her tone is comforting and compassionate. I wish I had that trait, making people comfortable just with my voice.

She hangs up and stores the phone in her purse. I give her a thumbs-up.

We park in front of the bungalow, and I motion for her to leave her phone in the car but to bring Brandi's in so we can have Dave check it. If it's really Brandi's, he should be able to pull up any data we couldn't find and then disable it in a way that will make it look like it just ran out of a charge. I just hope Grace is up to the ruse. She's looking more frayed by the minute.

XXXIII

GRACE

Grace's throat tightened with anxiety as she entered the safe house. Jenny was clearly giving her the stink eye. Kevin explained their plan to her and Dave while Grace went to throw some clothes into a backpack. When Kevin finished, Grace approached Jenny. Stumbling over her words, she apologized for ditching her at Walmart, but Jenny was pure ice.

"Right," she said, then turned and walked away.

Dave gave Grace a sympathetic look. "She'll get over it," he whispered. She's up for a promotion, and you made her look bad."

"If it's any consolation," Grace said in her direction, "I'm not normally like this, running away, taking crazy risks. It's like all the rules have changed now that I'm worried about bad guys, a missing sister, and the FBI. Back home, I'm just a simple New Yorker living what used to be a very dull life."

Dave nodded. "I get it. People are thrown by the intrigue, by our bizarre protocols. I just wish you had spoken up about your fears. We're trained to help you through it."

"I didn't realize I was having a problem until I just decided to take off. I suppose that probably happens too."

"Yeah, but when it does, somebody usually ends up getting hurt."

Grace leafed through a magazine, trying to stay out of Jenny's way while she waited for Kevin to get ready. He eventually emerged from his room with his backpack.

"Let me see what you're carrying, 'cause we're going to be hiking for a long time."

Since Grace wasn't above pleading, she said to Dave, "Doesn't it make more sense for us to fly into Supai in a helicopter instead of hiking in?"

"That would be up to the boss. I'd call him."

"Do it, Kevin! I'm sure Anton will have money to fly in. That means if Brandi's there, he'll have access to her before we do. That could be dangerous."

"So, now you're making it about her instead of the sweat quotient?"

"Kevin, that's not it!"

Jenny walked into the living room, making eye contact with Kevin, not Grace. "She's right. Save a few bucks, and it might cost you a life."

"Thanks," Grace said, knowing that Jenny certainly wasn't worried about her comfort.

Jenny's remark seemed to convince Kevin to call Lewis and get the okay. When he hung up, he said, "They're gonna have a pilot meet us at the trailhead, but it'll be early, probably before five AM."

"I can live with that," Grace said.

Jenny managed to nod in their direction as they left.

KEVIN

When we get to the car, for Anton's benefit, we talk about where we're going, leaving out the part that we're taking a helicopter. Then we settle into an uncomfortable silence.

"You wanna listen to music? It looks like this car has satellite radio."

Grace nods. "Sure."

"Any particular kind?"

"You choose. I'm probably going to take a nap."

I can't tell if she's serious or just trying not to talk. Either way it suits me. Conversation is way more taxing when you think someone is listening. I put on some mild Salsa music without cranking it up to my normal volume. She puts her seat back and closes her eyes.

She's like that for almost the whole three-hour trek. By now, without the cloud cover we have back east, the stars are out. It's so stark and glittery with the moon backlighting the mountains that I'm tempted to wake her up and share it, but I don't.

It's hard not to watch her sleep. It's the first time I've seen her when her face isn't distorted by anxiety. Her lips are slack, her eyebrows un-furrowed, her lashes resting on her cheeks like a child. For the first time I realize how vulnerable she is, how much she's depending on me to pull this whole thing off. One thing I know for sure. I never, ever want to see her hurt or betrayed, a feeling that's unfamiliar and gut-twisting.

We drive up I-17, turn onto I-40, and by about 11:00 PM get to our hotel in Seligman, the historic beginning of Route 66. After I nudge her awake, she stumbles, disheveled and incoherent, toward our rooms.

Before I turn in, I call the helicopter company. The guy on call says that the pilot will meet us at the landing pad on Hualapai Hilltop at 5:00 AM tomorrow. I have a hard time getting to sleep. When I do, I dream of falling out of the sky.

XXXIV

GRACE

Blue water was all around. Deafening noise. The water was only up to her knees, but Grace was scared of drowning. She sensed movement behind her, but before she could turn to look, someone pushed her head underwater. She fought and thrashed for as long as she could, but it was no use. Bubbles swirled around her head, and she resigned herself to death. Then there was pounding, like someone operating a jackhammer on the road.

She opened her eyes, her heart racing. Someone was pounding on the door. On shaky legs, she stumbled out of bed to look through the peephole at a wide-angle view of Kevin grinning. When she opened the door, it banged against the chain. "What do you want?"

"Time to get up."

"It's the middle of the night."

"Yup, four AM. The trailhead is an hour away. We've gotta get going."

"You could've called," she grumbled.

He chuckled. "We're on the down low, remember?"

Grace shut the door in his face and got dressed. When she appeared in the lobby, fifteen minutes later, he handed her a cup of coffee he had made in his room. "It's watery and lukewarm, but it's got caffeine."

They walked through the unlit parking lot in the dark, hanging onto each other and trying not to trip in any of the football-size holes in the dirt. Once they were in the car, it felt like it was still the night before. They sipped their muddy coffees in silence while they drove to the Havasupai Trailhead.

When they arrived, Kevin motioned Grace to get out of the car with her phone in her backpack so he could call Lewis James. He was obviously irritated when he caught up to her moments later.

"No point worrying about your phone anymore. There's absolutely no cell service here."

"So, you don't know if Lewis sent in backup?"

"Nope. And according to my research, Supai only has part-time tribal police who usually don't stay overnight in the village."

"Who handles crime at night?"

"I have no idea."

He swore when he stubbed his toe on a rock in the dark. Pulling out his phone flashlight to read the signs, he saw one that said *Heli pad* with an arrow pointing to a set of stairs cut out of the stone on the canyon side of the parking lot.

Kevin helped Grace down to a broad shelf in the mountain. They could barely see him, but a pilot was walking around a little orange and white helicopter doing the aeronautic equivalent of kicking the tires. They were almost upon him when he turned around and jumped.

"Oh man, don't sneak up on a guy like that." With a grin he pumped Kevin's hand. "Morning. I'm Joe."

"Thanks for coming out this early, Joe," Kevin said.

"Yeah, usually I don't start until ten, but your boy, Lewis, said you wanted to get an early start."

Joe pulled two folded-up pictures of Kevin and Grace from his shirt pocket. "When he paid for your tickets, he faxed me these." His hoarse laugh turned into a cough. "I think he was worried someone would try to impersonate you."

Joe gave Kevin a business card. "The pick-up is at the Tourism Office near the café. Anybody else who wants a ride outta town has to leave before dark, but since you're cops, I can come get you anytime."

Grace grinned at being called a cop as Joe helped her into the helicopter, a little four-seater job. As they strapped in, he said, "You guys are in luck. You're going to get to see the sun come up."

Once airborne, they saw a line of purple in the east widen and gradually brighten into pink and gold. As they elevated over the canyon walls they were met by a blinding, orange sun. Joe took a pass by the falls, all three of them. Grace grabbed her brochure and pointed out the names to Kevin. Mooney Falls was the one usually pictured in the travel brochures. It was very narrow, dropping 200 feet—higher than Niagara. New Navajo Falls, to its west, poured out over lush overgrowth. Grace was most curious about Havasu Falls, which was closest to the village, because that was the one, she'd seen in her dreams.

At about 100 feet high, it was an aquamarine sheet of water pouring from a red bluff into a series of plunge pools. When the sunlight hit the water, it looked like an iridescent light show, streaming and bouncing down the cliffs. The travel brochures were completely unable to capture the water's color. It was as turquoise as the gemstone and completely awe-inspiring. No wonder Robin came here to recharge. It was like stepping into heaven.

As they approached the village, they passed corn crops, peach trees, and horses in corrals. Two odd rock formations towered above the highest cliff, looking like soldiers guarding the canyon. But getting closer, the sense of awe evaporated.

Below was a run-down, little town, scattered with rust-colored, clapboard houses. A grocery store, café, and tourist center made up the center of the town, each building more ramshackle than the next. Parked outside the hotel were a dozen or so golf carts— apparently the only mode of transportation besides horses. Only the school didn't look like a picture taken in the 1950s. Because it was so early, there were only one or two houses with lights on and not a single person anywhere.

Surprisingly, the ride took less than ten minutes, a far cry from hiking for eight hours. Kevin slid open the door of the helicopter just before they landed, so a cloud of dust enveloped them. The natural beauty of the land sharply contrasted with the reality of humans eking out an existence: poverty within paradise. Maybe the people in Supai would view New York City the same way—a grimy trap alongside the stunning skyscrapers and the magic of Broadway.

As they landed, the dirt kicked up into a cloud of grit that Grace could taste in her mouth.

KEVIN

I grab Grace's hand to help her out of the copter, and we're off the landing pad walking toward the café before Joe shouts goodbye. Brushing the red dust off my shirt, I open the door and follow her inside.

We enter a large, empty room housing a dozen picnic tables. There are some donuts, bagels, hardboiled eggs, and fruit set out on a counter next to a pot of coffee. A native man with a wizened face and long, Willie Nelson braids appears from a room behind the counter. He starts putting out granola bars and cold cereal.

"Everybody still asleep?" I ask.

"Yep," he says, pulling out jelly packets and sugar from a cupboard under the counter.

"Do a lot of people stay here at the inn?"

"It's full right now."

"I guess they're the ones who don't want to rough it at the campgrounds, huh?"

He says nothing.

Grace tries to put cold cream cheese on a bagel. It stays in a big mound and tears up the bread.

"Do you know the Blackbears?"

"Ponah and Howi?" He motions to his left. "They're down the road. Number twenty-two."

I glance at my watch which reads five-thirty. "What do you think, Grace? Is it too early to pay the Blackbears a visit?"

Grace chuckles.

"Well then, what do you want to do next?"

"How far is the hike to Havasu falls?"

I turn to our new friend and ask.

"Two miles down the road."

Grace slides off her chair. "Let's go."

She finishes her bagel while I buy four bottles of water and a few snacks. We pass Ponah and Howi's house on our way toward the falls, but nobody's stirring inside. There are sparse trees here and there, lots of cactus and lots of red dust. The dirt road has no tire tracks.

Grace kicks up dust as she walks. "It's weird to be in a place without cars."

I can already feel sweat pouring down the middle of my back. I don't want to think about what it will be like at noon. "Tell me again why we're here," I whine.

Grace pulls her hair up into a ponytail. "It's a vacation, courtesy of the Federal Bureau of Investigation."

As we walk over the river on a rickety wooden footbridge, we start to hear the genuine roar of water blasting through the canyon. Grace grins and starts running down the path. We turn a corner and there it is, one hundred feet of pounding water.

Since we're both wearing shorts and water sandals, we dump our backpacks on the shore and stride into the water which is icy cold. We're able to wade out quite far before the lake descends into deep plunge pools and scattered mineral plateaus. By the time we're up to our knees, I notice a change in Grace. She gets wobbly and pale. "Are you okay?" I ask, grabbing her arm.

She nods, but I know she's not.

I walk her back to shore where she collapses onto the red gravel. "What's happening?"

She takes a deep breath. "Panic. I'm having trouble breathing." She puts her icy, trembling hands on mine. "Do you think you could say a little prayer for me?"

"Uh—I'm sorry?"

Her eyes tear up. "It's just, I'm so afraid something bad is gonna happen."

"Or not."

She doesn't respond.

"Grace, I would pray with you, but I'm not sure how to. What you fear may not even happen."

As soon as I say it, I know that's only an excuse. I just don't want to talk to God. I could do the little condescending *there, there* for her sake, but I don't want to. My face reddens as her eyes bore into me. "Besides," I say with a half-laugh, "God's not gonna listen to me. In His book, let's face it, I'm a jerk."

"No, you're not." Her blue eyes are wide and childlike.

"Come on, Grace. By now you must know I have a ton of anger, and I can't forgive people."

She puts her hand on her chest. Her breath is ragged. "You just have to work through that." She gasps and gulps air.

"If I even want to."

"You've just got issues, like everyone else."

She stops talking and tries to slow down her breathing.

I wish what she thought was true. I shake my head and grin. "I can't pray for you, but I can listen."

She nods, grabs both of my hands and closes her eyes. We sit like that for a while. It feels good to hold her hands, smooth and cool from being in the water. But I don't want to be thinking about her when we're supposed to be praying, so I focus on the top of the waterfall.

I can't imagine how awesome the view must be from a hundred feet above the canyon. It's too bad nobody can hike to the summit. Numerous signs say the rocks are unstable, so the area is completely blocked off. But now it looks like something is stirring up there. Maybe it's a coyote or a wild goat. *Watch out little guy; don't go near the edge!*

I try to focus on the few words Grace is praying since I told her

I'd listen, but I'm mesmerized by the movement at the top of the falls. I don't think it's anything four-footed. There's red on it, so maybe it's a wild turkey, a really huge one.

It ventures out onto a precipice to the left of the falls.

It's a person—a person wearing a red shirt—a woman.

And it looks a lot like Brandi.

XXXV

GRACE

She knew it was dumb to ask Kevin to pray, because if he had ever had any faith, by his own confession, it was in the toilet. But hers wasn't much better. She was choking on anxiety. The fact that they were stranded in a beautiful, treacherous place wasn't helping.

But she just needed somebody to hear her prayer and amen it. She didn't speak immediately after grabbing Kevin's hands, but then she said out loud, "God, help us find Brandi. Keep her safe from Anton. Help us get out of here in one piece. We wanna go home, God. Amen."

KEVIN

Could it be? Even though it's far away and the sun is practically blinding me, I'm almost sure it's her. But what is she doing? Why is she alone and putting herself in such obvious danger?

She comes out onto the ledge and looks around, as if satisfying herself that she's alone. Then she inches closer to the edge of the falls. Suddenly, she slips, landing on her back. A few rocks break off and plummet into the pounding spray 100 feet below.

I squeeze Grace's hand hard until she opens her eyes. "Look," I say, pointing to the figure.

She squints and stares as she stands up. "Is that—"
"Yes!"

"Why is she up there?"

"I think she's planning to jump."

"But she'll be killed!"

Instead of responding, I take off into the water. Grace is right behind me. Both of us try to yell but we can barely hear ourselves above the roar of the falls.

"Oh, God," I say, suddenly not ashamed to pray, "don't let her…"

But it's too late. She drops off the cliff feet first. Five seconds later she disappears into the pounding spray.

GRACE

As soon as she saw Brandi at the top of the falls, all the pictures of the last month came tumbling out like a movie on fast forward. She knew Brandi was going to jump.

Kevin jumped into the water, and she was right behind him, slapping the water with clumsy strokes. Brandi came down like a boulder dropped from a cliff and disappeared under the water instantly.

Grace pounded her way toward the falls, but couldn't see anything above the spray of her own thrashing.

Take a deep breath, she heard.

A deep breath? Then a scene with her old voice teacher flashed into her mind. *You've got the best breath control of any of my students. Your lungs must be a third bigger than anyone else's.*

Take a deep breath.

She took a huge breath and dove down.

KEVIN

I look behind me but don't see Grace anymore. *Where is she? God, I can't lose them both.* I just keep swimming as hard as I can, but I'm not a stronger swimmer. I didn't learn until I was an adult. Swim classes, another thing Dad nixed.

I keep pushing on toward the falls until the spray raining down on me feels like a million tiny needles. I try to judge where Brandi might have fallen, but the swirling current could have taken her anywhere. *Why God?* I scream inside my head.

The next thing I know, I'm caught in a massive vortex pulling on my legs. I take a deep breath and get sucked under the falls.

GRACE

When Grace went underwater, everything quieted down. She could see the blue-green bubbles floating up and felt like she was being propelled without any effort. But to where?

She let the current pull her and tried to remain calm, believing she would have the air she needed to find Brandi. But then she got a glimpse of Kevin.

What was he doing? His arms were flailing and yet he just kept going down. Grace swam after him, but the water was getting darker the deeper she dove, and she had lost sight of him. She just tried to swim in his general direction when she felt something brush past her.

Brandi?

Grace could see she was floating—like she'd gotten knocked out by her fall.

She took off after Brandi. But what about Kevin? How could she reach them both?

KEVIN

My lungs are bursting and still I'm going down. What was I thinking, jumping into the water like I was some kind of lifeguard? Ten-year-olds swim better than I do. And now, the big, tough New York detective is gonna drown, because, like a fool he tried to save someone else. Real smart.

That thing about your life flashing before you—it's true.

Everything slows down. I keep thinking, *I just wanted to tell her
I love her.*

GRACE

She didn't want to make the decision, but she had to. It was
instinctive, automatic. *Brandi's why I'm here. I was the reason she
was kidnapped. I have to make it right.*

She spun around and headed toward where Brandi had floated
by, reaching out her hands and swinging them, wildly, in every
direction. She couldn't hold her breath anymore, so she kicked her
way to the surface, took a deep gulp of air and went back down.

When she did, she bumped into a spongy, red thing, a red thing
with arms. She grabbed at it, but it swooshed away. She kicked
her feet and tried again. She managed to grab a handful of hair.

With her lungs bursting, she heaved herself upwards towards
the light. When she hit the surface of the water, she gulped a huge
mouthful of air. With Brandi's head in the crook of her elbow, she
swam as fast as she could toward shore.

She didn't go far before hitting the ledge of a limestone plateau.
She pushed Brandi forward, heaved her halfway up onto the hard
surface, and then climbed out on the terrace herself. Hooking her
hands under Brandi's arms, she dragged her completely out of the
water, dreading the worst. When she accidently dropped her onto
the ledge, Brandi screamed out in pain and started retching water.
The disgusting sounds were glorious.

But Grace didn't have time to help Brandi or even introduce herself. She jumped back in the water and swam toward where she saw
Kevin go under. Taking a huge breath, she dove down. The minerals
stung her eyes and made the water cloudy. She couldn't see him.
She surfaced, breathed and screamed as loud as she could, "Kevin!"

No answer. Down she went again, but desperation and fatigue
were taking control. Her arms and legs felt like cement. How could
this be? How could she have sacrificed him to save her?

Each time she surfaced and yelled out his name, she could see Brandi lying on the limestone terrace. *I saved someone who wants to die instead of someone who wants to live. How could it turn out like this?*

Dread inched up from her gut, but she pushed it away and swam closer to the falls. Still, she couldn't get through them. Even underwater, the falls felt like getting pelted by rocks. She tried to skirt around them, going deeper each time she dove. Her underwater vision was terrible because the water was so turbulent. Up to the surface, she'd breathe, shout his name, and dive down again. Twice. Three times. Four times. She stopped counting but kept diving.

KEVIN

He saved others, but he can't save himself.
 Your billows swept over me.
 Forgive us our trespasses as we—
 He saved others, but he can't save himself.
I'm five years old, and my dad's standing over me with a belt, my mom grabbing his arm. Cassie is crying in the other room; the dog is barking.

"No, John," my mother cries.

"Get away," he shouts, pushing her hard.

When I pee my pants, the belt hurts worse. The buckle catches my shoulder on the last whack. Then I'm floating and my shoulder slams against a wall, a rough wall made of stone. Frantically, I reach out, claw at it and swim up, pushing myself higher off each jutting ledge until, finally—air!

I don't know how, but I'm alive. The sound of the falls is deafening. I can't figure out where I am. Then it dawns on me—I'm *behind* the falls. I try to climb up onto the ledge but my left shoulder aches so bad it takes me four tries. Then in the distance—

"Kevin!"

"Grace," I call out. Not sure that she can hear me, I call again and again as loud as I can, "Grace!"

GRACE

She heard her name but couldn't tell where it was coming from. *Wishful thinking?* Her arms and legs felt like jelly. She half dog-paddled, half floated toward another limestone shelf twirling around a dozen times to see if he was in the water. Then she caught sight of Brandi, far away, standing up and pointing to the falls. Again, she heard her name. She stared into the falls and saw someone walking.

Walking?

She got to the little plateau and tried to climb up on it, but her arms and legs were so tired, she could only hold on, trying to catch her breath. She didn't know how long she hung on there, but eventually someone was beside her.

It was Brandi.

She didn't do anything. She just stayed by Grace's side. "He's behind the falls," Brandi said. "He's safe."

KEVIN

It takes me a while, crawling along the rock face, to get to a place where I can drop down into the water without getting pounded to death by the falls. Grace and Brandi are maybe seventy-five feet away from where I am. It's impossible for me to use my left arm to swim, so I lean to my right side, doing a one-stroke, floating combination.

It's slow going, but I'm getting there. I can see them side by side bobbing in the water, holding onto the ledge and each other. Brandi's red shirt is the only way I can tell them apart.

GRACE

When Kevin got to them, Grace realized he was having as much trouble as Brandi—something with his shoulder which was scraped and bloody beneath his torn shirt. She was eventually able to pull herself onto the limestone ledge in the middle of the lake, but neither of them could do the same.

So they floated there, both of them holding onto the ledge with one hand. How could she get them to shore safely? Her mind shuffled through a dozen scenarios, but taking them one at a time was the only thing that made sense. Only Brandi wasn't going to be safe no matter what she did. Wanting to kill yourself was nowhere near safe.

Brandi's vacant eyes were so sad, so tortured. At least Grace could get her where she wouldn't just float away to die. Kevin's voice jarred her. "Help Brandi get to shore."

"Is that okay?" Grace asked her sister, sliding off the terrace into the water.

Brandi nodded.

Grace slipped her arm around Brandi's waist and swam her towards the shore. Brandi didn't resist, neither did she help. She was just—resigned. Grace found herself praying with every stroke. *We were this close in the womb, God. Take some of my hope and faith and put it into her. Let her feel how loved she is.*

When they got to wading depth, Grace helped Brandi up so that she could walk. For the first time she saw that Brandi was covered in scrapes and bruises. Her arm was crooked, and she was using her opposite hand to support it.

Brandi stumbled a few times, but Grace managed to grab her before she hit the ground. Each time she did, Brandi would cry out in pain. Finally, they found a patch of grass, and Grace helped her sit down.

She then turned to go help Kevin, but saw that he was already wading toward them. Grace ran to him, and he put his arm on her shoulder, leaning on her as he half-stumbled, half-walked.

When they got to Brandi, they both fell down like they'd swum a marathon. They were about eighty yards from where Kevin and

Grace had started out, so once she caught her breath, Grace walked to the place where they had left their stuff, gathered it up, and tried to hurry back.

She twisted open a bottle of water and gave it to Brandi. After she'd taken a few long gulps, she handed it back to Grace, all the while staring at her. Without warning, she started sobbing. Grace didn't bring any tissues in her backpack, but she still had the napkins from breakfast, so she handed them to Brandi.

"You want some water?" she asked Kevin.

"No thanks, I think I've swallowed enough for a lifetime."

None of them talked while Brandi sat, crying into the napkins, her shoulders shaking. Eventually Grace asked gently, "What's going on with your arm? What can I do to help?"

"It's not my arm," Brandi said. "It's my collarbone. I broke it in the accident, and now it's worse."

"Would it help to put your arm in a sling? I've got an extra t-shirt we could use."

Brandi nodded, so Grace went to work tearing her shirt into two long strips. She tied them together around Brandi's neck and gently helped her put her arm into the sling. Brandi thanked her with her eyes.

Grace turned her attention to Kevin who was obviously in terrible pain. "Is it broken?" she asked, pointing to his shoulder.

"No. When I slammed into the canyon wall, it got dislocated. It used to happen when I was a kid. I can pop it back in, but I need help to do it."

Grace forced back squeamish thoughts. "Tell me what to do."

He started to stand up, but he couldn't do it alone, so she pulled him up by his other arm. "Just hold onto me so I can stay steady," he said. I have to bend all the way back to do this."

While Grace supported him, he let his arm hang down. Then he arched his back and let his arm twist around toward his back. With a violent motion, he swung his shoulder and arm up. It took a few excruciating tries, but eventually, his arm hung normal again.

"That's it?" she asked. "You're all right now?"

He winced. "Not exactly. It'll be sore for a week, but at least I can use it."

"Thank you," Brandi said, in a small voice. "You both almost got killed trying to save me. I thought nobody would be here at this hour. I'm so sorry."

Grace wasn't sure what to do next. She didn't know Brandi at all. Just because they had the same genes, she was tempted to say the kind of things that would make her feel better, but she realized that might be a mistake. She hadn't lived Brandi's life. How could she know how she felt? But she wanted to understand.

"Why Brandi? Why did you jump?"

Brandi was quiet for a few moments then said, "My life is a lie. What's the point?"

XXXVI

KEVIN

This doesn't fit into the plan at all. I was prepared in the event that we might never find Grace's twin, or that she wouldn't want to know Grace, or that someone would try to keep them apart. But I never thought that I'd have to deal with some unstable, suicidal girl.

What now? Get her to a hospital—a shrink? Take her back to the Heisman's, Mama B, her friends, anyone who could talk some sense into her? I've worked on psych cases before, but not with someone who seemed totally normal and then tried to jump off a 100-foot waterfall.

I know I'm over my head, so I do the only thing that makes sense to me: get moving. "I think we'd better head back to town—get Brandi looked at, and figure out what we're gonna do next."

"Is that okay?" Grace asks Brandi whose face is back in the napkins.

It takes her a while to respond, but finally she blows her nose and says, "I need to go back to the Blackbear's. Robin will be looking for me soon, if she isn't already."

Grace nods. "All right, let me help you up."

Brandi pushes herself up off the ground with her good arm with Grace leaning in to steady her. Then Grace shoulders both our backpacks.

"Whoa, I can carry my own," I say.

"I think you should help Brandi instead. The ground is uneven and there's that rickety bridge."

We walk back to town together. It makes me sad that our journey is coming to an end, because I've felt more alive in the past few weeks than I have in years. This girl has gotten to me, and I don't want to let her go.

GRACE

Grace was having trouble walking ever since she'd gotten out of the water. Somewhere, while she was swimming, she had slammed her foot into a rock. It hadn't hurt much while she was in the cold water, but now, with every step, a burning pain was shooting from her ankle up through her calf. She walked behind Brandi and Kevin so they wouldn't notice. There were already enough injuries in this party. Beyond that, her heart was breaking for Brandi. She kept searching for the right thing to do or say, but she was drawing a blank. Sharing a womb together for nine month more than two decades ago didn't help her know how to comfort this stranger— this stranger who was alive, but just barely.

If I ever get my hands on Lena, she thought, *I will choke the life out of her! It's her fault that Brandi's a mess.* She longed to see Brandi return to that confident girl who performed at the Black Swan— that girl that was so filled with fun and hope—and music. Lena had set her up for this misery the moment she stole her from the hospital. It was one thing to have some jerk like Anton on the outside threaten you. It was something else when family betrayed you.

But while she was savoring her righteous indignation, a dark thought squeezed in. *You did this, Grace. If you hadn't shown up, she never would have known. She would have been able to live out her life in unsuspecting ignorance. If anyone's to blame for what just happened, it's you.*

She tried to push the thought away, but it seemed to scream louder with every painful step. *Grace, the protector? What a joke.*

You couldn't save Mimi. Her career is ruined. You thought coming here would "save" Brandi? You made her try to kill herself. Kevin just almost drowned! No one is safe around you!

"I think we need to stop for a few minutes," Kevin said, pointing to a picnic table a few yards away.

"Good idea," Grace said, dumping the backpacks on the table.

She sat down, glad to take weight off her foot. They passed the water bottle around. "That's the Blackbear's house," Brandi said, pointing to number 22 up the road.

Just what I need, Grace thought, *to meet more strangers.*

As if reading her thoughts, Brandi said, "You'll like them. They're beautiful people."

From the corner of her eye, Grace could see Kevin give her a once over, his gaze resting on her foot. "What did you do to yourself? Your ankle is huge."

"It's fine," Grace said, but when she tried to swing it up to look at it, she could barely stand the pain.

Brandi examined it too. "It may be broken, or at least severely sprained. You shouldn't be walking."

"We're a screwed-up bunch," Grace said, grimacing.

"Maybe I should go on ahead to see if the Blackbears have something to carry you on," Kevin said.

"That's all right. I can make it there."

Ignoring me, Kevin turned to Brandi, "Do you mind staying with her?"

"No."

As he stood to leave, Brandi put her hand on his arm. "Do you think we can keep what happened back there between us? I know it was an impulsive, stupid thing to do. I don't know what I was thinking."

Kevin glanced at Grace, looking for guidance, but she was in too much pain to think clearly. "I'll agree to that," he said, "if you'll agree to talk to somebody when we get out of here."

"I promise, I will," she said. "I'll probably tell my friend Robin

anyway, but I just don't want to make it a big deal and get everybody involved."

"It *was* a big deal," Kevin said.

"I'll talk to a shrink, really. God knows I need one."

Kevin pointed to all our scrapes and bruises. "How will we explain these injuries?"

"We went under the falls and got knocked around," she said.

"With our clothes on?"

"People do it."

He looked at her doubtfully, but then shrugged and set off for the Blackbear's.

Brandi handed Grace back the water bottle, and they sat without speaking for a while, the birds squawking around their heads. Grace noticed Brandi was staring at her. "What's going on?" Brandi asked.

"Nothing, just hurting a bit."

"I don't know if this is a twin thing or just natural intuition, but I'm pretty sure you're lying."

Grace laughed, and Brandi smiled too. "You remind me of my sister," Grace said, "*our* sister. She always wants to see my face when we talk about rough things because she believes she can *read my eyes*."

"What's her name?"

"Mimi."

"That's sweet. How old is she?"

"Seventeen. She's graduating high school next week."

"Well, she's right. Your voice sounds all upbeat, but you look terrible."

Grace's eyes welled up with tears, with one sliding down her cheek. "If you had died back there, it would've been my fault."

Brandi didn't say anything for a while. She just picked lint off the only dry thing on her body, Grace's ripped-up t-shirt sling. "Why do you say that?"

"If I'd never come here, and you'd never found out about me, you'd just be your regular self, without any cares."

"You think I lived a carefree life until you came along?" Brandi shook her head and chuckled. "Are all New Yorkers that naïve?"

"I saw you that night at the Black Swan, up on stage, singing and playing. You looked happy."

"You did, huh? Well, maybe Mimi needs to teach *you* how to read eyes. My mom's an alcoholic, the band is always fighting, I can't pay my bills, I just broke up with my drug dealing boyfriend. Yeah, my life is peachy."

"But finding out your mom kidnapped you couldn't have made it better."

"No. But that's on her," she said, staring off into the trees.

"There were a lot of things that drove me to find you, Brandi, things that would take too long to go into right now, but besides all of that, I think I was being selfish."

"It's selfish to try to find your twin sister?"

"Well, yeah, if you don't stop to think how it all might play out."

"I would've done the same thing."

When Grace didn't say anything, she went on. "Look, there's a lot you don't know about me. I'm not the chill, happy-go-lucky type. I've been suicidal before. I've got scars up and down my arms from cutting myself in middle school. Smoked weed up to a year ago. I haven't exactly been a *good girl*. But when I lost my best friend over Anton, when I saw how he was preying on the Native kids, I started to get mad. I started to clean up my act."

She shifted in pain, trying to adjust her sling. "Having the car accident really shook me up. Then when Kevin told me all that stuff about my mother, it just kinda threw me over the top, so I took off."

Her eyes darkened as she looked into Grace's. "Robin and I got here late last night. I couldn't sleep because of childhood memories that kept popping up in my head—memories that started to take on new meaning. By the time the sun came up, I was a basket case. I wasn't planning to jump. I just wanted to find some peace. But then—I can't describe it—the thought came in. It was almost comical, in a sick kind of way. Sort of, *it'll serve her right to live with this.* As soon as I jumped, I regretted it. That's me. Jump first, think after. In that split second, I knew hurting her by hurting myself meant I was still paying the price. Thank God you guys were there. That's all I can say."

"You believe in God?"

"Yeah, sort of. I'm surrounded by all kinds of Christian-types, the Blackbears, Robin. They're always praying over me and such. I guess you two showing up at the falls proves that God is at least somewhat interested in helping me."

Grace smiled. "I think He is."

They didn't say much after that, just waited for Kevin to come back. Brandi helped Grace to elevate her leg on the backpacks. After that she lay back and closed her eyes for a while. Campers started to come out of their tents, rumpled and groggy, quizzically looking at them sitting on the table in their wet clothes.

One longhaired, blond kid started talking to them, offering Grace a squashed granola bar which she declined. He seemed to want to know her life story, which she was certainly not about to share. While they were talking, he glanced at Brandi and did a double take. "Hey, you're twins!"

It was the first time anyone besides Kevin had ever seen them together. It sounded—normal. Brandi looked at Grace and grinned.

"Yes, we are."

KEVIN

When I get to the Blackbear's house, I see an old dude sporting a grey ponytail standing outside. He's petting a skinny horse who's eating out of a bucket.

"Are you Howi Blackbear?" I ask.

"Who wants to know?" he says.

"Kevin Jacobs." I hold out my hand for him to shake.

He looks me over. "You don't look so hot."

"I know. My friend and I were playing around at the falls, and we got pounded into the rocks. She's got a sprained or broken foot. I left her back there with her, uh, sister Brandi. I guess she's a friend of your granddaughter, Robin."

"We were wondering where that girl went. They came in yesterday and nobody could find her this morning. How do you know her?" he asks, clearly suspicious.

"Oh, I just met her. I'm here with her sister. We came to see her from New York."

"You came to see her *here*?"

"Yeah, well, it's a long story. But, anyway, she sent me here to get some help for Grace. That's her sister."

Howi begins to look positively menacing. "Are you that rotten boyfriend of hers?"

"No, sir, I just need some help."

He gives me another once over and goes into the shed. When he comes out, he's pushing a wheelbarrow. "The golf cart's not working. Try this."

I want to say, "You're kidding!" but think better of it. "Thank you, sir. We'll return it very soon."

Since my dislocated shoulder isn't happy about pushing it empty, I can't imagine how I'm going to push it with Grace inside. But as I walk back, I try to review my strategy. I need to get the girls back to the trailhead, see what kind of medical help Grace needs, and cash in on Brandi's promise to talk to a shrink. Anton hasn't shown up yet. He's the wild card. But as soon as the FBI arrives, we'll be home free. Until then we should stay hidden.

I'm halfway back to the girls when I hear steps behind me. They're getting faster as they approach. My gun is in the backpack with Grace, my phone is useless, but I can still throw a mean right hook.

I drop the wheelbarrow and whirl around. It's Howi coming down the road at a trot. When he gets to me, he's wheezing, so it takes him a minute to catch his breath.

"My old lady said I need to help you. She's the boss."

"That's the best thing I've heard all day," I say.

Howi picks up the wheelbarrow as if it's a toy and pushes it alongside me. We walk in silence for a few minutes. Then he asks, "Is Brandi in some kind of trouble?"

"No, but there are some jerks who might try to hurt her—that old boyfriend you mentioned, for instance."

Howi frowns. "I just might take a shovel to his head."

I chuckle. "Not a bad idea."

Howi looks straight ahead while we're walking. "Who are you, really?"

"What do you mean?"

"You're not just the friend of a sister, or whatever you said. Who are you?"

This guy is a no-nonsense, straightforward dude, so I say, "I'm a New York City detective."

"I figured."

I smile. "How'd you know?"

"The way you hold yourself, the way you turned around when I came up behind you. It's the training. Twenty-some-odd years ago, I worked as a sheriff for the Bureau of Indian Affairs. That was before the arthritis and emphysema kicked in, and I couldn't run no more."

"Pleased to meet another officer of the law."

He grins.

"It seems like law enforcement is kinda lax out here, though."

"True. Not enough guys to be impartial cause everybody's related."

"Who's the sheriff in charge right now?"

"Jim Richards, but he's not here all the time."

"So I've heard."

"Mr. Detective, why are you *really* here?"

In the few minutes we have, I fill him in on the essentials.

He shakes his head. "Twins, eh? Pretty convincing, I guess. How's Brandi taking it?"

"Not very well. She's pretty fragile."

"That them over there?"

I spot the girls sitting at the picnic table where I left them. It looks like Grace is talking to some camper while Brandi sits off to the side watching them. "What is wrong with that girl? She's like a child who needs to be told not to talk to strangers."

Howi shakes his head. "An innocent."

When Brandi sees me, she nudges Grace and points. Then she takes off toward us. Howi puts the wheelbarrow down while she hugs him with one arm. He pats her on the back. "Okay, okay."

By the time we get to Grace, the camper has walked off. Howi does a barely perceptible double-take of the two girls. Then a slow smile spreads across his face. "We've come to fetch you. Think you can hop into this fancy transporter?"

Grace smiles and hobbles over to it, plopping her bottom into the wheelbarrow. She scoots forward so her right leg is on the ground in front. "I can use my good leg to help."

We begin our comical journey back—me with my bloody shoulder, Brandi with her homemade sling, the old man pushing, and Grace with her foot out like a clam, scooting us along.

When we get to the house, Brandi walks in first while Howi sits on a lawn chair outside to catch his breath. In a minute, Robin and the grandma come out. Robin is a beautiful girl with an athletic build, a round face, and long black hair. The grandma is wizened and stooped. She rushes over to Howi, bending down to look into his eyes. "You all right?"

He nods, breathing hard.

"I just told you to go with him, not to push the wheelbarrow. Come in out of the sun, you old goat."

Robin helps Grace who is hopping on one foot. We step into an immaculate but old-fashioned little house that smells of breakfast. There are lots of rugs and doilies, animal skins, pottery, and a huge dreamcatcher on the wall. They have air conditioning, thank God.

Robin helps Grace into a recliner and tilts it back so she can elevate her ankle. The grandma brings ice waters in on a tray. Brandi and Robin disappear into a back bedroom, which makes for some awkward conversation between Grace and me and the Blackbears.

The grandma looks Grace up and down. "My, my, I don't know who you are honey, but you gotta be related to our Brandi."

Grace grins, but as she shifts in the chair, her smile morphs into a grimace of pain.

"Something's wrong with that ankle, darlin'. I'm gonna get you some ice and one of my own concoctions to help the swelling. You'll feel a difference in no time."

"Thanks, Mrs. Blackbear."

The grandma waves her hand like she's swatting a fly. "Oh honey, call me Ponah."

I turn to Howi who is beginning to breathe normally. "Do you have a land line here?"

"Yeah, but if you're thinking of calling the sheriff, he ain't here yet. He flies in at noon."

"No, I need to speak to someone else."

"Be my guest. It's in the kitchen on the wall."

On my way into the kitchen, I meet Ponah who offers me breakfast. "Oh, thanks, but I've already eaten."

"Nonsense," she says, as she fills up a plate on the counter.

I dial Lewis' office number, but it just keeps ringing, no message, no pick up. Then I try his cell. Same story. Finally, I realize the calls are probably not going through. Nothing more to do but carry my plate into the living room and start eating.

By now, Ponah is working on Grace's ankle with her concoction, which looks like a red, mushy mud pie. Grace also has a plate of food which she is balancing on her lap, and they are talking like old friends. Howi sits in the other recliner with his eyes closed.

When Brandi and Robin come back into the living room, Brandi's eyes are red and Robin is holding her hand. Ponah, who obviously doesn't miss a trick, goes into the kitchen, brings out a cup of coffee and sets it down on the coffee table in front of Brandi. She lays her hand on top of Brandi's head for a moment, then leans down to kiss her. No words, but it's understood that she loves the kid.

Robin sits down on the coffee table and addresses her grandparents. "Brandi's gonna be leaving soon with Grace and Kevin."

Howi opens his eyes to slits. "You don't have to if you don't want to."

Robin gives him a shushing look. "Gramps."

But Brandi lays her hand on Robin's arm. "It's okay."

She turns to Howi. "I need to go with them, Gramps. We have a lot to talk about."

Ponah looks up from her work on Grace's ankle. "It's all right, honey. We understand."

Almost to herself, Brandi says, "They're telling me my mom is a freakin' liar and a criminal."

Everyone is silent for a moment. Then she adds, "Maybe she's passed on some of that to me."

Robin flings her black hair away from her face, her eyes flashing. "You're not a liar and you're definitely no criminal!"

"Really? 'Cause I've lied lots, and I hooked up with Anton even after you told me he was bad news."

Robin snickers. "That doesn't make you a criminal girl, just stupid."

"If it makes you feel any better," Grace pipes up, "I just broke up with a pretty crappy boyfriend, too."

Grace just broke up with a boyfriend? How did I not know this?

Ponah smiles as she continues to coat Grace's ankle with her slop. "Now, now, you young folk all make mistakes. Ain't that right, Howi?"

He nods solemnly, his eyes closed again.

"Maybe that's what happened to your mom. Maybe she just made a bad mistake."

There's a long silence. I, for one, don't buy that explanation, but I'm not about to get into this discussion.

Brandi looks down at the floor. "In the letter, she said she fell for the wrong guy."

"What letter?" Grace and Robin ask at the same time.

"She left me a letter in the safe at her house."

Now she has everyone's attention. Foolishly, I go into police mode. "Did she say where she was going?"

"Why do you want to know? So you can arrest her?" Brandi snarls, stomping out of the room.

When Robin tries to follow, Ponah grabs her hand. "Give her space, honey."

At this point, Howi comes to life and thrusts himself out of his recliner. As he walks out the door, I hear him mumble, "I'm going out to feed the chickens."

Ponah stands up and looks at me. "I should clean up your shoulder. If you wait much longer, it'll get infected from the algae."

She walks into the kitchen and returns with a wet towel and a pair of scissors. She cuts my sleeve vertically and gently scrubs the abrasions. Then she pats them dry and applies a smelly mixture that feels cool and prickly. Afterwards, she disappears into a back bedroom while I go back to the kitchen to try the phone again. Nobody's answering—not the pilot or Lewis. I'm about to slam the phone down when Robin walks into the kitchen with the breakfast dishes. "Hi," I say, hanging up the phone like a gentleman.

She flashes me a big, white smile and carries the teetering pile of plates to the sink.

"Uh, Grace and I met your mom a few days ago. She asked us to tell you to call."

She starts filling the sink with soapy water. "You see what the phones are like."

"Is there anywhere else in town better than here?"

"Probably the tourist center. Those lines don't go down as much."

"That's where we have to pick up the helicopter. If you're leaving soon, you're welcome to fly out with us."

"I don't have money to fly."

"Don't worry. It's on the government's dime."

She smiles as she starts to wash the dishes.

"Did Brandi tell you what happened at the falls?"

She turns to look at me, her hands covered in suds. "Yes."

"You think she's gonna be able to handle all this?"

"She's stronger than she thinks. But she doesn't like manipulation, so be honest with her."

"She probably already thinks I'm a con artist. Did she tell you I went to the store?"

"Yes. She even thought you were kinda cute, until she realized that you and Grace are an item."

I blush, wanting so much for it to be true. "We're not an item."

Robin flashes her white smile again. "Brandi's hurting, not blind."

At that moment, I hear the front door open. Poking my head through the doorway I see Howi walk into the house with three guys behind him—Anton and his two apes.

XXXVII

GRACE

"Well, whadaya know. I finally found you!"

Grace looked up into the eyes of Anton. Suddenly, the air seemed to go out of the room. Howi had an awful look on his face, his fists clenched at his side.

Anton gave Howi an unnecessary shove onto the couch. "Sit down, old man."

Anton and his boys all seemed to wear the same sneer, like little replicas of each other. "Hey baby," he said planting a hard kiss on Grace's mouth.

Grace started to speak but then stopped. Her mind raced trying to remember the southwestern lilt of Brandi's accent. *Come back vocal training!*

"What happened to you?" he asked, pointing to her foot.

"Just twisted my ankle," she said, trying to deemphasize the *k*, and lose the unconscious Brooklyn *oy*.

He tilted his head and stared at her for a second, looking like a dog who's heard a high-pitched whistle. "Where's your punk friend Robin, your twin, and the pretty boy?"

"They went to the falls," Grace said, trying to keep her answers short.

"Well, let's get going. I've got a surprise for you."

"What surprise?"

"It wouldn't be a surprise it I told you."

281

Pretending to be Brandi was a kneejerk, impulsive act, an attempt to protect her. But Grace needed to act fast before anyone came back into the living room. She took the mud pack off her ankle and stood up. To her surprise, she only felt a small twinge when she put weight on it.

She glanced toward the kitchen and saw a small patch of Kevin's shirt in the doorway. Remembering that his gun was in her backpack on the floor, she made sure not to grab it. "I'll need a little help," she said.

"I gotcha baby," Anton said as he put his arm around her waist. "Where's your stuff?"

"I didn't bring anything."

He stepped back and looked at her again, full in the face. She could see his small mind growing doubtful. "I don't remember that shirt you're wearing."

"It's Robin's."

"So, you came here without any clothes?"

"Just a little dirty laundry that I don't need. I left pretty fast. Had that cop breathing down my neck."

At that, his face turned hard. He motioned for the boys to help her. "Get her in the golf cart. I'm gonna have a look around."

He started strolling through the living room on his way to the kitchen when one of the guys said, "You want me to go to the falls?"

"Not yet. Let's check the house first."

No one knew how it happened, but at that moment Howi jumped off the couch like he was twenty-years-old and tackled Anton. The goons were so surprised it took them a few seconds to react. They let go of Grace and lunged for Howi. They grabbed him and slammed him into the china closet which rattled like all the glass was breaking. Anton started to pick himself up off the floor, cursing like crazy when Kevin charged in from the kitchen, plowing into Anton from behind. Down they both went, breaking a lamp as they fell. The other two guys turned around and started to charge Kevin. But Howi was on his feet again and body slammed them both. All three went down.

Grace stood there, frozen with fear, until she saw that in the melee her backpack had been shoved across the room close to her feet. She grabbed it and pulled out Kevin's gun. It felt so cold and ugly, she almost dropped it. But then she heard Kevin shout her name. Instinctively, she dropped the gun to the floor and kicked it over to him. Kevin grabbed the gun and shoved it into Anton's face.

"Get up!" Kevin shouted.

Anton put his hands up and slowly rose. Kevin turned his attention to the other two who were also showing him their hands. "You three get over by the door and face that wall. Now!"

With all the commotion, Ponah and Brandi dashed out of the bedroom. Howi was trying to get up off the floor. Ponah screamed his name and ran to him.

"I'm all right, woman," he said, brushing her off. But he was unsteady and had a gash over his eye.

When Anton saw Brandi, he gave a little laugh and sauntered to the wall. He still looked so cocky that Grace wanted to punch him in the mouth. Kevin kept yelling until the three of them had their hands and feet spread-eagled against the wall. "Howi, you got any rope to tie these goons up?"

Howi stumbled into the kitchen and yanked open a drawer. "Better than that."

He pulled out a handful of thick, plastic cable ties. Kevin told him to tie their hands behind their backs. Then Kevin ordered them to turn around while he searched them for weapons. They were all packing, so he dumped their ammunition on the coffee table and kicked their guns into the kitchen—except for Anton's. He kept that one loaded and stuck it into his waistband. He told Robin to grab three chairs from the kitchen and put them in the center of the living room. Then he made the prisoners sit down while Howi cable-tied their feet together.

Brandi, Robin, Ponah, and Grace stared like scared rabbits, while

Kevin barked with the authority of a military officer. This was a side of him Grace had never seen. Even Howi was precision-like in his actions. Was it possible they could kill these guys if they needed to? And how could Anton still be wearing a smirk like he wasn't really worried?

Once the guys were tied up, Kevin said to Robin, "Take the golf cart outside and drive your grandma and the girls to the café. See if you can find a phone that works."

He pulled a paper out of his pocket. "Call this number. It belongs to a federal agent. Tell him I've got Anton and need backup *now*. Then try to find someone in law enforcement. Anyone, I don't care if it's the mayor! Just get somebody down here. And call the helicopter service."

Ponah, regaining her composure, stood tall. "I'm not going anywhere."

Kevin glanced at Howi, but he just shrugged his shoulders. "All right, you can stay here, but I want the girls to go."

"I hate to leave you—" Grace started to say.

"Go!" he shouted.

Robin drove them to the center of town. She tried the door to the police station, but it was locked. Next door was the tribal office. Robin was in there for ten minutes. When she came out, she said, "They're going to send some of the tribal leaders to the house."

They went to the café and watched Robin talk to the guy who ran the place. She gave Grace and Brandi a thumbs-up and disappeared behind the counter. The clock on the wall said ten-thirty. *How could so much have happened already?* Grace wondered.

Grace sat down at the counter with Brandi. "You okay?"

Brandi gave her an ironic smile. "Sure."

"How on earth could you have dated someone like Anton?" Grace blurted out.

At first, Brandi looked defensive, but then her face softened.

"He wasn't always this way. When I was a kid, he was my protector. We both had it pretty rough. Ray was a jerk, and Anton's mother wasn't any better."

Everybody's got a backstory, Grace thought, *but still.*

Brandi brushed invisible crumbs off the counter. "What about your—our—parents?"

How could she answer that? Grace wanted to gush, *Nothing like the creeps you've known.* But then she knew Brandi didn't need any Maddox family propaganda to make her feel worse. "Our dad died from cancer when I was eighteen. He was a good guy—a musician, a little eccentric. Mom's kind of an ancient, hippie-type—over-protective, a clutter junkie. She's an art teacher."

Brandi, who'd been staring out the window, turned to face her sister. "That's cool. I'm minoring in fine art."

"She used to do shows before Dad died, but then she got too into us—Mimi, really, with her schedule."

"What kind of schedule? What does Mimi do?"

At that moment, all Grace's grief about Mimi came flooding back. "Uh, she plays the violin."

She couldn't say more than that. But Brandi, who seemed to have intuitive superpowers must have picked up on something. "Is she okay?"

"She had a car accident a week ago and needs some surgery on her hands."

She nods. "That stinks. And you, what's your deal?"

"I play the piano and sing a little." Grace laughed. "The night you didn't make it to The Brass Mill, the night you had your accident? I went up there and sang. Nobody knew the difference."

Her eyes widened. "Get out."

"It's true. I asked Larry to sing lead while I did backup vocals. Of course, we just sang covers, none of your original stuff."

She shook her head. "You're a gutsy little thing, aren't you?"

"No more than you."

She frowned. "I'm not gutsy."

"You took off on Kevin."

A smile spread across her face. "That was fun."

They didn't talk for a few moments, just watched people in the café getting their coffee and snacks. "What's gonna happen now, Brandi?"

"What do you mean?"

"Well, I came out here to find you. Now that I have, what do we do? Just go our separate ways, knowing we both exist?"

Brandi stared out the window again, a faraway look on her face. But after a few moments, she turned back to Grace. "Unless you want something different."

Grace laughed. "If I could, I'd put you in a suitcase and take you back home with me."

"What's stopping you?"

Grace's eyes widened. "You'd come to New York with me?"

"Well, not *forever*. But school's out for the summer. I'm sure I could get time off from the store."

Grace wanted to hug her, but then remembered the broken bones. "That would be awesome."

She didn't get any more words out because Robin ran into the café with a terrible look on her face.

XXXVIII

KEVIN

As soon as the girls leave, I go back to the phone in the kitchen, all the while keeping my eye on Anton and his boys. They're nowhere near each other, but at one point they look like they're trying to communicate. I yell from the kitchen, "Howi, make sure those jerks don't talk."

Ponah calls back, "Can they at least have a drink of water?"

Women! What is *wrong* with them? "Not now, Mrs. Blackbear."

Instead of trying to reach Lewis, I decide to call Dave at the safehouse. Miraculously, it goes through.

"Hey Dave, it's Kevin. I'm here in Supai with Anton and his boys, but I can't get Lewis or the pilot. What can you do for me?"

"You're breaking up, Kevin."

"We're in Supai and we need to get out!"

"Are the agents there with you?"

"*Nobody's* here," I shout. "It's like we disappeared off the face of the earth. I need a helicopter, I need Lewis, and I need a team."

Silence on the other end.

"Dave?"

The line is absolutely dead. I slam the phone down and hear Anton snicker from the living room. I want to go clock him up the side of his head with my gun, but thinking of Grace makes me hesitate. Something's obviously wrong with me. Next thing you know, I'll be offering him a freakin' drink of water.

"What's so funny?" I bark in his face.

He doesn't say anything, just grins like an idiot.

I lean against the wall, trying to look as calm as a clam. "It doesn't matter how long we have to wait. It's cool in here, and we're just gonna sit around the parlor and have a good old time."

I turn to Ponah. "We won't be offering our guests water because then they might have to use the bathroom, and we can't have that. Frankly, I don't care if we have to wait a week."

Anton sneers. "You think you're pretty slick, don't you? We'll see who comes looking for us first—your guys or my guys."

"Another word out of you and you'll be sitting outside. It's only about a hundred and ten degrees out there. An hour in the sun will make you want to drink your own sweat."

"You want me to go check on the girls?" Howi asks.

Ponah grabs his arm. "I don't want you walking anywhere in this heat."

She's right. He looks awful.

"Stop babying me!" he snarls.

Untouched by his tone, she looks at me. "I can go check on them. I'll take Minnow."

"Minnow?"

Ponah gestures toward the pasture outside. "The horse. She only lets *me* ride her."

"Dumb animal," Howi mutters.

"That would be great, 'cause I need Howi here with me."

He straightens up, looking pleased.

After she leaves, I sit down facing Anton, my gun in my lap. "So how did you get into this business, Anton? Was it passed down by dear, old, uncle Ray?"

He looks like he wants to spit in my face. "You told me not to talk."

"Not unless you're spoken to."

Frankly, I'm getting bored babysitting these goons. Maybe Anton can tell me something about where Lena's gone.

"Aren't you supposed to read me my rights?"

"Why? You're not under arrest. We're just visiting until the others get here."

"Then why are we tied up?"

"Because you and your thugs hurt my boy, Howi. And you were carrying, and that's against the law on the reservation. But, hey, that's not my business. Like I said, we're just visiting."

"Who exactly are we waiting for?"

"The Feds. They're the ones that have a problem with you, not me. Apparently, they've been looking at you for a while. Once I hand you over, it'll be quite a feather in Agent James' cap."

An ugly sneer begins to play on Anton's lips. "Agent James? Agent Lewis James?"

"None other."

"Man, have you been played," Anton said.

GRACE

Brandi stood up, alarmed. "What's wrong, Robin?"

"I just hung up with AirWest. Their helicopter crashed with four people on board. They're sending out another one to look for it. They don't know when they'll be able to come for us."

Grace stood up too, her brain in alarm mode. *What else is going to happen? Who else is going to get hurt? Am I a walking disaster from birth that sucks people into harm?*

She felt light-headed, and her heart was pounding—something Brandi immediately noticed. "Sit down, kid. You look awful."

At that moment Ponah walked into the café, sweat glistening her face. Robin ran to her. "Is everything okay, Gram?"

Ponah wiped her face with a red kerchief. Then she saw Brandi hovering over Grace. "That's what I was just about to ask you."

Before Robin could finish telling her about the helicopter crash, Grace butted in. "The people on board were probably FBI agents. How are we gonna get out of here, especially now, with Anton?"

Ponah patted her arm. "Hold on honey." Then she turned to Robin. "Did you talk to the sheriff?"

"No, but some tribal leaders are going to the house."

"Good. Supposedly, the men have everything under control, but I don't know how long they think they're going to be able to keep those boys tied up."

"Is there any other way out of here, besides hiking the trail?" Grace asked.

"You can rent mules to ride on, but they don't go any faster." She looked at the clock on the wall. "You'd have to wait till morning, though. They've already left for the day."

Fear closed Grace's throat. "We can't keep Anton and his boys tied up till then."

Ponah nodded. "I agree. Your Kevin won't even let me give them water. He's a jumpy one."

"Probably because Lewis isn't here. What will happen if he was on that helicopter?"

Grace couldn't hold in the tears any longer. Robin and Brandi stood there looking awkward, but Ponah knew just what to do. She took Grace in her arms and let her cry it out. After a while, she started to rock her, talking softly in a low, scratchy voice.

When Grace calmed down, Ponah gave her the red kerchief. She tried to wipe her tears and snot off Ponah's shoulder which made the girls laugh.

"These shoulders have been soaked with tears too many times to count."

Brandi smiled. "They're probably still wet from mine."

Ponah nodded. "What we need to do right now, girls, is pray. We need to pray for those people in the helicopter, for ourselves, and even for Anton and those other boys."

Robin smiled, shaking her head incredulously.

"And why not?" Ponah asked. "God loves them too, you know."

She glanced around the room which had pretty much cleared out. "This is as good a place as any to pray. Anybody want to start?"

Brandi grabbed Grace's hand like they were little kids and closed her eyes.

KEVIN

"What are you talking about?" I growl.

"Agent Lewis James, the chemist from Washington? Yeah, he knows all about me and my dirty deeds. And if you believe that, you're dumber than I thought."

"I'm telling you, Anton, you keep it up—"

He interrupts me. "Lewis James has set you up. He's been trying to keep me quiet for a while now. He must have planned this whole thing."

I start to feel sick in the pit of my stomach. "Tell me what you're talkin' about before I duct tape your mouth shut. You've got duct tape, right Howi?"

Howi opens a drawer in the China cabinet. "Sure thing."

I pull up a chair alongside Anton. "Let's hear your little fairy tale, before I lose patience."

For once, there's no smirk on his face. He's deadly serious. "When Lewis James came out here four years ago, he got friendly with my Uncle Ray. He asked Ray to be his eyes and ears, being that he knew a lot of shady dudes in Phoenix. He knew Ray was on probation and that the cash earnings from the club didn't always get logged on the books. He said he would ignore that if my uncle kept him informed with what was happening in the drug trade, which Ray did. When 25i hit the scene, James got really interested and started watching its distribution."

"Yeah, he watched you and your uncle distribute it."

"No! Ray wouldn't get involved. He was selling Spice, but that wasn't illegal yet, and he was selling weed, figuring legalization was right around the corner. But he wouldn't touch 25i 'cause that stuff can kill people."

Anton looks at his guys for confirmation, and they both nod.

"That's right," Blondie says. "Ray never dealt that stuff. He was strictly a leaf man."

I grin at Howi. "One lies and the other swears to it."

Anton's face flushes. "I'm telling the truth. One night, after a few drinks, Agent James brags to Ray that he could make it himself if he wanted to. Pretty soon, the stuff starts flooding the whole Arizona market. Ray had his suspicions but didn't say anything. When the Phoenix PD starts questioning him, Ray gets *mysteriously* killed in an accident."

The veins pop out on Anton's neck as he continues. "James knows I'm onto him. He started gunning for me about nine months ago."

"So, you're the innocent victim in all of this? Gimme a break!"

"I admit I still sell Spice, even though it's illegal now, and weed too. Sometimes we'll get a bad batch and people get sick, but they never die, and we've *never* sold 25i."

"And I suppose you hunting down Brandi was just because you wanted a date?"

He composes himself and lowers his voice, looking almost embarrassed. "I wanted Brandi to go away with me. I'm selling the Black Swan. I wanna get out of Phoenix before the same thing happens to me that happened to Uncle Ray. I figured if we could get away for a few weeks, she would see that I was different, that we could start over."

"And you just brought muscle and guns with you because that's how you roll as a reformed man?"

"Knowin' that James is after me? Yeah, I thought this might be a set up."

"Then why did you come?"

"I want her back, man. She's the best thing that ever happened to me."

I turn away from him in disgust and go into the kitchen where no one can see me. His story is preposterous, the desperate ploy of someone who's run out of options. I've seen his kind a thousand times. Smart enough to cook up a story and dumb enough to think anybody would believe it. The part about Brandi is the stupidest. He wants to run away with her to a new life? He must think I'm an idiot! Sure, she's beautiful and smart, with enough personality to make it interesting, but who would risk walking into a trap just to convince a woman to leave the state with you? Unbidden the thought comes up, *you would, if it was Grace.*

I grab a glass of water, feeling just a twinge of guilt that the guys in the living room haven't had anything to eat or drink for hours. All right, maybe men, like women, can be swayed by emotion, by desire. But this guy is a thug. How could he ever think she'd go back to him? A typical narcissist—all ego and arrogance.

But I can't shut out the niggling inconsistencies in this case. Like, no matter how many people were out searching for Anton, he always eluded us. I assumed it was because Anton was tracking Grace's phone, but it just as easily could have been Lewis tracking Anton, keeping him out of range until he could get to him first.

Lewis is obviously a cold fish, hard to read, but that's not uncommon with Feds. I didn't pick up a bad vibe with him, but—ever since I took this case, my intuition has gone haywire. It's because of Grace. One minute she's so lovable I can't keep myself from fantasizing about her. The next minute I want to wring her neck.

Getting back to Lewis, the most damning factor, the one that makes me really wonder if Anton is telling the truth is that he promised backup and had plenty of time to make that happen. Yet here we are, me and a guy in his 80s, completely alone against the world. If Anton *is* telling the truth, that means that when Lewis gets here, he'll try to shut him up for good. The last thing I want to do is have to protect those jerks in the living room.

XXXIX

GRACE

Robin started with the Lord's Prayer, and Ponah and Grace joined in. Brandi didn't seem to know the words. Then Grace said a few words about the people in the helicopter. Ponah prayed that the tied-up guys would straighten out. Then she added, "And dear, sweet Jesus, Grace and Brandi have lost so much by being apart all these years. Heal their hearts."

Something settled down inside Grace. Maybe Brandi felt it too because she squeezed Grace's hand.

Afterwards, they all sat down, while the guy at the counter gave them cold, bottled waters. "Anybody wanna see if they need volunteers to help search for survivors of the crash?" Robin asked.

"I can't do anything," Brandi said, "but I'll go with you."

Ponah downed her water and stood up. "I'll look up the mule train schedule."

Grace stood too. "Can I just go back to the house?"

Ponah nodded. "Take the golf cart."

Grace stepped inside the house where it was mercifully cool, but the three guys looked miserable bound to their straight back chairs. The TV was on with the volume turned up loud. Howi was watching it when his eyes were open. Kevin popped his head out of the kitchen and looked relieved to see her. She met him in the kitchen and whispered, "Joe's helicopter crashed carrying three other people. We think he may have been transporting Lewis and some other agents."

Kevin's face hardened, and he cursed under his breath. "How are we gonna get out of here? And what do I do with these goons?"

"I had the same reaction. But that was before I realized that people we know may be injured or dead. Have a little perspective."

She tilted her head and grinned. "And Ponah said to give the guys water and untie them."

"No way! Until I have back up, I'm not taking any chances."

"Kevin, they're sitting in there watching *The Price is Right* with Howi. How dangerous can they be?"

"You have no idea. Anton just fed me a cock and bull story that Lewis was responsible for his uncle's death, that he's the chemist behind the killer drugs, and that he's going to kill him as soon as he gets here."

Grace looked straight into Kevin's eyes. "It's not impossible."

He shook his head. "You believe him?"

"Listen, I haven't liked Lewis from the start. He's pushy, he has no compassion for Brandi, and he's never been around when we needed him."

"And you think Anton is better?"

"No, but Brandi must have seen something good in him."

"That's just girl talk," he spat out, turning to stare out the window.

"Excuse me?"

He mimicked her in a girl's voice. "'Untie the boys, they're not dangerous. Brandi must have seen something good in him. Naïve, do-gooder, girl talk!"

Grace's eyes flashed and she raised her voice. "Compassion isn't naïve and neither is giving someone the benefit of the doubt."

He ran his fingers through his crusty, damp hair. "Look, I just want to get out of this hell hole and go home."

"Leave this vacation paradise? Why, I thought you were having the time of your life!"

He looked at her like she was crazy, but eventually a small smile flickered at the corner of his mouth.

She feigned shock and said in a perfect southern drawl, "Well, dear me! Here I am spouting optimism—just like a girl."

At that moment, there was a loud rap on the kitchen door, and they both jumped. Kevin opened the door with his gun drawn, and they found themselves staring into the faces of three large Native men. They were the stateliest guys Grace had ever seen, but they all stepped back at the sight of the gun. "We heard you needed some help from the tribal council," the most ancient of the three said.

At the sound of his voice, Howi had entered the kitchen. He shook each man's hand. "This is Art Fox, Earl Harjo, and Matt Shepherd," he said to Kevin. "They represent our government."

Kevin put the gun back into his waistband. "I'm sorry for greeting you with a gun. I didn't know if it was more of Anton's people."

He showed them his detective badge and explained the reason for his presence in Supai. "I have some men who are wanted by the police in Phoenix."

He pointed to the three stooges in the living room. "They should be locked up until Federal agents arrive to arrest them. Since I haven't been able to contact your local police officer, I'd appreciate it if you'd open your jail for them."

Art Fox shook his head. "We don't arrest non-Indians."

Kevin's jaw tightened. "I'm not asking you to arrest them, just to hold them until the authorities get here."

At that point, Howi invited the men to walk out back so they could talk privately. Before he closed the door, Grace could hear him speaking in another language.

Kevin stood there looking at the door for a while. Then he grabbed a glass, filled it with water, found a plastic straw and walked into the living room. He offered each of the guys a drink of water. They all accepted and expressed thanks. When the tribal councilmen and Howi walked back into the house, none of them looked very happy. "They'll take them to the jail," Howi said, "but they won't keep them overnight. If the police don't come by nine this evening, they'll release them."

Kevin looked incredulous. "What if the Feds don't get here by then? Where's the reciprocity? I'd hold people for them if they needed it."

"Maybe, but if you couldn't charge them under your jurisdiction, you'd have to release them, too. It's the same here."

Kevin nodded, grudgingly.

"Let the men take them to the jail," Howi went on. "That way *they* have to feed them, not us. If the police aren't here by nine, we'll have to take them back."

"That's ridiculous!"

"But it's the way it is," Howi said.

Kevin angrily cut the ties on the guys' feet but not their hands. The Native men led them out. Just as Anton was leaving, he looked at Kevin. "You know we are all just sitting ducks here."

"Yeah, yeah," Kevin said, giving him a shove towards the door. "That's your problem, not mine."

Once they were gone, it seemed easier to breathe in the house. Kevin and Grace ended up sitting on the couch together, watching *Family Feud*. After a while, Grace dozed off. When she awakened, Kevin had his arm around her, and her head was on his chest. He was leaning back on a pillow, snoring softly. Grace tried to slip away, but he woke up with a start. Instantly, his hand went to the gun in his waistband. "You okay?" he asked.

"Yes, I just want to change my clothes. They feel caked with limestone. In fact, I'd love to take a shower."

"Towels are in the bathroom closet," Howi said from his chair.

While Grace walked to the bathroom, she noticed that, although her ankle was stiff, it didn't hurt at all. *I'd love to take Ponah home with me,* she thought.

Home. What was it going to be like when they got there? How

would Eve handle the news of Brandi, and how would Brandi handle them? Would she stay for a while or just turn around and return to Arizona? What would happen to Lena when they found her—if they found her?

And then there was Kevin. She didn't want him to disappear. Thank goodness she was done with Ben. But there was still so much to worry about—Mimi's graduation and surgery, Jay's recovery. She stepped into the shower feeling overwhelmed. It was like she'd broken into a million pieces, with nothing to pull her back together.

But God's kindness had helped her find her sister. She hoped He would continue to help.

KEVIN

We sit down on the couch and it's not long before Grace starts nodding off, doing the head-bob thing. I put my arm around her and let her lean into me. It feels so good, so right, to have her here. Within a few days we'll be home. What then? Hopefully the Feds will catch Lena and then the courts will take over. But I'll be going back to Carlton Hines and Bob and my buddy Freddy and salsa dancing at the clubs and going to Cassie and Dan's on the weekend and hating my father—normal life again. But is it? *This* is normal—Grace by my side. How can I tell her how I feel? What if she doesn't feel it too?

The Maddox family will be unhinged for a while. Once it hits the news, it'll be a zoo. People will be after them—and me too probably—for interviews. They'll want to write books about this. Will Grace and I be able to find time to be together? I have to talk to her before we leave Arizona, but I don't know what to say. *Please don't walk out of my life,* sounds whiny and desperate.

Grace eases herself off my chest, and I startle awake. I realize I've been dreaming I was drowning. It seems like it happened in another lifetime, even though it was only hours ago. *He saved others; but he can't save himself.,* is playing on repeat in my head.

Grace heads to the bathroom for a shower. When she returns she still looks bruised and rumpled but also fresh and beautiful, which make me feel like a scuzzball. I push myself off the couch and say, "Me next."

Once the water hits me, the feeling that I'm drowning comes back. I know it's my imagination, so I steady myself and take a deep, wonderful breath. I scrub my aching shoulder, but even that feels a little better. I'm so afraid Grace won't feel the way I do, so I push it out of my mind. By the time I get out of the shower and into clean clothes, I can hear Ponah and the girls chattering. They have obviously returned and are excited about something. As I walk into the living room, Robin declares, "They found the helicopter."

I glance at Grace who appears stricken. "Lewis James and two other people were killed in the accident. The pilot survived, but is in rough shape. They just LifeFlighted him to Flagstaff Hospital."

"Do they know who the others were?"

Grace's eyes fill with tears. "Probably Dave and Jenny. Sounds about right, since everyone who gets involved with me gets hurt."

She pushes herself off the couch and walks outside, the screen door banging behind her.

Robin makes eye contact with me and shrugs. "They think it was engine failure. If it hadn't been them, it would've been someone else. It could've been us on our way out of here."

I nod and follow Grace outside. She's leaning on the fence near the horse corral watching Minnow eat hay. I walk over and lean on the fence next to her. She picks up a piece of hay and starts tearing it into little pieces. "I can't imagine what their families are going through right now. It makes my stomach sick."

"It's awful, I know, but Grace, it's not your fault—or mine. It just happened."

"Right."

"I'm serious! You can't keep blaming yourself for every bad thing that happens."

She stands there, watching Minnow swish her tail and munch

on sweet hay. "This whole trip backfired. We don't know what to do with Anton. We don't know if Lewis was dirty. I can't even think about Dave and Jenny. What a mistake."

"How can you say that? You saved your sister's life!"

"Yeah, after I gave her a reason to kill herself. And you—you almost died."

"Also not your fault. But why am I trying to talk you out of your guilt? You even think you were responsible for Brandi's kidnapping when she was a baby."

The glare she gives me is withering, but I keep pressing.

"I'm sorry Grace, but pretty soon you'll make yourself responsible for earthquakes and tsunamis. Leave something for those of us who never feel guilty at all."

Grace opens her mouth, apparently thinks better of it, then closes it and stares at the horse. I want to put my arms around her and tell her it's all going to be okay, but I already know where that leads, so we both remain silent for a long moment.

It's time to change the subject. "Have you ever heard the phrase, *He saved others, but he couldn't save himself?*"

"I think it's from the Bible," she replies, still not looking at me.

Minnow swishes her tail and chomps without a care in the world.

"I kept hearing those words while I was thrashing in the water, when I was sure I was going to die. What does it mean?"

"I'm pretty sure it was a mocking statement people threw at Jesus while He was hanging on the cross," Grace murmurs, almost to herself. "Something like, *Why doesn't he do for himself what he did for everybody else?*"

We remain leaning on the fence without talking, without looking at each other, for another few minutes, then I break the silence. "You know, Grace, you and I are more alike than you realize. You always feel guilty when people get hurt, and I'm always trying to save them. We're a couple of self-appointed superheroes."

"What a pair," she murmurs.

At around 7:30 PM, Howi and Ponah's phone rings. It's Matt Shepherd, the councilman.

"Some FBI agents are waiting for you down at the café," he says, then hangs up without another word.

While walking to the jail, the pain in my shoulder reappears, a grim reminder of this morning's escapade. It's getting cooler, maybe all the way down to 90, but the heat still saps my energy. As I approach the jail, I see Dave and Jenny standing outside. I quicken my pace and surprise myself by hugging them both. "I'm so glad to see you guys. We thought you went down in the helicopter."

"We were supposed to be on that transport," Jenny says. "But at the last minute, Lewis had two other guys go with him. He told us to take the next ride in."

"Were they FBI?"

"I don't think so. I never saw them before."

Anton's story niggles at the back of my mind while we talk about the accident. Pretty soon the tribal police come marching out of the jail with the guys. All three look rumpled and miserable. Anton, who's lost his bravado, gives me a desperate look. "Did you tell them about Lewis James?" he asks.

"James is dead, punk. Make sure you don't end up the same way."

Even so, I take Dave and Jenny aside. "You might as well be prepared. Anton is gonna try to convince you that Lewis James was dirty. He says Lewis was making the 25i himself, that he had Ray killed and was gunning for him."

They both give me an odd look—wide-eyed, but absolutely devoid of any other expression. "We'll investigate it," Jenny says. Then she drops the subject completely.

The helicopter lifts off, and I can taste the cloud of sand it kicks up. I listen to the fading *thwack, thwack, thwack* of the rotor blades mingling with the distant murmur of the falls. I look up at the few stars starting to poke out of the darkening sky. Dusk falls quickly. I head back, leaving a lonesome stillness in my wake.

XL

GRACE

At about ten-thirty, Grace and the others boarded a helicopter sent in especially for them. There were tearful goodbyes with Howi and Ponah and promises to visit again. When they landed at the trailhead, it was completely dark save for the stars pinpricking the velvet black sky. Kevin and Robin pulled out flashlights to find their cars.

Brandi and Kevin decided to ride together so they could talk about legal stuff, while Grace rode with Robin. They all agreed to drive through the night instead of spending money on a hotel.

Just before 3:00 AM, they arrived at Brandi's apartment in Phoenix. Brandi and Robin shared the bedroom while Kevin and Grace camped out in the living room. The little black-and-white cat who managed to completely avoid Grace when she snuck into Brandi's house, meowed around them for at least an hour until Brandi took it into her room and shut the door. When Grace opened her eyes the next morning, she realized it had been a week since she left home. One week.

She lifted herself off the couch and stepped over Kevin, who was still sound asleep on the floor. She made her way into the kitchen where she found Robin rifling through the fridge looking for food. Together, they threw together scrambled eggs, toast, and coffee. To keep from disturbing Kevin and Brandi, they took their breakfast out to the tiny deck outside the kitchen.

Robin curled her legs up under her in the canvas camp chair and sipped her coffee. Grace was curious about her fifteen-year friendship with Brandi, so Robin regaled her with stories about their escapades, their brief falling out, and how she'd come to her rescue, two days ago. After a long silence, Robin added, "I'm glad Brandi's going back to New York with you."

Grace searched for the right words. "You think she's, uh, stable enough?"

"Brandi's a survivor. She'll do all right."

Grace said nothing, but Robin must have read her mind. "She told me that she jumped off the falls."

"I wasn't sure you knew."

"Brandi wasn't herself that morning. She'd been up for two days straight, was in pain, and had just gotten the biggest shock of her life."

She took another sip of coffee and went on. "I should've known and kept better tabs on her, but I was tired from hiking in and out of Supai two days in a row. Thank God you were there at the right moment."

"I just don't want to stress her out. When we get to New York, emotions are going to run high."

"You girls talking about me?" Brandi asked, walking onto the deck. She was munching on a granola bar and carrying a container of blueberry yogurt.

"You bet," Robin said.

"So, Grace, you think I'm a whack job you're gonna need to babysit?"

"I didn't say that—"

"Yeah, you kinda did. Look, I promised pretty boy I'd go see a shrink, and I will. I just don't want to be analyzed like a specimen. I already feel like a bug on a slide."

Grace smiled. *Talk about feeling like a specimen? Try having blue dreams.*

"I'm actually more worried about your mom than me." Brandi said. "How is she taking all of this? I can't imagine what she's feeling."

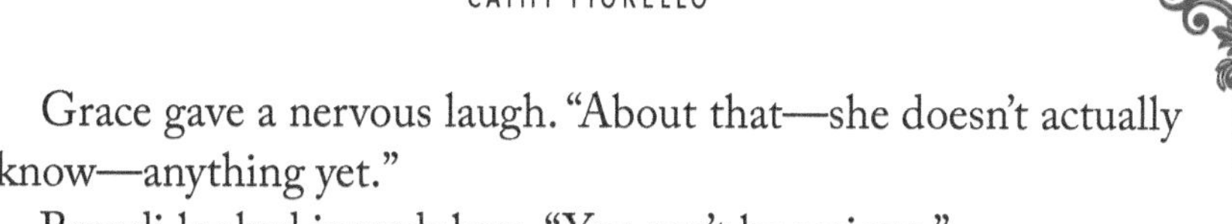

Grace gave a nervous laugh. "About that—she doesn't actually know—anything yet."

Brandi looked incredulous. "You can't be serious."

"I didn't want to get her hopes up before we knew anything. Kevin and I came out here on sort of a false pretext to protect her. After we found out you were real, you disappeared. And if you remember, by the time we finally met, we were kinda incommunicado."

"Let me get this straight. You're just gonna call her up out of the blue and say what, I *found my twin sister, you know, the one you thought was dead?*"

Grace felt herself getting defensive. Maybe she hadn't handled things well. "I'll figure out a way. Mimi knows. She'll help."

Brandi grew quiet, a pensive, almost frightened shadow crossed her eyes.

Could she be scared of meeting our mom? Mom's such a marshmallow. Then again, her role model for motherhood was Lena.

Grace's defensiveness melted. "It'll be okay Brandi. She has a really strong faith. She's really quite an amazing lady. You're going to love her. And she'll love you!"

Brandi shook her head. "Something you thought was true your whole life, and then you find out it wasn't? Hopefully she'll handle it better than I did."

Grace leaned in to her. "How was it when Kevin told you?"

Brandi's typical bravado was gone, and she looked fragile as a child. "At first it seemed like a sick joke—something Anton might cook up. I didn't want to believe it, but a part of me knew it was true."

She ripped the top off the yogurt container and stirred its contents for a full minute. Robin stood and walked past Grace, giving her a half-smile that seemed to say, "Be patient with her."

"My mom and I never really connected. It was like she... *couldn't*. Maybe the secret strangled her; I don't know. She just got crazier and crazier. Eventually, booze left no room for me."

Grace almost started to feel sorry for Lena. *Almost.* "Do you think she made it to Mexico? Is she capable of being able to disappear?"

Brandi gave a grim smile. "Oh, she's capable, all right. If they don't catch her at the border, they'll probably never find her. I just wish—I just—well, I wish a lot of things."

Grace's heart ached for her. All their holding her hair back while she puked wouldn't erase this pain.

Brandi let out a big sigh then seemed to brighten up. "Getting back to your mother, I think you're gonna be in a ton of trouble when you start talking. How many lies have you told in all, Grace?"

Grace put on the most innocent look she could muster. "I tried not to lie to her."

Brandi took a big spoonful of yogurt and snickered. "Tried?"

"I have lied to other people, though, and I've done some things that might be considered illegal."

"My sister, the felon. Like what?" Wow, *sister* sounded great in Brandi's mouth.

"Besides impersonating you a few times, I broke into your apartment and took some of your stuff, and I ran away from police protection."

Brandi choked on a mouthful of yogurt. "You stole my stuff?"

Robin, who'd just come back outside, laughed out loud. She put more toast, butter, and jam on the table between them.

"Not really *took*—more like *borrowed*," Grace said, picking up a piece of toast, "so I could figure out where you were."

Brandi put her feet up on the other chair. "Sounds like you have an aptitude for crime. And here I thought you were the good one."

"Oh, I'm definitely not the good one. That distinction goes to Mimi."

"Who's Mimi?" Robin asked.

"Mimi is Grace's little sister. She's got some major problems right now, poor kid. She's a violinist whose hands got mangled in an accident."

Grace stopped chewing. "Did Kevin tell you about the accident?"

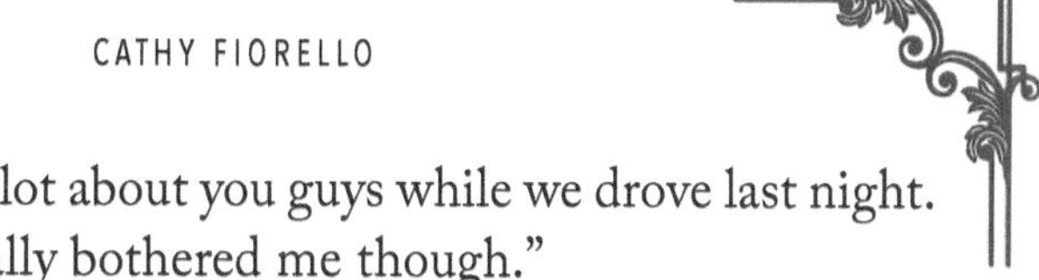

"Yeah, he told me a lot about you guys while we drove last night. One thing he said really bothered me though."

"What?"

"That you think you're nothing special because your sister is so good. I guess he's talked to Mimi about it, too."

"She's a prodigy, for crying out loud. What a meddler he is."

Brandi turned to Robin with a grin. "He also showed me some of Grace's YouTube videos. She's got some jazz magic going on."

Grace blushed. "They're just my college recital. I've gotta take them down."

"Don't you dare," Brandi said, shaking her yogurt spoon at Grace. "I have a feeling you're ten times better than what you think you are."

Grace shook her head and put her feet up on the chair next to Brandi's. Their feet looked the same, except Brandi's were tan and Grace's were white as milk. She tried to stretch out her ankle which was still a little sore.

Brandi nudged her foot with her own. "I've been meaning to ask you; did they name me—you know—before I was taken?"

"Yes. They called you Faith. We were Grace and Faith."

There was a long pause. Then Brandi said, "I like that."

Robin picked up the breakfast plates. "When should I start moving in my things?"

Brandi started to help her clean up. "Today if you want."

Grace held the kitchen door open for them. "You're moving?"

"Yeah, into the apartment. We've always talked about it, and now that Brandi's going back with you, I might as well look after the place and take care of the cat."

"But what if Anton comes looking for Brandi?"

"We're getting an alarm put in. My dad's in the business."

Brandi put the dishes in the sink. "Anton isn't as dangerous as he likes people to think."

Grace put the jam and bread in the fridge. "He seemed pretty dangerous to me."

"He just needs to get out of the business and start over. I know he can be a good guy."

Robin started to run the water in the sink. "If that's what he wants."

Grace peeked into the living room. "I'd better wake Kevin. We've got lots of stuff to do before we fly out."

"Could you do something for me first?" Brandi asked.

"Sure, what?"

"Would you read my mom's letter."

KEVIN

When I wake up, I have no idea where I am, but then a furry body with a motor rubs up against my arm. I put out my hand to pet the critter. It gets a real charge out of that and starts walking across my chest.

Grace is gone, but there are voices in the kitchen, so I throw on a shirt and walk that way. I catch a glimpse of myself in a mirror. I can't believe how terrible I look! I haven't shaved in days, and my upper body and face look like I've been in a cage fight. I try to comb my hair with my fingers, but nothing will settle down. Oh well, let Grace see the real me.

When I walk into the kitchen, everyone jumps, then starts to laugh. "Quite a jittery crowd. Where's the coffee?"

Grace hands me her cup. "Here, finish mine. It's my third, and I'm starting to get on my own nerves."

I taste it. Too much sugar, but it's coffee. After some small talk, Grace asks if I'll pick up her stuff at the bungalow, and Brandi asks for a ride to the Heismans'.

I grab a piece of toast from the table. "Sure," I answer them both. "But we should drop by the police station first to see if they want statements about Anton and Lena."

Brandi twists her hair with her fingers and avoids my eyes. "What's going to happen to her?"

"The Feds will probably extradite her to New York. Once she's charged, it'll be up to the courts. That is, *if* they can find her, which right now looks like a pretty big, if."

"They won't make me testify against her, right?"

"Probably not, Brandi, but that's way down the line."

Grace puts her arm around her. "You won't have to do anything alone. We're a team now, right?"

Brandi nods. "I just don't know how I feel about her. Part of me wants her to get help, but part of me hates her because she's hurt so many people."

I glance at Grace who meets my eyes with a knowing smile. "Believe me, I get what you're saying, Brandi. Maybe while we're on our way, I can tell you a little of my story."

We walk back into the living room to get my keys. "Have you ever heard what the ancient Romans used to do to murderers?"

XLI

GRACE

After everyone left, Grace settled down in the living room to read Lena's letter. She pulled it from the envelope and tried to study the loopy handwriting of the woman who destroyed her family. She didn't feel an ounce of compassion for her. But because Brandi asked, she wanted to understand.

September 23, 2016

Dear Brandi,

You're an adult today—21. I hope I never have to give you this letter, but if you're reading it, it's because you've found out some things. Just let me say, everything I've ever done, I've done for you. Don't forget that, and don't judge me. You haven't lived my life.

When I lived in New York, I did everything humanly possible to have a baby, but my body betrayed me. Frank was no help, skirt-chaser that he was. Ironically, I was a Lamaze instructor, teaching granola moms to deliver naturally while their yuppie husbands helped out. It was like salt being rubbed into an open wound.

One day a couple came into the class. They were going to have twins—two, when I couldn't even have one! I decided I wanted one of those babies. You may think I'm a monster, but it was because my life was so unfair. That night, I told Frank we had to get married because I was planning to adopt a kid.

After we did, I shipped him out to Phoenix to work for Ray Morgan. I didn't need him around, asking questions.

The day you were born, I went to the hospital in the middle of the night with a gym bag. When I got to the neonatal unit, you were there without your sibling. I almost lost my nerve, but I knew you were mine. You made me want you, so you see, it wasn't my fault. I put you in the gym bag and drove straight through to Ohio, 12 hours, stopping only once for gas. The gym bag was like a little bassinet. You were out of view, sleeping on Baby Tylenol the whole way except when I fed and changed you. When I felt guilty, I told myself it was for your own good, because with them you just would have been one of a pair, but with me you'd be special.

When I got to Arizona, stupid Frank believed everything I told him. He never asked about adoption papers or a birth certificate. You don't really need them until you go to kindergarten, so when you were five, I paid one of the doctors at Phoenix Children's Hospital to sign off on the certificate. Of course, I had to sleep with him, the ass. But even though I had it, I was always afraid to pull it out in case someone would accuse me of it being a fake.

In those first few weeks I knew what was going on back east. The family was upset, but didn't they have at least one healthy baby? When the national news started carrying the story, I got worried. The mom was whining and crying on TV. I knew I needed to do something, but what? At the hospital where I worked, we served a very poor, maternal population. In the ER we would get babies who were malnourished and one step away from full dehydration. And sometimes a scared teenager would deliver a baby at home, not know what to do with it, and just drop it off at the hospital. Well, God saw my situation. You probably think it's wrong to bring God into this, now that you're so holy with all your "Christian" friends, but how else could I explain it? I wasn't going to give you back and go to jail. I didn't want to run all over the country with you to keep you hidden. And then there was Frank, who, even though he was stupid, would probably figure it out eventually.

I was working the graveyard shift in the ER, and early one morning I went out for a smoke. There by the door was a box with a naked newborn who was dead, probably from exposure. Maybe if I'd taken her in and we'd worked on her, she would have survived because she was still warm. But the idea popped into my head so fast, I couldn't do anything but follow my instinct. I put the box in my car, left work and stopped on the way to get three bags of ice. When I got home, I woke up Frank and told him to take the next few days off, that I had to take a trip. He was all pissed off saying he didn't know how to take care of a baby, and I couldn't just leave him like that. But I told him, "Hey, you said you wanted a kid, so deal."

I don't know how I did it after staying up all night, but I drove from Phoenix to Indianapolis on only a few hours of sleep, stopping just to pee, eat, and buy ice. Two days later, I was in Manhattan. I still had your baby bracelet which I put on the kid before I dropped her in the Central Park Reservoir. Then I went to a payphone and called the police.

Well, they bought it, and the danger was over for me. Say what you will, Brandi, but I did it all for you, to give you a good life. When Frank left me high and dry, I had to do it all on my own. Ray helped out when we got together, but I knew you hated him, so I never could be happy.

I made a plan a long time ago of what to do if anyone ever came looking for me. So, try to be happy. No matter what anyone says, I'm your mother. I raised you, supported you, gave up everything for you. Remember that.

Mom

Grace put down the letter and immediately went outside to breathe some fresh air. It was hot already. The sky was blue and cloudless, and the cacti across the street were blooming pink and red. But Grace felt shaken and slimed. Lena's delusional refrain, "I did it all for you," was especially creepy. What was it like being raised by Lena? What was it like *being* Lena—always looking over her shoulder, haunted by what Brandi would think when she found out the truth. Her secret ate away at her so that she couldn't even love the daughter she'd stolen.

XLII

Grace took a long shower before she started making calls, both to wash Lena's sickness off her and to prepare herself to talk to Eve. As the spray pounded her face and body, she tried to pray, but was ashamed of how childish and foolish her prayers sounded.

Oh, God, keep mom from having a heart attack.

Don't let bad things happen anymore.

I'm scared.

After climbing out of the shower, she went into Brandi's room to find something to wear. She smiled when she realized she was doing what she'd always yelled at Mimi for doing —borrowing clothes without permission. She dressed and braided her hair, then started looking through Brandi's books, photos, and makeup.

What am I doing? I can't put it off any longer.

Please, God?

She dialed Mimi's number—no answer.

She dialed Pastor Dan—no answer.

Cassie's number—right to voicemail.

All right, all right. I get the picture, she muttered to God.

She called Eve, who picked up on the first ring.

Eve's voice bordered on panic. "Where have you been?! I've been so worried about you."

Grace grinned. *Yell as much as you want. Be as protective and annoying as you can be—I will never complain again.*

"I'm sorry you couldn't reach me, Mom. Some places in Arizona don't get cell service. How's everything going over there?"

"What's wrong?" Eve asked immediately.

"What do you mean?"

"You don't sound like yourself. Something's wrong."

Grace paused. This was going to be harder than she thought. She wanted to proceed slowly, but Eve's mom-antennae were vibrating. "Nothing's wrong. In fact, everything's going really well."

"I don't believe you. You know you could never lie to me, Gracie."

She was right. Better jump in. "Can we FaceTime, Mom, you and me and Mimi?"

"Just tell me, Grace. You're in trouble, aren't you?"

"No, Mom, I'm not. but I want to talk to both of you together. What's she doing?"

"What she's been doing every day since you left—lying on the couch watching Netflix."

"Can I talk to her for just a minute before we video-chat?"

"Grace—"

"Please, Mom, it's important. Just let me talk to her."

Grace could hear her walk the phone into the living room. "Put that thing on pause. It's your sister."

"Hey, Gracie."

Mimi sounded drugged, like she had, in fact, been watching Netflix nonstop for ten days straight.

"How ya doing, kid? You okay?"

"My hands hurt. When're you coming home? I need you."

Grace's heart ached, but she tried to be upbeat. "Good news, Mi, I think we're coming home tomorrow. Listen, I've gotta tell Mom about Brandi. I finally met her and she wants to come back to New York with us. But Mom has to be prepared. I wanted Dan and Cassie to be there with you guys when I told her, but I can't get them to pick up. If it's just you two, do you think she'll be okay, or will she flip out and have a heart attack or something?"

"I think she already knows something's up."

"What? How?"

"She's been talking all weird since last Sunday."

"What's she been saying?"

"Pastor Dan preached about some prophet seeing a bunch of bones in a graveyard that connected to each other and turned into an army. Ever since she heard that, she keeps asking me, *Can these bones live, Mimi?* I ask her, *What bones?* and she says, *The bones of this family.*"

"Maybe she thinks it has to do with your surgery, that you'll get your hands back the way they were."

"Oh yeah, she thinks that too, but this is something else. Weird, huh."

"Maybe God's been preparing her?"

There was no enthusiasm in Mimi's voice. "Maybe."

"Where's your faith, girl?"

At that, she started to sound like a whining nine-year-old. "I'm just overwhelmed, Gracie. I need you here."

"Tomorrow, Mi."

"What if Brandi doesn't like us? What if it's weirder than it was without her?"

"Oh, believe me, it will be. But don't worry, Mi. God is all over this."

"Where'd you get all this God talk? It's not like you."

"Let's just say God's done a number on me. He cares, He's got our backs—has from the beginning."

"Just come home," Mimi pleaded. "That's all I want."

"Okay, you ready? Hang up and FaceTime me back."

Grace prayed like crazy while she waited for the call. When their faces came up on her phone, love tightened her throat.

"What's this about?" Eve demanded.

Grace swallowed hard. "Mom, get ready for an amazing story."

XLIII

KEVIN

Carlton yells at me till he's blue in the face because I haven't been in touch. When he finally shuts up long enough for me to tell my story, he is completely speechless.

Well, I think, *that's a first.*

It doesn't last long, though, because next thing, he's asking me a hundred questions, firing them at me like a machine gun. I try to answer every one, but a few times I say, "I'll have to talk to you in more detail about that one."

"Put it in the report, Kevin. You're writing everything up, right?"

"Just making notes right now, Chief. I'm kinda recovering from a few bumps and bruises."

There's a long pause, but before he hangs up, he says, "Great work, Kevin. I mean it. Really, really good work."

"Thanks, sir." I'm too surprised to say any more.

After I pick up our stuff at the bungalow, I head back to Brandi's apartment. I've been trading voicemails with the Feds. It seems like nobody knows who's in charge anymore. My phone rings just as I'm turning onto Brandi's street. The call is from Lewis James' office.

"Kevin, this is Jenny."

"Hi Jenny, sorry I didn't see you at the bungalow. Dave said you were on another assignment."

"Yeah, I'm trying to make sense of Lewis's office. It's a total mess!

He barely kept records. We can't even tell what he was working on. The only case we know anything about is yours."

"You'll figure it out."

"I probably shouldn't be telling you this, but there are lots of inconsistencies, if you know what I mean. It'll take a while to follow all the threads. But that's not why I called."

She pauses. "I have bad news about Lena Benedict. She slipped through."

"What? She's a little old lady, for Pete's sake."

"She must have had another passport and a disguise. They found her car in Mexico, stripped clean."

I shake my head. "Brandi called it. I guess she's smarter than we thought."

"I don't say this often, but the woman must be an evil genius."

"Any chance we'll find her?"

"The Federales have her picture, but by now, she could have slipped out of Mexico, too. I'm sorry."

"My boss isn't gonna be happy, but I guess that's your problem now."

"Like everything else. You going back anytime soon?"

"Tomorrow."

"It's been nice working with you, Kevin. At least we've got Anton in custody. Tell Grace no hard feelings." She chuckles. "That girl's got guts."

When I get back to Brandi's apartment, Grace is in the bedroom with the door shut. I shower and shave and wait for her to come out. In the meantime, I look up that Bible verse on my phone, *He saved others, but he cannot save himself.* Like Grace said, it was some guys mocking Jesus while he hung on the cross.

What a bunch of scum to mock somebody who can't fight back!

Won't fight back. I wonder where that thought came from.

I start working on my report for Sergeant Hines, but like an itch I can't get rid of, I keep thinking of those jerks taunting Jesus—guys He somehow thought were worth saving. They figured if He was really a king, he wouldn't be up there bleeding to death. Or maybe they just wanted to see one more miracle.

Like me.

I've always challenged God to change my dad, get me out of trouble—as if He owed me something. But now, He's done something really miraculous. He kept me from drowning.

"Thank you," I whisper.

And just like that, a torrent of words burst out. "God, I really hate my dad. I want him to come crawling to me, begging for forgiveness."

Pretty soon, I'm blubbering for no reason.

Afraid that Grace will see me, I go into the bathroom and sit on the floor. I'm such a hater. It feels like black ink leaking out all over me. And I can't stop crying.

I sit there for... I don't know how long. Eventually, I pull myself together, stand up, and look in the mirror. I laugh at my bloodshot eyes and scraped up face, but somehow I feel—better.

GRACE

Grace set her phone up on Brandi's dresser which left her hands free to start picking at the skin around her fingernails. "Mom, I'm not getting the nightmares anymore."

"That's great honey."

She looked into Eve's eyes—so expectant, so kind. She looked at Mimi sitting close by, with her mutton chops in her lap, and then she started crying. As soon as she did, Mimi did too. There they were wailing, while Eve was looking at them like they'd gone crazy.

"What's happening?" she said slowly, looking first at Grace and then at Mimi.

In between great, hiccupy sobs, Grace said, "I don't know how to tell you—"

"She found the baby, Mom!" Mimi blurted out.

Eve looked bewildered. "What baby?"

Grace choked back sobs. "Your baby."

"My baby? What are you talking about?"

"The baby you lost. The twin. She's alive. I found her."

Eve's face turned white.

"Oh God, help her, Mimi!" Grace cried out.

Mimi threw her arms around Eve and started saying, "It's okay Mom, it's okay," while she patted her back like she was burping an infant.

"Go get her some water," Grace yelled.

Mimi jumped off the couch and ran toward the kitchen.

Grace moaned. "I knew we shouldn't have done this without Cassie and Dan being there."

Eve just kept staring at her like she was an alien.

"Mom, say something!"

Her voice was no more than a whisper. "You found her? You found Faith?"

Grace nodded while Mimi came screeching back with a glass of water between her wrapped up paws that she nearly dropped on Eve. "Drink it, and calm down, Mom, just calm down."

Eve looked at her with those eyes, the *mom eyes*, and said, "Mimi, maybe *you* need to calm down."

As soon as she said that, Mimi started crying again, which made Grace start crying too. The only one who had even an ounce of composure was Eve. "Tell me everything," she said, looking like a queen.

Looking like a strong and beautiful queen.

KEVIN

When Grace finally comes out of Brandi's bedroom, she looks like a complete train wreck. Her eyes are red and puffy with mascara running down her cheeks. She walks straight into my arms and stands there for a while, totally spent. Fortunately, she doesn't seem to notice I'm a little off my game, too. I'm happy to hold her in my arms, but she motions for us to sit on the couch.

"I called my mom," she says between sniffles.

The thought hits my brain, *What was she thinking?* Even I know you don't wear eye makeup when you're announcing to your mom that you've found your long-lost sister that everybody thought was dead. But I at least have enough sense to keep that thought to myself. Instead, I look into her dazed eyes and ask, "How did it go?"

"She knew, somehow she knew."

"What? How could that be?"

She shakes her head and just sits there for a while. "She told me the weirdest story. She said for a long time she couldn't shake the feeling that when she walked into my room, she would see my sister there with me. She knew it was crazy, but she couldn't talk herself out of it. She ended up going to a shrink who told her that was the way she was processing her grief, and the feelings would go away eventually. They didn't.

"One day she woke up thinking, *A mother knows when her child has died because something in her dies too.* When she told Dad, he said, *She's still alive in you, and that's why you keep looking for her.* She accepted that and lived with those feelings off and on ever since."

Grace's eyes fill with tears, and one of them escapes onto her cheek. She takes a deep breath. "It had been a while since she'd thought about the baby, but when we came here, those feelings came back with a vengeance. She prayed for peace, but peace never came. What do you think of all this?"

I grin. "When it comes to your family, Grace, I try not to speculate. What's normal for you people makes my mind do flip-flops."

She wipes the tears off her face but keeps clinging to me.

"Now that you told her, how's she doing?"

"She's pretty much in shock. Mimi on the other hand is a freakin' basket case, so Mom's trying to take care of her."

I chuckle. "She's just like you, always taking care of someone else."

"I'm not always taking care of someone else."

"No? Care to impersonate Brandi again in some threatening situation?"

She brushes me off. "Mom wants to talk to Brandi as soon as we can set it up. Brandi's anxious to talk to her too."

"You guys are gonna have some kind of reunion when you get back."

"I'm scared, actually."

"Why?"

"What if it's not what we expected? What if we can't meld? Like Mimi said, what if it's stranger than it was without her?"

"Grace, I can already see a bond between you and Brandi."

Suddenly, she punches me in the arm. "And you. Who gave you the right to tell her my secrets—like the way I compare myself to Mimi?"

"Oh," I say with mock seriousness, "we had quite the conversations, your sisters and I."

"Talking behind my back? How dare you!"

"You wanna know why I dare to? Because you are a phenomenal person, and you don't even know it. You think you're not as talented as your sisters, but that's a lot of bunk. You are every bit as talented and beautiful and wonderful…"

I don't get another word out because she kisses me, smack on the mouth.

I'm so surprised that I barely return it. Finally, I come to my senses and kiss her back with everything I've got. Afterwards, I try to say something, but she cuts me off by putting her two fingers against my lips. "I know," she says.

And then she kisses me again.

XLIV

GRACE

They all gathered for pizza that night at the apartment—Robin's parents, Howard, Rosie, the band members, Kevin and Grace. At first, it was awkward because no one knew what to say or do. But then Kevin pushed the couch and chairs to the wall, put on some salsa music and started dancing with Grace.

She was so klutzy that he had to work hard to make her look good. Soon the Blackbears were dancing, and they knew what they were doing. Even Howard and Rosie got up and did some white bread thing that had everyone smiling.

But the highlight of the night took place behind closed doors when Brandi and Grace video-called Eve and Mimi. Brandi was as nervous as a bride. She wore her best blouse and kept asking Grace if she looked okay.

Grace tried to reassure her. "You could be tricked out like a hooker and they wouldn't care."

While everyone else was chowing down on food in the kitchen, the twins made the call. Eve and Mimi were both sitting on the couch like they were on display too. Mimi was finally wearing something other than pajamas, and Eve had makeup on.

Brandi sat on the bed next to Grace, her body ramrod straight, like she was posing for one of those old-time photos. With shaking hands, she kept twisting the bottom of her shirt. All Grace could get out was, "Mom, meet Brandi," and everyone started crying.

Then they all laughed, then started crying again. Not much intelligible was said for a long moment, just those tears of grief and joy which needed no other language to be understood. Brandi used up half a box of tissues, hiding her face in them much like she did with the napkins at the waterfall. Eventually, she looked up and was able to let out a shy, "Hi."

Through her tears, the look of love in Eve's eyes was absolutely priceless. Grace didn't know if Brandi had ever seen a look like that from Lena, but when she locked eyes with Eve, there was a visible change in her body language. It was like her awkward, self-protection melted. After that, Grace watched Eve's eyes drinking in every feature, every gesture and word, the same way Grace had when she'd first seen Brandi on the lipstick cam. Mimi just kept looking from Brandi to Grace, over and over as if she couldn't trust her eyes.

They seem strangely surprised that Grace and Brandi looked so much alike, even though they hadn't even tried to milk their resemblance at all. Grace had fixed her braid again, and Brandi was wearing her hair down, curled for the occasion. Throughout their conversation, Eve kept touching the screen. Grace was worried that Brandi would think Eve had mental issues, but she seemed to take it all in stride.

"You're wearing a sling, dear. Did you break your arm? Does it hurt?"

Brandi shook her head. "No, not really. I broke my collarbone in an accident, so the sling is supposed to keep me from using the arm. Grace hooked me up at the reservation by making me a sling from a T-shirt she tore up."

"You were on a reservation?"

Brandi gave Grace the same look she did when Grace had said Eve didn't know why she was in Arizona. "Uh, I haven't told them all the details yet."

She looked back at Eve. "Your daughter is quite the trip. She's like the most impulsive, determined person I've ever met."

"She's also a thief," Mimi said. "The shirt she tore up for you was mine."

Eve smiled. "Impulsive, determined, yes. But without her, this miracle would have never happened."

Grace grinned. "Who's the good daughter now, Mi?"

Eve laughed and patted Mimi's arm. "When does your flight arrive tomorrow?"

"Two."

Eve touched the screen again. "I don't know how I'll ever sleep tonight."

Grace couldn't stand it anymore. "Ma, you're creeping me out! You'll get plenty of time to touch her when we get there."

Brandi laughed. "Her manners aren't very good, Mrs. Maddox."

All of a sudden there was an awkward silence. Brandi blushed. "Uh, I'm not sure what to call you."

"You can call me whatever you want."

Grace decided to change the subject. "Brandi's a musician, Mom. She's in a band and writes her own music."

"Cool, do you play anything?" Mimi asked, putting her mutton chops behind her.

"Guitar, some drums, bass."

"You should bring your guitar with you."

"I'm planning to." Brandi paused. "I hear you're getting an operation soon?"

Mimi's face fell. "Yeah, Mom and I are going to Ohio to some big-name surgeon."

"I believe you're gonna get it all back, Mimi," Brandi said with surprising conviction.

Mimi was unable to disguise her cynicism. "What makes you think that?"

"If you have half the spunk your sister has, you'll do it. And I can help, too. I've broken fingers three separate times. They give you special exercises to gain the strength back."

Mimi didn't look hopeful, so Grace chimed in, "Wouldn't it be great if we all ended up playing together?"

"I'd love that," Brandi said.

After a few minutes, Eve said "Would you girls mind if I had a few words alone with Brandi?"

"No," both Mimi and Grace said, although that was the last thing Grace wanted to do. But they said their goodbyes, and Grace went back to the party. Brandi was in her bedroom alone for another half hour. When she came out, her eyes were red and swollen. Grace hurried over to her. "You okay?"

"Yeah. We talked about my mom. She told me to forgive her, if I can, and try to pray for her. I said I didn't know if I could. But then your mom said, *Maybe we can do it together.* What a lady! I've never met anyone like her."

Grace grinned. "You have no idea."

And then she gave her twin sister the first hug of her life.

XLV

GRACE

Early the next morning, Robin drove them to the airport. Kevin looked preoccupied and unsettled. Brandi looked scared. Grace kept cracking jokes, misplacing her ticket, and running to the restroom. They said their goodbyes, hugged Robin, made plans for their next time together—hopefully in the fall—then Brandi and Robin walked off to talk by themselves while Kevin and Grace tried not to stare. When they returned, both girls had tears in their eyes.

The trip was long and bumpy, but nothing could wipe the smile off Grace's face. She and Kevin sat next to each other, stealing moments of conversation when Brandi slept. They weren't ready to share their feelings for each other with anyone else just yet. It was like a beautiful secret they held between them; warm and intimate. Every once in a while, Grace would catch him staring at her. When she did, his smile was so dazzling, she'd get lightheaded. Brandi must have noticed because whenever it happened, she'd grin and elbow Grace.

Sometimes, when Brandi was awake, Grace would see her staring off into space, her eyes far away. While Kevin tried to do paperwork, she and Brandi would tentatively compare notes on growing up. Grace tried to keep it light, fearful of stirring up too much emotion. She kept reminding herself that only a few days ago Brandi had tried to kill herself. Maybe Brandi picked up on Grace's concern because she asked her for Pastor Dan's phone number and said she was going to meet with him until she found a therapist.

KEVIN

I try writing my report on the plane, but sitting so close to Grace, knowing what is happening between us, makes it impossible to concentrate. I can't believe that in the span of a few weeks, this girl has turned my life upside down. I glance from her to Brandi and find myself grinning. For the first time, I feel like I've been part of a genuine miracle.

Grace mostly focuses on Brandi, but occasionally she flashes me a smile or squeezes my hand. I can't describe how I feel when she does that. It's like someone sees down into the real me, past all the defenses—and, finally, likes what she sees.

GRACE

By the time they got to JFK, all three of them were jittery. Kevin had sworn his boss to secrecy so that no press or police would show up when they arrived. They wouldn't be able to keep their reunion a secret forever, but for now, they were just an ordinary family meeting each other at the airport.

Grace's newfound courage, albeit foolish and impulsive, had caused her to see herself differently. She'd decided, after the night at the Black Swan, that she was going to put together a jazz band and play some gigs. If she had been good enough to play weddings with her father at fifteen, she could do it again. And hanging out with criminals—and breaking the law herself—made her wonder if she might have a future in police work. She certainly had experience working a *protection detail* with Mimi. Maybe someday she could get paid for doing it.

And then there was Kevin.

They passed through their gate and took the escalator down to the baggage claim. Grace's stomach was doing flip flops. Brandi said hers was too, so they grabbed each other's hands. They were going to meet their family. Together.

In the distance, Grace could see Mimi, Dan, Cassie, and Eve waiting for them, looking like they couldn't stop smiling if they tried. Mimi came running up, all tears and embraces.

But not Eve. Looking calm and beautiful, she watched them come to her. Her brown hair was piled on her head; her Hippie skirt floated below her knees. She kissed Grace and held her tight for a moment.

After that, she turned to Brandi, and with infinite tenderness, said, "May I hug you?"

Brandi nodded and fell into her arms. It was such a personal, holy moment that the rest of them had to turn away.

Kevin and Grace walked over to the baggage carousel to wait for their suitcases to circle round. Soon Mimi, Cassie, and Dan joined them, talking excitedly about how well Jay was doing in rehab.

They all kept their distance from Eve and Brandi for a while. At one point, Grace glanced over at them. Brandi was sobbing on Eve's shoulder.

Let it all out, sis. You've got years of comfort due you.

Once their suitcases wobbled through the rubber flaps, they grabbed them and headed for the door. Eve had her arm around Brandi and was talking quietly to her as they walked. It was clear they had their own thing going.

Grace waited for the niggle of jealousy to rise up, that familiar twinge that she was not enough.

But it didn't come. Not at all.

ACKNOWLEDGEMENTS

M any thanks to:

My editor and publisher, Mike Parker, for his gentle, but expert, treatment of *Dreamreader*;

My mentor and friend, Gail Kittleson, for her encouragement and for the laughs;

The beta readers, Ruth Wagner, Elizabeth Patterson, and Karie Fiorello for the hours of attention they paid to this book;

Kathleen Patterson, who prays me through just about everything;

My tender Savior who has rescued me from the brambles that surround and the thorns that draw blood.

ABOUT THE AUTHOR

A family therapist and church musician by day, Cathy Fiorello is a voracious reader and scribbler of stories and poems by night. She has been published in *Haruah—Breath of Heaven, Ruminate, Families, the Frontline of Pluralism, Connecticut Literary Anthology, 2021* and *ChristianDevotions.us.* She received Honorable Mentions in the *Writer's Digest* Short Story Contest, *Ruminate's* Janet McCabe poetry contest, and won first place in the Greater Philadelphia Christian Writer's Conference poetry contest.

Cathy and her husband Sam have twenty-two people in their immediate family: five children, their five spouses, and twelve sparkling grandchildren.

Connect with Cathy online at:

www. cathyfiorello.com

also available from

WordCrafts Press

27 Words
by KL Palmer

Canelands
by Gerry Harlan Brown

Angela's Treasures
by Marian Rizzo

Paint Me Fearless
by Hallie Lee

The Restless Earth
by Alan Cockrell

www.wordcrafts.net

www.ingramcontent.com/pod-product-compliance
Lightning Source LLC
Chambersburg PA
CBHW022310310726
48973CB00001B/289